GW00732200

WHEN DUTY WHISPERS LOW

A TODD INGRAM NOVEL

JOHN J. GOBBELL

Severn River
PUBLISHING

Copyright © 2002 by John J. Gobbell.

All rights reserved.

No part of this book may be reproduced in any form or by any electronic or mechanical means, including information storage and retrieval systems, without written permission from the author, except for the use of brief quotations in a book review.

Severn River Publishing
www.SevernRiverPublishing.com

This is a work of fiction. Names, characters, businesses, places, events and incidents are either the products of the author's imagination or used in a fictitious manner. Any resemblance to actual persons, living or dead, or actual events is purely coincidental.

Gordon W. Prange, *Miracle at Midway*, 1982, McGraw-Hill, Inc., Chapter 44, Japanese Order of Battle, used with permission of the publisher

ISBN: 978-1-951249-79-3 (Paperback)
ISBN: 978-1-951249-88-5 (Hardback)
ISBN: 979-8-715712-0-59 (Hardback)

ALSO BY JOHN J. GOBBELL

The Todd Ingram Series

The Last Lieutenant

A Code For Tomorrow

When Duty Whispers Low

The Neptune Strategy

Edge of Valor

Dead Man Launch

Other Books

A Call to Colors

The Brutus Lie

Never miss a new release! Sign up to receive exclusive updates from author John J. Gobbell.

SevernRiverPublishing.com/John-J-Gobbell

*To the allied forces who courageously
defeated the enemy in the solomon islands
campaign of World War II*

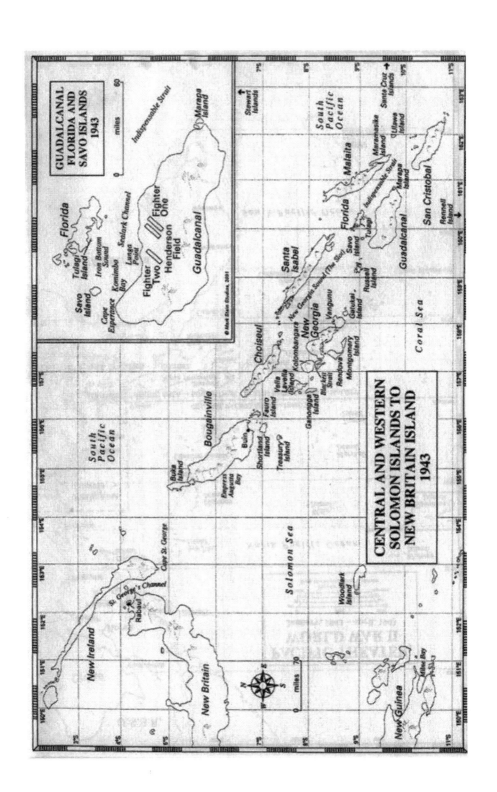

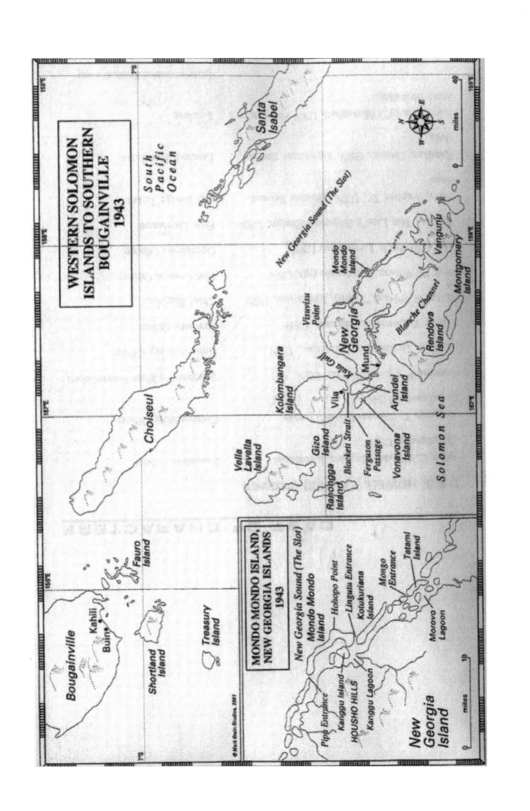

CAST OF CHARACTERS

USS *Howell* (DD 482) (RICOCHET)
Alton C. Ingram, Lieutenant Commander, USN, "Todd," Executive Officer
Jeremiah T. Landa, Commander, USN, "Boom Boom," Captain
Leonard P. Seltzer, USN, "Leo," Boatswain's Mate 2nd Class
Luther T. Dutton, Lieutenant, USN, Gunnery Officer
Louis B. Delmonico, Lieutenant, USN, Replaced Luther Dutton as Gunnery Officer
Henry E. Kelly, Lieutenant, USN, "Hank," Chief Engineer
Jack W. Wilson, Lieutenant (j.g), USN, "Jack," Fire Control Officer
Carl Offenbach, Lieutenant, USN, Operations Officer
Ensign Walter Edgerton, Ensign USN, "Hot Lips," First Lieutenant
Early, Stephen W., Yeoman 2nd class, USN and bridge talker
Katsikas, Dmitriy, Signalman 1st Class, USN
Eric Monaghan, Pharmacist's Mate 1st Class, USN, "Bucky"
L. A. Briley, Quartermaster 2nd Class, USN

PT 72
Elton P. White, Lieutenant (j.g.), USN, "Tubby," Commanding Officer
Winston Fuller, Ensign, USN, "Sir Winston," Executive Officer
Tommy Kellogg, Lieutenant (j.g.), USN, original skipper of *PT 72*

PT 94
Oscar K. Bollinger, Lieutenant (j.g.) USN, Commanding Officer
Ralph Thomas, Ensign, USN, Executive Officer
Dominic Gambino, Radarman 2nd class, USN, "Bambino"

PT-88
Tommy Madison, Lieutenant (j.g) USN, Skipper

USS *Hitchcock* (DD 357)
Roland De Reuter, Commander, USN, Commanding Officer

USS *Pence* (DD 452)
Ralph Druckman, Commander, USN, Commanding Officer

HMNZS *Kiwi*
Gordon Bridson, Lieutenant Commander, Commanding Officer

Guadalcanal (CACTUS)
Marc Mitscher, Rear Admiral, USN, "Pete," Commander, Air, Solomons, under Halsey.
Field Harris, Brigadier General, USMC, Mitscher's Chief of Staff
John Mitchell, Major USAAF, Commanding Officer, 339th Fighter Squadron, P-38 pilot
Tom Lanphier, Capt. USAAF, P-38 pilot

Other USN
Theodore R. Myszynski, Captain USN, "Rocko" Commodore DESRON 12, aboard USS *Whitney* (AD 4) "Fishbait."
Dexter A. Sands, Rear Admiral, USN, Commander battle group aboard light cruiser USS *Santa Monica*
Otto Deveraux, Captain, USN, Commander DESDIV 11 aboard *U.S.S. Barber*
Lieutenant (j.g) Oliver P. Toliver III, USN, "Ollie," Ingram's friend, ordnance liaison officer for the 14th naval district in San Francisco

Pacific Fleet Headquarters, Pearl Harbor, T.H.

Chester W. Nimitz, Admiral, USN, Commander in Chief, Pacific Fleet, CinCPac.

Commander Edwin T. Layton, USN, Pacific Fleet Intelligence Officer to Admiral Nimitz

Michael T. Novak, Commander, USN, Head Combat Intelligence Unit (CIU) of Intelligence Center, Pacific Ocean Area (ICPOA),

Robert L. St. Clair, Major, USMC, head of base brig, Pearl Harbor.

Augustine Rivera, Chief Warrant Officer, USN, Criminal Investigation Division, Works for St. Clair

San Pedro, California

Helen Ingram, Captain, USA, Todd Ingram's wife

Mrs. Peabody, Helen's next door neighbor

Laura West (Dutton), Luther's wife. pianist NBC Symphony Orchestra

Steve Bullard, Motorcycle Officer, San Pedro Police Department

Roberta Thatcher, NBC Orchestra Manager

Rutherford T. Moore, M.D., Colonel, USA, Helen's superior officer at Fort MacArthur Dispensary, San Pedro, California

Robert L. Thorpe, Sergeant, USA, Moore's secretary

Washington, D.C.

Dr. Joshua Landa, Jerry Landa's younger brother at Department of Terrestrial Magnetism in Washington, D.C.

Frank Ashton, Captain, USN, Joshua Landa's Boss; Liaison to subsection of Section T of the Carnegie Institution's Department of Terrestrial Magnetism

Long Beach, California

Larry Dunnigan, Admiral, USN, COMCARDIV 15

Bruce Klosterman, Lieutenant, USN, Dunnigan's aide.

Imperial Japanese Navy

Isoroku Yamamoto, Admiral, Commander in chief of the Combined fleet

Watanabe, Yasuji, Captain, Yamamoto's aide and one of his closest friends

Kanji Sugiyama, Lieutenant, Torpedo Officer, *I-1*

Omi Heijiro, Yamamoto's orderly

Jisaburo Ozawa, Admiral, Commander, Third Fleet

Matamome Ugaki, Vice Admiral, Yamamoto's chief of Staff

Tomoshiga Sajejima, Vice Admiral, Commander, Eighth Air Fleet, Rabaul

Kanji Takano, Captain, Fleet Ordnance Officer under Vice Admiral Tomoshiga Sajejima

Ryunosuke Kusaka, Admiral Commanding Officer, Southeast Area Fleet, Rabaul

Takeo Kotani, Flight Warrant Officer, Pilot G4M2 Bomber no. 323

Ryozo Enomoto, Commander, Captain, Destroyer *Matukaze*

PREFACE

The period of February, 1943 to June, 1943 was a relative 'quiet time' in the Pacific War. Both American and Japanese forces were reeling, in a manner of speaking, from the massive expenditures of ships and manpower in the lower Solomons campaign, the Japanese suffering the worst end of the bargain. Japan's loss of Guadalcanal was not just a tactical set-back, but a major strategic one as well to say nothing about what happened at Midway in June, 1942.

At this time, thirteen *Essex* class carriers, quickly followed by another block of eleven, were rapidly coming off the ways and preparing to steam for the war zone. Eventually, they would become the major weapon for Admiral Chester W. Nimitz's drive across the Central Pacific. But for the time being, Admiral William F. Halsey, Jr., Commander of the South Pacific Area and South Pacific Force, was down to just one carrier, the others having been either sunk or damaged in the bloody battles in the Lower Solomons from mid-1942 to early 1943. Thus, Halsey instructed his surface forces in the Solomon Islands to "...keep pushing the Japs around," a stalling tactic until new carriers, capital ships, and auxiliaries arrived.

Admiral Isoroku Yamamoto, Commander in Chief of the Combined Fleet of the Imperial Japanese Navy, realized the same thing. His headquarters weren't aboard the monstrous battleship *Musashi* in the remote Truk Lagoon by accident. Presumably, the *Gensui* was there to be close to the front. But another reality for Yamamoto was that he'd come under close scrutiny by the General Staff in Tokyo because of the Battle of Midway debacle. Thus, Truk was a good excuse for escape when the Allies invaded Guadalcanal in August. 1942. But things did not go well for Yamamoto's forces. The Japanese were forced to give up Guadalcanal with a great loss of men and material. The pressure from Tokyo became greater, the outrage more pointed. Yamamoto needed to do something. Quickly. Something that would throw the U.S. Navy off-balance; something that would allow him to re-group, to re-capture Guadalcanal and press on with Japan's grand strategy of cutting off the American supply lines to Australia; a critical element for the ultimate success of Nippon's Greater East Asia Co-Prosperity Sphere.

Accordingly, Yamamoto developed "Operation I," a series of massive, Pearl-Harbor-sized air raids designed to cripple Allied bases in the lower Solomons and New Guinea. Temporarily shifting his headquarters from Truk to Rabaul, Yamamoto 'borrowed' hundreds of aircraft from commands all over the Pacific in order to carry out the attacks. Himself a Navy flier, Yamamoto helped brief his aircrews and, wearing dress whites with sword, waved to his pilots as they lumbered off the runway and headed southeast.

About the same time, the Allies added a new element to the Pacific War – the proximity fused anti-aircraft projectile. It was a weapon developed in the strictest secrecy that had a devastating effect upon the enemy. When introduced to the fleet, the proximity or VT (variable time) fuse had a predicted kill probability of about fifty percent. At the war's end, the probability had advanced to eighty percent, an amazing achievement for a device that was only conceived in 1940.

These elements, all seemingly disconnected, are what Todd Ingram met when he returned to the South Pacific in February 1943. His story follows.

So nigh is grandeur to our dust
So near is God to man
When Duty whispers low
Thou must.
The youth replies, I can!

Ralph Waldo Emerson

PROLOGUE

28 January, 1943
 IJN *Musashi*
 Truk Atoll, Caroline Islands

His quarters were two levels below the *Musashi's* bridge. Wearing only a loin cloth, he sat near an open port hole, fanning himself and writing in his impeccable calligraphy. In spite of the giant battleship's air conditioning, he enjoyed the evening's sea breeze, for it gently carried the aroma of beach, dying kelp, and vegetation from the nearby islands. His pen strokes were those of a piano player-- precise, bold, his poetry exact and expressive.

But, for a moment, his hand shook as he bent to his task. He sat up and held his hands out, fingers splayed. With a grunt of satisfaction, he noted his right hand wasn't shaking as much as before. Lately, he'd been feeling tired, so the fleet medical officer had injected him with a combination of vitamins B and C, which seemed to help. He rubbed his right arm and, for a moment, listened to a gull squawk out on the lagoon. A ship's whistle blasted in the distance; then the gull brayed again, perhaps a protest, he thought, perhaps a mate stealing its food.

Born in 1884, the future Admiral of the Imperial Japanese Navy's

Combined Fleet grew up in the Niigata prefecture on the Sea of Japan. Yamamoto was the family name, and the child was given the name Isoroku, which means fifty-six in Japanese, because that was his father's age at the time Yamamoto was born. Yamamoto grew to become a slight man: five feet three inches tall, weighing 130 pounds at most, having a rather delicate bone structure to his face, and the sensitive fingers of a pianist. He graduated from the Etajima Naval Academy in 1904. A year later, he lost the middle and index fingers of his left hand as a result of a turret explosion aboard the battleship *Nisshin* in the battle against the Czarist Navy at Tsushima Straits. As a young officer ashore, Yamamoto was known in Shimbashi's geisha district as *Eighty Sen.* normally, the geishas charged one full yen for a manicure. Because of his missing

Fingers, Yamamoto demanded a break. His charge: eight tenths of a yen.

He spent six years in America, the most recent period from 1926 to 1928, as a Naval Attaché, assigned to Japan's embassy in Washington D.C... During that time, he took an English language class at Harvard. Extra curricular activities included a taste for gambling. American poker, which he played well, was his specialty and he had an even stronger taste for Johnnie Walker Black Label Scotch. He'd been a gymnast in his younger days and, still the athlete, took up bowling in the United States, beating many a local hustler. He took particular delight in trouncing those who thought they were fleecing a little Jap.

Later in his career, Yamamoto learned to fly, working his way to senior command in aviation billets, ultimately commanding the aircraft carrier *Akagi*. Then he *became* head of the Navy's Aeronautics Department.

In 1939, Isoroku Yamamoto was promoted to his Navy's highest office, Commander In Chief of the Combined Fleet. Comparable to Field Marshal, this office carried the honorific, *gensui*. In 1940, he began planning *Operation Z*, the Imperial Japanese Navy's attack on Pearl Harbor. As with Admiral Heihahiro Togo's attack against the Czarist Navy at Tsushima Straits, (the original *Operation Z*) Yamamoto's assault on Pearl Harbor was similarly structured: With both nations in a state of undeclared war, *Operation Z* was a surprise attack on a harbored fleet. Both *Operations Z* turned out as designed: bold assaults, wildly successful, decisive victories...

...his brow was knit. Since last May, things had gone badly: The Coral Sea,

Midway, and now, the Solomon Islands, 1,300 miles to the southeast. Over 50,000 men had been committed to Guadalcanal. The campaign went poorly, and now he was obliged to evacuate the tiny fraction that remained. The rest had all been killed on land or at sea. Worse was the loss of face. He needed to work up something that would smash the Americans once and for all.

But...he needed relaxation. Simple relaxation away from this ship and even away from this job. He'd been out here since last August, and it was beginning to wear on him.

....breath in ...breath out...

Golden evenings like this on the lagoon calmed him. He'd had a good dinner: raw sea bream and broiled sea bream, rice cake soaked in *ozoni*, a holiday soup each complimented by chilled beer. And the talk at the table had been lively.

And yet, the *gensui* felt empty...his thoughts drifted...there has to be a way to get back at the United States Navy before they gain too much momentum. *But what?*

...Chiyoko... With his self-imposed exile, he'd hadn't seen Chiyoko Kawaii, his mistress of nine years, since last August, six long months. He missed her and thought of her daily. During that time it seemed everything was going wrong with this war. His comrades were dying by the dozens; and the Americans kept coming, no matter how many of their ships were sunk, how many planes were knocked from the sky. *As at Tsushima Straits or Pearl Harbor, we need a decisive victory. How can I make that happen?*

A last shaft of golden sunlight burst into his stateroom, shining on his admiral's's uniform. Yamamoto gazed at it for a moment, then realized his hand was once again steady. Drawing a deep breath, he returned to his meticulous calligraphy. He dipped his pen and bent over the paper. For ten minutes he painstakingly wrote:

> Looking back over the year
> I feel myself grow tense
> At the number of comrades
> Who are no more

PART I

Cowardice, as distinguished from panic, is almost always just a lack of ability to suspend the function of the imagination. Learning to suspend your imagination and live completely in the very second of the present minute with no before and no after is the greatest gift a soldier can acquire.

Ernest Hemingway
Men At War (1942)

1

29 January, 1943
   His Majesty's New Zealand Ship *Kiwi*
   Two miles west of Cape Esperance
   Guadalcanal, Solomon Islands

The night was clear with a half-moon rising in the eastern sky, its light shimmering off the verdant mountain-jungles of Guadalcanal. Cape Esperance, Guadalcanal's northwestern prominence, lay two miles ahead. There was a bit of wind off the island, making the water whitecap. There was no ground swell to speak of, and the horizon was sharply defined; one could see quite a distance. For example, Savo Island lay ten miles straight off the bow, the features of its dark, brooding volcanic peak well outlined as it thrust fifteen hundred feet into the sky. Eight months earlier, Savo Island had been the site of a horrible disaster, where the Japanese Navy sank four Allied cruisers and one destroyer in just thirty minutes.

   Kiwi searched in an elongated race-track pattern, her sistership, HMNZS *Moa*, steaming obediently 1,000 yards off her port beam. They were 700 ton corvettes built by Henry Robb Ltd. Relatively small, *Kiwi* and her sisters were just 150 feet in length, and were powered by a recalcitrant 2,600 horsepower triple-expansion steam engine. With a top speed of only sixteen knots, these ships were much slower and less than half the size of their big-brother American destroyers. Used primarily for antisubmarine warfare, they carried a four-inch anti-aircraft cannon mounted on a raised platform on their foredecks, which made them a bit top-heavy. Elsewhere, their anti-aircraft suite was augmented by twenty millimeter cannons.

Kiwi's captain, Lieutenant Commander Jeremiah Bridson, was a man of elephantine proportions. Ship's company stood out of his way, not only from discipline and respect, but also from self preservation. The deck gratings rattled whenever Bridson thumped about his bridge, his men feeling the vibration and instinctively stepping aside in the nick of time. Even so, Bridson was well-liked by *Kiwi's* seventy-two officers and men. And his reputation for tom-foolery was legendary south of the equator.

But now, with the moon up and seas moderate, Bridson crammed his bulk in his Captain's chair, put his feet up and drank coffee, thanking his lucky stars that he was in the Navy and not over there on Guadalcanal, slogging around in bug-infested muck, chasing Japs. Still, Bridson had long ago learned that complacency invited disaster. He forced himself to raise his binoculars and once again sweep the horizon, as did the eight other sailors on his bridge.

While peering into the dark reaches of Guadalcanal's shoreline, he kept in mind a message received from the Yanks: They predicted that a Japanese cargo submarine would land on the 26th, 27th or tonight, the 29th, supposedly right into Komimbo Bay, now three thousand yards off their starboard quarter. Bridson had snorted contemptuously when he first read the message. But his Squadron Commodore had recently told him about the Yanks' supersecret radio intelligence facility in Hawaii -- Fleet Radio Unit, Pacific, (FRU-PAC) -- which did marvelous things, providing solid intelligence that most of the time was bang-on. And this message, he knew, had originated from FRUPAC. So he took it seriously, demanding that his officers keep their eyes peeled.

Piiing, piiing.

But damn, it was boring. The sun had set two hours ago and there hadn't been a peep on the bloody sonar for the past four days. And it seemed Thursday was going to be a bust as well. It showed in the crew; they had become damned irritable. Thank God tomorrow evening they were due to be relieved by the corvettes *Arabis* and *Arbutus*.

Piiiing. Piiiing.

Bridson drummed his fingers, watching the moon and listening to the sonar. The continuous, monochromatic pinging nearly drove him mad on quiet on nights like this.

Hadley, his twenty-five year old executive officer, stepped into the tiny shack. "Captain. Request permission to reverse course."

Bridson sat up, seeing Cape Esperance a mile ahead. Hadley was a little early, but what the hell. Change the pattern. Besides, turning was something to do. "Very well, Number One. Signal *Moa*, please."

"Aye, aye, Captain." Hadley shouted to the signalman aft, "Stokes. Take up yer light and tell *Moa* to stand by for one-eight turn."

"Aye, Sir."

Piiiing. Piiiing. Bridson wished he could go below and listen to records. He had a new Jerome Kern album that he'd only heard once.

Stokes clacked his signal light. "*Moa* acknowledges, Sir."

"Very well," called Hadley. "Stand by execute! Left standard rudder, steady up on course two-four-zero."

Obediently the ships leaned into their turn to port. Bridson watched the *Moa* swing across her bow when he heard, "*Piiiing - bloop.*"

"What the hell?"

Piiiing - bloop. Down doppler. The contact was headed away. "Get with it, Riley!" Bridson shouted into the sonar shack.

A surprised Riley shouted up through the sonar shack's open hatch, "Sonar contact! Possible submarine, bearing one-eight-five. Range, fifteen hundred yards."

Bridson jumped from his chair, his feet thumping on the deck grating. "Eric!"

Hadley needed no prodding. "Shift yer rudder. Steady up on one-eight-five. Close up to action stations, submarine."

Kiwi heeled into her turn to starboard while Bridson yelled back to the signal bridge, "Stokes. Signal *Moa,* 'follow me!' Number One, increase speed to fifteen knots."

"Aye, Sir. Fifteen knots."

Men raced throughout the ship to man their action stations as the *Kiwi* steadied on her new course and speed. After a few moments, Hadley, now wearing helmet and sound-powered phones, called, "All stations manned and ready, Captain."

"Very well." Bridson had his binoculars up, scanning the area before him. "Bearing clear." No surface ships were on the sonar bearing.

Damn! The message was bang-on. We've got the bastard right in Komimbo Bay. Piiiing, Bloop.

The speaker clicked. It was Riley again with, "Bearing now one-six-five, drawing left, range seven-fifty. Down doppler, stern aspect, strong echo."

"Damned near on it," said Bridson. "Guns, stand by to roll depth charges!"

"Standing by, Captain," said *Kiwi's* gunnery officer.

"You okay with this, Guns?" asked Bridson. Ralph Carlson was a brand new junior Lieutenant gunnery officer, and Bridson had yet to see him in action.

"Standing by, Captain," Carlson repeated.

"Very well, Guns, set depth for two hundred feet."

"Aye, aye, Sir."

Piiiing, bloop.

"Bearing steady on one-six-five, range, four hundred, shifting to short scale."

The pings pulsed very quickly now. *Kiwi* was nearly on top.

Stokes called from the signal bridge. "Signal from *Moa,* Captain. She also has sonar contact."

"Very well. Tell *Moa* we're dropping soon and to make her run as soon as possible."

"Bugger's playing a dangerous game laying this close to the beach," Carlson muttered. The risk was that the submarine could be trapped against the shore.

"That's why we set 'em so deep, Guns." Bridson raised a hand in the air, then dropped it. "Guns, roll one! Roll two!" *Kiwi* launched a seven-charge pattern.

With the corvette a mere five hundred yards off the beach, Hadley kicked in full rudder and spun *Kiwi* back out to sea.

WHRUMP! The charges went. Being set so deep, they didn't raise a water column.

Kiwi opened the range to seven hundred yards as *Moa* dropped her depth charges. "Riley!"

"Captain. Yes, Sir. Regained contact. Range six hundred yards, bearing one-six-five. and..."

"And what, damnit!"

"Sounds like she's blowing her ballast tanks, Sir."

"Good God." Bridson jammed his binoculars to his eyes.

Carlson saw it first. "Submarine! Red ten." Ten degrees off the port bow.

Bridson adjusted the fine focus and gasped with the rest of his men. Even partially submerged, he could tell the submarine was enormous, easily twice the length of his little ship. With a high, rounded conning tower, landing barges were strapped to her flanks; she was most likely a cargo submarine, probably a troop carrier. "Big bastard -- Number One! Head right at the bloody thing, full speed. All forward mounts, commence fire!"

Immediately, the four inch gun belched out a round, with the twenty millimeter and fifty caliber guns chattering away.

"Five hundred yards," called Riley.

The submarine's forward hatch popped open and silhouetted figures raced for her deck gun. But they tumbled to the deck as the fifties hit them, only to be replaced by others.

"Captain, it's the Chief Engineer." The watch messenger handed Bridson a sound powered handset.

Bridson jammed it to his ear. "What is it, chief?"

"What the hell are you doing to our ship?"

"Shut up. There's a weekend's leave in Auckland dead ahead of us!" With that, Bridson bracketed the phone and yelled, "Mr. Hadley, I have the conn."

"Yes, Sir."

Two hundred yards.

The Japanese submarine lay before them making very little headway. Her port side was exposed; a classic T-bone. Something whizzed by Bridson's ear and he realized the Japanese now had soldiers on deck in full packs with rifles. Suddenly the submarine's deck gun blasted, the round passing fifty feet above the *Kiwi*.

One hundred yards.

"Stand by!"

Fifty yards.

"Hang on!" Bridson slapped his palms on the bridge bulwark and locked his elbows.

CRUNCH! *Kiwi* dug into the submarine's port ballast tank.

The submarine rolled heavily to starboard, spilling dead and wounded off her decks into Komimbo Bay.

"Back full," roared Bridson. "Right full rudder."

Like insects, Japanese troops, many in full field packs, popped from the hatches and jumped overboard as the *Kiwi* wiggled herself away. Bridson whiffed the heavy odor of diesel oil as it poured from the submarine's ruptured tanks. As she backed clear, the *Kiwi's* twenty-millimeter rounds pounded the submarine's deck gun area and conning tower. One mount in particular pumped shell after shell into the landing barges. Suddenly, the barge strapped to the port side caught fire, giving the scene an eerie glow.

As the light flickered, Bridson yelled, "Rudder amidships, ahead full!"

Bullets zipped past their head, some clanging into the *Kiwi's* superstructure as she gathered headway. Once again the engineroom phone buzzed. Bridson grabbed it, instinctively knowing it was his Chief Engineer. "What!"

"Captain. You're not ramming again?"

"You bet I am. Now tell me, any damage?"

"Not sure."

"All right, let me know. Say, you have any time to come up, Chiefy?"

"Too busy keeping this bugger glued together. Why?"

"You should see this bastard. She's a football field."

"Then stand off and leave it to the damned deck gun!"

"Take us all night, Chief. I say hit her again! It'll be a week's leave." With that, Bridson jammed the phone in the bracket and ordered, "Left full rudder."

Another round erupted from the submarine's deck gun and screeched harmlessly overhead. If anything, the *Kiwi's* gunfire intensified, mercilessly knocking down anyone coming out of hatches to man the submarine's guns.

Hadley pointed to diesel smoke pouring from the submarines exhaust vents aft. "She's gathering weigh, Captain. Looks like they're trying to beach her."

"We'll fix that," muttered Bridson. *Kiwi* steadied on her course with Bridson yelling, "Stand by to raaaaaam!"

CRUNCH!

"Damnit." They'd hit twelve feet aft of the first hole. Bridson had wanted to saw the sub in half by hitting her in the same place. "Back full, right full rudder."

Bullets clanged around them. "Arrgh! Jesus," yelled Carlson, clutching his shoulder.

Bridson saw blood seeping out of his gunnery officer's right arm. "Better go below and see the quack, Ralph."

"And miss all this? I'm fine, Sir. It's a clean wound."

Bridson thought, *you'll do fine, Ralph. All you have to do is live through all this muck they call a war.* "Here, Stokes. Run a battle dressing around Mr. Carlson's arm."

"Aye, Captain."

"Ahead full, rudder amidships!" The phone buzzed. Once again, Bridson ripped the phone from its bracket. "This better be good, Chief."

"Only if you like a flooded forepeak, Captain."

"Is it progressive?"

"Can't tell."

"Well, find out. And we're going in again."

"Captain, I don't want to walk home."

"Come on, Chief." Then he yelled for all to hear. "Once more for a fortnight!" Shoving the phone in bracket he said, "Left full rudder."

"Good God!" said Hadley.

"What?"

"It's a bloody *banzai* charge." Hadley pointed as *Kiwi* steadied up, the submarine once again before her.

Bridson raised his binoculars to see a pair of Japanese officers waving swords in the air. What they were screaming, Bridson couldn't tell. "Faster, damnit," he urged. Because she was turning so tightly, the *Kiwi* hadn't gained more than ten knots headway. Then he spotted one of the vee-shaped holes he'd put in the submarine's ballast tank. He ran over and grabbed the helmsman's collar and pointed. "Head right for that one!"

"Right, Sir." The helmsman eased in a bit of left rudder then steadied up.

"Stand by to raaaam!"

With an awful screech, *Kiwi* lunged up and rode over the submarine, shoving her halfway under. Bridson looked over the bulwark to see more Japanese soldiers scrambling through hatches and running about the submarine's deck. Just as Bridson realized they were trying to board his ship, the *Kiwi's* men, now armed with rifles and pistols, poured a murderous volley into them, knocking the soldiers into the water. Then, from the conning tower, a Japanese officer ran toward the corvette, screaming and waving a sword in the air. As *Kiwi's* bow plunged back into the water, the officer leapt and miraculously grabbed the corvette's stanchion with one hand, still waving his sword with the other. The *Kiwi* bucked up and down, and finally the Japanese officer lost his grip and tumbled into fuel-oil saturated water.

Leaving a glistening odorous wake, the submarine miraculously gathered headway and again plodded toward the beach, just one hundred yards away.

Bridson grabbed the phone and buzzed the chief engineer.

The chief engineer raged, "Look what you've done to my ship."

"Tell me," said Bridson.

"Forepeak. Chain locker. Pyrotechnics locker. Bosun's locker. Forward fresh water tank, all flooded. Crew compartment bulkhead leaking badly. I'd say we're done for the evening."

"Right." Bridson bracketed his phone and said, "Cease fire, all guns." Then, "Stokes. Signal to the *Moa*."

"Sir!"

"'*Take over, you deserve some of the fun.*'"

"Aye, aye, Sir." Stokes ran off to clack his signal lantern. As he did, Bridson watched the submarine. She was nose-up on a coral outcrop, about twenty-five yards off the beach. "Looks like they've got her aground, Eric."

Hadley squinted through his binoculars. "I think so. Look at the diesel exhaust pour out. I'd say he's trying to drive her further up the beach."

Bridson sighed. Suddenly he felt very tired. "Take the conn, Eric. Stand off the beach and keep us out of *Moa's* way while we assess our damage."

"Aye aye, Sir - Blimey!" Hadley's binoculars snapped to his eyes.

"What the devil is it?"

"There." Hadley pointed. "What the hell?"

Bridson found the spot. It was larger hole was just forward of the sub's conning tower. Bubbling up amongst the diesel fuel were sheets of paper, thousands of them, tablet-size.

"Think they're going to dump leaflets on us?"

"No," said Bridson. "Secret weapon. They've finally figured out a way to beat us."

Hadley dropped his glasses and looked at Bridson.

"Paperwork, Number One. They'll kill us with paper work."

2

24 February, 1943
  U.S.S. *Howell* (DD 482)
  Kula Gulf, Solomon Islands

...at dawn's red glare, sailor beware.

High overhead, aircraft engines resonated among the reddish-pink clouds. Frantically, Todd Ingram tried to pick out the death-messengers, their droning a macabre reverberation in his ears.

Where the hell are they?

Ingram's eyes darted among the breaking day's overcast. His adam's apple bounced as he swallowed, trying to force back whatever gnawed deep in his stomach.

Almost straight up now, flying southeast.

Jerry Landa, standing one deck below on the port bridge-wing, called up, "Maybe they can't see us."

Don't count on it, captain.

The seas were high, and with a formation speed of twenty knots, the groundswell made the four destroyers roll drunkenly. Ingram braced himself against the main battery director rail, steadying his binoculars as he searched the clouds.

Just then the sun rose, its upper edge peeking between clouds and horizon, bathing the four wallowing destroyers in a rich golden-yellow elixir and making Ingram's lieutenant commander's gold leafs gleam like the ancient beacon of Alexandria. It was as if someone had turned on stage lights.

Up the curtain, thought Ingram, his grey eyes flicking momentarily to the other *Fletcher* class destroyers. They steamed in a diamond formation, each of their five, five-inch thirty-eight guns at READY AIR, their single-barrel guns pointed defiantly, almost straight up, like needles from a pin cushion. *Barber* was in the lead, steaming 1,000 yards ahead of *Howell* and carrying Otto Deveraux, Commodore of the four-ship Destroyer Division Eleven (DESDIV 11). *Issac* and *Griffith* were on either wing, with *Howell* in the tail-end charley slot.

"What's their course?" Landa's even white teeth glinted in the new day.

Ingram jabbed the sound-powered phone mike-button and called down to Lieutenant jay gee Tubby White, the CIC evaluator. Traditionally, *Fletcher* class destroyers posted their executive officers to CIC and their gunbosses to the bridge. But Landa wanted it the other way around, so he could have Ingram close-by for input.

"Jap's course is one-five-zero," reported White. He was filling in for Luther Dutton as gun boss on this patrol.

"Tubby says they're still on the same bearing, Captain. About three-three-zero. Speed: one thirty," said Ingram. "Range: now six thousand."

Next to Ingram was his talker, Vogel, who asked, "What do you think, Sir?" A first class storekeeper, Vogel had recently joined the *Howell*. He was a quiet dark-haired kid who kept to himself and read a lot. In fact, Ingram discovered Vogel had two years of college before he'd been drafted.

"I honestly wish I knew. You can never tell with Japs."

Vogel swallowed twice. This was his first time in combat. "Maybe they'll keep on going."

Ingram raised his binoculars. *Don't bet on it.*

The routine of the past few days had become a monotony. Up at 0430 for general quarters (GQ). At daybreak, look for Japs. Seldom did they attack and rarely in force. When they did go by, it usually was a sortie heading south to Guadalcanal. But Ingram had to agree with Landa's intuition. This time, something was different.

A pilot-house speaker screeched over the talk between ships (TBS) circuit: "*Gillespie, this is Crabtree. Speed: thirty. I say again, speed: thirty. Stand by, execute. Ricochet. Over?*"

Howell's OOD, Lieutenant Carl Offenbach, grabbed the pilot house mike and snapped, "*Ricochet, Roger, out.*" He ordered the lee helmsman, "All engines ahead, flank. Indicate turns for thirty knots."

Engineman second class Earl Bannister repeated the order in a deep Southern accent as he shoved the lee helm's gleaming brass handles to flank speed. Bannister bent down and twirled the engine indicators to 300, reporting back to Offenbach, "Sir, Main Control acknowledges all ahead flank, three-zero-zero turns for thirty knots."

"Very well." Offenbach caught Landa's eye for a nod of approval.

The uptakes in the *Howell's* stacks squealed as her boilers hungrily gulped air, feeding the fires that generated steam to the turbines producing 60,000 horsepower. Almost immediately, Ingram felt the acceleration, as machinist's mates in the engine rooms cracked their throttles, making the ship dig in her twin screws.

The *Howell's* lumbering motion became a desperate rise and plunge, the bow burying itself in crystal blue water, then rising to shake itself free and spew white-green foam over the forward five-inch mounts.

Desperately, the men on the bridge swept the sky with their binoculars, searching in vain for the source of the rumbling engines. A bit of spray whipped over one lookout, a signalman; he lowered his glasses and started wiping the lens with tissue paper.

"Dimmit! Keep an eye out, sailor," Landa snapped.

"Y-yes, Sir!" The signalman quickly raised his binoculars.

Landa looked over his shoulder to Ingram. "Japs are laughing at us. They can see us, but we can't see them."

"Maybe headed for Rendova," Ingram said. He gulped the last of the coffee he'd been nursing since before daybreak, when they had called general quarters. Jamming the cup into a gear locker, he took a deep breath, trying to ignore the burning that erupted in his belly.

"Rendova? No dice. They're pissed and looking for us. Wouldn't you be?"

Ingram nodded. "Probably circling. Looking for a hole to dive through."

"Anything new on air cover?"

Ingram called down to CIC. "Tubby, what's the story on air cover?"

There was a muffled conversation, then White came on the line. "CACTUS says they vectored four Wildcats. ETA, twenty minutes." CACTUS was the airstrip on Guadalcanal's Henderson Field.

"They're late," muttered Ingram. The F4Fs were supposed to have been overhead at dawn.

"What can I tell you?" White said, sounding testy. It was as if he'd been taking lessons from Luther Dutton, an MIT electronics whiz, now on loan to the *Barber* to replace their gunnery officer, who had been stricken with a bad case of malaria.

"Four F4Fs enroute, Captain. ETA twenty minutes," Ingram groaned.

"Dammit." Landa swept the skies to the southeast with his binoculars, looking in vain for the Navy fighters. "Call 'em and tell 'em to shake a leg, Todd."

"Yes, Sir."

They all bitched. Even his talker, Vogel, stood beside him and muttered under his breath. Ingram couldn't blame them. They'd been at this for a week, dashing up and down the Slot from Tulagi and back, seeking enemy supply barges and trying to sink them. Embarrassing to the U.S. Navy was that the Japanese miraculously evacuated their remaining troops from Guadalcanal two weeks ago. Like Churchill at Dunkirk, Admiral Isoroku Yamamoto, Commander In Chief of The Combined Japanese Fleet, had used anything that floated -- from barges to submarines to destroyers -- rescuing 11,000 starved, emaciated soldiers during the nights of February first through the sixth, disembarking at Cape Esperance.

Ingram felt like they'd been at general quarters round the clock, which was close to the truth. Early last evening, DESDIV 11 had bushwhacked a Japanese supply convoy, sinking three armored one-hundred foot barges off Kolombangara and damaging a destroyer. That's why, he was sure, the planes were searching them out: retribution.

Vogel thrust a finger into the air. "Holy smokes!"

Ingram saw it at the same time. A speck plunging through the clouds; the morning's new sun glinting off its canopy. "Off the port bow, Captain," Ingram said.

The TBS speaker screeched. Landa stepped in the pilot house, fiddled with knobs, gave an acknowledgment, then stepped onto the port bridgewing. "Otto is ordering us to come right to unmask batteries." He grinned up to Ingram. "Actually, we got a bottle of scotch riding on who gets the first bogie today."

Offenbach ordered right rudder, and the *Howell* began slogging drunkenly through the waves, allowing all of her five gunmounts to bear on the target.

Ingram keyed his mike. "Jack?"

"On target and tracking," said Jack Wilson, the main battery director officer. Throughout the ship, the five-inch gun mounts shifted into "automatic" and pointed at the speck. They were synchronized with the ships gunfire computer, which received its target range, elevation, and bearing information from the main battery director atop the pilot house where Ingram stood.

As the *Howell* skidded through her turn, Ingram spotted three Bno-- five more specks diving one-by-one through the clouds, their engines screaming. The first plane was halfway down, displaying the familiar low-wing silhouette of a "Val," a single engine Aichi D3A1 Navy (Type 99) dive bomber, its fixed landing gear helping to slow its dive. Underneath the Val's bellies was a 500 kilogram bomb, a 100 kilogram bomb slung under each wing.

Landa raised his hand, then dropped it. "Commence fire!"

Ingram shouted, "Commence fire, all batteries!"

In turn, Jack Wilson crouched inside the director and barked the order to his pointer, Ernie Williams.

A ruddy-complected second class fire-controlman, Williams' eye was pressed to powerful gyro-stabilized sight, its cross-hairs centered on the lead Val. He jabbed a foot treadle.

All five gun mounts belched death at the planes, the muzzle-blasts slamming Ingram from all directions. Two seconds later, the forty-millimeter mounts opened up, followed by the strident crack of the twenties. Smoke momentarily obscured the formation, as all four ships hammered away.

Soon, the sky was studded with little black puffs ranging among the diving Vals.

"How many?" called Tubby from CIC.

Ingram pressed a hand against his headphone. The damned guns were so loud; conversation was impossible. He could hardly think. Finally, he managed, "What?"

"How many Japs?"

Ingram inhaled cordite-laden smoke from the forward gun mounts. He coughed for a moment, then rasped into the microphone, "Hard to tell. They're coming one by one through a hole in the clouds. I'd say fifteen or so."

The first Val passed through 5,000 feet, and at about 3,500 dropped its bomb at the *Barber*. The pilothouse speaker squawked, "Maneuver independently!"

"Come right ninety degrees, Carl!" Landa yelled.

The *Howell's* rudder whipped over, throwing her transom to port. Leaning almost twenty-five degrees, she lunged though the waves, her decks glistening with water. Then her rudder dug in and the *Howell* snapped through her turn like a jaguar skidding around a lumbering water buffalo.

WHOOM! A water-column rose three hundred yards off the Howell's port bow.

"Rudder amidships!" barked Offenbach.

The gunfire noise was incredible. Ingram was astounded he could hear Offenbach at all.

Apparently the helmsman hadn't, for Offenbach ran into the pilot house and right up to the helmsman. "Dammit! I said rudder amidships!"

WHOOM! Another bomb cascaded fifty yards off the Howell's port beam.

"I have the conn," Landa shouted. "Mr. Offenbach, stay in the pilot house and relay orders."

"Aye, aye, Sir. Captain has the conn."

The cannons pounded away, with one plane disappearing in a greasy red-orange blast, pieces whipping in all directions, throwing smoke and steam. Yet on they came. Another bomb was released over the *Howell*. "Left standard rudder," Landa shouted.

The ship rolled into her turn, the bomb smacking the water fifty yards to starboard. As the screaming Val pulled out of her dive, the two forward forty-millimeter mounts chattered away, eating into its wing root. Smoke poured out, then incredibly, the wing snapped off and the Val spun horribly around its axis, parts spewing before it thumped into the water.

"Steady on three-zero-zero."

"Three-zero-zero, aye, Sir," came the response from the pilot house, as another Val pushed over and headed down in an eighty degree dive.

"Jeez, how many of these bastards!"

Furiously, the guns of DESDIV 11 laced the sky with shrapnel as a dive-bomber plummeted, its 1,070 horsepower Kensei engine screaming at them. This one looked like it was locked on the *Barber*.

Ingram fine-tuned the binoculars focus and made out the pilot, pitched forward in his seat, held by shoulder straps, his eye pressed to his bombing-telescope.

"Left standard rudder!"

On came the plane, holding its dive longer than the others. Yes, it *was* headed for the *Barber*, which at that moment leaned to port, beginning a frantic turn to starboard.

The pilot must have noticed, for he pulled back on his stick a bit, easing from the dive. After two more incredibly long seconds, the bomb lunged clear, and the Val began its pull-out. The combined fury of DESDIV 11 clawed with all its might at the turning Val, which leveled out and raced for safety.

"No!" Ingram heard a voice that he knew was his own.

The bomb, as if attached to a guide wire, raced directly for the *Barber*. Time seemed frozen. Like magic, the bomb found the destroyer's aft funnel and disappeared inside.

CRACK!

The *Barber* erupted in a belching plume of dark, smoking, flame. The shock wave hit Ingram in an enormous, ear-piercing explosion which hammered Kula Gulf and the surrounding islands. Tons of spinning debris and flame spewed into the air. A column of smoke rose two thousand feet, hovering over the spot the proud little *Barber* had occupied only moments before.

Ingram forced his mouth to close, swallowing several times. "No." A look at the bridge told him they too, were mesmerized. Ingram's eyes were dumbly fixed on the smoke column. It soon cleared, showing...nothing. He felt light-headed -- the *Barber* no longer existed. His eyes watered. And it wasn't from the smoke.

Finally, he swept the sky with his binoculars. No more Vals. "Cease fire."

Landa looked up to Ingram with an ashen face. "Luther was aboard."

Luther. *Good God*! Ingram felt an emptiness he didn't believe possible. It seemed there was no depth to it.

Griffith and *Issac* ceased fire, the silence as loud as the recent air attack. Ingram looked back to the *Barber's* pall of smoke and pressed a hand to his ear phone, as White made another report. "Commander Kilpatrick, aboard *Griffith,* has assumed duties as Division Commodore."

Tears ran down Landa's cheeks. "Good God. Luther."

Ingram wiped his own tears, wondering why Landa was crying.

3

24 February, 1943
   U.S.S. *Howell* (DD 482)
   New Georgia Sound (The Slot), Solomon Islands

The planes swooped in low from the Eastern horizon, heading directly at the three remaining destroyers. *Issac* opened fire with her forward forty millimeters, as Tom Kilpatrick, *Griffith's* skipper and new acting Commodore, screeched over the TBS, "Cease fire, damnit!"

An F4F wildcat roared past the *Howell* at masthead level, wiggling its wings. Another zipped over doing a victory roll, then a third. "Do not shoot! They're friendlies," Landa shouted, spittle flying from his lips, as his face turned crimson. To Ingram he muttered, "Jerks should know better than to point their noses at us."

They'd hove into the lee of New Georgia Island and the groundswell abated as if someone had pulled the switch of a giant wave-making machine. The wind also dropped and the three remaining ships steamed in a column over a remarkably smooth, glass-like surface. *Issac* was in the lead, followed by *Griffith*, then *Howell*.

Ingram swallowed his bile. *Bastard wildcats are twenty minutes late.*

The F4Fs flew on, eventually forming up and circling the smoke-column marking the *Barber's* grave. They orbited twice, then ran back over the three destroyers, spreading out, two wildcats to port, one to starboard.

Kilpatrick came back on the TBS, his voice calm, official this time, ordering a search for *Barber* survivors. Gracefully, the three destroyers reversed course, leaving *Howell* in the lead position.

Ingram shuddered for a moment, wondering if they would find anything. Or worse, if they did find something, what it would look like.

"Seems like they've finally done their arithmetic and discovered one of us is missing." Landa watched the Wildcats passing lazily overhead at 2000 feet. "How long do we have them?"

Ingram called Tubby White in CIC, hearing the crisp rattle of voices over the radio net in the background. "Two hours," White said. "They apologize for being late. Apparently jumped by Japs on the way up. Lost one of theirs."

Ingram relayed the message to Landa, whose binoculars were riveted on the *Barber's* death pall. "Hope the poor bastard was able to bail out."

"Nooooo." Sitting straight up in his bunk, Ingram fumbled for the bulkhead light switch and flicked it on. *Ease up.* His chest heaved, and he willed to slow his breathing. Sweat ran down his face and torso; the bunk covers were shoved in a rumpled heap at his feet.

"Damn." He looked at his little wind-up alarm: nearly ten-thirty. Another hour and a half to Tulagi.

The dream was so vivid, reliving the *Barber's* explosion. When Ingram had turned in, he'd expected the dream, and it came as scheduled. That brand-new 2,100 ton ship blown to smithereens before his eyes. And with her, 322 officers and men.

Including Luther Dutton, the MIT whiz kid. It had taken months to break through Dutton's New England facade. Once inside, Ingram discovered a talented man with a warm sense of humor. Luther was married to a concert pianist, who had been featured in a recent issue of *Collier's*. To round things out, Luther had played the violin like a maestro, often entertaining the ship's company on the fantail while anchored on balmy evenings. Luther's wife, what was her stage name? Laura West.

She'd played piano for them one night at a USO performance back in the States. It was just before Ingram had shipped out. He and his wife Helen had sat listening, arm in arm, the theater dark, the audience bound to rich, melody-filled moments. At the concert's end, Luther joined his wife on stage, playing *Die Meditation*, their music seamless, beautifully crafted, as if they'd practiced this one piece all their lives.

In fact, Ingram owed Luther Dutton money, thanks to Hank Kelly, the ship's engineering officer. It was on their last night at the Pearl Harbor O Club. Waiting to catch a flight for Brisbane Australia, Kelly dared a moping Ingram to try calling Helen from the lobby payphone. There must have been at least two hundred officers that hot sweaty night, yelling and singing over raucous music, as Ingram dug four quarters from his pocket, walked to the cramped booth, and shut the accordion doors. The vent fan in the little dark-brown cubical didn't work, making it swelter and smell of cheap beer. He dropped in his money, dialed the operator and, to his surprise, was immediately connected with Helen in San Pedro, California. Helen sounded like she was trapped in a giant clamshell, with some ghoul fiendishly turning the volume up and down.

Nobody believed Ingram and he actually had to hand the phone to a wide-eyed Luther Dutton. Hank Kelly and Tubby White also took their turns to verify it was Helen. Each grinned as Helen spoke with them, promising to call their loved ones. Ingram had used all his change, and borrowed another four quarters from Luther. As Todd and Helen lingered over one another's words, Luther ran to the bartender to break a two dollar bill to feed the damned phone. Finally, the operator cut in with a priority call; she gave Todd and Helen just five seconds to say goodbye.

Exacting his *quid pro quo*, Luther Dutton tallied Ingram's phone bill and drew up the IOU for ten dollars on an O Club bar napkin before all present. Cat-calls rang from the rafters as Ingram signed, vowing to repay Luther the next day.

But their flight schedules were advanced, and they shipped out early the next morning on different airplanes. Then fate struck a cruel blow. *Barber's* gun-boss came down with a serious case of malaria, and Luther Dutton was given temporary orders to become *Barber's* gunboss. In the meantime, Tubby

White, a blond, portly lieutenant junior grade, was upgraded as *Howell's* temporary gunboss.

Luther's plane had arrived ten hours earlier, and he was gone by the time Ingram reported to the *Howell*. Now Ingram would never see Luther again.

And his IOU lay at the bottom of the Kula Gulf...

Ingram rose and padded to his desk. In the corner was an eight by ten framed picture of Helen, beautiful, smiling, signed '*all my love.*' She'd given it to him the night he caught the airplane for Hawaii. "Hi, hon." He looked at her for a moment then forced his eyes to the safe. Rubbing a hand over his chin, he ran the combination, pulled out his wallet. Then he buttoned a shirt, stepped into his trousers and shoes, snatched his garrison cap, and headed topside.

It was a blazing moonlit night. Water swished down the starboard side, and the *Howell* barely rolled, following *Issac* and *Griffith* at 500 yard intervals. Ahead, Savo Island silently stuck its menacing 735 foot peak into the night. Raising his eyes to the sky, Ingram studied the stars, the Southern Cross quite clear: a million dollar view.

He thought of Luther and that crazy telephone call. The explosion flashed before him, and his stomach surged. *Hold on, damnit.* He stepped in shadows beneath the starboard motor whale boat, both hands desperately grasping the bulwark. It took all his will power to keep from retching. Finally, his belly decided to cooperate and he stood, looking from side-to-side, half-expecting to see someone smirking.

He took two deep breaths, wishing he could stop the sweating. After a moment, he leaned on the bulwark and gazed into the glowing phosphorescent wake, its luminescence making his face glow like a Peter Lorre horror film.

Twenty feet aft, Jerry Landa climbed through a deck hatch from the forward boiler room. Hank Kelly, wearing oil splotched engineer's overalls, emerged after him, and the two stood talking on the main deck, the wind ruffling their hair, a shard of light occasionally bouncing off Landa's perfect white teeth.

Ingram shook his head. Jerry Landa: A skipper's skipper. He had an instinctive gift of leadership with a sharp sense of humor. At times however, that was off-set by an explosive temper. But Ingram had learned to deal with it and either kept his Commanding Officer out of trouble or crawled in a hole when it wasn't safe for any one around. In a way, Ingram and Landa were cultural contrasts. Landa, from a stevedoring family, grew up in Brooklyn and went to the Merchant Marine Academy. Ingram grew up in Echo, Oregon, a small railroading town near Pendleton, and attended the Naval Academy. The unmarried Landa was flamboyant and ashore, had acquired the nickname "Boom Boom," presumably because, when the party was at a fever pitch, he told barroom jokes mimicking the sounds of human flatus. Oddly, Landa didn't like to be called "Boom Boom," although he enjoyed calling others by nick-names. Ingram on the other hand was married with him and Helen living quiet lives. Their goal, after he left the Navy, was to live on her fathers avocado ranch near Ramona, California.

Ingram concentrated on the swishing water. Somnolent. Calming. He felt better. *Let it go, Todd.* But how to get rid of the abject cowardice he felt. It had been with him since his escape from Corregidor last May. In retrospect, it seemed like he'd been fighting himself more than fighting the Japanese. Oftentimes, he'd just felt like cutting and running. And yet, Admiral Ray Spruance had deemed it proper to personally decorate Ingram with the Navy Cross and call him a hero. *Me, a real phony. If they only knew.* He slapped his palms on the bulwark and tried to concentrate on the low shape of Guadal-canal as it grew above the horizon, the scent of honeysuckle taunting his nostrils.

Damnit. There's plenty to live for. Helen's image poured through his mind. He saw her clearly, almost as if she stood before him now. She was tall, five eight, slender with dark brown hair pulled back and tied at the neck. But it was Helen's eyes that always drew him in: dark brown, quick, intelligent, absorbing; entirely warm and consuming.

Four months previously, the *Howell* had been hit by a suicide bomber on her fo'c'sle while screening the carrier *Enterprise* in the Battle of The Santa Cruz Islands. Landa suffered a serious lung puncture wound, and eventually recuperated in the U.S. With the others, he returned to duty aboard the *Howell,* just as she emerged from overhaul in Brisbane, Australia. During the overhaul, Ingram was given a special behind-the-lines assignment in Mindanao. There, he suffered cracked ribs and serious internal injuries at the hands of the Japanese, but accomplished his mission and rescued Helen Durand -- who in a way, rescued him. Later they were married and had two months of recuperation and honeymooning. Indeed, she was all he needed...

Landa walked up. "Not you, too."

Ingram's head spun and he nearly stuttered, "Me too, what, Skipper?"

Landa leaned beside him on the bulwark. "Down. Morale. Piss-poor. Nobody's talking. Seeing the *Barber* go up like that."

"Sometimes it gets to you."

Landa nodded.

"I wonder..."

"What?"

"Maybe I should write a letter to Luther's wife. You know? Better than a telegram on a Friday afternoon?"

"Good idea."

Moments passed, then Landa said in a sharp tone, "Not on my watch, Mr. Ingram."

"What?"

"I've got a ship to run. If we show any fear or hesitancy or unwillingness to jump in and do it, then the crew is going to act the same way. Everybody. Officers--"

"I didn't mean to--"

Landa held up a hand and cut him off. "Don't be a sap. No, you don't mean to. Nor does anyone else. But I've toured my ship. I just finished the forward boiler room with Hank Kelly. Morale down there, like everywhere else, is lower than a dachshund's balls. We've lost our edge, damnit. "And to me, that means we lose next time Tojo comes calling."

"Jerry--"

"Listen. We've been out of this fracas for four months, both of us wounded, and yet, here we are again, with our same ship and same crew, more or less. We have to get our arms around this thing, Todd, before it gets us."

"Aye, aye, Skipper. Tomorrow morning, I'll put a note in the Plan Of The Day prohibiting any display of poor morale: punishment for such offense resulting in restriction to the ship for fourteen days on rations of stale bread and water. Furthermore, I will order all officers to--"

"Todd, just shut up."

Ingram puffed his cheeks. "Sorry."

"You know, I did something dangerous while I was recovering."

"What?"

"I read a book."

"Sure."

"Damnit. It was fiction. Hemingway."

Ingram grinned with the realization that Landa usually read seedy detective novels.

"He has a new one, it's called *Men At War*."

"Umm."

Landa studied Ingram to make sure he wasn't pulling a face. Satisfied, he said, "He talks about cowardice. Basically, he says, you have to put your imagination in neutral. No looking forward, no looking back. Just neutral. Live for now and for the time of your next meal. That's it." Landa waved a hand in the air. "No wives or girlfriends, no civilian job, no real estate deals, no mom or dad. Nothing."

They stood for a moment, forearms braced on the bulwark, each lost in thought. Landa was right, of course. Ingram wondered if Landa knew about his nightmares. Maybe Landa knew about his fear, his pills. *Stop it!* "Live for today, only," he said.

"'Fraid so. Tough on guys like you who are married. If you look forward to your sweetheart, you're screwed."

"Tougher on Luther."

"Damnit. Will you listen to me?"

"Okay."

"Remember John Halford?"

"Off the *Bass*?" John Halford was the CO off the destroyer U.S.S. *Bass* who, after eighteen months at sea, was sent home to teach engineering at the U.S. Naval Academy.

"That's him. Pretty good skipper. I met him in the O Club right after we pulled into Noumea from Stateside. The *Bass* was just coming out of overhaul -- her aft deckhouse had been badly mauled in that Savo Island fracas.

Halford was telling me about it. Sounded awful, lots of gore. So I asked John, 'How do you stand it? How do you keep your sanity in all this?' Guess what he said?"

Ingram kept silent.

"John said that he considers himself dead. That there is nothing to look forward to. Just dead. That's it. No imagination to fill in the blanks and drive you crazy."

"He married?"

"Yeah."

"Well? Did he write to his wife?"

"I think so."

"A one sided conversation?" Ingram scratched his head. "What happened when he read her letters?"

"Never opened them. Tied them in a bundle and kept them in chronological order to read on his way home."

"I wish I had his will-power." Water swished down the side, the wake hissing in the night. Ingram watched it, his eyes becoming unfocused.

"Todd?" Landa waved a hand before his face.

"What?"

"I said, 'Helen's worth going home to, I grant you that.'"

Ingram reached for his wallet.

"I don't want pictures now."

"No." Ingram pulled out a ten dollar bill, smoothed it on the bulwark, and flicked it over the side.

Landa watched it flutter into the wake, as if throwing ten dollar bills into the New Georgia Sound was the most normal thing a Sailor could do. He slapped Ingram on the back. "Buck up, Todd. Go write your letter. But remember, our chances of getting through this are good. Just don't think about it."

"Right." Ingram turned to walk forward, then stopped. "What you say makes sense, Skipper. It's hard for me to accept it, but I understand what you're getting at."

"Okay."

"In a way you're lucky, Jerry."

"Oh?"

"No wife, No kids. Nobody to think of."

"A perfect warrior."

"You know what I mean."

Landa shrugged, then nodded out to sea. "What was the ten bucks for?"

"A friend." Ingram touched his cap. "Permission to lay below?"

Landa returned the salute. "Sleep well, Todd."

Landa watched him go, then stared at the sea's glassy surface. Ingram was right. He could pump out crap about getting wrapped up in loved ones. But there are times, he knew, when you have to think of yourself and survival. Not to get sidetracked with a wife. Yes, I am lucky, he thought. No wife. No family. No dog, no mortgage, no Sunday paper in front of a roaring fire while drinking freshly brewed coffee, the scent of bacon and eggs wafting from the kitchen.

There was Josh, though. Jerry Landa's mother had died giving birth to Jerry's younger brother. Growing up in Brooklyn, the boys were close and their father, a stevedore, raised them as best as he could, keeping the family together. Josh was clearly the smarter of the two, showing great potential. Both Landa and his father made sure the boy studied and made good grades. Landa had just graduated from the Merchant Marine Academy and was slated for sea duty when his father fell into a ship's hold, breaking his neck, killing himself. All of Landa's extra money went to properly raising Josh. And the kid rewarded the memory of his father and older brother by earning a scholarship to MIT. Landa was very proud, as Josh hit home runs everywhere he went, becoming a *wunderkind* of sorts, earning his Ph.D. in electronic engineering at age twenty. He was now with a government agency working on secret electronic stuff he couldn't talk about.

Except there was one thing Josh leaked to his older brother when they got together a few weeks back while Landa was recuperating in San Francisco. They'd had drinks, with Josh loosening up and telling his worries over a top secret new device called the proximity fuse. That it was being rushed to the fleet too quickly, that it might be inaccurate and worse, unsafe.

Josh could never hold his booze, Landa knew. And here the kid was again, eyes red, weaving on his barstool and slurring, "...gotta tell you I'm worried 'bout that damn thing, 'cause yer first on the list to receive them." He burped. "Destroyers gettum first."

"What should I do?" Landa prodded.

"Be careful. Radar might set 'em off. Make 'em blow up in your gun barrels or sumthin'. Be careful. Stay with your regular time fuses until the proximity fuses are proven. You swear?"

"I swear," Landa said to his little brother, the MIT genius.

And now, Landa thought, how neat. Unlike me, Josh doesn't have to catch a Jap bullet. *Damnit. Like Ingram, I got something to live for, too.*

Landa straightened his cap and moved forward. One of his Sailors stepped aside as he mounted the ladder to his sea cabin. The ship took a roll as Landa said under his breath, "Or, maybe, to die for."

4

25 February, 1943
   Rawlings & Sons Piano Repair, Inc.
   Silver Spring, Maryland

"You going home, Josh?" Four gold stripes gleamed on Frank Ashton's sleeve as he reached over Joshua Landa's shoulder to jerk the blackout curtains shut.

Josh's heart raced as he carefully nudged a gray crate further under the lab bench with a foot. "Not yet," he croaked.

At six-two, two hundred pounds, the Navy Captain dwarfed the twenty-eight year old Josh who buttoned his coat tighter against the cold outside. Hunching his five-foot nine-inch bean-pole frame further over the lab bench, he made a show of scribbling in his journal. *Can Ashton see the damned crate?*

"What's keeping you so late?"

Josh didn't want to be kicked off this job. If he were, his exemption would be canceled and it would be straight into the Army, MIT Ph.D. notwithstanding. *Show respect.* He cleared his throat and said, "Just a couple of tests. Won't be too long."

"...well, don't forget the drapes, Josh. We'll sure get in Dutch if some block warden pounds on the door and finds out what we're really doing."

Josh flipped switches on an oscilloscope, then turned on a speaker and said, "No, Sir, mustn't tip the Nazis. We just fix pianos. That's all we do here. Old man Rawlings has been dead for years, but that's okay. His wastrel sons preserved his ears in formaldehyde. Perfect pitch, that's their secret. Here, listen to this. High 'C.'" He ran the gain up, making the speaker screech.

Ashton covered his ears until Josh turned off the audio. "You really shouldn't be here alone."

Josh spun and faced Ashton, his hands jammed on his hips, his feet spread.

"I worry about you," Ashton said, jabbing Josh's shoulder.

"You tell us we're in a race against time. You tell us to produce. You say we're wasteful. You tell us."

"Josh. Hey, I'm on your side." Ashton offered his signature easy smile.

"...can I help it if my partner is home with pneumonia? The damn job finally got to him. How can I go home when you throw all these impossible deadlines at me?"

"I just don't want you getting overtired. And look," Ashton swept a hand across the laboratory, "everyone is gone."

"All I do is test glass. When do I get to test the fuse?"

"You're not ready. In due time. But not now."

"But you won't listen to my theory."

"Which one is it now?"

"Radar interference." *Damnit*. Josh wished he hadn't lost his temper. Casually, he reached over and closed his journal.

"Radar interference is not your bailiwick." Ashton paused for a moment, then said, "Say, have you been doing anything on your own?" His eyes dropped to Josh's journal.

Josh gave a crooked grin. "No, sir.'" He threw a mock salute. "Just glass. Twenty, thirty, fifty thousand 'Gs.' we have it in all sizes. Then crunch, crunch, crunch. Do you realize, Captain, how many little kids can't decorate their Christmas trees with light bulbs because of all the glass we're crunching up?"

Ashton thought about that. It was true. The demand for hardened glass vacuum tubes had virtually wiped out any remaining civilian glass supplies for the rest of the war. He pat Josh on the shoulder. "Go on home, Josh. Relax. You need it."

Josh pointed toward the stairwell. "I'm not alone. Gordon's downstairs."

"Gordon is not a scientist." Ashton said, referring to the civilian security guard in the downstairs lobby. "And you know the rules. I want people working in pairs, never alone. You must have backup." Ashton studied the workbench. Metal boxes, wires, tools of all sizes and shapes, beakers and bench vices absorbed every square inch. He wondered, how can Josh get anything done?

Josh tried again. "If I'm right, we'll save money in the long run, lots of it."

Ashton pointed to a sign over the doorway which read:

I DON'T WANT ANY DAMN FOOL IN THIS LABORATORY TO SAVE MONEY. I ONLY WANT HIM TO SAVE TIME.

Merle Tuve, the lab director had authored the sign. Josh knew what it said and, without looking, shrugged, "All I'm trying to do is--"

"You have to walk before you can run, kid. Give it a while. We'll get you going on the whiz-bang stuff soon enough."

"Okay." Josh heaved a sigh, knowing he couldn't fight it. Technically the blue-blooded Ashton was Josh's boss. His Naval lineage went back to his great grandfather, who stood alongside Farragut in the Civil War's Battle of Mobile Bay. Administratively, Josh's real boss was Herb Randall at the Carnegie Institute's Department of Terrestrial Magnetism. Like Josh Landa, Randall was one of the new *wunderkinds* in military electronics. Both of their doctoral studies were in radar, a field that was explored up to 1936, then cast aside as a luxury. But after war broke out in Europe, the science was resurrected, primarily by the British, who used radar to defend England against the Nazi *Luftwaffe* in the Battle of Britain.

By the luck of the draw, Josh had missed being assigned to Randall's staff, now housed in a likewise surreptitious building over on Georgia Avenue, the sign on that building announcing USED CARS. There, Randall rubbed elbows with the lions of the physical sciences: Merle Tuve, Richard Roberts, or even the oft-visiting Vannevar Bush, Chairman of the National Defense Research Committee and President Roosevelt's personal scientific appointee. Also, on Georgia Avenue was Navy Commander Deke Parsons, who Josh admired, especially when compared to this spit-wad standing next to him.

Josh tapped the gray crate with his toe, making sure it was out of sight. Then he slumped his shoulders and ran a hand through thick sandy hair, pushing it from his forehead.

Finesse it. With a sigh, he said, "All right Captain. I'll wrap it up and start first thing tomorrow morning."

Ashton clapped Josh on the shoulder. "Good. Now, look. I won't be seeing you for a few weeks."

"Oh?"

"Out to the South Pacific: Tulagi."

"Hey, my brother's out there. In the Navy, that is."

"Is he on a ship?"

"The *Howell*. A destroyer. He's the skipper."

"Well, I'll be a monkey's uncle. I'm going to visit the *Howell*. How about that?"

"Well, please give him my best. His name is Jerry."

"I'll do that. And Josh?"

"Yes?"

"I'm going to tell Gordon to come up here in ten minutes and throw you out if you're not done." Again, the signature smile. By comparison, Josh's teeth were dull, the lowers very crooked. It had bothered him ever since his teens. Jerry, the well-built football player with the championship smile. Girls followed him everywhere. Josh, the anemic ninety-pound weakling with terminal acne. Girls couldn't run fast enough to clear the room.

Ashton pulled on his grey kid gloves, straightened his blouse, and then arranged his peaked hat with a tilt, emulating an old salt with years at sea. Picking up his briefcase he winked and said, "Good night."

Josh switched off the oscilloscope and speaker, tossed his journal into his briefcase, and began throwing tools in the drawer. "...night. Have a good trip."

"...thanks." The door closed but Josh walked over and opened it, hearing Ashton's loud, confident footsteps going downstairs. His voice echoed with

Gordon's as they bid each other good-night with the front door slamming behind Ashton, Gordon throwing the double locks. To make sure, Josh raised a corner of the blackout curtain and watched Ashton climb into his gray Plymouth coupe and drive off.

Quickly, Josh turned on the oscilloscope, rearranged his tools, then grabbed his journal and swept aside junk and extraneous litter. While the scope warmed, he flipped switches to turn on the speaker, and then made a journal entry in careful printing:

January 25, 1943

1.) COMMENT; ASHTON'S TEST INSTRUCTIONS (COPY ENCLOSED) DO NOT PROVIDE FOR REMOVING THE TETRYL BOOSTER. FURTHER, ASHTON'S INSTRUCTIONS HAVE THE USUAL BOILERPLATE B "DO NOT DEVIATE FROM THESE INSTRUCTIONS WITHOUT EXPLICIT WRITTEN PERMISSION." I SHOULD POINT THIS OUT TO ASHTON AFTER RECEIVING OFFICIAL AUTHORIZATION TO TEST THIS FUZE.

2.) COMMENCING TEST OF MARK 32 FUZE AGAINST EXTERNAL RADAR INTERFERENCE. WILL BEGIN IN THE 100 CENTIMETER BAND.

Carefully, Josh reached under the bench and pulled out the wooden crate. It was somewhat larger than a shoebox with: TOP SECRET B MARK 32 FUZE B TOP SECRET, stenciled in black letters on top. It took ninety seconds to remove four large screws and ease off the lid. Inside, packed in shredded newsprint, was a gleaming fuse. Josh took a deep breath, cradled the fuse with both hands, and reverently lifted it from the box and set it on the bench.

About the size of a pint milk bottle, the mechanism was streamlined, yet menacing looking. Just beneath a cone-shaped nose cap were machined threads that allowed the bottom two thirds to fit inside a five-inch 38 caliber projectile. Essentially, this fuse was a miniature radar set. Made from hardened plastic, the nosecap housed the antenna. Beneath was a small compartment packed with four, pencil-thin vacuum tubes. A wet cell battery was housed below that. At the base was a two ounce tetryl booster charge. When fired from a gun, a five inch cannon in this case, the wet-cell activated and brought the fuse to life, sending radar beams out against an aerial target.

Forcing himself to exhale, Josh carefully set the Mark 32 fuse in a jig, then bent close to examine it. Tuve and his boys had done it! The physics were judged insurmountable when the project began just two years ago. The fused projectile, when shot out of a cannon, sustained set-back forces equivalent to *20,000 times the force of gravity*. If that wasn't hard enough, everything had to work while the projectile was in flight, spinning at *500 revolutions per second*. The beauty was that the fuse was designed to blow up in the *proximity* of the airplane's path, nullifying the usually erroneous range estimate from the fire control team on board ship. Now, all the shipboard gunners had to do was to aim the shell properly. The Mark 32's circuitry would do the rest, triggering an air-burst within seventy feet of the airplane, knocking Japanese and German airplanes from the skies like clay pigeons on a skeet range.

This fuse had been designated for the Dahlgren test range down river on the Potomac. But with Herb Randall's help, Josh had intercepted a shipment and carved this one out for 'further inspection at the glass-ware substation as stated on the packing slip.

Footsteps tapped on the main stairway. He checked his clock. *Damnit! Gordon!* Ten minutes. Where had the time gone? Quickly, he ran over and locked the door.

He carefully unscrewed the cap, then the base-ring, removed the keeper, and exposed the vacuum tubes packed below the nosecap. There, off to the side, was the elegant little thyratron, its tube made of hardened glass. Tiny wires ran from the thyratron down to the booster charge at the fuse's base.

Knuckles rapped on the door. "Dr. Landa?"

He called over his shoulder, "Done in a minute. Just wrapping up."

Safety first, as Ashton said. Josh carefully unclipped the thyratron wires making sure they were pulled well away from the fuse. With a pair of alligator clips, he connected a tall battery to the amplifier. Two other alligator clips served to connect the amplifier to the oscilloscope, making it hum in a steady monotone -- its white horizontal curser ruler-straight across the grid-work of a green cathode ray tube. Uncapping his fountain pen, Josh scratched notes in his journal, the black ink flowing across the page.

Gordon knocked again, louder. "Dr. Landa. Please."

"Okay, okay. Keep your shirt on!"

Now for the thyratron. Quickly, he reached for a screwdriver, not realizing he had knocked a small metal base ring-plate against the thryatron's wires.

Hurry! Josh's face was inches from the fuse as he reached to unclip the amplifier. Worse, he was unaware that the oscilloscope had begun to warble.

"Dr. Landa!"

"Go away!"

"Captain Ashton left instructions." The doorknob rattled.

"What?" Josh's eyes flicked from the oscilloscope to the metal base ring-plate. "Noooo!"

The oscilloscope cursor wiggled horribly across the screen, the speaker warbling louder and louder. Inexplicably, Josh reached to turn down the gain. In a millisecond he realized his mistake, that he should have gone for the plate that completed the thyratron circuit to the booster charge.

Too late. The last thing he remembered was an impossibly white-hot flash and something tearing into his head.

5

3 March, 1943
San Pedro, California

Helen had just turned on the Kraft Music Hall when the phone rang.

"Helen, it's Laura."

"Really?" *That must have sounded stupid.* Reaching to the radio, Helen eased down the volume, not wanting to lose Bing Crosby entirely. As she did, the realization hit her that she was speaking with Laura *West* Dutton, the concert pianist and wife of Todd's shipmate.

"I can prove it, honest," Laura laughed. She lived in Beverly Hills, a fair distance, which made the connection sound scratchy.

Having just finished dinner, Helen had laid a fire, its crackle helping to mask the occasional rumble of an oncoming storm. "How good to hear from you," she said.

She eased back in the overstuffed chair, letting Fred, her gray tabby cat jump in her lap and curl up.

"The honor's all mine, Helen. Luther and I enjoyed our time with you and Todd."

"I'm flattered you remembered." Just before Todd and Luther shipped out three weeks previously, Laura had given a USO sponsored piano concert at the Long Beach Naval Shipyard base theater. Surprisingly, it was a sell-out, the crowd wildly cheering at the program's end. She did an encore, then the crowd called for another. To their surprise, a Navy lieutenant in dress blues rose from the audience, mounted the stage and opened a violin case. It was Luther Dutton. He nodded and they began Laura's second encore: *The Meditation*. The crowd was ecstatic.

Later, the Ingrams and the Duttons had drinks at the Villa Rivera Hotel in downtown Long Beach. At the theater, Laura wore rimless glasses and her sandy hair was pulled-back into a bun, her air professional, almost arrogant, a perfect match for her husband. But as she walked in the Villa Rivera, she whipped off her glasses and undid her hair. The change was phenomenal, with Laura's smile now vulnerable, open and genuine. Helen, a tee-totaler, drank only ginger-ale while the others had cocktails. Laura on a dare from Luther, had a martini that night. Soon, she was smashing sentences as if calling a tobacco auction. Then she got the hiccups and began a laugh which soon had them all going

And now, it was almost as if they were back in the Villa Rivera. Helen asked, "You still a one martini girl?"

Laura chuckled, "I remember one thing that night. You said you were going to take up piano."

"Well..."

"Did you?"

"Well, this place has a piano and I've been practicing. Running scales, you know: do, re mi? Chopsticks?" Todd and Helen had rented a two bedroom furnished home on Alma Street three houses away from San Pedro High School. The view of Los Angeles Harbor was breathtaking and it was only a five minute drive from her duty station, the Fort MacArthur Base Infirmary. The furniture was mahogany, and an ancient, out-of-tune, upright Gulbrandsen piano, stood in the corner.

"You started lessons?" Laura asked.

"Not yet."

As if on cue, Fred rose, stretched, then hopped onto the floor. He walked over to the piano, jumped on the bench, then the keyboard. Discordant notes sounded as Fred sauntered up the keyboard, a feline glissando. When he reached the end, the gray tabby squarely planted his hind feet, and loosed a crescendo as he hopped onto the widow sill. From there, he bound onto the floor and disappeared into the guest bedroom.

Hearing the cacophony, Laura said, "Good God, hon, you do need help."

"That's Fred."

"What?"

Helen told her.

Laura laughed. "Sounds like Fred is coming along just fine. But what about you? You promised you would take lessons."

"Haven't gotten around to it yet." That night at the Villa Rivera Helen had vowed to resume her piano and they'd shaken hands solemnly. "I have a study guide. That's what I use."

"No. Get a teacher. You'll thank me in the long run."

"Teachers are expensive."

"All right. Then I'll come down and give you lessons myself."

"Anytime."

"Seriously, how 'bout dinner some evening. I'm bored."

"I'd love to. By the way, when's your next concert?"

"Actually, I'm out of the concert game for a while. I just signed with the NBC Orchestra. But they have me standing by and there's nothing on right now. And that's why I'm bored"

"NBC! That's keen."

"Thanks. How about next Saturday night?"

"Well, okay. I'm clear."

"Good. It's settled, then."

"Your best bet is to take the Pacific Electric to downtown L.A., then transfer to the San Pedro line."

Laura yawned, "No thanks, I think I'll drive."

"Oh." Helen remembered that Luther and Laura had driven up to the Villa Rivera in a light green, 1941 Cadillac convertible with gleaming white sidewall tires.

"Any good restaurants down there?"

Helen thought for a moment. "Olsen's. Great fish, abalone, even a steak now and then."

"Okay. Maybe we could go someplace for a drink before dinner?"

"That would be Shanghai Red's"

After a pause, Laura said dryly, "I just want a martini. I'd rather not get raped."

It was Helen's turn to laugh. "Oh, no. The police station is practically next door. We couldn't be safer."

"I'll take your word for it."

Static clicked for a moment, then Laura asked, "Uh, you heard from Todd?"

"Just one letter, one page. It sounded like he was in a hurry. " Helen bit her lip. She didn't mention that Todd had finished his letter with best wishes from the wardroom and that Luther Dutton was gone for a couple of weeks, filling in on the *Barber*. "You?"

"...nothing. Damnit. Just nothing. It's driving me crazy. How often do you write?"

"I...I try to get something out once a day. Keep things going. You know?"

They hung up, looking forward to Saturday night.

A loud, stuttering meow ranged from the guest room, a sure sign Fred had trapped a bug of some kind. Helen rose, shivering. Even with the fire and the ancient floor heater going, it seemed the old bungalow was still damp. It didn't help when Pacific storms whipped around the Palos Verdes Peninsula to buffet the house with forty knot winds.

"...what are you up to?" Helen muttered. All she could see of Fred were his eyes, gleaming in the dark. She padded to the guest room door and pushed it open. The room was small, perhaps ten by twelve and furnished with a single bed, dresser, and bedside table with lamp. But it had become a storage facility for Jerry Landa, the consummate ship-bound bachelor. In addition to suitcases and boxes and boxes of stuff ranging back to high school, the room held Landa's skis, golf clubs, chemistry set, and punching bag. The tiny closet was stuffed with his civilian clothes and to round things out, a steamer trunk had shown up just this morning. Apparently, it belonged to his brother and for lack of room anywhere else, ended up at the foot of the bed.

Helen flipped on the overhead light and stepped in, just as a gust of wind smacked the house, making kitchen dishes rattle. "...cockroach?"

Fred walked to the window, rose on his hind legs and pawed at the roller blind. Suddenly, the blind snapped up, going 'flap-flap-flap' at the top. The terrified cat spun around, all paws pumping furiously on the hardwood floor, failing to gain traction. Finally, Fred hurtled into the living room and hid behind the piano.

"You dope." Helen eased between two large boxes and reached for the blind, noticing a driving slantwise mist outside, not quite a rain. After drawing the blind, she clicked out the light and closed the door. Fred peeked around the piano and she said, "Boo!."

Later, her ablutions done, Helen crawled into bed, the cat curling at her feet. Taking up her pad she penned a note to Todd. After a page of chat she finished with,

"...they test fired Fort Macarthur's guns again last Friday. Everything: 14 inch, 6 inch, machine guns. Jeepers, those things put out a roar. But then both of us heard worse when we were 'out there.' Even so, the ground bucked all the way down to the infirmary. Kids at the high school were wide-eyed. I heard a couple of classroom windows broke.

They didn't warn us. I wonder why? When I got home our dinning room window was cracked all the way across. You know, the one with the BB gun hole, so I hope we get a new one courtesy of Uncle Sam. I have a call into the landlord.

My new boss at the Fort infirmary is a Colonel Moore. He called today, saying I've been promoted to Captain. So watch it buddy, I'm catching up to you.

By the way, Railway Express came by this morning and delivered a steamer trunk that belongs to Jerry's brother. Why would they do that? You should see it. It's a big green thing. The only place for it was at the foot of the guestroom bed, and it almost blocks the door. I'll tell you, all that junk in there. Can you ask Jerry to maybe find another place to store his stuff?

Mom and Dad send their love. He can't wait for you to get back on the ranch and run the tractor. Think I'll go up there next week.

Oh, I almost forgot to say, Laura Dutton just called, you know, as in Laura West Dutton. We had a good chat and she's coming down next Saturday night for dinner. She's threatening to teach me piano. Maybe I'll pour molasses in the keyboard. She seems okay, not taken up by her fame and all that. I hope the four of us remain good friends after this is all over.

Ummm. Time for dreamland. Wednesday night. Missed Bing Crosby when Laura called, and it's raining outside with the storm getting raucous. It scares Fred, his ears lay back every time a gust of wind hits the house.

I miss you honey and ache for you to come home soon. Going to curl up now and dream of you.

All My Love

Helen

...glissando. Racking her out of a graceful sleep. Up the keys. *Damnit, Fred!*

She'd forgotten to close the keyboard. In the gloom, the dial of her alarm clock read three-thirty-five.

"...uhhh." Helen lay back, and, cocking an ear to the outside, heard neither wind nor rain. The storm was down. *Thank Heaven.*

Another two keys thudded. Helen groaned and after a moment, whipped her covers off, the cold biting through her nightgown. "I'll kill 'im." She rose and marched through the living room toward the --

The guest room door swung open. A figure stood in the doorway.

Helen's mouth opened. She tried to scream.

Just then, the guest room blind zipped up, going 'flap-flap-flap,' back-lighting the figure. With that, Fred streaked past the apparition, through the living room and disappeared into the bedroom.

"...who...who," Helen gasped. She reached down to the coffee table and grabbed a brass ashtray made from a five-inch cannon powder case.

Whoever it was, looked back at the window. Helen could see it was open. But his face was covered by a dark balaclava. He had broad shoulders; it had to be a man. He took a step toward Helen and hesitated.

She found her voice and screamed.

The man turned, and, in two steps, dove cleanly through the guest room window.

A small zephyr rustled the bushes at the window. To Helen it felt like a 150 mile per hour typhoon.

"My God!" Flipping on the living room light, she raced in the guest room, hit the light and slammed down the window. Making sure it was locked, she pulled the blind down and ran back to the living room.

Tears ran as she grabbed the phone and dialed the operator. "Police! My God. Police. Hurry!"

6

6 March, 1943
U.S.S. *Howell* (DD 482)
Tulagi Harbor, Solomon Islands

With no wind, the sea was flat in Tulagi Harbor; almost mirror-smooth. Cruisers, troopships, sea-going tugs, and destroyers, stood brooding over their anchorages, chains slack, wisps of black smoke lazily rising from a stack and curling to the sky. It had rained earlier, and the late morning was thick with humidity, sweat, peeling paint, wilted salt-caked clothing, jungle rot, green slime-coated leather boots, and worst of all, un-predictable electronic equipment.

Lieutenant (j.g.) Elton P. "Tubby" White wiped his brow and stepped back to the quarterdeck, a shady area beneath the 01 level catwalk; a spot occasionally graced by zephyrs. He peered south toward Guadalcanal, where clouds gathered over the mountains, promising yet more rain. Two hours to the next storm, he figured.

WAP! Tubby slapped the back of his neck. One more of at least ten billion Solomon Island-type mosquitoes had landed on his neck. "Damnit!"

The specter of malaria was too horrible to contemplate and he'd smeared repellant everywhere. Tubby was the in-port officer of the deck for the morning watch. He was five nine and a compact two hundred five pounds. Tubby's uniform consisted of cut-off khaki work trousers, a sweat-soaked sleeveless shirt, and a pith helmet providing shade for his large, oval head. A .45 automatic, dangling from a web belt, completed his ensemble. He'd played guard at USC and his fine blond hair was cut short, emphasizing a round face and oversized lower lip some took for a sign of ignorance. But what Tubby lacked in looks was more than made up for in IQ, which got him into trouble. Like the time he disassembled a Ford model "A" and reassembled it on the second story of USC's Bovard Hall. Everyone knew it was Tubby yet, somehow, they couldn't pin it on him. Or the time during Christmas break, at the downtown Broadway Department Store. He'd found a job as a mail clerk in the pneumatic tube dispatching station. On Christmas Eve, Tubby stuffed white mice into the message capsules and sent them squeaking on their way. His satisfaction: muted screams and telephones jangling stridently in the outer office. But Tubby overplayed it. He'd run out of mice and was dumping confetti into the tubes when, an enraged supervisor burst through the door and fired him on the spot. Accordingly, Tubby was almost suspended from USC and had to work hard to achieve the Dean's amnesty. With great restraint, Tubby concentrated on his studies and earned his B.S. in mechanical engineering, his stunts notwithstanding.

A pair of F4Fs blasted over the *Howell* and flew on to skim the *Issac* and *Griffith's* mast heads. A couple of Marine hot-dogs, he supposed, but Tubby was glad to see them out and around, waiting to pounce on Japs.

Two more Wildcats rose off Guadalcanal and joined the first pair to fly a slow orbit overhead, a CAP (Combat Air Patrol) pattern. Even with the fighters buzzing overhead, Tubby still felt vulnerable sitting here. And he was sure the others did too. They were in Tulagi to take on fuel and ammunition. Right now, a fuel barge was moored alongside with two thick hoses snaked over fore and aft, pumping NSFO -- Naval standard fuel oil. The humidity-laden day was getting hotter, and the whole atmosphere seemed sticky, almost greasy, as the heavy, fuel oil fumes vented from the *Howell's* tanks.

They were sitting ducks, and Admiral Halsey's standing orders were that all ships were to keep up steam, so they could get underway at a moment's notice, even if it meant slipping anchor. Halsey also stipulated that all ships be at condition III watches: all guns manned for defense against air attack.

To clearly state his views on the situation, Halsey had ordered a forty-by-sixty foot bill-board erected at the entrance to Tulagi Harbor for all to read:

KILL JAPS. KILL JAPS, KILL THE YELLOW BASTARDS. IF YOU DO YOUR JOB YOU WILL KILL THE SONS OF BITCHES.

Tubby peered at Halsey's sign, thinking of the first time he'd seen it: incredulity and shock. But later, he'd seen the wrecked ships limp into Tulagi and offload their maimed sailors, some living, others forever muted under canvas tarps. And he'd been in CIC when the *Barber* went up. He could still hear and feel the WHACK against the *Howell's* superstructure. It was like being stuffed into in a fifty-five gallon oil drum with the neighborhood thug hitting it with a baseball bat. And all those guys gone, among them, Luther Dutton, an officer he admired, in spite of his MIT bullshit.

The gravity of the situation really sank in when Tubby learned of Japanese atrocities from old-timers in the crew. Take Mr. Ingram, for example. He was an okay guy, reputed to have survived the worst of what the Japs dished out at Corregidor in the Philippines. For sure, Tubby knew the part about Ingram's escape from Corregidor was true. The night the 'Rock' fell to the Japs, Ingram commandeered a thirty-six foot launch and made it with ten other guys all the way to Darwin, Australia under the cover of night; an amazing voyage of 1,900 miles, most of it through Jap-held territory. That was in May of last year, and he'd been awarded the Navy Cross last August. And then, for some reason, Ingram was reputed to have been given a purple heart, arising from a more recent secret mission in the Philippines.

But Ingram didn't pin on his medals until a couple of weeks ago. That was when the *Howell* rejoined the squadron from Brisbane. Rocko Myszynski stepped aboard for a dress inspection. Before the entire wardroom, the exasperated Commodore of DESRON 12 shouted to Ingram that he was out of uniform. Uncharacteristically, the flamboyant Myszynski made everyone stand at attention while Ingram ran below to his stateroom, rummaged around, and returned four minutes later, the Navy Cross and Purple Heart affixed with the rest of his campaign ribbons, which included four battle stars. But getting Ingram to talk about Bataan or Corregidor, or the rest of the Philippines, was like speaking to a blank wall. Ingram would unfocus for a moment, then look right through you. With that, he would change the subject. Sure, he and 'Boom Boom' Landa would talk about more recent actions and lessons learned from the Battles of Cape Esperance or the Santa Cruz Islands. The latter inflicted considerable damage to the *Howell's* fo'c'sle, killing twenty-two men and seriously wounding Landa, earning him his own Purple Heart.

Tubby checked the clock, 1047, and wondered when his orders would come through. He'd put in for PT boats back in the States, and they'd posted him to the *Howell*, on a temporary basis, so the San Diego detailer said, until a spot opened up for him in the Solomons. He'd been aboard the *Howell* since she'd come out of the shipyard in Melbourne. Eight weeks, damnit.

Even with the Wildcats flying overhead, they were sitting ducks. That's what these cans were. With their weight-saving aluminum superstructures, these damn destroyers were prone to burning like Roman candles when hit with something hot, like burning fuel. He shuddered again when he thought of the *Barber*. But the fact that the PTs carried 3,000 gallons of 100 octane gasoline somehow didn't bother him. Fast and maneuverable, the PTs could dodge Jap bullets. They were powered by three V-12 supercharged 4M-2500 Packard engines. Each one produced 2,500 horsepower, more than enough juice to get out of a Jap's way, and dish some back to him, too.

Tubby shifted his eyes to the crew as they shuffled back and forth. Barely speaking, and looking furtively toward the sky, they didn't act like sailors. They looked more like fugitives: men on the run. Tubby put their morose mood down to the fact that Rocko Myszynski was sending them on another raid tonight to hit the Vila airstrip on Kolombangara Island. He'd already seen three or four of the other ships ease past in the last hour.

As if to validate Tubby's thoughts, he heard a 'clunk' off to port. It was the light cruiser, *Sioux Falls,* belching black smoke from her forward stack. Having just housed her anchor, white water frothed beneath her screw guards, and she gathered way. The 12,000 ton ship glided past, while men walked her 608 feet length, stowing gear, getting ready. Launched less than three years ago, the *Sioux Falls* had just joined the fleet, sporting new dazzle camouflage. To Tubby, she seemed a floating porcupine. Guns bristled everywhere: her main battery consisted of twelve six-inch forty-sevens pointing to the sky from four triple mounts; elsewhere, twelve five-inch thirty-eights were housed in six twin mounts; and an untold number of forty and twenty millimeter cannons stuck out from every other corner aboard the ship. Spinning atop her foremast were the secret new air search and surface-search radar antennas. The *Sioux Falls's* bow-wave grew larger as she increased speed, heading into Iron Bottom Sound. The scuttlebutt was that the *Sioux Falls* was to be joined tonight by her sisters *King City* and *Santa Monica,* along with the destroyers *Armstrong, Fruehauf, Mutz* and *Lyon.* Further inshore, the *Hanscom, Dale, W. E. Dunalp, Caldwell, Redmond* and *Cummings* were getting up steam. Tubby raised his binoculars. Sure enough, through the anchored ships, he spotted at least four other ships gathered out on the Sound, radar antennae twirling, guns at the 'ready air position' dark, menacing.

Tubby shook his head slowly. Battleships carried over 2,700 officers and men; the light cruisers, 1,200; destroyers, 300 plus. But PT boats carried just two officers and ten men. And that suited Tubby just fine. No oceans of gold braid (and gold bricks) to get in his way. Just step on the gas and stomp Japs.

He checked the clock again, 1105, his heart soaring that this could be his last watch aboard the *Howell.* PTs would be a lot better than hanging around here. *Look at these guys!* The *Barber's* loss had left an indelible impression of anger and revenge, unsatisfied by two subsequent runs back to Kula Gulf. Without targets, the crew hadn't an opportunity to vent their rage. And now, it seemed to Tubby, they had become distant, withdrawn.

And Landa's situation wasn't helping. When they returned to port, the skipper was really down about something. Then Mr. Ingram had told them, quietly, that the old man had received a telegram that his kid brother had been critically injured in the States. The point was that the old man took it out on everyone else. At lunch yesterday, one of the ensigns at the other end of the table had said something offhanded about poor morale. The old man flew into a rage. "There will absolutely be no poor morale," he yelled. Landa's face turned red, as pieces of Chicken ala King spewed from his mouth, "I will not tolerate poor morale. We need every one of those sonsabitches to give it their all, and damnit," the Captain smashed down a fist, "I'll not put up with backsliders."

Strange thing about Landa, Tubby thought. His reputation in the Fleet was top-notch. Friends, fellow skippers called him "Boom Boom" because, Tubby supposed, Landa loved to shoot the ship's guns. (Indeed, there were some peace-time skippers who cowered in the pilot house from the sharp CRACK of the five-inch gun when it went off.) Off watch, Landa's calling card was a broad, impossibly white Pepsodent grin, unmasking a mouth full of perfect teeth; a grin that disarmed all who stepped within ten yards. Indeed, Landa was known for being a fun loving, hard drinking sailor, the kind Tubby wanted to sail with.

So thought an elated Tubby when he received his orders to join the *Howell*. As things turned out, the Jerome Landa he served under was a good skipper, all right. But gone was the signature smile. Gone were the backslaps and practical jokes. When not on the bridge, the man spent most of his time in his sea cabin.

Seltzer, the sandy-haired petty officer of the watch, stepped up and sounded six bells over the 1MC: 1100: half hour to chow. Seltzer was a bean-pole second class boatswain's mate who, Tubby understood, knew Ingram pretty well. In fact, he'd heard Seltzer had been on that secret mission with Ingram, but neither spoke of it.

Seltzer caught Tubby's eye. "Any word from the XO on when we take aboard ammo?"

"Not yet."

They watched as a dark-blue splotched PBY lifted off from the harbor and headed east. "Daily mail to Espiritu Santu," Seltzer said.

"Yup."

Seltzer's eyes tracked the PBY as it disappeared. "You know, Sir, Tom Crane, the flight engineer on that plane, is a friend of mine."

Tubby started to move off.

"Tom said they always bring back a case of scotch. Maybe more."

"No kidding?"

Seltzer looked from side to side. "That stuff goes directly to the Tulagi O Club and disappears. Top brass gets it all."

"Really?"

Seltzer's eyebrows went up.

"Yeah, I may know a guy or two over there who might look the other way," Tubby said quietly. "Maybe on mail call we--"

Redding, a stocky second class boiler tender known as the 'Oil King', emerged from the after fire room hatch like a spider crawling from a drain pipe. Sweat dripped down his face as he walked up and said, "All topped off, Sir. You can shove the barge off."

White took in Redding's tobacco stained teeth and fuel-oil splotched dungarees. How do those men survive down there when it's so damned hot up here, he wondered? He'd heard temperatures pushed 115 degrees at times in the boiler and engine rooms, maybe more." Very well," he said.

The fuel barge crew was already recovering their hoses. That done, Seltzer and Redding passed their lines over, and the fuel barge chugged off into Tulagi's humidity-laden haze. White watched it go, breathing a sigh of relief, thankful once more the Japs hadn't caught them with their pants down.

Redding gave a yellow-toothed grin and reached to his breast pocket. "Okay to light up, Sir?

"Yeah, I don't see why—"

"---Sir, looks like an ammo barge is approaching," Hardy, the messenger of the watch said.

"What? Better hold that cigarette, Redding." Tubby said.

Redding grumbled as he stuffed Chesterfields back into his pocket.

Seltzer pointed to an LCM plowing its way toward the *Howell*, a red baker flag at her staff. "We expecting an ammo barge, Mr. White?" he asked.

"I---." The LCM slowed, and an officer poked his head above her bulwark. Sun glinted off of a silver collar device. The man's hat bore scrambled eggs. White gasped, "Damnit. A full Captain!"

The LCM backed down, its twin diesels roaring. Black smoke poured from exhaust pipes as her twin screws bit the water. White grabbed the quarterdeck phone and rang the wardroom. No answer. None from the bridge, either. "Hardy, damnit. Get the Exec. Shit; the Captain--Everybody. " He slapped Hardy on the butt. "On the double. Go!"

"Sir!" The messenger ran forward, keys jangling at his duty belt.

Seltzer quickly moved aft to help the LCM moor alongside. White turned to Redding. "Give Seltzer a hand."

The LCM's bowline snaked through the air and landed at Tubby's feet. He caught it, stooped to pass it under the lifeline, spun it around a cleat and tied it off. When Tubby stood, he was within eighteen inches of the Navy Captain, a broad grin stretched across the man's face. The captain saluted the flag on the fantail; then saluted Tubby White. "Permission to come aboard, Sir?"

"I...I, of course, Captain. Here, let me." Tubby offered a hand to help the Captain jump over the life line. "We should part the line first, Sir."

"No, that's okay." The Captain nimbly leaped over the lines and alighted on the deck. He held out a hand. "Hi. Frank Ashton."

"Tubby White." He took Ashton's hand. In his late 40s or early 50s, the captain had close-cropped salt and pepper hair, and a set of teeth that nearly matched Landa's for brightness and perfect alignment. He wore neither blouse nor tie, but his tailor-made khaki shirt and trousers were neatly pressed making Ashton look as if he'd stepped from a Brooks Brothers ad.

"I'm sorry, Sir. I---we weren't aware you were coming. If you don't mind holding on for a moment, I'll have the Captain or XO. "

"Good morning, Sir. Jerry Landa." Landa walked up and saluted.

"Hi. Frank Ashton." Returning the salute, he shook Landa's hand. "I...I...have you heard about your brother.?"

"As far as I know, he's critical. Do you have any news?"

Ashton looked down. "Nothing new. I'm sorry. What a terrible thing. He was the best."

"What the hell do you mean *was* the best?"

"Sorry. I didn't mean it that way."

"What's wrong with him?"

"All the doctors can say is that he suffered a brain injury. Then an infection set in."

Landa jammed his hands on his hips and nodded.

After a long moment, Ashton said, "Your ship is beautiful. These new *Fletcher* class destroyers are really tops." He swung around, taking in the *Howell*. "Say, do they really call you 'Boom Boom?'"

"We try our best, Sir."

"Well, she looks brand new to me."

The crew gathered like onlookers at the scene of a head-on collision. With a glance from Landa, they moved on and he said, "Well, she was little dented. Got into a fracas or two with the Japs. We just got out of the yard."

"Heard all about that. And well done. That's why I'm here."

Ingram broke through a knot of sailors. "All right. Carry on." He saluted Ashton and introduced himself.

"Did you come in that, Sir?" Landa pointed to the LCM.

"The name's Frank. And yes, that's my cab. We have some ammo for you, *Griffith* and *Issac*."

They peered into the LCM's well to see several pallets of olive drab five-inch gun projectiles; stacked nose up, deadly. Suppose we call away a work party?" Ashton said.

"The sooner, the better," agreed Landa. "Excuse me." He stepped over to Tubby White, palmed his elbow and moved him away. "Why didn't you let me know he'd arrived?" he hissed.

"Captain, he just pulled up without warning. I didn't know."

"You goldbrick." Landa's teeth were clenched. "We had word of this at 0800. Don't you read the message board?"

"I---" Tubby looked wildly at Ingram.

Landa seethed, "as far as I'm concerned, Mister, you can have your damned PT transfer, the sooner the better. Now call away a work party and get that ammo aboard. Better get the chief gunner, too." His hand tightened on White's elbow.

Tubby White jerked his elbow away and stood at attention. "Yes, Sir. Will there be anything else, Sir?"

Landa unclenched his fists, spun, and walked back to Ashton, who flipped pages on a clip board.

Ingram moved over and said, "Not your fault, Tubby. The radioman forgot to post the message. I'll fix it with the skipper."

White glared at Landa and rubbed his elbow. "Sonofabitch."

"That's enough. I said I would fix it," said Ingram. "By the way," he said more softly, "your transfer came through about a half hour ago. This is your last watch aboard the *Howell*. So when you're relieved, go have chow, pack your gear and *adios*."

"Yes, Sir. Thank you Sir,"

"Forget it, Tubby. The Captain's had bad news about his brother."

Tubby White's face said *so what*?

"Better call away that work detail." Ingram patted Tubby White's shoulder, then joined Landa and Ashton as they moved forward to the wardroom.

White watched Ashton lead the way, grinning and returning salutes as he went, waving his arms, laughing. *God, now there's a leader. The kind of guy you'd follow anywhere.*

As for Landa, he thought, I'll fix that bastard.

Seltzer walked up, brushing off his hands. "Mr. White, Sir, about my proposal for that scotch?"

"Later, damnit."

"Yes, Sir."

7

6 March, 1943
   U.S.S. *Howell* (DD 482)
   Tulagi Harbor, Solomon Islands

As tradition dictated, Landa, the ship's commanding officer, took the head of the table for the noon meal. Ashton sat to Landa's right, a chair normally reserved for Todd Ingram, the executive officer. So Ingram sat to Landa's left, the rest of the officers arranged in the usual order of seniority with Edgerton, the boot ensign, sitting in the far corner.

Landa toyed with his food. The others were quiet, too. Maybe it was the heat, Ingram thought. Their faces were flushed, in spite of three mighty fans, giving it their all. Thankfully, a cold bean salad was the main course served along with a semi-viscous tomato soup of dubious origin.

From courtesy, all waited for the ranking officer, Ashton, to begin the meal. He rubbed his hands and said, "Looks good." He raised his spoon with a flourish, slurped loudly and said, "What? Cold soup?"

At the table's end, Ensign Edgerton lifted a full spoonful and swallowed. "Owwww. Cheez!" He fanned his mouth furiously, and his face turned red.

"Here." Kelly shoved over a glass of water.

"Joke's so old," Ashton laughed, "I didn't believe anyone would fall for it. I should apologize."

"Don't," said Landa. "He's headed for a lot worse. Might as well get used to it."

"What's his name?" Ashton asked.

"Edgerton, Sir," Ingram told him.

"Mr. Edgerton. Where you from, Sailor?"

"Cuyahoga Falls, Sir," Edgerton gasped. "That's in Ohio,"

"You bet I know where Cuyahoga Falls is. I'm from Sioux Falls."

"I'll be damned," Edgerton blurted,

Kelly grinned. "Me too, Sir."

"Where?" asked Ashton.

"Sioux Falls. You know South Euclid?" Kelly said.

Ashton sat back. "I'll be damned. That's where I grew up. Tell me, Mr..."

"Kelly."

"Mr. Kelly. I haven't been back in twenty years. Do the Tanner Brothers still have their hardware store?"

"I'll be damned," said Kelly " As far as I know, they do."

Ashton eyed the rest of the table. "For the rest of you unfortunates, the Tanner Brothers gave free candy, summer employment to neighborhood kids, shelter to hobos, and had the hottest stove in winter. The grown ups would sit by the cracker barrel and talk politics, religion, women, and every other damned thing under the sun. We called it the..." He snapped his fingers.

"...Spit and Argue club," said Kelly

"That's it. The Spit and Argue Club." While the others ate, Ashton kept talking. Soon, he was reminiscing about his first duty assignment out of the Naval Academy. "...she was the *Lindsay*, an old four stack destroyer." In a single, fluid motion Ashton loaded more bean salad on his plate, took a bite, then continued, a far off look in his eye. "Along came World War I and we found ourselves bouncing in the North Atlantic on convoy duty. Now you guys may have a legitimate gripe about what's going on down here, but, I'll tell you, the North Atlantic in winter is not my idea of a good time. And still," he smiled, "we got two German U-boats."

"Really?" said Kelly.

"Caught the first one on the surface at night. Damn fool was up-moon. Didn't see us coming..."

Something struck Ingram. Ashton, Ashton. Yes...he'd heard of this senior naval captain who still looked as if he'd stepped from a recruiting poster. He was a favored son, reputed to be in line for the top job at the Bureau of Ordnance. And the Ashtons were a well known Navy family; hell, the guy's great grandfather had stood beside Farragut at the Battle of Mobile Bay.

Ashton stabbed the air with a fork. "...we ran over him and laid a pattern of six depth charges. But God, it was stormy. Waves with short periods and steep troughs. I don't know how we rolled them off. In fact, one depth charge pitched off the ready rack and slid around the deck. Took four men to grab hold and wrestle it down. They were scared. I don't blame them. So was I. Four hundred and fifty pounds clanking around. Then they set the fuse and shoved it over. Turns out that was the one that got him." With a grin, Ashton fashioned an explosion with his hands. "Whump! Right away. The Jerry's stern shot in the air, hung there for a moment then went straight down."

The plates were cleared and the conversation became animated, with the officers hurling questions at Ashton.

Seltzer knocked and walked into the wardroom wearing his hat, duty belt, and side arm. Standing at attention, he said, "Captain, the Officer of the deck sends his respects and reports the hour of twelve hundred. The chronometers have been wound and compared, and he would like to submit the noon position and fuel status reports." Seltzer handed over two slips.

"And the OOD is...?" Landa asked.

Seltzer said, "Mr. Foreman relieved Mr. White about fifteen minutes ago, Captain."

"Is the ammo aboard, yet?"

"Almost. About twenty rounds to go, Captain."

"Very well. Please give Mr. Foreman my compliments. And tell him he may light the smoking lamp when finished loading ammo." Landa pocketed the noon status slips.

"Yes, Sir." Seltzer turned and walked out.

"Excuse me, Captain." Ingram rose and followed Seltzer down the passage way. "Leo?"

Seltzer stopped and turned. "Sir?"

"Where's Tubby?"

"Damned if I know. What's with the Skipper, anyway? His little gig on the quarterdeck went over like a turd in a beer pitcher."

"It's his brother."

"Don't matter."

Seltzer had pushed beyond the limit, but Ingram let it pass. He and Seltzer had joined the *Howell* last September and fought side-by-side in the Battles of Cape Esperance and the Santa Cruz Islands. Later, while the *Howell* was in the Brisbane shipyard, they had been parachuted into Japanese-held Mindanao on a top secret, near-fatal assignment. By now, their times in combat had forged a bond of mutual trust. Ingram said, "He'll get over it. We just have to be patient. It's Tubby I'm worried about. He didn't show up for chow. Usually, he's the first one to the hog trough."

Seltzer shrugged.

"Okay." Ingram left Seltzer, headed down the ladder into 'Officer's Country' and walked to Tubby's stateroom. Sweeping aside the curtain, he looked in. Empty.

He retraced his steps and bumped into Tubby White.

"Excuse me, Sir." White stepped in, flipped his pith helmet on the desk, pulled a dufflebag from the overhead and threw it on the bunk.

"You going up for chow?"

"No, thank you, Sir." White yanked opened drawers, dug out his clothes and stuffed them into the duffle.

Feeling Ingram's eyes on his back, he turned and added, "A stores boat is standing by to give me a hop to the PT base." He paused, "If that's okay with you, Sir."

"Come on, Tubby. You don't have to walk off like this."

Tubby stuffed soiled laundry atop clean shirts and trousers. "All I need are my orders, Sir."

Ingram pushed his toe through a patch of rust on the deck. When first built, Officer's Country in the *Fletcher* class destroyers had dark-green linoleum decks, haze grey bulkheads and white overheads. Good for habitability, bad for fire prevention, as many had learned in the past few months. In fact, BuShips had passed orders for all ships to immediately remove all flammable materials such as linoleum, wood paneling, and interior paint, which had to be scraped to bare metal. So now, everything was a dull rust-brown, giving one a repressed feeling, which perfectly matched Tubby's demeanor at the moment.

After a long pause Ingram said, "As you wish, Mr. White. You may pick up your orders in the ship's office." He turned and walked aft.

"Mr. Ingram?" Tubby's head poked in the passageway.

"Yes?"

"I'm sorry. You've treated me swell. I don't have it in for you. But I can't let that jerk--"

"--don't forget to say goodbye to the Captain." Ingram headed down the passageway.

A baize green cloth covered the wardroom table, and the chairs were rearranged classroom style, facing the starboard side where Captain Ashton stood before a portable blackboard. He scrawled on the blackboard, TOP SECRET, then said, "Need I say more?"

His eyes swept the wardroom. "Okay, let's start from the top. Admiral Isoroku Yamamoto is the guy, who you know, runs the whole Jap Navy. And, in case you didn't know, it's this jerk who planned the Pearl Harbor attack. But now, Mr. Yamamoto is one angry sonofabitch. He is angry because we kicked him off Guadalcanal two months ago."

A few smiled.

"You're proud, and rightfully so. This ship distinguished herself admirably in the Santa Cruz Islands battle and at Cape Esperance. So now, Mr. Yamamoto is swinging at anchor in Truk Lagoon, trying to figure out a way to knock us on our butts and eventually kick us out of Guadalcanal." Ashton paused for a moment. "Except for the *Barber* incident, it's been a quiet time. We believe something's coming our way, but we're not sure what it is exactly. But, you can bet the Japs will throw everything at us, except maybe Tojo's limousine. So what we're trying to do right now is figure out a way to stop the bastards. Cold. In their tracks.

"Now, for the past two years, a special office of BuOrd, simply called Department 'T,' has been working on something to counter the enemy air threat." Ashton smacked a fist in his palm. "And now, I'm happy to tell you that we've done it. I--"

A clean-shaven Tubby White knocked softly and stepped in, a large envelope tucked under his arm. He was dressed in clean khaki's. His shoes were shined; even his belt buckle was polished. "Excuse me, Sir."

Landa looked up. "Yes?"

"Sorry for the interruption, Captain. Permission to leave the ship, Sir?" Tubby said.

Landa stood, took Tubby's hand and said, "Of course." He flashed his best grin and said, "Good luck in those floating hundred-octane bombs, Tubby."

Ashton coughed politely and sipped coffee, while the other officers said their good-byes. There was a good round of handshakes with cat-calls following Tubby as he walked out.

Landa waved a hand to Ashton. "Sorry, Sir."

"It's okay. You, *Issac* and *Griffith* are my first clients, so to speak, especially since," Ashton glanced at his watch, " you're underway for the Blackett Straits this evening. So I have two more calls this afternoon."

Landa nodded.

"Gentlemen," Ashton asked in a crisp baritone. "They've sent me all the way from Silver Spring, Maryland, to indoctrinate you into the use of the Mark 32 proximity fuse."

Ingram looked around, seeing more than one officer sitting pitched forward in his chair.

Ashton's chalk squeaked on the board as he drew a picture of a five inch projectile, then, an expanded view of the fuse that sat atop the projectile ."The Mark 32 proximity fuse is, in reality, a miniature radar set. After it leaves the gun-barrel, it sends out radio waves just like a radar transmitter. At the same time, a receiver in the fuse senses the echoed waves as they bounce back from a target. When the shell is closest to the target, it goes off, spreading a lethal pattern of shrapnel. Right now, we estimate the kill ratio to be about fifty percent, compared to the ten percent of your current Mark 18, mechanical time fuses."

"You gotta be kidding," said Lou Delmonico, a dark, wavy haired lieutenant who was *Howell's* new gun boss. He'd been aboard only a few days to replace Luther Dutton. They all began talking, with Delmonico asking, "What fires the fuse?"

"Basically, there's an oscillator that receives the reflected waves from a target." Ashton sketched as he spoke, "The outgoing and incoming signals interact to create a ripple signal. Thus, when the projectile closes the target to within seventy feet, the ripple pattern triggers a thyratron tube. Now, that's really a switch which sends an electric current to a condenser which, in turn, sets off an explosion in the tetryl detonator here," Ashton smacked the board, breaking the chalk. Tossing the broken pieces in the tray, he brushed off his hands and continued, "That, in turn, fires the projectile's main charge. Boom!"

"You mean we don't have to set fuses?" Ingram asked. In addition to aiming the gun, fuse setting was one of the trickiest parts of the air defense problem. Projectiles were set to explode at a pre-set time. If the ship's gunfire control computer calculated correctly, the shell would explode when it arrived at the target. Otherwise, it would detonate uselessly before or after the target, leaving the familiar puffy black smoke puff in the sky.

"No." Ashton folded his hands. "No fuse setting. In a way, that's why some of us call the proximity fuse the variable time or VT fuse, because we don't have to calculate the time of flight. The fuse's radar signal does it all."

"Yikes! No excuse for your guys missing now." Chief Engineer Hank Kelly smacked Gun Boss Lou Delmonico on the arm.

A hub-bub arose with everyone talking at once. Someone whooped with, "So solly, Cholly. Sayonara."

Landa turned and gave his officers a sour look. Ingram put two fingers in his mouth and whistled loudly.

"How can you be so sure?" Landa said after they quieted.

"Believe me, Jerry, we tested this fuse at Dahlgren until the cows came home. And we kept testing after that. It's ready. And it is effective. And it is safe to handle. We made sure of that."

"But you have no experience in the fleet. You---"

"Actually we do." Ashton interrupted, looking at his watch again. " The *Helena* shot down a Betty using VT ammo a little over a month ago," he pointed northwest, "right up The Slot."

Quiet descended on the wardroom. Landa crossed his arms and looked at the deck, his lips pressed white. After a minute he looked up . "...but the set-back would ruin your little radar set. A cannon punching out a shell at twenty thousand Gs. Then it spins at---"

"Believe me, Jerry. It works. And Rocko Myszynski has bought into the VT fuse and will incorporate it into squadron doctrine in the next few days."

"I wouldn't know about that; we're too busy fighting Japs," Landa said softly.

"I beg your pardon?"

"Sorry Captain. Just talking to myself."

"I see." Ashton reached into his briefcase and produced a thick folder of papers. "Here's Commodore Myszynski's doctrine draft regarding DESRON TWELVE using variable time fuses for anti-aircraft warfare. He's asked me to give a copy to you and the other skippers for comment." Ashton dropped the folder on the wardroom table, his gaze on Landa. "Are there any questions?"

"No, Sir. I don't think so," said Landa.

"Then, I thank you." Ashton quickly wiped off the chalk board, stuffed his material in his briefcase, and walked out.

The others stood, but Landa said, "Hold on. Remain in your seats, please. I want to go over a few things about tonight." Then he walked out after Ashton.

Delmonico poured coffee. "What the hell gives, XO?" Ingram shook his head. "Damned if I know." He grabbed his cap and headed out to find it had begun raining. In fact, the storm was heavy, with water sheeting down the decks. Momentarily, he took shelter under the starboard motor whale boat as a cloudburst grew to a roar. When it lightened, Ingram saw Ashton and Landa talking thirty feet further aft, standing in the open, oblivious to the rain. They were nearly nose to nose and were red-faced; and it wasn't the oppressive humidity, Ingram could tell. Men ducked past, as if the two senior officers were pedestrians blocking a Manhattan sidewalk during a blizzard. Their conversation grew more animated. Suddenly, Ashton stepped back and pointed a finger at Landa. Landa gave a retort.

Ashton threw his hands in the air and walked aft to the LCM, where he gave a short whistle and twirled a finger over his head. Saluting curtly, Ashton stepped through a break in the lifelines as Foreman saluted back. The LCM's twin engines cranked, as Ashton dropped to the LCM's well deck.

The crew quickly took in her lines, and with a roar, the LCM quickly backed away and was lost to sight, as another cloudburst swooped in.

Landa turned and walked forward, shaking his head as he passed Ingram.

Ingram had to yell against the pounding rain. "What is it, Jerry?"

Landa swept on, yelling as he went. "...it's all hocus-pocus. Bunch of butterfly catchers in white lab coats running around setting off firecrackers. Damned if I'll let them use the things on my ship."

"Why not?"

"I can't tell you."

"What?"

"Look. All I can say is that they're unreliable. And that other radars can set them off in our gun-barrels. They just haven't been tested enough." Landa walked faster waving his hands in the air. "Imagine that. Trying to shoot down a Jap when another ship lights you up with his radar. Boom! No thanks, Buster."

Ingram walked fast to keep up. "But what if it's true? What if the VT fuses do have a fifty percent reliability factor? That's far better than the Mark 18s."

"Bullshit."

8

6 March, 1943
  U.S.S. *Howell* (DD 482)
  Tulagi Harbor, Solomon Islands

Rain pummeled the *Howell's* main deck as sailors lined up for the evening meal. But many took comfort in the downpour because the storms drove away the mosquitoes; the drawback was the insects' furious return when the weather turned fair. But this storm lingered. Lightning crashed, bringing the caustic scent of ozone. Thirty knot winds blew through sunset and into twilight.

Tom Kilpatrick, the division commodore riding in *Griffith*, signaled underway time for 1900. So they hurried chow and set anchor detail at 1830. On the bridge Landa paced athwartships from one wing to the other to the other, snorting and shoving his way past watch-standers, glancing at the radar repeater as he passed through the pilot house. Wearing slickers, Ingram was crouched in the port bridge wing, staying out of Landa's path. As custom dictated, the port wing was Ingram's fiefdom when the *Howell* weighed anchor. The starboard bridge wing was reserved for the Officer of the Deck (OOD), Carl Offenbach, and the captain. Tonight, when the anchor was raised, Offenbach would conn the ship, and Landa would be perched in his skipper's chair, keeping a sharp eye until they were well into Iron Bottom Sound and clear of other ships.

Always at Landa's elbow was Early, his talker, a balding, rather officious, bespectacled second class yeoman. Plunging after his Captain with sound-powered phones mounted on his ears and chest, Early played it to the hilt, bumping into senior ratings and officers, elbowing them aside. Curses ranged behind him as his long telephone cord trailed on the deck, inevitably snagging a foot or curling around a hatch dog.

A particularly heavy burst of rain exploded over Ingram, drawing him into his own world of sound and water and oblivion, the visibility dropping to a few yards. At least, Ingram thought, anyone ashore working for the Japs wouldn't see them go. Water leaked down his back, and for a moment or two, the half dozen men gathered on the fo'c'sle were lost to view. Young Edgerton, the hot soup-drinking boot Ensign, stood among them, as newly appointed First Lieutenant.

Landa stomped out onto the bridgewing, just as the cloudburst storm eased, the visibility lifting to a hundred yards. With a nod toward the fo'c'sle he said, "How's Hot Lips holding up?" In the six or so hours that had passed since the noon meal, Ensign Edgerton had acquired his nickname, an honorific often bestowed on small ships. Like 'Boom Boom' Landa, 'Hot Lips' was a name that would, in all likelihood, stick for the rest of Edgerton's life.

"Hasn't floated away yet. Chief Murphy will take good care of him."

"What do you think, Todd? We ready for war?" It was a frayed joke that had gone over well in earlier times.

"All night long, Captain." Ingram raised his binoculars, peering into blackness.

Someone shouted in the pilot house. Landa ran in. Ingram followed right behind, finding ten or so men in a group.

Ingram peered over Landa's shoulder at the deck mounted, waist-high, radar repeater, red and green indicating lights blinking merrily. But now, the cathode ray tube (CRT) a gigantic, black glass eye, was dead. No green cursor swept a 360° path around the scope.

"What do we have, Carl?" Landa asked quietly.

Carl Offenbach was the Operations Officer whose department was responsible for the radars. He grabbed a phone handset and punched a button to CIC. After a terse exchange, he bracketed the phone and said, "Pretty sure it's the magnetron, Captain. Edwards is on his way down to the radar room with a new one. Should be on-line in ten minutes, tops."

"Hmmm." Landa didn't want to get underway in this muck. Picking their way among ships in Tulagi Harbor in zero visibility could end in disaster. Ingram thought about tonight's Munda bombardment group anchored nearby: the *Andrew Hanscom, Dale, W. E. Dunlap,* and *Caldwell*, all due to get underway at 1730. He sure didn't want to plow into one of them.

"How was your shore leave, Carl?" Landa asked.

Offenbach looked up, water dripping from his cap. "Sir?"

"What? You didn't go ashore?"

The question, of course, was absurd. While in a war zone, no one was granted shore leave. But then Offenbach was one of the new ones aboard; not used to Landa's 180E mood swings. "I'm not sure that---"

"How about you, Todd? Have a good time"?

The Captain's eyes sparkled and Ingram realized Boom Boom Landa had somehow put aside his anxiety over his brother and re-joined the *Howell*. "Actually, no shore leave for me, Captain. Too much paperwork."

"I see." Landa's eyes darted around the pilothouse. "Anybody else go ashore?"

One or two shook their heads, 'o.'

"Well, that's good. You men are lucky, you know."

Offenbach's face said, *What the hell have I gotten myself into*?

Except for the occasional crackle of a loud speaker, a macabre silence descended. "Yes, very lucky, I'd say."

Ingram rolled his eyes.

"Think of it as pure hygiene," Landa said,

"What?" said Offenbach.

"Thank God none of you did go ashore. I'm proud of you. Excellent. Excellent. This is good for the war effort." He looked at Early, his yeoman-talker. "Remind me to write a memo to Admiral Ernest J. King. In it, I'll say what a great job you are all doing. And thank God you're not Germans, like *Leutnant Offenbach* here. You'd be in terrible trouble."

Offenbach straightened and absently whipped off his hat, while the others stood about with stunned faces.

"You see, if you were among Mr. Offenbach's kinsmen now serving with the *Kriegsmarine* in the European theater, you'd be flat on your backs, thermometers in your mouths with temperatures of one hundred and two degrees. Maybe more. Yes siree. The South Pacific is the proper place for the likes of Commander Jerry Landa, mosquitoes, rain, Japs, everything. The hell with Europe."

Ingram looked at his watch and gave Landa a look: *Damnit Jerry. It's almost 1900.*

"You see, the Frogs have got the German's number. Right, Mr. Offenbach?"

"...I don't--"

"What the Frogs have done in places like Le Havre, La Rochelle, or Marseille, is to stock their whorehouses with hookers infected with crabs, gonorrhea, and *syph*. This is great stuff. Imagine some U-boat skipper when, in the middle of the Atlantic, he hears," Landa faked a German accent, "*Herr Kapitaine. Leutnant Dumkopf cannot relieve the watch because he is versmitten mit der krabs und der klapp. Sieg Heil*!"

"Mr. Offenbach." Landa twirled a finger in the air. "Until I read that fleet intelligence briefing a few days ago, I always thought the Germans were smarter than the French. But now we learn the Frogs have dreamed up a new deadly biological weapon. Kill Germans with the clap!"

Snickers ranged in the pilothouse. Even the corners of Offenbach's mouth turned up.

"See? We're just damned lucky here. No whorehouses, nothing to infect the ship. No crabs, no oozing sores, no raging temperatures. No shanker mechanics telling you to bend over. Just 314 healthy fighting men." Landa squared his shoulders. "Right, Mr. Offenbach?"

Just then the radar flicked on; the cursor marched around the scope, making Offenbach's face glow green. "You bet, Captain," he said.

Landa clapped Offenbach's shoulder. "Nice to have our little secret gadget back."

Ingram smirked at the irony. Whether Landa liked it or not, he *was* the morale officer. And now, he seemed his old self. "Time is now 1854, Captain," he said.

"Early, please call the fo'c'sle and tell Mr. Edgerton to heave the anchor to short stay." Landa stepped through the hatchway and disappeared into the rain.

Ingram was dreaming of tomato soup when the phone over his bunk buzzed. He yawned and checked his little wind-up alarm: 1036. They were in a moderate seaway with long, rolling groundswells giving a delicious, mind-numbing motion to the *Howell*, beckoning him to sleep, back to...

The buzzing became strident. Ingram ripped the phone from the bracket and growled, "XO."

"Mr. Ingram?" It was Landa, yelling.

"Captain?"

"Get your ass up here."

"Sir?"

"Now, damnit."

"Give me a min—"

"Don't bother to dress. I said now!" The phone crashed down, breaking the connection.

Already in a tee shirt, Ingram quickly steeped into trousers, shoes, threw on a light raincoat and ran for the companionway where he "...oof," bumped into Hank Kelly, obviously on the same expedition.

"What's up, XO?" asked Kelly.

"Damned if I know." A tight-lipped Ingram charged up the ladder, with Kelly following.

In thirty seconds, they climbed three decks to the bridge level, emerging in a vestibule that forward, gave to the pilothouse and aft, to the Captain's sea-cabin. Before stepping to Landa's door, Ingram ducked outside. The storm was gone, and stars glittered overhead in a stygian, moonless brilliance. Dead ahead were the silhouettes of *Griffith* and *Issac* as they plowed west in a column through the Solomon Sea.

Landa's door was closed. Ingram walked up and knocked, while Kelly stood behind.

"Enter!"

Ingram opened the door. Unlike his stateroom on the main deck, the Captain's sea cabin was small, functional, set up so the captain could step to the bridge at a moment's notice. The room was furnished with a bunk, a small functional desk, a stainless steel washbasin, and a stainless steel toilet. The tiny bulkhead light was on, with Landa sitting at the edge of his bunk, elbows propped on his knees, chin resting in his hands.

"Captain?"

"That sonofabitch. Nobody does that to me and gets away with it." Landa's eyes were dark and malevolent.

"Sir?"

"Hear that? You nincompoops. How the hell am I supposed to sleep?"

"Captain. I don't---"

"Shut up and listen, damnit!"

A rattle, then another. Then a whole cascade sounded overhead, as the ship rolled.

"Well?" growled Landa.

"Sir, I don't understand."

"Come here. Damnit."

Ingram walked toward Landa.

"There." Landa peered at the overhead.

Ingram looked up, hearing a clanking sound, metal glancing off metal. He looked at Kelly, who covered his mouth with a hand, knowing exactly what it was.

"Ball bearings," said Landa. "That fat little bastard stuffed ball bearings in my ventilation duct. Look here. See the chipped paint where he unscrewed the inspection plate?" He pointed.

"Who?"

"Lieutenant junior grade White. That's who!" roared Landa, slamming a fist against the bulkhead. Even as he yelled, the ship took a pronounced roll to port and a group of ball bearings rattled and clanked though the air duct.

Kelly's hand was still clamped over his mouth, his eyes betraying the broad grin stretching under his palm.

Landa growled, "Where did that son of a bitch get the ball bearings, Mr. Kelly?"

Kelly gave a muffled, "No idea, Sir."

"Well, listen to those sonsabitches. Pretty big bastards, I'd say." As if to emphasize his point, more bearings clanked and rattled as the ship heeled to starboard.

"Yessir."

"You'll take an inventory immediately, Mr. Kelly."

"Yessir." Kelly looked at Ingram. Both knew the task was impossible. In a little more than three hours, they would be at general quarters, poised to enter Ferguson Passage.

Landa pointed. "Mr. Kelly, get a ship fitter up here on the double. He's got just ten minutes to get rid of these frigging bearings."

The *Howell* rolled gracefully to port: ball-bearings obediently plinked their way through the ventilation duct.

"Move!" yelled Landa.

Kelly dashed out of the sea cabin, his feet clanking furiously as he descended the ladder.

From the pilothouse, the lee helm clanged with an engine order, and the ship's motion seemed less pronounced. Landa and Ingram locked eyes, knowing they had slowed. As in confirmation, the telephone over Landa's bunk buzzed. He yanked it from the bracket. "Captain."

He listened, then said, "Very well, I'll be out." Landa replaced the phone and muttered while pulling on his pants, "*Griffith* thinks she has a sonar contact. Tom Kilpatrick wants to talk to me."

Then Landa bent to tie his shoes and smirked, his head pitching from side to side. "Tubby White, huh? Great hot-dog practical joker, huh? Do you still have his file?"

"No, Sir. It's gone." Ingram stood at parade rest realizing Landa was putting on a great show. Tubby's stunt was fantastic and the word would get around quickly. The best thing Landa could do was to harness his famous temper and show indignation against a cause that would soon blow over. Yet, Ingram dared not acknowledge to Landa that he knew of the ploy. *Play it out.*

"Just as well. Two can play that game." Landa swore softly.

The *Howell* rolled drunkenly to port in a large swell; the ball bearings obediently ricocheting on their journey across the Captain's sea cabin.

9

6 March, 1943
>   Fourteenth Naval District Headquarters,
>   Pearl Harbor Naval Station
>   Territory Of Hawaii

Mike Novak nearly rolled the jeep because he had to wash his hands. Caroming around a corner, he spotted his destination: the Detention Center at the end of the block. Novak tromped it, pulling a churning dust-cloud through a platoon of marching Marines.

Novak had just left Captain Howard O'Grady, Chief of staff to Admiral Charles A. Lockwood, Commander Submarines Pacific (COMSUBPAC). The O'Grady meetings had become a ritual, with Lockwood often present. And O'Grady treated him like a submariner, because Novak once was. Proudly, he wore his dolphins, even though he would never again put to sea in a submarine. Novak had been at the top of his game in 1938 as Lieutenant Commander Michael T. Novak, captain of the submarine *S-42*, stationed in Pearl Harbor. But one day, while body surfing, he'd had an argument with a ten foot wave and the hard, sandy bottom won. A broken back laid him up for six months, giving Novak a medical discharge. Now, after recall, the six-two, sandy-haired Novak was a full commander in charge of the Combat Intelligence Unit (CIU) of the Intelligence Center, for the Pacific Ocean Area (ICPOA). In essence, it was Novak's job to give O'Grady the CIU's findings, so Lockwood's submarines could do their job, which, formally stated, was:

DESTROY ENEMY SHIPS AND SHIPPING BY OFFENSIVE PATROLS AT FOCAL POINTS.

It was the *FOCAL POINTS* part of the mission statement where Novak came into play. Novak told O'Grady of the latest Japanese naval and maritime ship movements. O'Grady and Lockwood would then lay out plots and signal their submarines where to intercept the enemy.

Novak's input was from the Fleet Radio Unit Pacific (FRUPac), housed in the same dingy cellar as his group. Side by side, they lay beneath the Fourteenth Naval District Headquarters Administration Building. It was a high security area called "The Basement," which featured the most recalcitrant air-conditioning system ever attempted by man. Those who spent any time in the Basement invariably came out with arthritis or whooping cough. For just six hours, one's reward could be uncontrollable wheezing.

FRUPac, lead by Commander Joseph J. Rochefort, was a group of highly skilled radio operators, cryptographers and linguists responsible for breaking and translating Japanese codes. Using new and sophisticated devices such as key punch machines, (they used from two to three million punch cards per month) sorters, collators and high speed printers, FRUPac employed every trick to accomplish the task. Last June, Rochefort caused a stir after cracking key elements of the Japanese Navy's five-digit code labeled JN 25. Thus Rochefort predicted with devastating accuracy, the disposition of Admiral Isoroku Yamamoto's forces when he attacked Midway Island, just 1,200 miles northwest of Honolulu. The architect of the Peal Harbor sneak attack, Yamamoto's Combined Fleet vastly outnumbered the U.S. Navy at Midway three to one. But Rear Admiral Ray Spruance, armed with Rochefort's predictions, surprised Yamamoto and sank all four of his attack carriers. This not only denied Yamamoto the ability to attack

Midway, but nullified his capacity to conduct offensive operations in the future.

Today's meeting had gone well. FRUPac had recently cracked the Japanese "Maru Code," a special code exclusively used for Japanese merchant ships. Last night, Novak had plotted some radio intercepts and learned the exact track, including course and speed, of the *Jamaica Maru*, a tanker of 27,500 tons. Fully loaded, she had just left Soerabaja, bound for Yokohama via the Makassar Strait. Thus, Makassar Strait became the *Focal Point* where O'Grady and Lockwood would tell their submarines to take care of business.

As usual, Novak wrote the coordinates on the palm of his hand with his Parker 51 Fountain Pen, a retirement gift from his shipmates aboard the *S-42*. Next, he would drive to SUBPAC headquarters and read the data to O'Grady. With that, O'Grady and Lockwood would dispatch their submarines, while Novak washed his hands. No records; easy to get rid of. All he had to do was step in the head and turn on the water.

It began some years ago, when Rochefort and his translator-linguists started breaking Japanese codes; the simple ones were followed by more complex codes, including the Japanese "Purple" or diplomatic code. American translations of the purple code allowed Secretary of State Cordell Hull to know exactly what Japanese Ambassador Kichisaburo Nomura was going to say as he waited outside Hull's office on December 7, 1941. Along the way, Rochefort discovered the Japanese Achilles' heel: they were, to the point of arrogance, recondite about their language and believed no outsider could fully understand its nuances, let alone their codes. But Rochefort and his crew proved them wrong, with the Japanese having no idea that Rochefort was reading their mail at all levels.

But problems had arisen. Over the past few months, the Japanese had changed JN-25 by incorporating new additives. Novak's weekly intelligence estimates for Japan's Naval units were growing less and less accurate. Last week O'Grady had given a sidelong glance that told Novak he was losing credibility.

Late for his next meeting, Novak quickly excused himself from O'Grady's office and dashed down the hall to wash his hands, before anyone had a chance to see the incriminating coordinates written on his palm, like a high-schooler cheating on a physics mid-term. But the men's room was crowded with plumbers who wielded wrenches and blow torches and pipe dope. Novak didn't have time to run up to the next deck, so the thin, former basketball forward from the Naval Academy, raced for his jeep and headed for the Fourteenth Naval District Detention Center, hoping to wash up there.

The jeep screeched to a halt and he ran for the lobby. "Damnit," he wheezed, as he shoved open the double doors, promising himself to do something to get back into shape. But he was usually at his desk seven days a week. There was simply no time.

Novak walked in the main entrance and down the hall to a door marked FRUPAC SECURITY.

Inside, there was an inner office with a Marine behind a counter. Novak walked up and slapped down his ID. "Commander Novak calling for Major St. Clair." The thin, sharp-edged Marine, wearing two rows of ribbons with four battle stars, looked Novak up and down as if he were General Hideki Tojo.

Novak grew impatient. "I'd like to use the head, sergeant."

The Marine, whose bakilte tag read HEDGES, muttered something that sounded like "*momensar*." Then he cocked an eyebrow, picked up the phone and methodically dialed a three digit number, pausing by Novak's count, four seconds between each digit. Covering the mouthpiece, Hedges kept his eyes on Novak while he spoke in low tones.

Thirty seconds later, a stocky dark curly-haired, Marine major burst into the lobby, a cigarette dangling from his lips. His right hand shot out, "Mike. Glad you made it."

Novak offered his left, "Uh. Damned Basement gives me arthritis. How are you, Bob?" They shook, then Novak made a show out of rubbing his right elbow.

"You guys ever going to do something about that air conditioning?"

St. Clair turned to Hedges and the two Marines grunted at one another in a language only Marines understand. So ordered, Hedges raised a countertop section and Novak was passed through.

"Got a nickel?" asked St. Clair, as they walked down the hall. Novak handed one over then wordlessly stepped through the door marked 'men.'

Five minutes later, Novak walked out of the bathroom feeling much better, his hands scrubbed clean. St. Clair handed over a frosted bottle of Coke and said. "He's on the second deck. Got another nickel?"

Novak drank deeply, as St. Clair dropped the nickel into the Coke machine. He drew the fresh bottle out with a 'clank,' uncapped it, and said, "He loves Cokes and cigarettes. Come on."

At the top of a companionway, they paused before two Marine corporals, dressed in fatigues with holstered .45s.

"He's cleared," said Novak. The guards stood aside.

Halfway down a gloomy hall, St. Clair stopped before a door with a square window. Above, was a sign that said: ROOM B. "Take a look. It's one-way."

Novak peered through. There was a conference table, four folding chairs scattered around, and a wall-mounted blackboard. A Marine major was seated on one side of the table, his hands splayed before him. Wearing a shoulder holster and a .45, he was a slim, sinewy, dark man with a pock-marked face. Seated opposite the major was an Oriental dressed in American khakis. He looked to be short, stocky, his hair an overgrown crew-cut. A pack of Chesterfields and an ashtray lay before the Oriental who took advantage of both, blowing smoke in the Marine's direction.

St. Clair lit up his own Chesterfield and blew smoke on the window. "You feed them, cloth them, and they're ready to again take on the world. You ready?"

"Sure."

St. Clair nodded to Novak's chest. "You want to take-off your dolphins?"

"I want him to know."

"Okay." St. Clair turned and opened the door for Novak. They walked in, and the prisoner immediately stood and bowed.

Ignoring the Oriental, Novak said, "Major Rivera, this is Commander Novak."

Barely taking his eyes off his charge, Rivera looked up and nodded.

"How do you do?" Novak almost offered a hand, but realized Rivera was not going to reciprocate, his eyes again fixed on his prisoner. Instead, Novak bowed to the prisoner, noting that Rivera's eyes narrowed ever so slightly.

"Commander Novak," said St. Clair, "this is Lieutenant Kanji Sugiyama of the Imperial Japanese Navy, recently of the submarine *I-1*."

Sugiyama bowed again, with Novak and St. Clair following suit. Then St. Clair offered the Coke to Sugiyama who looked at it warily for a moment. When Sugiyama reached for it, he spotted the gold submariner's dolphins pinned over Novak's breast pocket. "*Ah, so.*" He broke into a smile, displaying a gold-capped tooth and bowed again.

Novak returned the bow and sat next to Rivera, St. Clair beside Sugiyama.

"Not bad. Submariner to submariner. A level playing field," St. Clair said.

"You sure he doesn't understand English?"

"Positive."

"And you, Major? asked Novak.

Rivera gave a snort.

What does that mean?

Where do you want to start?" asked St. Clair.

"I'd like to hear his side of the story. Just let him tell it."

"Okay." St. Clair leaned forward and spoke in Japanese.

Sugiyama sat back, blew smoke, and grunted something.

Lighting another Chesterfield, St. Clair said, "He's tired of telling it."

Novak tried not to show his discomfort at all the blue smoke. "Make him sing for his dinner."

"Like no more cokes or cigarettes?"

"Tell him you'll cut off his balls." Rivera spoke for the first time.

That startled Novak; it took seconds for him to manage, "Let' s just stick to cokes and cigarettes." In a way, he couldn't blame the major. He'd just read a report about a Japanese doctor in a POW camp near Batavia who had surgically removed the livers of two American airmen, then woke them and told them it was an experiment to see how long they could live. One died twelve hours later; the other fought it, living for four days. Here, in Hawaii, they offered cigarettes and Cokes and...khaki uniforms.

St. Clair spoke again, his tones soft, his hands gesturing in an intoxicating way that reminded Novak of a ballerina. Sugiyama responded finally, and spoke for a while. Then, his voice trailed off.

"Hadn't heard that, before. Lieutenant Sugiyama says he was torpedo officer aboard the *I-1*," St. Clair said.

"Where was he when the attack began?"

St. Clair spoke.

Sugiyama grabbed the frosted Coke and gulped. Then he talked.

"Control room. Apparently, they thought our cruisers and destroyers had passed by, and it was clear for them to enter Komimbo Bay."

"Tell him there were just two New Zealand corvettes."

St. Clair did so.

Sugiyama gave Novak a malevolent glance and crushed out a cigarette.

"You pissed him off."

"Sorry. Then what happened?"

St. Clair asked the question.

Sugiyama took another cigarette and pat his pockets. Novak took out a Zippo, leaned forward and flicked it. Sugiyama inhaled deeply, then muttered through smoke.

"He asks if you've been depth charged," St. Clair said.

Novak had heard a few practice depth-charges dropped at a distance in his S-Boat days. But he's never had to suffer through a real attack. In fact, the closest he'd been to combat was at home in Honolulu, eating breakfast with his wife on December 7, 1941, wondering about the commotion over at Pearl Harbor. Sensing what Sugiyama was driving at, he replied "Tell him many times."

Sugiyama nodded curtly, then spoke for a couple of minutes. When he finished, Novak noticed an involuntary jerk in Sugiyama's left hand, the one holding the cigarette. And his face was wan.

"They took so many depth charges that the main motors were thrown off their mounts. So the skipper battle-surfaced and they were immediately taken under fire. With Imperial Marines manning their deck gun, they were rammed five times."

"Too bad," said Rivera.

Bridson's battle report read that the *Kiwi* rammed the *I-1* three times, but Novak chose not to make an issue. "And then?"

St. Clair asked the question.

Sugiyama tried to act nonchalant as he spoke, but his face turned pale and his hand shook.

"The navigator, Lieutenant Mizota Kenryo, buckled on his sword and led a charge, just before they were rammed the last time. Sugiyama followed Kenryo but had barely crawled through the conning tower hatch when the destroyer struck, rolling the *I-1*, --- how far?" St. Clair asked Sugiyama a question.

Sugiyama stared at the table and mumbled something.

"Good God. She rolled sixty degrees on her beam ends. Sugiyama fell in the water with dead and wounded. Then he swam to the beach."

"Oh, my goodness," Rivera said in a falsetto.

They talked for another ten minutes, with Sugiyama becoming more congenial. To Novak's surprise, it was Sugiyama who offered the next question.

"Wants to know if we saw their surrender leaflets," said Novak.

Novak hoped he looked puzzled when he said, "All we found was a sunken submarine carcass."

Sugiyama seemed to be satisfied, then sat back and finished his Coke.

"We done?" asked St. Clair.

Novak leaned forward. It was a wild shot, but he was looking to do a favor for Lockwood whose torpedoes were suffering a horrible fifty percent failure rate. "One more question. Ask him if they have any premature exploding problems with their torpedoes."

St. Clair pitched the question.

Sugiyama spoke, then quickly butt-lighted a new cigarette and smiled.

Without inflection, St. Clair said, "He answers, 'We don't, but you do.'"

"Yikes," Novak said softly. Slapping his knees, he stood. "Okay. That's all."

"Take him back," St. Clair said to Rivera. He tossed a full pack of Chesterfields to Sugiyama and followed Novak into the hall.

After the door closed, they peered through, watching Rivera grab Sugiyama's elbow and shoving him out the far door. "What do you think?" asked St. Clair.

"He's one smart Jap."

"He took a bite out of your ass with the torpedo question."

"I didn't expect that."

"You want to see the stuff or wait 'till we deliver it?"

"What do you think?"

"Okay, let's go."

They descended two flights of stairs into a basement and showed their credentials to more Marines, Novak was sure, then had landed on Guadalcanal. Finally, they walked into a basement of more dismal appointments than where Novak worked. He asked, "Is this a cell block?"

"Just for hard cases." He walked up to a door guarded by two Marines with submachine guns. After showing their credentials, the Marines stepped aside. St. Clair pulled out a key ring and inserted one in a lock. Then he found a second key and inserted that in another lock. Silently, the door swung open. It was a well lighted cell. But there were no beds or bathroom accessories or anything one would expect to accommodate a prisoner. Instead, two eight foot tables stood against opposite walls. Elsewhere, crates and boxes were neatly stacked ceiling high. The place smelled of mildew in spite of two large electric fans whirling back and forth. "The Japs bombed the hell out of the *I-1*, hoping we wouldn't find anything. Damned hulk slid off the beach and back in the water. That's why this stuff is still damp." A new cigarette dangled from St. Clair's lips,

Novak walked over to a table and picked up a book with a red binding. He thumbed through it, occasionally stopping at a page, running his index finger over the Japanese *kana* characters.

"...a treasure," Novak said. "You sure it's JN-25?"

"I'd say. And here, look at this." St. Clair flipped to a page. "Dated January 20th." St. Clair waved an arm around the cell. "Hundreds of code-books. What they couldn't bury they tried to burn. And the salvage divers found a bunch more aboard the *I-1*"

"Can I take this one?"

"Sign a slip?"

"You bet."

St. Clair's hands went to his hips, his brow furrowed as he puffed on his cigarette.

"What?"

"What about Sugiyama. Do you think he bought it?"

"About the code books being surrender leaflets? I don't think so."

"Me neither."

"He's one smart Jap all right. Okay then. I don't want him mixing with other POWs."

"Naturally. What do you want us to do?" St. Clair's eyes were cold and there was something in his tone.

"What do you think?" asked Novak.

"I can turn him over to Rivera if you want," shrugged St. Clair.

A vision of the two American POW airmen dying without livers flashed across Novak's mind. That Jap doctor watched the whole thing. Novak realized what power he had. He could casually order Sugiyama's execution and nobody would care. All he had to say was 'shoot the sonofabitch.' And St. Clair would tell Rivera to blast that Jap with his .45, no questions asked.

"Send him a carton of cigarettes. I want to keep pumping him about torpedoes."

10

6 March, 1943
San Pedro, California

A horn honked.

Helen looked out the window. "Jeepers."

The afternoon fog had become thick. And now, in early evening, she could barely make out Laura's light green Cadillac. But through swirling mist, she could see the top was down. *She's crazy.*

Laura blasted the horn again.

"Okay, okay," Helen muttered as she ran to her hall closet. Laura honked once more, this time nearly sitting on the horn. Grabbing rain coat and scarf, Helen dashed outside, locking the door behind.

Wearing a thick overcoat and light green scarf that matched the Cadillac, Laura sat back, one arm propped on the door, the other casually draped on the top of the driver's seat. Artie Shaw softly played on KECA.

"Hi ya, toots," Laura feigned chewing gum and arched an eyebrow. "Wanna ride?"

"You bet. How long were you on the road?"

"Not bad. Couple of hours straight down Sepulveda."

Helen stepped in, finding the heater running full blast. It felt good on her legs, but the rest of her was cold.

Laura started the car. "We still going to hit the Hong Kong bar?"

"Shanghai Red's. Maybe, yes. Maybe, no. Friends tell me it's pretty wild there on Saturday night."

"You want to give it a shot?"

Helen shrugged.

"Aw, what the heck. Which way?" asked Laura, as she pulled out.

"Turn right and go down Seventeenth to Palos Verdes Street."

Laura zipped around the corner and stepped on it, easily shifting through the gears.

Wisps blew by as Helen clutched the arm rest and peered into the fog. She guessed the visibility at no more than fifty feet.

"This baby really moves out. Don't get to use it much with rationing and all. You want to drive?"

"N-n-no thanks." Icy wind blasted through every crevice in Helen's clothing, making her teeth chatter. She leaned close to the heater and rubbed her hands. "How do you stand this?"

"I don't."

"Then why?"

"You wouldn't believe the guys who whistle at me. And get this. A Sailor jumped in, while I waited for a light in Manhattan Beach."

"Laura!"

"It was all great sport. He was with two Marines, and they lifted him out like he was a head of cabbage. All the poor klutz was trying to do was to give me his address. Look." she pointed to a wrinkled envelope on the floor.

"You know? I'll bet you started it." Helen picked up the envelope finding an impossible scrawl on the back.

"Hi ya, toots," Laura grinned. Too late, she downshifted and ran a red light at Gaffey, then tromped it again. "Actually, you're right. It's the single guys you worry about. There was this soldier in a rain coat in Culver City. Now, he was spooky. Thousand yard stare. You know what I mean?"

"I know." Helen had seen plenty of thousand yard stares on Corregidor.

"Well. I peeled out when he walked up to the car. Laid rubber for a half a block. How 'bout that?"

Helen gave up wondering how Laura could afford to peel out or whatever, along with driving the thirty or so miles to San Pedro.

Laura hit the accelerator again. Helen braced against the dashboard, as the Cadillac swerved around a stake truck, with Laura yanking the gearshift down into third. The speedometer neared seventy-five, as they hit a bump, both bouncing a foot off the seat. A rational side of Helen wondered how ironic if she were killed in this fancy Cadillac convertible, on her way to dinner this Saturday night, in the relative safety of the United States, after all her near-brushes with death in the Philippines. But then her irrational side took over. Blood drained from her face and she yelled, "God! All I want is a nice meal, not the emergency ward!"

"Sorry, hon." Laura slowed to a more reasonable speed. It was a good thing, for a moment later, the Pacific Avenue traffic light burst out of the fog. It was Red. She hit the brakes, screeching to a stop.

A motorcycle pulled up next to Laura.

"Damn," she muttered.

Helen peered around to see a policeman wearing a broad smile.

"*Ubi ignis est*?" He tipped his cap, then reached out and clamped a hand on the top of Laura's door.

"What?" said Laura.

"My name's Bullard. Officer Bullard. And that's Latin, Mam. I learned it right back there," he jabbed a gloved thumb over his shoulder, "at San Pedro High School. Can't say I remember anything else."

"But Mr. Bullard, I don't---"

"That's okay, Mam. I'm not a civilian. You can call me Officer Bullard."

"Officer Bullard." Laura crossed her arms and looked straight ahead.

The light turned green. Cars piled up behind them, and Bullard waved them around. "Yes, Mam. And you know? That bit of Latin? *Ubi ignis est*? It means 'where's the fire?'" Bullard turned off his engine, eased from his motorcycle, and stepped close to the Cadillac. He looked down at Laura, his head cocked.

"Fire?" Laura mustered the courage to look at Officer Bullard.

"You're lucky that it's foggy, Mam. I saw you two blocks back, and I coulda swore you were doin' seventy. But then this stuff," Officer Bullard waved a hand at the sky, "swallowed you up and I couldn't tell for sure. May I see your driver's license, please?"

Laura dug in her purse and handed it over.

"Will ya look at that. All the way from Beverly Hills."

"I'm sorry, Officer Bullard. These hills are so steep and I don't live here, as you can see. I'm just not used to---"

"-- cause if I had had a chance to clock you at seventy, you'd be on your way to jail by now. To say nothing of wasting rationed gas." A dark moment passed as Bullard glared at Laura.

"Evening, ladies." Bullard leaned around, smiled at Helen, and tipped his cap. Handing back Laura's license, he waved two more cars around, then kick-started his motorcycle, and rumbled off with a flourish, disappearing into the fog.

"Bullard. Perfect name for a cop. Good looking, too." Laura stuffed her license in her purse.

"Not bad."

"Did you see him give me the eye?"

"Nonsense!"

"Then why did he drive off through a red light?"

Helen looked up, seeing it was true.

Laura, in a more sedate mood, followed Helen's directions to Beacon Street where they found Shanghai Red's. With the top down, they heard the clamor a half block away, where a discordant piano competed with the hubbub of loud voices. The only parking spot available was next to a police vehicle zone which served the station, almost next door to Shanghai Red's. Laura pulled in and pushed a button. "Watch this." A motor whined and the white canvas top rose from the boot and arched over into place.

"Amazing. They think of everything."

"Evening ladies." It was Officer Bullard, unloading two thick notebooks from his motorcycle's saddle bags.

"Officer Bullard. How are you?" Laura said, locking the top in place.

"You're not going in there?" Bullard jammed his hands on his hips.

"Well, I---" Helen muttered.

Laura shrugged.

Bullard beckoned with his index finger and walked them up to one of Shanghai Red's front windows. They peered in to see the place stuffed with men, mostly sailors. Thick, blue smoke pressed the walls and ceiling, making it nearly impossible to see to the back. "Well?" he said.

"What do you think, Laura?" asked Helen.

"I dunno."

Helen said, "I don't either."

"I do need to use the powder room."

Bullard said, "Well you could use ours...come to think of it, I wouldn't recommend that you use ours..."

Helen said, "Okay, let's freshen up here, then head to Olsen's."

"Good idea. Olsen's, a great place." said Bullard. "I'll wait right here for you."

"Thanks, officer." Laura flashed Bullard a broad smile.

"It's Jim," he said.

Helen rolled her eyes as if saying, *Oh, it's Jim now*.

Bullard opened the door and stood conspicuously in the entrance. After surveying the room, he stepped aside and said, "Looks okay for now. If you're not out in five minutes, I'm coming in. The bathroom's all the way in back and down a hall."

"Okay," said Helen.

Laura and Helen walked in, the smoke almost knocking them over. The piano plinked a nameless tune as they elbowed through a crowd of Merchant Marine and U.S. Navy sailors. Uniforms from allied Navies brushed against them while across the room, Helen recognized some Army artillery officers from Ft. MacArthur. Seated at the end of the bar were four Marines who nursed beers, their faces bored.

They squeezed their way to the back and found a hall lighted by a forty watt bulb. Following smudged signs, they passed a small kitchen and discovered the ladies room. Once yellow, it had faded to brown, the only ventilation an open window that gave on an alley. Oddly, the wall separating the men's and women's rest room was not complete to the ceiling. There was a foot of empty space that consisted of a tight wire mesh, leaving the occupants of the ladies room to hear sounds of drunken men going about their functions.

Trying to ignore the noise next door, Helen said, "Did I tell you about my burglar?"

"What? No."

"It was last Sunday night. After we talked."

"You're kidding."

Quickly, Helen told her.

"What did the cops say?"

"Actually, they were rather perfunctory. Walked around, couldn't find anything, then stood looking at me, scratching their heads. Then this one cop begins lecturing me on keeping my windows locked. He found one window with a defective lock. So I had it replaced."

"You should have called Officer Bullard." They both laughed, as Laura dabbed on lipstick.

Suddenly, the ladies room resonated with flushing toilets and loud, exaggerated groans from the other side. Someone wheezed as blue, cigar smoke shot through the wire mesh screen. "Air raid!" One of them called. Another giggled so much that he ended up gasping for breath.

"Jerks," Laura said.

The men having had their fun, banged open the door and caromed down the hallway to the bar. Their voices drifted away and it soon became quiet. But they heard a sink running and someone humming.

"Almost done, hon?" Laura said quietly.

Helen grabbed a paper towel to dry her hands.

The men's room door crashed open and someone shuffled in. "Sorry." It was a high-pitched male voice, that sounded as if he'd barely reached puberty. He said, "Hey! Shorty."

The other said, "Earle! How the hell are you? Say. Are you AWOL? I thought you was headed for the *Barber*."

Helen's head jerked up. The *Barber*. In a recent letter, Todd had told her Luther Dutton was riding the *Barber*. She cast a sidelong glance at Laura, who put on final touches of her lipstick, oblivious to the reference to her husband's ship.

A stall door crashed open and shut, the bolt clanging home. A belt buckle jangled. "Nope. I'm legal. Say, what are you doing here in Pedro?"

"Off to Lighthouse Street to find a cathouse. So what's with you? You AWOL or not?"

"Well, my plane had engine trouble on the way to Pearl. Took a week to fix it, then they sent the plane on, but get this: without me. They held me for three days..."

Dropping her lipstick in her purse, Laura tapped Helen on the elbow. "Stinks in here. See you outside, hon." She walked out.

Helen barely noticed, intent on the conversation next door.

"Yeah? How about that?" It was Shorty's voice.

"Turns out the damn *Barber* is gone, Shorty. Chief on CinCPac staff told me a Jap bomb got her magazine. Blew up without a trace. Everybody blasted to smithereens. Nobody got out."

"Jeepers."

"Man, am I lucky. And get this. I got orders to the *Dixie* here in Long Beach. Whoever snafued that plane's engine saved my life. I'd buy the poor bastard a drink if I knew who he was."

"That's awful about the *Barber*. Say, you wanna hit that cathouse with me?"

"Sure."

Feeling as if someone had kicked her in the stomach, Helen staggered for the door.

She had no idea how she made it outside, only that she was on the sidewalk, slumped against the Cadillac, Laura's arm around her. "Helen? Helen? What the hell?" She fanned Helen's face.

"Who was it, lady?" Bullard stepped close, his breath smelling of chewing gum. "Just point him out."

"What? No." Helen looked up. "I...I'm all right." She stood straight and looked into Laura's eyes. They were laced with mirth and mischief. Laura, the concert pianist from Beverly Hills out on the town in her snazzy Cadillac, without a worry, on a Saturday night. *Blew up without a trace,* the kid had said.

But then her mind raced. The kid could be wrong. This happens all the time, she reminded herself. Wrong ships. Wrong locations. People's names mixed up. Bodies with the wrong ID tags; she'd seen that plenty of times in

Corregidor's tunnels. Helen took a deep breath. Yes. It must have been a, "...mistake," she blurted.

"What?" said Laura and Bullard at the same time.

"...a mistake. Thought I saw somebody back there I knew on Corregidor," Helen lied, "But it's impossible. He's gone..." She pressed her fingers to her temples.

"You were on Corregidor?" asked Bullard.

She gave a sleight nod.

"I'll be damned."

Laura gave Helen a little hug. "It's okay, hon. I imagine that stuff stays with you a while."

"I'm fine now."

"Look, maybe you don't want to have dinner. I could..."

"No. Let's go. It's what I need." Helen took a deep breath.

"You sure?"

"You bet." Helen opened her door and stepped in.

"Keen." Laura walked around to the driver's side.

"Don't you worry about the fog, Mam. I'll escort you there myself." Bullard threw a leg over his motorcycle and kicked it into life. Leaning down to Helen he said, "Corregidor, huh?"

The Harley's engine roared, obliterating Bullard's voice. But Helen knew what he'd said and managed a smile and a nod. She only hoped she could keep it up for the evening.

11

6 March, 1943
   U.S.S. *Whitney* (AD 4)
   Tulagi Harbor, Solomon Islands

Captain Theodore R. "Rocko" Myszynski, Commodore of Destroyer Squadron Twelve (DESRON12) shook his thick, bald head. His eyes darted one way, then another, as Japanese twin engine "Betty" bombers zipped overhead, explosions reverberating around Tulagi Harbor. Myszynski cursed softly as a shockwave gnawed at the destroyer tender. Sitting alone in the spacious wardroom, his face was distorted by red night-lights. Deep, crimson shadows ranged across his skull; dark thick stubble on his lower jaw made him look like Lucifer's messenger. A bomb crashed nearby, making Myszynski wish even more he was on tonight's raid up the slot. But he'd been ordered to a conference with Major General Alexander Patch over on Guadalcanal tomorrow, and there was no getting out of it. With a scowl, he glanced at the bulkhead-mounted clock: 0325. Rocko lit his cigar stub, poured a cup of coffee, and sat again, trying to relax.

As usual, the harbor was blacked out. Myszynski cocked an ear, trying to pick out how many Betty's were out there.

Crumpf.

Half dozen he reckoned, each lobbing 500 kg bombs at anything looking like a target. Then he smirked. No secondary explosions from that one. Must have missed. But once in a while, the planes would find something, their victim burning and lighting the place up, illuminating a lot of targets. But the anti-aircraft fire was effective tonight, keeping them at bay.

Bomb flashes brightened the wardroom like a neon sign flicking on and off. Myszynski got up and pulled the blackout curtains over a porthole, then looked around sheepishly. The rest of the ship was at general quarters, yet Myszynski, with nothing to do in flagplot, had wandered off to the wardroom, looking for coffee.

"Damnit!" A mosquito landed on Myszynski's ear. He slapped at it, the concussion making his ear ring. He was so full of bug bites, he wondered if his face would be recognizable in another six months, when he was due to be rotated home. In a low voice, he mimicked an idiot, "Duh, Gloria? Do ya recognize me? I used to be your husband. Now, I"m a rolling, bug-bitten blob of suntanned protoplasm."

Crumpf, Crumpf. That didn't sound close either. *Better luck next time, Tojo.*

Mosquito bites or not, he missed Gloria and the kids. Jennifer his daughter, was seventeen and beautiful now. Young John was turning thirteen. He wondered if—

"Mind if I join you, Commodore?" Frank Ashton stood above him, cup and saucer in hand, wearing tee shirt, khaki trousers and shower sandals. Like Myszynski, the red lights gave Ashton's face a demonic cast.

"Please." Myszynski waved a hand at the chair opposite.

"How long does this go on?" Ashton sounded a bit nervous as he sat.

"Two or three hours, Frank. Every night for the last two months that I can remember."

"God." Ashton sipped and dabbed a napkin at his lips.

"Damnit!" Myszynski slapped his left ear. "Think I'd rather have the air raids than these damned mosquitoes. I'll tell you. I---"

"Commodore?" A messenger stepped in.

"Yes?"

The messenger, a nineteen year old radioman third class wearing dungarees and helmet, walked over and handed Myszynski a clip board and pencil. Myszynski signed, took his message and handed back the clipboard.

"Thank you, Sir." The messenger walked out.

Myszynski felt Ashton's eyes on him as he read the message. "Sonofabitch," he muttered.

"Yes?" Ashton ventured.

"Damnit! *Griffith. Howell* and *Isaacs* have been chasing a Jap sub twenty miles west of the Russells for the past two and half hours. Don't know if they got it, but they dropped," Myszynski slapped the flimsy with the back of his hand, "...thirty depth charges. Then the *Griffith* had an engineering casualty. Tom Kilpatrick says they lost lube oil to the starboard shaft. Had to lock it before she wiped a bearing. Now she's headed back here on one screw at twelve knots. Shit!" Myszynski's cigar stub rolled back and forth across his mouth. "Tom sent *Isaacs* and *Howell* on ahead: Jerry Landa is in command. Well, Landa can take care of things, I suppose."

A shadow crossed Ashton's face. "Is there anything I can do?"

"Sure. Go tell the Japs to hang around Vila Harbor for another hour."

"What?"

CRUMPFF! Light slashed through the wardroom curtains. The 8,325 ton *Whitney* shuddered. Ashton's eyes jerked toward the sound of water cascading close aboard.

"It's okay, Frank. You don't hear the one that gets you."

Ashton gave a thin smile and lifted his coffee cup. But his fingers shook and he put it back on the saucer. Then he grabbed the cup with both hands and drank. "Besides the sub contact, think your boys will get anymore business tonight?"

"That's what they're up there for. Business. Halsey told us to 'push the Japs around,' so we're pushing them around. What worries me now is that with this delay, *Isaacs* and *Howell* may be stuck up The Slot at daylight with a bunch of Jap Zeros running around. At first light they should be better than halfway home. 'Cause last time they caught us in the Vella Gulf with our pants down when we lost the *Barber*." He flicked his cigar ash toward an ashtray.

Crumpf! As if on cue, a bomb hit.

The invader's engines disappeared to the Northwest. Myszynski glanced after them. "So long, Tojo." He sat up in his chair and squared his eyes on Ashton, "How do you figure? Two weeks ago, they'd send one or two planes. Now we get a half dozen every night. Is that because you're in town, Frank?"

The all-clear sounded outside and Ashton tried a laugh. "I don't think they know me, Rocko."

Myszynski shifted gears. "Your proximity fuses may get a work out after all."

"How's that?"

"Take tonight's raid for example. We're hitting two airfields up there in the Western Solomons. Bob Briscoe has four cans bombarding the Munda airstrip about now. But the real show is with Dexter Sands. He's got the light cruisers *Sioux Falls, Santa Monica, King City,* and three cans. They run up The Slot, then cut down Kula Gulf to smack the Vila Stanmore airstrip on Kolombangara, in about," he checked his watch, "thirty minutes from now. Icing on the cake is that a dumbo report came in an hour ago saying there were two Jap cans anchored in there." A dumbo was a PBY twin engine amphibian used in the Solomons for night reconnaissance and ship harassment. "We planned this raid, figuring anybody trapped in Vila Harbor is going to up-anchor and am-scray west out the Blackett Strait."

"And that's where we had the little bastards. Because *Griffith, Isaacs* and *Howell* were supposed to run north through Ferguson Passage, to blockade the West end of the Blackett Strait and shut the door on anything that tries to escape from Vila." Myszynski bashed a fist on the table. Cups jumped.

With the raid over, Ashton's smile returned to full gleam, "Amazing."

"Trouble is now, they'll miss the rendezvous. Maybe the targets, too."

"Oh."

"The worst part is, the tables could be turned. If those two don't get out of there and haul ass, they could get caught in broad daylight by a bunch of pissed-off Japs." Myszynski grabbed a phone from it's bracket. "It's Commodore Myszynski in the wardroom," he growled. "Send a messenger down."

Shoving the phone into its bracket, he said, "Have to get aircover from *Cactus*; those boys are going to need it."

. . .

The night was clear and moonless, as the ship ground her way up the backside of a wave, then plunged into the trough, spewing white spray over the open bridge. But it was warm and the spray felt good, as Ingram, wearing only a short sleeved shirt, yanked a towel off his neck and wiped his binoculars dry. Training them north again, he picked out Kolombangara's 5,500 foot round peak. An extinct volcano, Kolombangara stood as a hulking silhouette against the Northern sky. To port lay Gizo Island, and to starboard, Vanavona Island. They were about halfway up the Ferguson Passage, Ingram reckoned. An hour earlier, they had spotted Briscoe's bombardment group on the radar as his four destroyers retired southeast back to Tulagi, their job finished.

They stood at general quarters, *Howell* leading the *Isaacs* with a vengeance at thirty-two knots, making up forty lost minutes. Earlier, they'd received the dumbo report, forwarded from Rocko Myszynski that two Japanese destroyers were anchored in Vila Harbor. And Landa wanted them.

Aft, Ingram saw *Isaacs* send a flashing light message through her red night-filter. Ingram leaned over the pilot house rail, picking Landa from the murk on the starboard bridgewing. The Captain was on the phone, arguing with Hank Kelly about why the ship couldn't go faster.

"Todd?" Landa looked up to the fly bridge.

Sir?"

"What do you think? Hank says thirty-two knots is all we get. His excuse is that we're too heavy and the ship needs a bottom job."

"Makes sense to me, Captain." Ingram didn't want to spar anymore with Landa tonight. First it was those damned ball bearings. Now, he was on fire about barnacles. The Captain should be concentrating on the mission.

"You may believe that bullshit when you get your own ship. For me, I'm going to talk to Kelly after this. These ships were originally rated at thirty-eight." As if everything had been said on the subject, Landa stepped into the pilot house.

With tons of extra equipment added to the original design, Ingram and Landa both knew the *Fletcher*s would never make thirty-eight knots. Landa sometimes liked to needle people when he was on edge and it was no use arguing with him.

"Blackett Strait in fifteen minutes," Landa announced from the hatchway.

Just then Katsikas, a first class signalman, finished clicking his flashing light from the signal bridge, then called forward, "Message from *Isaacs*, Sir. *'Trouble with number three boiler. May have to shut down and reduce speed to twenty-seven knots.'*"

Tonight, speed is everything, thought Ingram. In spite of the humid night a cold wave swept through him.

Landa said to Katsikas, "Very well. Ask *Isaacs* to keep us advised."

"Yes, Sir." Katsikas began clacking the reply on the signal lamp.

First the Jap submarine, then *Griffith*, now *Isaacs*. Ingram trained his binoculars, wondering why this raid was turning so sour. Off to his right he saw lights flash. Soon following was the rolling thunder of gunfire from Sand's group.

"Looks like Dexter is on station and going at it. We're about thirty minutes out, Todd. Think we ought to keep going?" said Landa.

Strange question, thought Ingram. If I had my way we'd grab a full load of fuel and head for the States. "Don't think we have much choice, Captain."

"Me, too. We're committed." Landa grabbed the phone and started arguing with Kelly again. He covered up the mouthpiece and looked up to Ingram, the starlight catching his broad, gleaming smile. "He's getting pissed. Should I remind him of who I am?"

"Skipper, I think we should---"

Suddenly, a brilliant light burst from the direction of the Vila airstrip. The entire sky lit up momentarily, turning the islands surrounding the Ferguson Passage into a bizarre moonscape. Ingram thrust his hand before his eyes. "What the--"

A terrific explosion rocked the ship, tearing at their eardrums. The echo reverberated for a few seconds, then disappeared. Finally, it died away, the only sound from the ship's uptakes, the foamy wake whispering alongside, and the crackle of the loud speakers.

Landa grabbed the TBS radio phone. "*Ovaltine. Ovaltine. This is Ricochet, Ricochet, over,*" he shouted. Landa tried several times, then handed the phone to Offenbach. "Keep trying. All circuits," he growled.

Secondary explosions lighted the sky and thundered in from the Vila airstrip. Then it was quiet and subdued on the bridge, as all within earshot, strained to hear any response to Offenbach, as he ran the code-signs for the light cruisers *Sioux Falls*, *Santa Monica* and *King City*. With a nod from

Landa, Offenbach tried the destroyers *Hanscom, Dale, W.E. Dunlap and Lyon* as well.

Landa jerked his head. *Get down here.*

Ingram stripped off his earphones, scrambled down to the pilot house and walked up to Landa. The skipper took Ingram's elbow and led him to a corner. "You think we ought to go in there? "

"Our orders are to rendezvous with the *Sioux Falls* group, who will provide us with maximum air cover for our exit from the Kula Gulf."

"I know, I know. But first light is now an hour and a half away. We're going to be stuck at the north end of the Kula Gulf, a good twenty or thirty miles away from those guys."

Landa was right. Rendezvousing with the *Sioux Falls* was the best of all worlds for mutual protection on the return trip.

"Ovaltine up on SecTac, Sir." Offenbach handed Landa the radiophone and said, "Apparently, our PriTac circuit was down."

"Thanks," muttered Landa. Grabbing the phone, he said, "*Ricochet, over.*" Static ranged from the speaker. He reached up and adjusted the squelch knob.

"*...interrogative Uncle Joe, over?*" Uncle Joe was the code name for *Griffith*.

"*Ovaltine, this is Ricochet. We held down a skunk for two hours, then Uncle Joe suffered an engineering casualty. Returned to Ring Bolt. Ricochet and Tootsie Roll are enroute to the party. Over.*" Ring Bolt was for Tulagi; Tootsie Roll for *Isaacs*.

The best Ingram could make out was, "*...reversed course, back in Kula...two enemy DDs destroyed...right in that sucker's magazine...big boom you probably...interrogative your posit? Over*"

"*Read you weak Ovaltine.*" Then Landa gave their position and asked, "*Shall we transit Blackett? Over.*"

"*...best chance...us. Cactus aircover at first light may extend to you. Mike speed shackle able-easy, unshackle. Can you overtake? Over.*"

Ingram scanned the shackle code chart mounted on the pilot house bulkhead. With a sinking feeling in his stomach, he turned to Landa and said, "They're at thirty knots."

Landa nodded. "*Ovaltine, we're at shackle able-x-ray unshackle. Tootsie Roll having boiler problems. We may have to go to shackle able-george, unshackle. Can you reduce? Over?*"

"*Negative, over.*"

"That bastard!" said Landa. "Dexter Sands is sitting fat and happy up on his gun-toting cruisers, leaving us for the Jap's to have for breakfast."

Offenbach leaned out the pilothouse. "Turn for Blackett Straits coming up in three minutes, Captain." The ship rolled heavily as she entered the Strait's turbulent waters. Ahead, the rounded bulk of Kolombangara obscured a quarter of the brilliant night sky, and Ingram sniffed at the rich odor of forest and soil and decaying sealife.

"Very well," replied Landa, "Carl, flashing light to the *Isaacs*. '*Intend to enter Blackett Strait and follow Sioux Falls Group. Can you maintain thirty-two knots?*'"

The radio speaker squawked with "*Ricochet, over?*" It was Admiral Sands bugging Landa for not responding quickly. Landa leaned against the bulkhead, the phone in his hand, seemingly unaware of Sands' admonition as Katsikas clacked out his flashing light message to the *Isaacs*,

Landa seemed in a daze, so Ingram coaxed, "Captain?"

"Yeah, yeah." Landa raised the phone. "*Ovaltine, this is Ricochet. About to enter Blackett Straits. Will proceed in accordance with OpPlan and attempt rendezvous. Over.*"

"*Ovaltine. Roger. Out.*"

The *Isaacs*'s red-filtered signal light winked at them again. And to Ingram, it seemed she was falling behind.

"Turn in sixty seconds, Captain," announced Offenbach.

"Very well," said Landa. All eyes on the bridge were fixed on the *Isaacs* and the bad news her flashing light was sure to bring.

Finally, Katsikas announced, "From *Isaacs*, Sir. '*Blown tubes in number three boiler. Have secured it. Best speed is twenty-seven.*'"

Complete quiet ranged on the bridge, the only sounds, that of water swishing along the hull. Landa blinked and said, "Lieutenant Offenbach, make turns for twenty-seven knots."

Offenbach replied, "Yes, Sir. Time to turn is now, Captain."

"Very well. Make it so." Landa climbed up into his chair, took off his hat and ran his fingers through his hair. He turned to Katsikas. "Signal *Isaacs* of our speed change and turn."

"Right ten degrees rudder," Offenbach ordered. "Steady up on course zero-nine-seven. All engines ahead flank. Make two-seven-zero turns for twenty-seven knots."

"Todd?" said Landa.

"Sir?"

"It'll probably be daylight when we exit the Kula Gulf. What would you do?"

"Stick close to the coast."

"Why?"

"Gut feel."

"My guts say the same thing. Let's plot this out." He jumped off his Captain's chair and they walked in the pilot house.

12

7 March, 1943
  U.S.S. *Howell* (DD 482)
  Visuvisu Point, New Georgia Sound, (The Slot)

Fires from the *Sioux Falls* Bombardment Group raged around the Vila Stanmore airfield, as *Howell* and *Isaacs* ran at twenty-seven knots through the Blackett Strait. The flames were a good beacon on an otherwise dark night, helping to direct their own shore bombardment, the two destroyers each lobbing a little over two hundred rounds without slowing.

By first light, the *Howell* and *Isaacs* exited into the Kula Gulf, hugging the shores of Arundel, then New Georgia Islands. An hour later, they were poised to round the New Georgia's Northwest tip, Visuvisu Point, and pass into The Slot for the run home on course one-three-zero true.

General quarters were relaxed, some slept at their stations, others fetched coffee and sandwiches from the galley.

"Todd? Todd?"

Ingram's eyes blinked open. With only two or three hours sleep over the last day, he'd been cat-napping on the deck of the flying bridge, head propped on a life jacket. He groaned and looked around, finding a flat, wind-rippled sea, with gray skies overhead. To the east, the top half of Kolomban-gara lay shrouded in clouds, the rest of the island a hoary mist.

"Wake up, damnit." Landa mounted the pilot house ladder, his face at deck level, within two feet of Ingram.

Ingram yawned, and smacked his lips.

"Is that anyway to greet your commanding officer?"

"Morning, Captain." Ingram rolled on his back, clasped his hands on his belly and closed his eyes. He'd been dreaming of Helen, her perfume; her fine, black silky hair---

"Mr. Ingram!"

"Yes, sir." He sat up, blinking his eyes. His back and thighs ached from laying on the cold, steel deck, and his right leg was asleep. He peered aft to see *Isaacs* steaming obediently in their wake at five hundred yards. But something didn't seem right. He glanced at their wake; it seemed less foamy.

"That's right. More engineering problems for the *Isaacs*. Our speed is down to twenty knots and we're falling further and further behind."

"Do we have a choice?"

"Mmmm, we do have to stick together. Although I don't see why Dexter Sands didn't come back for us."

"Dexter Sands --- "

"Yeah, I just talked to him. He's thirty-five miles ahead and says that Rocko has ordered air cover for us. But I think that's bullshit. Whatever air cover there is, Dexter Sands will hog for himself. We're on our own."

Ingram shook his sleeping leg and looked up to the sky. "Why do I feel so loved?"

"Yeah. When do you think the Japs will hit?"

"Oh, around nine."

"How so?"

"That's how it was on Corregidor. They never started anything before nine. They don't like to get up in the morning." With a groan, Ingram stood.

"How we doing ammo-wise?" asked Landa.

"Down to about half."

"Okay. We set for anti-air?"

"Yes, sir. Fusing is complete on all able-able-common."

"Okay." Landa began descending the pilot house ladder. As an afterthought, he asked, "And we're using mechanical time fuses?"

"Uh no, Sir. Actually, we have mounts fifty-four and fifty-five dedicated to proximity fuses."

Landa's voice turned to a low growl: "I thought I ordered no proximity fuses."

"But Captain, there aren't enough mechanical time fuses for all our rounds."

"Fine. Shoot up all our time fuses. Then, if we're still shooting, use the proximity fuses."

"Don't you think we should---"

"That's an order, Mr. Ingram. Don't try my patience. Mechanical time fuses only. Do you understand?"

Ingram felt foolish rubbing his leg while being chewed out by the Captain. But he had to keep massaging if he wanted to stay on his feet. "Yes, Sir. Mechanical time fuses only."

"Better make it quick. I've got a feeling the Japs are becoming less lazy these days." He disappeared down the ladder.

Ingram jabbed his sound-powered phone talk button and called for Lou Delmonico.

"CIC."

"Lou, I just talked to the skipper."

"Yeah?"

"He wants all mechanical time fuses."

"What?" Delmonico sounded incredulous. "Not in all mounts?"

"Including mounts fifty-four and fifty-five," Ingram said.

"Shit!"

"Do it!"

"Yes, Sir."

The ship teetered on the side of a wave rolling heavily to starboard. The empty five-inch shell casings, kicked out from the night shore bombardment, rolled and clanked about the decks.

"And Lou."

"Yeah?"

"Tell your boys to police the brass."

"Yes, Sir."

A moment later Leo Seltzer, mount fifty-two's gun captain, exited the hatch and jumped on the 02 deck. Three of his gunners followed suit. Soon, gunners from the other gun-turrets jumped out and started picking up the shell casings, passing them for stowage amidships. Seltzer looked up to Ingram, his palms spread upward.

Ingram drew a finger across his throat. 'No proximity fuses.'

Seltzer shook his head slowly, then turned and shouted at his crew to move faster.

A Mitsubishi "Rufe," a single engine Zero with a float and wing pontoons, caught them two hours later as they ran down The Slot, close to the thickly wooded coast of New Georgia. Buzzing monotonously, the Rufe flew in a slow orbit 15,000 yards away, tantalizingly close. Everyone knew he was a spotter, and after twenty minutes, a frustrated Jerry Landa shouted, "Mr. Ingram. Let's try and shake his damned feathers."

"One round, Captain?" The slant-range of the five-inch was 18,000 yards, meaning the current fire-control problem had little chance of success.

"Yeah, see what happens."

Ingram called up to Jack Wilson in the Main Battery Director. "You on target?"

"On target and tracking."

"Give him one round from Mount fifty-one."

"One round, aye." Five seconds later, mount fifty-one erupted with a belch of smokeless powder. Much to Ingram's surprise, the round exploded close to the Rufe. The plane wobbled for a moment, regained its attitude, and plodded on. But it grew smaller.

Delmonico reported from CIC: "Trouble."

"What, Lou?" Ingram looked down to see Early, Landa's talker, passing the same report to the Captain.

"Air search radar picking up a whole potful of bogies. Looks like...sono-fabitch..." They heard him counting. "...forty or so!"

"Jeepers," said Wilson.

"Range?" demanded Ingram

"Bearing two-six-two, twenty-two miles. They're over Visuvisu Point headed our way -- Wait. They've split. One group is headed on down The Slot toward the *Sioux Falls* Group. The rest are peeling off to circle us."

Ingram couldn't see anything but clouds; the bottom appeared to be about 2,500 feet, the Rufe flying right beneath it. "How many, Lou?"

"Twelve, maybe thirteen, not counting the spotter."

Landa sounded General Quarters just to make sure everyone was awake.

"Gunnery Department manned and ready, Captain, " Ingram said.

Landa gave a thumbs up, his mouth spread wide in his signature 'Boom Boom' Landa grin. "Here we go, Todd."

Ingram punched his talk button. "How's it look, Lou?"

"Aww, shit. Coordinated attack. They're spitting into four groups of three planes each, hitting us from all four directions. Recommend *Isaacs* take on bogies designated Able through Fox. We should take on the rest; bogies George through Love."

The sky fairly rumbled with the sound of aircraft engines. As they passed overhead, some planes soared on, while others drifted off to the right or left.

"You have the feeling they can see us, but we can't see them?" Landa asked.

"I wouldn't be surprised. Sometimes--- there!" Ingram pointed at three single- engine Val dive bombers plunging beneath the overcast. "Jack! Do you have them?"

"Director Fifty-One, aye. On target and tracking."

"Director Forty-Three?" Ingram checked aft to see three more Vals attacking from the starboard quarter.

"Director Forty-Three on target and tracking."

The forty and twenty millimeter gun-stations reported in as well. Landa, with the TBS phone to his ears, raised a hand in the air. "Commence fire!" His hand sliced to the deck.

Both destroyers simultaneously belched gunfire from their five-inch, forty, and twenty millimeter gun mounts--Ingram almost knocked over from the muzzle blasts.

The first Val pulled from her dive and zipped overhead, the bomb over-shooting. It hit two hundred yards off the *Howell's* port quarter, raising a huge plume of bluish-white water. Ingram caught the second Val in his binoculars, seemingly headed straight for him. But mount fifty-two roared, and the Val disintegrated before his eyes.

The third Val caromed toward them. On the bridge, Landa yelled, "Left standard rudder. Steady on zero-three-four." Both destroyers pivoted quickly and were now abeam of one another.

The turn and the combined firepower seemed to throw off the Val's aim -- he had to raise his nose a bit to compensate. Mounts fifty-one and fifty-two blasted away, their shells exploding around the Val as it plummeted, growing larger and larger in Ingram's vision.

The Val released its bomb, which mercifully fell short. Landa and his watchstanders cheered and grinned, their fists in the air. Ingram looked over to see *Isaacs* taking care of her sector. The Vals were arching up into the clouds, out of gunsight, apparently regrouping to try again. Ingram was surprised to see half the Vals still had their 500 kg bombs. Apparently they weren't releasing unless they were sure.

The best news was that he counted only seven out of the original twelve.

The Vals regrouped and dove though the clouds again. This time two were lined up on the Howell's starboard bow. "Commence fire!" Ingram shouted. Mounts fifty-one and fifty-two roared at the dive bombers as they screamed down.

Suddenly, a Val zipped over Ingram's head from the opposite direction. It was at no more than fifty feet, it's engine howling. He pivoted as the Val ran past. Then he turned and watched, horror stricken, as a black death-messenger raced directly at him.

The bomb soared on a steady course, as Ingram lived a lifetime. It crashed through the maindeck and plunged into *Howell's* after engineroom. Seconds passed --- a dud?

The explosion was blinding. A wave of heat and brilliance blew past Ingram, knocking him on his back...

...smoke and steam enveloped the ship. Ingram reached to his head, finding a sticky wetness. He opened his eyes.

He was laying on his side, crunched against a stanchion, a leg dangling over the pilothouse bulkhead. Then his hearing returned. Screams intermingled with a loud hissing noise. Someone yelled and pulled at his shirt. Vogel, his talker; his lips were moving but Ingram couldn't hear over the terrible hissing.

The mainmast hung by one forward shroud on the port side; the other forwards had snapped, as if they were brittle rubber bands. The air search antennae had fallen off and crashed into number one stack. Ingram looked aft, trying to see through the white smoky hell. Finally, a gust of wind cleared the deck.

Ingram looked aft in abject horror. "Nooooo!"

The ship had broken in two! The bomb had sliced the *Howell* neatly in half. The aft section capsized onto its starboard side. Men blown into the water were swept under as the ship's upper works slammed down upon them. Sailors posted topside spilled out of their battle stations, some screaming, others lifeless dolls.

Jack Wilson climbed halfway out of his gun director and toppled down, dazed or wounded, Ingram couldn't tell. He caught Wilson by the shoulders and clumsily lowered him to the deck.

"My God, those guys," Wilson gasped. Catching his breath, he said, "We gotta do something!"

Large bubbles gurgled from the *Howell's* aft section and it settled fast.

Then the mast groaned directly above. Metal screeched, and what was left of the mast's upper works swayed in an obscene, convoluted orbit.

Someone cursed beneath. Landa wobbled to his feet, apparently uninjured, as others around him groaned and tried to stand.

Suddenly, there was a great blast of air. Ingram watched *Howell's* after end slip beneath the waves, her depth charge racks and flag staff the last things in view. Ingram racked his brain. Were the depth charges set on safe? He couldn't remember. Twenty...thirty...forty seconds passed. The water swirled where the Howell's aft section had been. Desperate swimmers groped for anything that would float amidst a quickly growing pool of fuel oil. But mercifully, if one could call it that, the depth charges didn't detonate.

Ingram stumbled to the after ladder and climbed down to the bridge. What was that sound? He walked up to Landa. The two men shouted at one another, neither able to understand the other. Ingram twirled a finger in his right ear, and he discerned the horrible sounds of the wounded and dying.

Landa's face was beet red and he shout at dazed sailors. Then he grabbed Ingram's lifejacket and bellowed.

"What?"

"Air cover!" Landa shrieked. "Dexter hogged the air cover."

"You don't know for sure."

"I'll kill the sonofabitch."

13
---

7 March, 1943
   U.S.S. *Howell* (DD 482)
   The Slot, Solomon Islands

The Vals, satisfied that *Howell* was done for, concentrated on *Isaacs*, driving her across The Slot toward Santa Isabel Island as she furiously fought off the air attack. Meanwhile, a rain squall settled about the *Howell,* cloaking her from two Vals that wandered back to check her condition.

Landa, Offenbach, Early, and Wilson stumbled about, pushing aside wreckage, trying to stand, or lean, only to slump to the deck in pain. It took several minutes for Ingram to galvanize himself to do something productive. The rain brought him back. A gentle, cleansing, nourishing rain that, to the uninjured, helped carry away shock, pain, noise, filth and gun smoke.

Ingram stood for a full thirty seconds, his face turned to the sky. The rain washed him, as men with gaunt eyes stumbled past, going nowhere on a wrecked ship. For a moment he heard locomotives chugging through Echo, Oregon where he grew up. After school, he would go down to the rail yard, beckoned by the mournful whistles of the Union Pacific. The engineers knew him and let him ride to Pendleton and back, shoveling coal for his fare. His parents never found out...

But then he opened his eyes, seeing gray, and hearing groans. Metal screeched again as the swaying mast hove into his view. The last forward shroud would soon part, and then the mast would fall.

A bell rang. Ingram looked over the bridge bulwarks. Mount fifty-two's crew stumbled out, walking like zombies. The radio squawked in the pilot house. Power! The radiomen must have patched in the emergency batteries.

"Shit!" Landa stood next to Ingram.

"The men..." Ingram waved a hand aft.

"Take care of the living first," Landa said. "Early! Get over here." He pulled his talker to his feet. "Status report." Landa grabbed a sound powered phone and punched up Hank Kelly in Main Control.

Offenbach lurched out of the pilothouse, a deep cut running across his forehead. Blood ran into his eyes. Ingram grabbed him by the collar before he stumbled into the starboard pelorus.

"Lemme go, damnit!"

"Where you going?" Asked Ingram.

"The Doc," he said hoarsely. "All I need are a few stitches. The rest of me is fine."

"Okay." Ingram led Offenbach through the vestibule into the Captain's Sea Cabin. "Here."

"Huh?"

It was clear Offenbach had no idea where he was, so Ingram pushed him on the bunk. "Stay here." He found a pillowcase, shoved it on Offenbach's forehead, then clamped the Lieutenant's hand over it. "Wait for a Doc to come and stitch this up. Then you're going back to work."

"Deal." Offenbach laid back.

"You should---"

Just then, he heard a sharp 'twang,' then a series of high-pitched tearing noises, like finger nails ripping on a blackboard.

"Look out!" Landa screamed from the signal bridge.

Ingram rushed outside, seeing men scatter as the mast fell backward. With an ear-popping crash, it landed along the starboard side of the 01 level, ripping through the forty-millimeter guntubs which had, moments before, been evacuated. With more screeches and groans, the mast came to rest: the after end propped on the 01 level, the mid section on main deck with about fifteen feet or so, hanging over the starboard side, immersed in water.

"Sonofabitch!" Ingram said. "Anybody under that?"

A corpsman popped out on the main deck to look for injured. The mast gave a shriek, metal grated on metal. Another five feet or so slipped under water.

"Damn. It's going over the side!"

"Good riddance," said Landa.

Ingram cupped his hands and shouted to a few men gathered on the main deck. "Stand clear! The mast is going!" The men dashed for hatchways and ladders. Seconds later, there was another 'twaaaang' as an aft shroud parted. The mast slipped further, ripping shackles, pins, and turnbuckles from their mountings.

Suddenly, a sailor ran aft on the 01 level toward the after torpedo mount, and began picking his way amongst the mast's wreckage.

"Hey! You! Stand clear!" Ingram shouted. "Didn't you hear the Captain?"

The man waved over his head, while foraging through a hopeless tangle of yardarm, shrouds, halyards, and an impossibly twisted surface search radar antennae. Another wire snapped; a signal halyard drew taught, and whipped over the sailor's head, just as he leaped down to the main deck.

Ingram recognized the sailor's sandy blond hair. "Seltzer. You crazy bastard. Get out of there."

"Shit. What's he doing?" gasped Landa.

Rigging screeched; an IFF antenna flashed over the side as if yanked by a crazed monster beneath the ship.

"My God," said Ingram. "He's going after the flag."

Early whipped off his headphones and raced down the aft ladder to the 01 deck to help. Then Katsikas joined in. Then others surged toward the aft ladder.

"That's enough!" bellowed Landa.

With Early and Katsikas' help, Seltzer pulled aside more wreckage. For a moment, he was lost to view in a sea of junk, but finally he popped up, holding the United States flag over his head with a grin.

"Get out of there!"

As if jumping the high hurdles, the three quickly dashed over wreckage for the sanctuary of the forward deckhouse.

Seltzer, the flag wrapped around his shoulders, was the last to bolt thorough the hatch when the final shroud parted with a "crack," its end slashing through the bulwarks as if it were a slab of cheese. The mast upended, and with a final groan of protest, sank out of sight.

Seltzer, Early and Katsikas climbed to the bridge and walked up to Landa. Wordlessly, Seltzer handed the flag to Landa, stepped back, and drew to attention. Early and Katsikas did the same.

Landa turned the flag over in his hands. His lips moved and his eyes grew misty.

Ingram's chest heaved, and he had trouble swallowing as he looked over this unlikely threesome.

"Thank you." Landa said softly. Offenbach shuffled out and stood beside Ingram, a bloody pillowcase wrapped around his head.

"It was Leo's idea," Early said.

"You gallant, crazy men. I salute you." Landa did so, and after they returned it, he extended his hand and they shook.

"I almost had the commissioning pennant, Sir," Seltzer said, "but then you and Mr. Ingram was yelling. So..."

"It's a good thing you did," Ingram laughed.

"Okay." Landa passed the flag back to Seltzer and nodded toward the gun director. "Think you men can jury rig the flag up there?"

"You bet, Captain." The three scrambled up the ladder to the pilot house, then crawled up the gun director and started bending the flag to the aft section of the fire control antenna.

The rain pounded harder, roaring and dimpling the water around them as the ship drifted. Ingram sighted the pelorus across the bow; it appeared to line up with their direction of movement. He caught Landa's eye.

"Better pass the word," Landa said. He called to Early, "Damnit, get back down here and put your phones on."

"Sir." Early scrambled down and hurriedly jammed on his sound-powered phone gear.

"Tell all stations to hang on. We'll be grounding soon, most likely on New Georgia."

Landa grabbed a phone and rang Hank Kelly. "How's that bulkhead holding up?" It was a seriously ruptured after-fireroom bulkhead that now constituted the ship's transom. "Yeah, yeah, well keep shoring. Say, listen. We're pretty sure we'll be running aground soon. So watch that bulkhead, and be ready to evacuate the fireroom if it splits when we hit. Got it?"

Turning to Ingram, Landa said, "Engineering department got off relatively easy. All men in the after engine room were lost. Two killed in the after fire room. But that's it for them. Both firerooms wrapped up the boilers and got out of there. Apparently, the main steam lines are ruptured. The diesel-generator took shrapnel through the block, so it looks like a goner. Most of our casualties are from the gun crews and aft repair parties that went down with..."

He stuttered for a moment. Then, "Hank wants help down there pounding in strongbacks. Any ideas?"

"How 'bout our First Lieutenant? Maybe some of the deck force?"

"Good idea. Where is he?"

"Combat?"

"Early, ask Mr. Delmonico to find Mr. Edgerton and tell him to lay to the bridge."

"Yes, Sir."

"Our only source of power is the emergency batteries."

Ingram opened his mouth to speak, but then noticed Early's ashen face. "What is it?"

"Captain," Early said. "Mr. Delmonico reports that Mr. Edgerton was a check-sight observer on mount fifty-four."

"Ahhh, shit."

Instinctively, Landa and Ingram looked aft in the rain, almost as if they could see the young ensign walking toward them. "Damnit! A great kid," said Landa.

Ingram turned his face to the sky, his tears mixing with clean fresh water, running down his shirt, washing grime away.

The rain let up for a moment. Looking around, Ingram spotted a thick patch of trees to starboard. "Land, about 200 yards, Jerry." Then the mist closed in. "We might want to drop anchor when we hit."

"Right, call away the anchor detail."

A bright orange-yellow coral head sweep past just beneath the surface. Then another, closer.

Suddenly, static ranged on the TBS and they heard a faint, *"Ricochet, Ricochet, this is Ovaltine, Ovaltine, over."* It was Dexter Sands, calling from the *Sioux Falls.*

"What shall I tell him, Sir," asked Offenbach.

"Think of something."

Offenbach picked up the hand set and pressed it to the blood-soaked pillowcase wrapped around his head. *"Ricochet, over."*

"Ricochet?" Dexter Sand's voice was incredulous, as if he really didn't expect an answer. *"Authenticate, over."*

They heard a scraping, then something thumped. The ship lurched.

An incredulous Offenbach stepped into the pilot house, looking for the day's authentication chart.

"Let me." Landa snatched the hand set from Offenbach and said, *"Ovaltine, this is Ricochet, Over."*

"Ricochet. Interrogative authentication. Over."

"Look, Dexter, we've had our ass blown off; everything behind the after fireroom is gone. We're on emergency power, have suffered well in excess of a hundred casualties, and have lots of injured men. I don't have time to screw with your fucking authentication code, because we're about to run aground on New Georgia Island. Where, I don't know, because we've lost our mast including my radar. And it's raining like hell. Needless to say, we need lots of help. Oh, by the way, thanks for the air cover. Ricochet, out." Landa bracketed the phone just as the *Howell* hit another bump.

Landa walked on the bridgewing as the *Howell* hit bottom. She turned sideways for a moment, then skipped over coral, scraping mud banks. Ahead, the mist parted. The area was heavily wooded and sloped gently down to a mangrove swamp, about one hundred yards distant.

The ship lurched and they pitched forward. Something, perhaps a coral reef, screeched and bit the *Howell's* bottom. With a final groan, she stopped for good.

Landa stood high on the bulwark step, put two fingers to his lips and whistled to the fo'c'sle crew. He sliced his hand across his neck and yelled, "Let her go!"

With a sledgehammer, a boatswain's mate on the fo'c'sle smacked the pelican hook's stopper, and the anchor fell free, smacking the water, and dragging its chain with it. The brakeman on the fo'c'sle set the anchor chain and quiet descended; the only sounds faint static on the pilot house loud speakers, thumping rain, and groans of the wounded.

With no mast, the *Howell* seemed naked. And her new aft end was the forward bulkhead of a gutted after engine room, where the shredded main deck hung only six feet above the water. Aft of that, there was no more U.S.S. *Howell*. It was...gone, sunk in the New Georgia sound: rudder, screws, three five-inch gunmounts, one forty and ten twenty millimeter gunmounts, the after berthing compartments, and the depth charge racks...gone. And, by Ingram's guess, approximately 125 men, who had moments before been living, working, fiercely loyal destroyer men dedicated to doing their jobs.

What remained was the forward end; its bow raised on a coral reef one hundred yards off the mangrove swamps of New Georgia Island. Remarkably, she was on an even keel.

Landa rubbed stubble on his chin. "I'm putting those guys in for a bronze star."

"No argument from me," Ingram said.

"Do you think Dexter Sands will ever speak to me again?"

"You were pretty brutal."

"Yeah, I was. Too bad." Landa shook his head. "Let's collect our casualty reports and figure out what's going on."

14

7 March, 1943
    U.S.S. *Howell* (DD 482)
    Mondo Mondo Island, Solomon Islands

Ingram checked his watch:1522. Damn! It seemed a crisis rose every two minutes, with everyone rushing from one emergency to the next. Landa had scheduled an officer's meeting long ago and still, it hadn't happened. And, the rain didn't help. Everything was slippery, with spilled fuel-oil making it worse as he picked his way among the main deck wreckage.

Suddenly, the ship gave a terrible screech. Then, it slid back, bumping along the bottom. Lurching to port, the bow skewed out to where *Howell's* starboard side was nearly parallel to the thickly vegetated shore. Then something caught her, perhaps another coral head, and she suddenly jolted to a halt. It was like being in an earthquake, Ingram realized: deep rumbling, shaking and terrifying uncertainty, followed by euphoric moments of gratitude and relief that the earth hadn't swallowed him up. A long five seconds passed before he dared to look over the starboard bulwark and check on the anchor chain. As he suspected, it was taut. That was what saved them. The anchor had dug in, keeping the bow from sliding out further.

Suddenly, Hank Kelly ran past Ingram and dove down the after fireroom hatch. Hearing a whistling noise, Ingram leaned over the hatch. A great blast of air roared in his face. Down below, the after fireroom was lighted only by battle lanterns, their hoary-white beams stabbing at the machinery. Sweating, filthy bodies darted about. Indeed, it looked like Lucifer's workshop.

Kelly's voice echoed up, "Secure. Secure. Get the hell out of here!'

Soon, eleven oil-soaked men erupted from the boiler room. Kelly was last to crawl out, his arms loaded with maintenance logs. He leaned over, slammed down the hatch and kicked the dogs tight.

Ingram said, "That's it?"

"Bulkhead let go. Worse, a coral head punched us though the bottom just beneath boiler number four. It's all flooded now, boilers three and four, half submerged. Nothing left but to get the hell out."

"Next line of defense..?"

"Up here." Kelly paced quickly to the forward engine room hatch. With a toothy grin, he stepped in the hatchway and held his face up to the rain, pausing to let it wash away some grime. "What's the movie for tonight?" And then he was gone.

"Keystone Cops." Ingram called after him. A thunderclap followed as he walked to the passageway to check on the wardroom, now converted to an operating theater.

He stepped in, finding Bucky Monaghan and two other corpsmen in blood-spattered surgical garb, standing over a patient splayed on the table. Earlier, Monaghan, their leading pharmacist's mate, had triaged the worst cases, deciding which of the scalded and shattered men should first be cared for; leaving others aside, to perhaps die.

"Hello."

The three looked up, then stepped back, taking off their masks. Monaghan nodded curtly. "Care to pitch in and give a hand, Sir?"

"Seriously?"

"Sorry, we just lost Redding." Monaghan's shoulders slumped and a set of forceps clanked as he threw them into a stainless basin. He waved at the inert form on the table. The man's mouth and eyes were wide open. "Internal injuries. Poor bastard bled out. I just couldn't find it all."

Ingram stepped up and closed Redding's eyes. He tried to speak. But words didn't come.

Monaghan's eyes glistened.

"...not your fault," Ingram managed.

"...I know. But tell that to Redding." Monaghan swallowed. "His last words were, 'God bless you.' Can you imagine that coming from Red? He swore like a...a friggin' bosun's mate." Monaghan exhaled deeply and leaned on the wardroom table. "'God bless you.'

"Better check on the guys below," he said to his two corpsmen.

"Okay, Buck." The corpsmen gathered medical supplies and walked out.

Ingram said. "You need anything?"

"Bottle of gin would do nicely."

Ingram pat Monaghan on the shoulder and walked out.

He stepped down the companionway to the next deck, an area given over to officer's staterooms and chief quarters. Now, without power to run the lights, blowers and exhaust fans, it was dark and the air was stale. In a macabre dance, flashlights bobbed up and down the midships passage-way as Monaghan's corpsmen darted in and out of staterooms, injecting morphine, patching wounds, wrapping broken limbs, doing their best to comfort their patients. As Ingram walked by, he could see in the faint light that some of the wounded had accepted their fate stoically, laid back and were quiet. Others moaned occasionally; a few cried. Taking a quick count, Ingram found twenty-two bunks full, including his own. Of the twenty-two, four had sheets drawn all the way over their heads. That was two more since the last time he'd been down here.

Continuing his walk forward, he stepped into the chief's quarters and walked among listless men, some sitting and muttering to one another, others sipping cold coffee and staring into space. Then he mounted the ladder and stepped onto the fo'c'sle.

With a vengeance, lightning flashed and thunder burst so harshly that seemed to raise him off the deck. And the rain poured harder, carving thousands of perfect little craters on the water. He found Chief Murphy standing at the bow, looking over the side. A twenty-two year veteran and ex-China sailor, Murphy's eyes were wide and round, his face the color of chalk.

"What do you think?" Ingram had to shout to be heard. His teeth chattered and he knew it wasn't from the rain.

"Don't look good. Where are we, Sir?" Murphy yelled back.

"Looks like Mondo Mondo, but we're not sure until we get a fix. And we can't do that until this storm clears." Mondo Mondo Island was one of a series of heavily wooded narrow islands forming a barrier off the northern coast of New Georgia Island.

Chief Murphy bent over the life line again, peering down.

"What is it?" asked Ingram.

"If this is Mondo Mondo, then the bottom is steep to." Murphy waved a hand aft. "The bottom drops off suddenly. This means, if the ship slides again, then we'll be afloat. Hard to see from here, but there's a bunch of coral heads where the bottom falls off. I'll bet we're wedged in among some. They could break and we could slide free."

"I don't think we want to do that. That slide punched a hole in the aft boiler room. They had to secure it. And the bulkhead let go."

"Shiiit," said Murphy.

"What?"

"I was hopin' we'd sort of slip back to sea. You know? Sort of like being launched again? And then just get towed home."

"Maybe, but with that bulkhead gone, we'd probably go down. Can you drop the port anchor?"

"...Todd?"

Ingram looked up to the bridge.

Landa gave a loud whistle and waved him up.

Waving back, he asked. "Chief?"

"Yes, Sir, we can drop it." said Murphy.

"Okay. Better do it and keep the scope short. In the meantime, I'm headed aft for officer's call." said Ingram.

"Yes, Sir."

For some crazy reason, Ingram thought of 'Hot Lips' Edgerton, sipping soup in the wardroom just a few days ago. And now, the young man was gone, trapped in a gun mount. *Welcome to World War II, Hot Lips.* He wondered if Chief Murphy had seen his teeth clacking. Not from the cold,

Ingram was sure. Running up into the rain, he took the aft companionway, two steps at a time.

Except for three officers who went down with the Howell's aft section, they were all there. Ingram took in their faces, realizing they mirrored his own. They had all aged over the last twelve hours. Their eyes were dark and deep-set. Pale lips were pressed in near grimaces and without sleep, faces were shriveled. Kelly seemed the worse off. His light sandy hair was terribly thinned, almost white.

"Okay, XO, why don't you start?" Landa said.

Ingram reported on his tour and finished with, "I told Chief Murphy to let the port anchor go."

"Makes sense." Landa turned to Kelly. "Okay Hank. Tell us what we have."

Kelly slumped against the aft bulkhead, hands stuffed in his oil-splotched coveralls, talking as if he were somewhere outside his body, his voice hollow. "...after fireroom is flooded and secured. That's it for boilers three and four. The space is useless. Main control is okay; we're shoring that bulkhead to make sure. Generator number one looks decent, but there's no steam for it. Boilers one and two in the forward fireroom have ruptured steam lines and we're trying to figure out a way to fix that. Plus, it looks like both boilers, especially number one, have shifted on their foundations and may be unsafe to operate. If there's any hope, it's with boiler number two. That's where we're concentrating right now. Fixing the steamline and a million other things so we can send steam to generator number one.

"As for the diesel-generator..." Kelly waved a hand.

Landa's eyebrows went up.

"...shrapnel penetrated both the block and crankcase. Looks like the crankshaft is cracked. We don't have a prayer."

A collective groan ranged among the officers.

"Emergency power?" Landa asked.

"We have ten, six-volt batteries in emergency radio, Captain. Otherwise, it's battle lanterns, and flashlights. So far, there's juice. Maybe for six or eight hours for the big, six-volt batteries. Depends on how well we conserve power. After that..." Kelly shrugged.

"Okay, Hank." Landa said. "Offenbach, where's your flute?"

"I beg your pardon?"

"You ready to march in the Minute Man Parade?"

Offenbach blinked, as he figured out what the Captain meant. A corpsman had stitched his head and wrapped a neat dressing around his brow, where just a spot of blood leaked through.

"Looks like Gunga Din to me," said Wilson.

Offenbach silenced Wilson with a glare that said,'I'm a lieutenant, you're a lieutenant (j.g.).'

"What is the story on the radios?" asked Landa.

"As some of you may have noticed," Offenbach said sarcastically, "the mast is gone. So, we jury rigged an antennae to the aft stack. No contact with anyone via TBS, which is to be expected. We're guarding that circuit right now and trying not to transmit in order to conserve power. But the bad part is that we can't get Tulagi on CW. We're trying all circuits. Nothing yet. Could be this damned storm, could be the antenna. Just don't know."

"Okay." Landa eyed Delmonico. "Gunnery?"

"All gunmounts forward of frame 155 are operable, at least in local control. We lost two of the waist twenty millimeters. So only two are left. One on each side. These are most easily manipulated, since they're essentially a manual cannon anyway. And thanks to mother nature a few minutes ago," Delmonico nodded toward the beach, "both five inch guns and both port side forty millimeters can be brought to bear, covering us from an attack from the sea."

"But only in manual control?" Landa asked. The hydraulically operated five-inch and forty millimeter guns were cumbersome to crank around in manual control.

"Yes, Sir," said Delmonico. "No power."

"Small arms?" asked Landa.

"Sir?" asked Delmonico.

"Against an attack from Mondo Mondo Island."

Ingram looked out the port hole. The bow was next to a small beachy area of perhaps ten feet or so. The rest of the coast was tall trees and mangrove swamps. "Hard to see where the Japs can get through, Captain." Delmonico turned to Wilson. "Jack?"

"Most of our small arms stuff went down with the aft end, Captain. But the midships gunlocker has ten Springfields, five of the new M-1s, two Thompson sub-machine guns, five BARs, and fifteen .45s."

"Ammo?" said Landa.

"About two clips each, Captain."

"All right. What about--"

"BOh," said Wilson.

"Yes?" From Landa.

"And a case of grenades."

"Are you finished, Mr. Wilson?" said Landa.

"Yes, Sir."

"Then I want a plan, within a half hour, of how and to whom we distribute these weapons. Understand?" Landa's eyes flicked to Delmonico.

"Yes, Sir."

"I want the Deck Division to launch the whale boats and all life rafts. Then inventory the survival gear and have it all ready to go. We might have enough diesel fuel to tow everybody down The Slot?" It was a rhetorical question and Landa looked at Kelly.

"I'll check, Captain," said Kelly.

The sound powered phone buzzed. Ingram picked it up. "Bridge."

A voice crackled, "Sir, Templeton in Radio Central. We have CW contact with *Ring Bolt*."

Ingram covered the mouthpiece and reported, "They've got Tulagi on CW." Then he asked Templeton, "Have they acknowledged our SITREP?"

"Just did, Mr. Ingram."

"They've got our SITREP. Anything else you want, Captain?"

"Send beer and sandwiches."

"That's it for now," Ingram said to Templeton. "By the way, how are the batteries doing?"

"Plenty of zip, so far, Sir," said Templeton.

Ingram had another thought. "Templeton?"

"Sir?"

"Send *Interrogative, Tootsie Roll*." Landa nodded his approval to inquire about the *Isaacs's* fate.

"Aye, aye, Sir."

Tulagi. They'd made contact with home base, 140 miles away. Help should arrive, soon. The pilothouse seemed lighter, the storm not so intense, their wounds less serious, the ship more comfortable.

As if in confirmation, the rain stopped. Soon a bolt of golden sunlight stabbed though the starboard side portholes. Then the clouds swept to the northwest, leaving the afternoon crisp and pure.

They piled out onto the starboard bridge wing, looking into the aquamarine blue waters of New Georgia Sound. Ingram sniffed the air: clean, ozone tainted, and wonderfully refreshing.

And before them, off the starboard side, was a heavily forested land, with the cone shaped volcanic peaks of New Georgia rising in the background. Offenbach nodded to Briley, one of his quartermasters, and they quickly took a round of bearings. Landa walked in the pilot house and leaned over Offenbach's shoulder as he plotted their position.

"Right here, Captain. Mondo Mondo Island," Offenbach announced.

"Okay, Carl," said Landa. "Get that to Tulagi ASAP." Then he stepped out on the bridge and stood next to Ingram. "When was the last time you had chow?"

"Not hungry." Ingram thought of Redding below on the wardroom table.

"Oh, yeah? I tell you, I could use a tall, cool bottle of Schlitz right now."

"Radio Central just called up, Captain," Offenbach's voice echoed from the pilot house. "Good news. The *Isaacs* made it home."

"Very well," Landa sighed. "God, all we need now is some---"

Suddenly, Wilson's arm jutted to the northwest.

"Damnit!" said Landa,

At first Ingram refused to look. But by the sound, he knew what it was and finally forced his eyes in that direction. A speck slowly circled the *Howell's* carcass, its engine, barely audible.

"Probably the same sonofabitch," Landa said.

Ingram's eyes narrowed on the Mitsubishi "Rufe," the single engine Zero with a float and wing pontoons; just like the one that had dogged them early this morning, now ages ago.

"Sound General Quarters," Landa said quietly.

With the ship so ripped up, it took five minutes to assume a semblance of general quarters. With the gun mounts manned and cranked around in the Rufe's general direction.

Then Ingram heard another engine, closer, its pitch much deeper. He groaned.

"What?" asked Landa.

"Hear that?"

"How can I not?" Landa peered to starboard, his binoculars scanning Mondo Mondo's treeline.

"Jack, you passed out the small arms?"

"Not yet," replied Wilson.

"Get to it," said Ingram. "Now."

"What's up?" Landa asked.

That damned engine. It was a diesel engine: a distinctive engine he'd heard ten months before, during his escape from Corregidor. "It's a Jap barge, Captain. A hundred footer. My guess it's coming down the inland waterway full of Jap Marines. If so, we can count on a night assault from Mondo Mondo Island."

15

7 March, 1943
   U.S.S. *Howell* (DD 482)
   Mondo Mondo Island, Solomon Islands

Four Marine F4Fs flashed overhead with a great roar. The men on the *Howell*'s bridge whooped and hollered as the Wildcats arched up and circled to the left. Three of them came down and were lost to sight on the other side of the tree line. Then their machine guns rattled, and something exploded inshore, nearly opposite where the *Howell* lay. Soon, a dark cloud of greasy smoke billowed up.

"Go gettum," yelled Landa. He leaned in the pilot house. "Carl, you have voice contact?"

"Trying, Captain." Offenbach twirled a dial on his receiver.

"Well, shove in your clutch."

"Yes, Sir."

Jack Wilson yelled and waved his helmet over his head, pointing off to the north. The fourth Wildcat had just gained the tail position of the Rufe. Little puffs trailing from the Wildcat's wings indicated the pilot had taken the float plane under fire. Then the Rufe panicked and peeled off to its left, and headed back toward the *Howell*. Easily, the Wildcat stayed on the lumbering float plane's tail, firing its six fifty-caliber wing-mounted machine guns. The pair descended to about fifty feet when a black puff of smoke suddenly belched from the float plane. For a moment, it arched gracefully up then rolled to its right and dove in, cartwheeling across the ocean, spewing parts as it went. The F4F flew on, doing a barrel roll over the *Howell,* as it passed overhead. A great roar broke out aboard the *Howell,* everyone cheering and thrusting their fists into the air.

Then the fourth Wildcat joined its partners, making strafing runs on the other side of Mondo Mondo Island.

"Got 'em, Captain," called Offenbach. He leaned over and spoke into the handset. "*Jubilee two-six, this is Ricochet, I hear you weak, but clear, over.*"

Static ranged, then the speaker rattled with, "*Ricochet, this is Jubilee two-six; we've taken a barge under fire and I think we destroyed it. But he'd already ducked into a mangrove swamp opposite you and is burning under the trees.*"

Landa grabbed the phone, "*Jubilee two-six, this is Ricochet, How far away is he? Over?*"

"*Jubilee two-six. Looks like a hundred yards or so of thick wood and overgrowth between you and them. Probably thirty to forty Japs in there. Over.*"

"*Roger Jubilee two-six. Any word on relief? Over.*"

"*Jubilee two-six. Word is Peter Tares enroute. You should be home for breakfast. How do you like your eggs? Over.*"

"*Over easy. Over.*"

"*Roger Ricochet. We'll stick around until our gas runs low.*"

"*Roger, Jubilee two-six. Thanks for beating up the barge. And good job on splashing that Rufe. We'll guard this circuit. Out.*" Landa walked out on the bridgewing and said to Ingram. "Looks like were going yachting tonight."

"We should plan how to transfer the wounded," Ingram said. "I wonder how they'll stand the pounding in PT Boats."

"You and Monaghan figure that one out," Landa said.

Just then, someone screamed in the jungle. A khaki-clad figure ran from the tree line right up to the ship and threw a...

"Grenade! Hit the deck!" yelled Ingram.

The grenade bounced on the fo'c'sle, rolled down toward Mount 51, and exploded.

Ingram yelled into his phone. "Mounts twenty one and forty one. Take that treeline under fire!" As the forty and twenty millimeter pumped shells into the trees, Ingram yelled up to Wilson, "Jack. Casualties?"

Wilson nodded and held up a finger, his other hand clamped over an earphone. Finally, he said, "Two men in mount fifty-one. Pointer and trainer injured by shrapnel. None serious."

Ingram leaned over the rail. "Captain? We might as well abandon the five inch mounts. Two men were injured in that blast. Grenades can punch holes in them."

"Make it so."

After relaying the order to Wilson, Ingram said, "Okay, Jack. Get those dammed small arms passed out. Set up your BARs in the forty millimeter gun tubs where they can see into the jungle."

"Got it!" Wilson disappeared down his hatch.

A sudden quiet descended. Landa called up, "Todd, since the starboard side is the engaged side, let's move all unarmed personnel or those not on gunmounts to the port side, out of the Jap's line of fire. No telling when they may start trying to pick us off with snipers."

As if in answer, a rifle shot rang out, and a bullet ricocheted off the director, a foot from Ingram's head. Two more shots plinked close by.

"Damn." Ingram turned to Vogel. "Come on!" Quickly, they ran down the ladder, taking the protection of the port side of the pilot house where they huddled beside Landa.

"What's taking Wilson so long?" Landa demanded. Just then, the forward forty-millimeters cranked out three clips of four rounds each. A scream ranged from deep in the forest.

Early and Offenbach ran in the pilothouse, dogged the starboard hatch, then the portholes. Soon, a shot rang out: a porthole shattered. Then another. Then a third. But when the shooting subsided, Offenbach quickly taped dark magazine pages over the shattered portholes.

The forty millimeters roared for another thirty seconds, then Landa yelled, "Cease fire." Turning to Offenbach, he said, "Call those jarheads and see if they can strafe the trees."

"Yes, Sir." Offenbach grabbed the phone and said, "*Jubilee two-six. Japs are sniping at us from close range. Can you strafe the trees without hitting us?*"

"*Without hitting you?*"

"*Affirmative.*" Offenbach rolled his eyes.

"*Ricochet, this is Jubilee two-six. Please be advised that we are United States Marines. Out.*"

"*I beg your pardon?*"

"Never mind, Carl," A smirk ranged across Landa's face.

They crawled outside and peeked around the corner of the pilot house.

The Wildcats formed up in line astern and headed for the *Howell*. At a thousand yards, the first one opened up with its six-fifty caliber machine guns. The pilot kicked a bit of rudder back and forth, walking a devastating line of fire just fifty yards before them. Giant divots, shot in the air, tree limbs cracked and tumbled, dirt and rocks flew everywhere. Smoke lingered as the plane flashed overhead, only to be replaced by the second Wildcat, then the third. Something exploded nearby as the forth Wildcat started shooting. A column of rich, black-red smoke roiled in the air. Then the last Wildcat swooped overhead and was gone. After a moment, the smoke cleared and one could see patches where trees had fallen.

"What do you think?" Landa swept the area with his binoculars.

"Japs had a damned flamethrower." Ingram nodded to where a fire flickered in the forest.

"Wouldn't want to be the guy with that rig strapped to my back," said Landa.

"No."

The radio crackled, "*Ricochet, this is Jubilee Two-Six. Everybody okay?*"

Offenbach swallowed a couple of times and looked at Landa, his eyes wide.

Landa grinned. "He's just screwing with you, Carl. Tell him that's all for now and thanks."

"Yes, Sir." Offenbach ducked into the pilot house.

Again, it was quiet. Absently, Ingram slapped at a mosquito on his ear. Then another on his forearm. He was almost glad to fuss with the mosquitoes, the absence of gunfire seeming delicious. He stepped in the pilot house and checked the bulkhead Seth Thomas chronometer. 1644. "What time is sunset?" he asked Offenbach.

"1819.

ZING! A bullet punched through the paper missing Offenbach's head by inches.

"Shit!" said Offenbach, dropping to the deck.

Landa, Ingram and Early scrunched down beside him, their backs braced to the bulkhead. "Looks like the Marines didn't get them all. We'll just have to do business from here," said Landa.

The phone buzzed. Offenbach reached up and pulled it from its bracket. "Bridge." Then, "Wait one." Covering the mouthpiece he whispered, "Radio has a message from Commodore Myszynski."

"Let's hear it."

"Go ahead." Offenbach nodded several times. "Very well, acknowledge, then sign off." Replacing the phone, he said, "Four boats of PT Squadron Nine enroute to pick us up. ETA 2330."

"So we hold out 'till then," Landa rubbed stubble on his chin, then said, "Todd, I have a feeling these guys are going to hit before that."

"When's moonrise, Carl?" Ingram asked.

Offenbach reached up to the chart table, pulled down the Nautical Almanac and looked it up. "2246, half moon."

"That's it, Skipper. They hit at 2246. That is if it's clear."

"So far, not a cloud in the sky. What if it's overcast?" Landa asked.

"I'd say, expect a parachute flare anytime after dark. But if it's clear, expect a 2246 assault."

"Okay. Carl, I want you to start burning every piece of paper on board. Begin with the code books and crypto stuff. I'll keep the decklog. Shove everything in boiler number one. Hank is ready for you. Todd, you and Monaghan get the wounded aft and on the port side and make 'em ready for transfer. Tell Delmonico to prepare to spike the guns as we pull off. I've already told Hank to open the seacocks and break the flanges." Landa looked at Ingram, his eyebrows up. "What else?"

"Small arms defense," Ingram said. "We should have pyrotechnics ready to go after sunset. And make sure all the boats and rafts are launched on the port side."

"Okay," said Landa.

"Oh, yeah," said Ingram. "Demolition charges. How about setting them for fifteen minutes after we shove off?"

"Makes sense to me. Carl, I want you to get the code machine, now. Take it to the fantail, or what's left of it. Have someone standby with a sledge to smash it if we're boarded. Otherwise, we take it with us and dump it over the side in deep water when we put to sea."

"Aye, aye, Captain."

Ingram was wrong. The Japanese attacked in a furious, screaming, raid at 2130, beginning with a white-phosphorous parachute flare. Then another. The *Howell's* forties and twenty's spit death into the trees, as yet another flare lighted the sky.

Suddenly, three men ran down the beach, throwing grenades. Two soldiers fell, the third lobbed his grenade on the foredeck just before he was cut down by BARs. The grenades exploded harmlessly, near the foredeck hatch. Then another screaming trio ran from the trees, throwing grenades. Two men made it back to the trees, the third soldier severed in half by a twenty-millimeter round. After the rippling explosions, a fire started on the fo'c'sle and a sailor ran out to douse it with a fire extinguisher. As he did, a shot rang out from the woods and the man fell, writhing.

"Sonsabitches picking us off, one by one." Landa banged a fist on the bulwark.

"How the hell can twenty or thirty Japs make so much noise and create so much fire?" Delmonico said. "You'd think a whole division was after us. You sure we can't use the five-inch, Skipper?" Both five inch mounts had been evacuated since they weren't effective at short range. The shells couldn't explode, since the fuses were set to enable after traveling 500 yards, far more than the fifty to seventy-five feet to the trees. And they didn't want any more casualties after the grenades had penetrated the relatively thin .25 inch steel plate.

"I don't think it's a good idea. How 'bout you, Todd?"

Something went 'THUNK' in the forest.

"We may have to," said Ingram.

The mortar round landed fifty yards beyond the ship.

"Jeez. Two more rounds and he has our range," said Landa

"Fire a flare, quick," ordered Ingram.

Delmonico gave the order then soon, a white phosphorous parachute flare rocketed up into the sky then popped open to light the landscape in a hoary brilliance.

'THUNK.'

Ingram pointed off to his right, where a wisp of smoke dissipated from the trees. He clamped Delmonico on the shoulder. "See over there. Hose that area down with all you got."

The mortar round landed twenty-five yards beyond the ship, raising a great white column of hissing water.

"Keep that area under fire." Ingram fastened his helmet strap and rose.

"Where you going? Todd." Landa shouted.

Ingram sat on his haunches and told him.

Landa finally said, "Okay. Go!"

Ingram ran down the ladder and forward on the port side, where the shapeless figures of mount 52's gun crew sat in the darkness, smoking cigarettes. He called quietly. "Leo?"

A figure stood.

Ingram moved close and said. "Find some volunteers. I want to get in your mount and crank out some rounds and hit that mortar."

Seltzer's eyebrows went up.

"Besides the muzzle blast and the racket, it's gotta kick up a hell of a lot of dirt somewhere. Maybe scare the crap out of them. We pop off four or five rounds then secure and run like hell," Ingram shrugged.

"Worth a try," said Seltzer. "We'll have to hand carry the rounds up from the magazine."

"They don't know that, Four, maybe five rounds ought to do the trick. We pass them up first, fire them off, before they start shooting back."

"Okay."

"I'd like to be trainer," Ingram said.

Seltzer cocked his head as if saying, 'you're crazy.'

"Nothing better to do." Ingram spread his palms.

"Your funeral." Seltzer walked forward.

'THUNK.'

"Hurry," said Ingram.

The mortar round exploded close aboard the starboard side, as they scrambled through the gun mount hatch. As *Howell's* twenty and forty millimeters fired back, Ingram called down the shell hoist to the handling room crew, "Hurry. We can't hold 'em down forever."

It took five precious minutes for the makeshift lower handling room crew to pass up five projectiles and five powder cases from the magazine. Finally, Seltzer eased into the pointer's chair saying, "Okay, where is he?"

Ingram put his head down to the gunsight's rubber eyepiece and spun the handwheels, training the mount to the right. One of Delmonico's flares lit up the night and he spotted the area. "On target!"

Seltzer cranked his wheels raising the barrel a few degrees, just as another mortar round shot out. "Ah, got the bastard--"

There was an explosion aft. The ship rocked as a shark worries its prey.

"Come on, Leo!" shouted Ingram.

"On target, load one round!" yelled Seltzer.

The powderman plunked his round on the tray. Then the projectile man followed with his fifty four-pound round. Together, they hand-rammed it. Then another man slammed the breach-block home. "Set!"

Seltzer peered in his sight, rolled in a bit of elevation and hit the foot treadle.

'CRACK.' Even without exploding, a great column of dirt, trees and bush rose in the pale light.

"Load and shoot." Ingram yelled, giving his training wheels a slight adjustment.

'CRACK!' Out went another round. They walked the fire back and forth as they cranked out the third forth and fifth rounds.

Again, quiet descended. Then, they heard something bounce on the maindeck. All Ingram could do was cover his ears. Even with that, it seemed a giant had hit the gunmount with a baseball bat. A piece of shrapnel ripped through the top right corner.

Ingram's ears rang as he crawled off his seat. Not knowing if he could be heard, he yelled, "Clear the mount!"

It seemed they understood for everyone scrambled out and ran aft, gaining the safety of the forward deckhouse. Ingram walked among them shaking hands and patting shoulders. He was surprised he was able to hear when Hardy, a third class gunners mate shook Ingram's hand and said to Seltzer, "Hey, Leo, we making Mr. Ingram an honorary gunner?"

"Hell, no. He's an officer," Seltzer said.

Ingram walked up to the bridge, finding several men huddled behind the bulwarks. Among them were a set of bright, shining teeth. Ingram sat and nodded toward Mondo Mondo, "If that damn mortar opens up again, I'm using both mounts."

Landa said, "Seems to have worked." He crossed his fingers. "No more mortar rounds."

Just then, the moon rose in the east, painting the *Howell* in an ashen, metallic sheen. Even with a half moon, everyone's features were ghost-like and surreal. Landa said, "May not need them. We're in voice contact with the PTs. They're about ten minutes away. I think we should start getting---"

Ingram held up a hand and rose to his knees.

"What?" Landa rose beside him.

A laboring diesel engine echoed over Mondo Mondo Island. Then it throttled down into silence.

"Bastards," hissed Delmonico. "Not again."

Landa sank down and put his head in his hand. "We gotta buy some time."

16

7 March, 1943
  IJN *Musashi*
  Truk Atoll, Caroline Islands

The Caroline archipelago lays approximately 3,000 miles southwest of Hawaii and 1,500 miles north of Australia, having a land area equaling two thirds of the state of Rhode Island. Stretching across an east-west axis of about 1,500 miles, the archipelago is as long as the distance from Baltimore to Denver.

Discovered by the Portuguese in 1527, the Caroline Islands were first named the New Philippines. Later, in 1685, they were taken over by Spain and renamed The Caroline Islands after Charles II of Spain. In 1899, Germany bought the Carolines after the Spanish-American war. A scant eighteen years later, Germany lost World War I, with the Islands going to Japan via a mandate from the League of Nations. A major provision of the mandate was that the islands were for peaceful uses only and were not to be fortified. But almost immediately, the Japanese closed the Carolines to foreigners and fortified them, the League of Nations mandate notwithstanding.

The Japanese' centerpiece was the Truk Atoll, laying toward the eastern end of the archipelago. Truk was actually a circular-shaped lagoon approximately thirty miles in diameter. Protected by barrier reefs, the pristine anchorage safeguarded six major islands: Tol, Udot, Moen, Dublon, Fefan and Uman. During the years before World War II, Japan constructed extensive fortifications making Truk Atoll Japan's *Gibraltar Of The Pacific*.

She was a monster.

Swinging lazily at anchor in Truk Atoll's Eton Anchorage, the 863 foot, 72,000 deadweight ton battleship was a monster. Easily the largest warship the world had ever seen, the *Musashi* was built by Mitsubishi Heavy Industries in the Nagasaki Naval Shipyard. *Yamato,* the lead ship of the class, was built in a gigantic graving dock at the Kure shipyard. Two more *Yamato* class battleships had been laid down, but only one, the *Shinano* was commissioned in Yokosuka, having later been converted to an aircraft carrier. The last battleship, simply called hull number III, was scrapped in her Kure dock to make room for more urgently needed ships.

In 1933, during the early design phase, Imperial Japanese Navy staff admirals decided the *Yamato* class battleships would engage in only a Pacific war; that Japan needn't be concerned over a Two-Ocean war, as was required for U.S. Navy ships. Thus, the *Yamato* class wasn't limited to size by the Panama Canal, an advantage the admiralty saw over the U.S. Navy. Therefore, Hiraga Yuzuru and Fukuda Keiji, the ships designers, were able to expand the beam to 127 feet, giving the *Yamato* class excellent seakeeping capabilities

Visualizing a Jutland type slugfest, Yuzuru and Kejii gave a lot of thought to the ship's armor. Her belt armor at the water line was manufactured in sections: each section was sixteen inches thick and measured nineteen by twelve feet, weighing sixty-eight and a half tons. Her decks had 7.8 inch amour plate, which were built to withstand a 2,200 pound amour-piercing bomb dropped from 10,000 feet. Unlike the *Titanic*, the *Yamato* class battleships had 1065 watertight compartments below the armor deck and another eighty-two watertight compartments above. Twelve Kanpon boilers delivered steam to four turbines which turned four propellers shafts, driving the *Musashi* and her crew of 2,500 through the water at a top speed of twenty-seven knots.

Newcomers had to be escorted when they boarded one of the massive battleships, least they become lost in her labyrinthine interior. But once inside the behemoth's superstructure, visitors were pleasantly surprised. They were greeted with air conditioning, linoleum decks polished to a deep luster and spotless white bulkheads. Brass fittings gleamed like bright diamonds in the officer's quarters. The wardroom, and lounge areas were appointed with dark paneled wood, deep leather sofas and other Western style furniture. Sparkling crystal, dinnerware and cutlery, was set in the wardroom which converted to a movie theater for nightly showings. The wardroom even had that rich aroma one finds in Western restaurants, a mixture of spices, fine cigars, leather and lingering cologne.

Her fighting and sea keeping capabilities were considered the best. The accommodations were the best and the food was the best. For this, her crew called her the *Musashi* hotel.

The *Musashi* eclipsed anything afloat in firepower. Each of her nine, 18.1 inch guns could hurl a 2,000 pound projectile over twenty-five miles. In fact, the gun turrets were so large that a special ship was built, just to carry them from the Kure shipyards to either the Nagasaki or Yokosuka shipyards.

But in a way, their massive guns created an Achilles heel. For example, the largest cannons used by the U.S. Navy were sixteen inch. When fired, the blast pressure to the atmosphere was 19.58 pounds per square inch. This meant a sailor could stand safely within one hundred feet of the gun's muzzle without any affect. On the other hand, the *Musashi's* eighteen inch guns delivered a whopping blast pressure of 58 pounds per square inch. Thus a man standing anywhere on the weather decks would have his clothes torn off, and, most likely, be knocked unconscious. Also, wooden shore boats cradled on the *Yamato's* deck would shatter. Accordingly, all humans, boats, airplanes, and other fragile equipment had to be stowed in special hangers when the ship's main batteries erupted. The blast pressure characteristics dictated that the *Yamato's* secondary battery consist of just four triple turreted 6.1 guns. As designed, the ships had no open anti-aircraft gun mounts.

Accordingly, the air-minded and more forward-thinking knew the *Yamato* class battleships' days were numbered; indeed that they were obsolete when they slid off the ways. For proof, one only had to look at the *Kido Butai's* devastation of the U.S. Navy's battleships at Pearl Harbor to realize that *Yamato* and *Musashi* were dinosaurs. There was a saying in the Imperial Japanese Navy's new upstart Air Arm. The three most useless items in the world were: The Great Wall Of China, the Pyramids of Egypt, and *Yamato* Class battleships. Thus, the great ships were destined to swing at anchor in some backwater, lest they blunder within range of American aircraft.

But still, she was a monster...

There was a knock at the door and Yamamoto looked up. Omi Heijiro, his round-faced chief orderly, poked his head around the door, his brows raised, "It's Captain Watanabe."

"Ah." Yamamoto stood. "Five minutes."

"Yes, *Gensui*." Heijiro bowed and closed the door with a soft click.

Yamamoto ran water over his face, then dressed. Soon, there was another knock.

"Enter."

Captain Yasuji Watanabe, his chief administrative officer and friend, opened the door, stepped in, and bowed. It was time for their evening game of mahjongg.

"Come." Yamamoto waved a palm at the conference table. "I saw Tsuji Masanobu today." He passed the mahjongg box.

"How'd he get past me?" Watanabe sat and began arranging the tiles.

"I know his boss. And he was sitting outside your office. You were busy, so I invited him up."

"I don't think I know him."

Yamamoto reached for a bottle of Johnnie Walker Black Label and two glasses. "He's a staff Major from the Seventeenth Army." Now on rest and recreation around Rabaul, the Seventeenth Army was the last evacuated from Guadalcanal a month ago. Navy destroyers and troopships successfully snatched the last thirteen thousand men from under Halsey's nose over a period of three nights.

"He was on *Ga-to*?" *Ga-to* was a play on Japanese ideographs for Guadalcanal: meaning starvation island.

Yamamoto grunted and spilled two fingers of Johnnie Walker in each glass. Tipping his glass at Watanabe, he sat back and drank. "I knew it was bad. But not that bad."

Watanabe shuffled the tiles around, while the *Gensui* stared into space.

"They're in horrible shape," said Yamamoto. "They've suffered every imaginable disease. They're terribly undernourished; their beards, nails, and hair have stopped growing. Their joints are horribly large and swollen and their buttocks are so atrophied that the anus is completely exposed and unprotected. He gave me this," Yamamoto passed over a dog-eared piece of paper. "It's from a soldier's journal that lay within reach of his body."

Wannabe picked it up, finding a page dated January 2, 1943:

Mortality Chart
  He who can rise to his feet: 30 days to live
  He who can sit up: 20 days to live
  He who must urinate while laying down: 3 days to live
  He who cannot speak: 2 days to live
  He who cannot blink his eyes: Dead at dawn

Watanabe slowly lowered his glass to the table.

"Drink, drink. This is not your fault."

"...all that and we lost..." It just slipped out. Watanabe couldn't help it.

"Yes. We lost Guadalcanal. Fifty thousand men. That's a price, all right. And now the Americans control the Eastern Solomons. I tell you, I was humbled by Masanobu's report. I sent him off to be showered, clothed, and treated to dinner in the wardroom."

Watanabe had barely noticed the thin frail looking Army major sitting with the junior officers near the aft bulkhead.

There was a soft knock at the door, Heijiro stuck his head in and said. "It's Captain Takano."

"Ah, good. Send him in."

"What?" said Watanabe.

"Do you know him?" asked Yamamoto.

"Yes, Sir." Watanabe had trouble checking his disgust. Captain Kanji

Takano was a flamboyant rising star who had just been appointed as Fleet Ordnance Officer under Vice Admiral Tomoshiga Sajejima. Rumor had it that he was to be appointed directly to Yamamoto, but Watanabe had been reluctant to ask. Also, Watanabe feared Takano was a spy. Some in Tokyo's high command were outspoken about Yamamoto's blunders at Coral Sea, Midway and now, Guadalcanal.

Captain Kanji Takano walked in, wearing immaculately cut dress blues with knife edge creases. He bowed to Yamamoto. "Good evening, Sir."

"Ah, Takano. Welcome. Thank you for coming. You've met Watanabe?"

The two naval captains faced one another and bowed stiffly.

"I hear you play poker, Takano?" Yamamoto's eyebrows were up, a gesture Watanabe recognized as an invitation. It was a gesture that disappointed Watanabe for he didn't know how to play poker, only mahjongg.

"I do, Sir." Takano smiled with a sidelong glance to Watanabe.

Pouring two fingers of scotch, Yamamoto handed Takano the glass and asked in a cowboy-accented English, his voice deep and throaty, "Well then, you like five card stud, partner?"

Delicately sniffing the scotch, Takano responded in the same language. "Ain't none better, uh, partner."

"I had heard you spoke English, Takano. But I didn't realize you spoke it so well. It's better than mine. Where did you learn it?" asked Yamamoto.

"University of Washington, Excellency." he paused. "And you, Sir?"

"Harvard." In Japanese, Yamamoto asked, "Ah, forgive me Watanabe. Do you play poker?"

"No, Sir," said Watanabe.

"I see...perhaps we could..."

"Pardon me, *Gensui*," but I can't play poker this evening."

"Oh?" said Yamamoto.

"I must stand the fleet communications watch," Takano check his wristwatch, "in ten minutes."

"I see," said Yamamoto. "Perhaps some other time."

"I look forward to that, *Gensui*."

What are we doing here? wondered Watanabe.

There was an awkward silence then Yamamoto said, "Very well. I'd like to ask you, Takano, if I am imagining that American anti-aircraft gunnery is becoming more accurate, that, perhaps they're shooting our airplanes down more quickly?"

"They have radar-controlled weapons, Sir," Takano said.

"Yes, yes," said Yamamoto. And their shooting has been decent, according to the reports I see. But in the last month I've had the feeling it's getting better. Why is that, do you suppose?"

"It hasn't occurred to me, *Gensui*," said Takano

"Did you see the fleet intelligence report that came to us via our Moscow Embassy? That the Americans are developing a new anti-aircraft fuse? One that is very accurate?"

Watanabe watched Takano fidget. Although the man was a brilliant ordnance officer, he was famous for in-baskets that overflowed with unopened documents.

"I haven't seen that one," Takano said.

"You know," said Yamamoto. "Maybe we can gather a little of our own intelligence. Of all the ammunition we confiscated from the Americans, there must a sample of the fuse somewhere."

Takano looked lost for a moment. "I've gone over those reports time and time again. I don't recall anything unusual." He knocked back his scotch in one gulp.

"I see," said Yamamoto. "Well then. Have we looked in --"

"--There might be something," Watanabe interjected. "The report just came in. Today, we severely damaged an American destroyer in the Kula Gulf."

"Excellent," said Yamamoto.

"Blew her stern off. She is the...the U.S.S. " Watanabe made a show of reaching for the answer although he knew it cold, "U.S.S. *Howell, Fletcher* class. They had to beach her."

"Beach her? Where?" asked Yamamoto, his eyes lighting up with possibilities.

A glance at Takano assured Watanabe the ordnance captain knew nothing about the *Howell*. "Mondo Mondo Island, *Gensui*, just off New Georgia Island. The report said the Americans are still aboard, but it looks as if they're trying to evacuate. "We're sending the destroyer *Matukaze* to back up a company of Imperial Marines."

"Um," said Yamamoto. "We should try to get the Americans off without them blowing up the ship." He turned to Takano. "Do you think you could head that up? Get someone down there to go aboard that destroyer and see if the Americans do have a new miracle fuse as our Soviet friends claim?"

"Of course, *Gensui*." Takano looked at his watch. He was scheduled to relieve in just five minutes.

"Go Takano," Yamamoto waved a hand. "Keep me informed through Watanabe here."

"Yes, *Gensui*." Takano bowed first to Yamamoto, then to Watanabe and walked for the door.

Yamamoto called after him, "And get a message to the *Matukaze*. Tell her to get the Americans off and to disarm all demolition charges."

"Yes, Sir." Takano walked out.

Watanabe sat at the card table, his palms pressed flat.

"Give him some slack, Watanabe," said Yamamoto, sitting beside him.

"Sir?" asked Wannabe innocently.

"He's a favorite son. And he's up for admiral. And don't forget, the man is a genius in ordnance. He has an MS in mechanical engineering."

"I see."

"No you don't. In reality I agree, the man is a fop. But I have no control over him. He's a cousin of Prince Konoye."

"Ah." Watanabe figured the evening was over so he started to box the mahjongg tiles.

"No, let's play." Yamamoto downed his scotch, then poured another three fingers, watching Watanabe spill the tiles and arrange them. "I have to play this game, Watanabe. Politics."

"I thought so."

"They're after me for...for..." Yamamoto waved a hand at the port hole. After a moment, he exhaled and said, "...so, I must do something."

"Sir?"

"The Americans." He toyed with a tile. "They keep replacing ships faster than we can put them down."

Watanabe extended the thought he knew ran through Yamamoto's head. *Worse, we can't replace our ships as fast as they are replacing theirs*

"Ahhh!" Yamamoto's eyebrows went up. After a moment, he said softly, *"Operation Z."*

"Sir?" *Operation Z* was the code word for the Japanese Navy's victorious attack on the Czarist fleet at the Battle of Tsushima Straits in 1905. With honor, the codeword, *Operation Z,* was again employed for the attack on the American Fleet at Pearl Harbor.

"...a heavy, decisive blow, like at Pearl Harbor. Like at Tsushima. We can hit Guadalcanal, New Guinea, a whole range of targets from...from..." He snapped the fingers of his right hand. "Rabaul, of course." He looked up. "My dear Watanabe. You've hardly touched your scotch."

Watanabe took another swallow. *Operation Z.* It had a magical lilt. He looked up to see Yamamoto's eyes gleaming.

"Massive air attacks," Yamamoto mused. "A hundred airplanes, two, maybe three hundred airplanes." He rubbed his hands together, then bent over to study the tiles. "We'll have to call this one *Operation I.* Call a staff conference tomorrow. Nine O'clock."

"Should I invite Captain Takano?"

"Yes, yes. He should be there."

"Yes, Sir." The alcohol ran softly into Watanabe's system, softening the horror of *Ga-to.* He held out an empty glass. *Operation I. Yes. Maybe it did have a chance.*

Yamamoto smiled and poured for his mahjongg partner. "The scotch agrees with you." It was a statement.

"Yes, *Gensui.*"

17

7 March, 1943
   U.S.S. *Howell* (DD 482)
   Mondo Mondo Island, Solomon Islands

"A PT Boat," said Ingram.

"Speak English," demanded Landa

"Send a PT up the inland passage. Hit 'em from behind. Keep that mortar off our backs."

"Makes sense to me." In weak moonlight, Landa's dark stubble and helmet made him look like a German soldier peering into No Man's Land at Verdun. They walked in the pilot house where Landa grabbed the TBS handset. "Carl, what's their call sign?"

"Boat Seven-Two."

Landa pressed the handset button, making the red button glow on the bulkhead mounted transmitter. "*Boat Seven-Two, this is Ricochet, over.*"

Static crackled on the speaker.

Landa muttered, then tried again, "*Boat Seven-Two, over.*"

Suddenly, a loud, grinding noise filled the compartment. A voice said, "*Seven-Two, over.*"

Landa clamped a hand over his ear and said, "*Boat Seven-Two. We have a problem. Japs have just landed a second barge-load of troops across the island. Can one of you divert, head into the inland waterway and shoot them from behind before they attack us in force? Over.*"

"*We can try, Ricochet. Interrogative your position, over?*"

Landa stared at the bulkhead, muttering, and drumming his fingers.

"What's wrong?" said Ingram.

"I've heard that voice, before." Then he keyed the TBS. "*About a hundred yards north of Hohopo Point, over.*"

The grinding noise filled the pilot house again. "*Ah, Ricochet, can you shoot a flare? Over.*"

"Affirmative. Red flare on the way." Landa eyed Ingram.

Ingram ducked out the hatch. "Louie. Shoot a red flare."

"Got it!" said Delmonico. Fifteen seconds later, a flare whooshed to the sky, popped its parachute and began its descent, trailing its red-phosphorescent brilliance.

The speaker crackled. "*Ricochet, we have you in sight. Please.*"

"Shit!" Landa roared. He stood there, his fists bunched, the transmitter button still red.

"Skipper! What the hell?"

"It's...it's," he sputtered.

"Damnit." Ingram wrested the TBS handset from Landa, keyed the mike and said, "*Boat Seven-Two, this is Ricochet. Say your last. Over.*"

"*Hi, Todd.*"

"Tubby?"

"*That's right.*"

"What are you doing there?"

"*My first night. I'm exec. Can you beat that?*"

Ingram cleared his throat. "*Roger Boat Seven-Two. Did you see our flare, over?*"

"*You bet. We have you in sight. Say, is the Skipper pissed at me?*"

Landa tapped Ingram on the shoulder, the look on his face saying, 'Gimme.'

Grabbing the handset, Landa said, "*Boat Seven-Two, this is Ricochet. Be advised, whoever takes the Inland waterway, that the Japs may have mortars and flamethrowers."*

White's voice came back, overly solicitous. *"Aye, aye, Ricochet, Sir. In fact, we are the ones assigned. We're now peeling off to head for the Lingutu Entrance. Three Peter Tares should be with you in four to five minutes, Captain, er Sir. Over."*

"Ricochet, out," said Landa. Then he hung up the hand set and muttered, "Fat little bastard."

Ingram looked away and ran his hand over his eyes.

Landa pulled his talker over. "Early, pass the word: abandon ship. All hands, except gun crews, lay portside aft for transfer to PT Boats." Then he turned to Offenbach. "How's the burn going?"

"Top Secret and Secret stuff is finished, Captain. So is most of the Confidential. Restricted is going into the boiler now. About ten more minutes should do it."

"Tell 'em to hurry." Landa said. "Todd, service and pay records?"

"Boxed up and ready to go," said Ingram.

"Personal gear?"

"Crew has packed one duffle each. Steward's mates packed officers one duffle each."

"Safes?"

"All emptied. I checked myself."

"Okay." Landa took a deep breath and looked around. Imperceptibly, his shoulders sagged.

"Captain?" Ingram asked quietly.

"Time to fly. Everybody off the bridge," said Landa.

"S'cuse me, Sir." Briley walked up to Landa.

"What?"

"Ship's deck log and ensign, Sir." Briley handed them over.

"Yes...very well, thank you, Briley." Landa thumbed the flag for a moment. "Now, let's put a nickel in it, it sounds like the PTs are getting close." In the distance, they heard the growl of engines.

Landa waited for everyone to step down the aft companionway, then lingered for a moment. At length, he followed the others, flag and log book clutched to his chest.

Ingram walked aft, finding the men crowded near the mangled remains of the quarterdeck. Monaghan and his corpsmen had his stretcher cases and wounded arranged, ready to go. Boxes and duffels were stacked up against the deckhouse bulkhead. Unfortunately, the engineers sleeping quarters were aft and had gone down with that section of the ship. So Ingram had made sure the men sleeping forward, shared clothing.

Landa walked up. "Don't set the demo charges until I give the word."

"Right."

"Who's going to do it?"

Ingram beckoned Delmonico over. "Louie, who sets the fuses?"

"Hardy." He pointed to a sailor waiting on the 01 deck above. "We've set the charges in the forward magazine. All he has to do is run down there and spin the dials. Kaboom! That should take care of it."

"Fifteen minutes?" asked Landa.

"Yes, Sir."

"How about setting a charge in the forward engine room?" Ingram asked.

"Don't think we need it. When that magazine goes, I wouldn't want to be within a mile of this ship."

"Okay, let's go with that," said Landa.

A PT Boat nosed up to the *Howell's* port side. Even at an idle, her triple Packard V-12 supercharged engines gave a loud, deep-throated rumble. Her sailors lowered fenders as she nudged against the *Howell*, their two decks about the same level. Mooring lines were tossed and cleated, the boat killing her engines. The next one idled up, and moored forward while the third moored outboard of the first PT Boat. All three were minus their torpedoes. A good idea, Ingram decided, since the eighty foot boats would be taking aboard quite a load of people.

He found Monaghan, moving about his stretcher cases. "All set, Bucky?"

"Ready."

"Take them aboard this one."

"Yes, Sir." Monaghan waved his men over and they began picking up stretchers.

Ingram found Hank Kelly talking to one of his chiefs. Both wore their trademark oil-splotched khaki coveralls, with Kelly looking scarecrow thin in the moonlight. "Hank, get your people on the boat forward. Make sure to stay out of the crew's way."

"Got it."

He stepped up to Offenbach and told him to do the same with his men in the outboard boat. The *Howell's* crew needed no urging, and soon, the three PT Boats were full, including the wounded. A knot of fifteen or so anxious men were all that remained on the destroyer. Landa pumped his fist in the air and shouted to the PT skippers. "Okay, thanks. See you in Tulagi. Now shove off!"

Gunfire broke out on the other side of Mondo Mondo Island. Tracers ripped across the sky. A forty millimeter round slammed into the main battery director, shredding the fire control antenna.

Offenbach said, "My God," his eyes propped wide open.

A few rounds ricocheted off the bridge. The men quickly crouched under the 01 catwalk and covered their ears as shells zinged over.

Offenbach sprang forward.

"Where you headed?" Ingram grabbed his shirt and pulled him to a halt.

"Our guys shooting at us. We gotta tell 'em to stop." Even as Offenbach spoke, two more forty millimeter tracers ripped into the pilot house clanging with a horrible noise. Then an enormous explosion on Mondo Mondo ripped the night with flames and debris flying in the air. "Shiiit." Offenbach tried to jerk from Ingram's grip.

Ingram held tight. "Carl. We're on the other side of an island. They can't shoot low enough to hit us down here. Leave 'em be." Ingram held tight as tracers flew and flames roiled to the accompaniment of a horrendous racket. He thought he heard screams and the stutter of a Japanese machine gun. But that was soon silenced. After five minutes, the gunfire rattled to a stop.

Like the rest, Ingram felt sheepish, as he tentatively stepped out from beneath the 01 catwalk. And the PT boats were gone. The gunfire had been so intense, he hadn't heard them start up and shove off.

"Carl. Crypto machine?" Landa demanded.

"Gone with the first boat, Sir," said Offenbach, his face still white.

To the south, a PT Boat's engines wound up and drew near.

"Okay, last boat on its way. Tell the gun mount crews to spike guns and lay aft." Landa called up to the 01 deck, "Hardy, got a flashlight?"

"You bet, Captain."

"Then do your stuff. Hurry."

"Sir!" Hardy ran forward into darkness.

The gun crews had no sooner assembled when the PT Boat materialized from the gloom. A white numeral 72 was painted under her bow. Painted in white script on the side of her cockpit was the name, *Little Lulu*. As *PT 72* throttled down, her fenders were kicked over, and she crunched to a hard landing against the *Howell's* port side.

Chief Murphy said gleefully, "Jeez, lookit that."

Tubby White, clad in life jacket and helmet, stood at the wheel. He killed the engines as soon as the lines were cleated, then stepped down from the bridge.

"Hi ya, Tubby," grinned Delmonico.

"Lou." Stepping to the PT Boat's starboard rail, White jammed his hands in his pockets.

"You okay, Tubby?" Ingram asked, as he signaled the *Howell's* men to board.

"Mr. White. Where did you learn to drive? I've seen better landings at the destruction derby," said Landa.

"My first time." Tubby's voice was a near whisper.

Landa opened his mouth to speak, but he was interrupted by rifle fire from Mondo Mondo Island.

"Some Japs are still alive over there. How the hell do you suppose anybody could live through that?" asked Delmonico.

"Somehow, they did, Lou. One of those bastards got our skipper." White waved to a canvas covered body laying on the aft deck, its booted feet sticking out from underneath. White spoke through clenched teeth, "Sonofabitch drilled Tommy Kellogg right through the forehead. I...I didn't realize it for a couple of minutes. Nobody was driving...we damn near went aground."

"So...now... you're in command?" Landa gasped.

"That's right, Captain. I'm the Captain." The two men locked eyes. Finally, White said, "I'm sorry about your ship, Sir. But are you ready to shove off?"

"Waiting for Hardy to set demolition charges," said Landa.

Something ripped through the night sky and popped over their heads, turning nighttime into day.

"Illumination shot!" yelled Ingram.

"Where's it coming from?" said Landa.

Another shot cracked open, the bright flare dancing on its parachute, turning the area even brighter. White jumped to his cockpit and yelled, "Wind 'em up!" The Packards had just coughed into life, when a cannon shell whistled overhead and exploded on the beach, raising a tall geyser of hissing water and sand.

"Hardy!" Delmonico cupped his hands around his mouth. Seconds passed. He yelled again. No Hardy. He looked at Ingram.

"Go!" said Ingram.

Delmonico ran forward, disappearing into darkness.

Another shell hit the island a hundred yards away.

"What the hell is out there?" yelled Landa.

White raised a pair of binoculars and looked out to sea. "Looks like a Jap can."

Ingram squinted to see a moonlit smudge about 7000 yards away. Just then, something flashed on its foredeck.

WHAM! A shell landed fifty yards to port, completely drenching them.

"Captain! Time to go!" White yelled.

"Not yet" said Landa. "Todd, damnit get aboard."

"But, Sir. I--"

"Now," yelled Landa.

Delmonico stumbled down the deck, caroming off bulkheads. His hand was clamped around his right shoulder and dark red blood seeped through his fingers. He lurched at Landa and collapsed into his arms.

"Where's Hardy?" Landa shouted.

A shell whistled and smacked the Howell's fo'c'sle, making the ship shake furiously.

White jabbed his fog horn. "Captain! We must go. You're jeopardizing this boat."

"Hardy?" Landa screamed in Delmonico face.

Delmonico face was very pale. Finally, he coughed and said, "Dead. Fo'c'sle."

"Did he set the charges?"

"Don't know." Delmonico eyes rolled back in his head and he passed out. Ingram and Offenbach caught him and pulled him aboard *Little Lulu*.

"Come on, Jerry!" Ingram hollered.

"Captain, damnit," shouted White.

Landa, jabbed an index finger at White. "I order you to stay here, damnit. I can't leave until I know if those charges are set. I'll be damned if I'm going to let my ship fall into the Jap's hands."

"Bullshit!" White called forward and aft, "Take in all lines."

His crew needed no urging, as another shell whistled overhead and exploded on Mondo Mondo, showering them with dirt and shell fragments.

"Last chance, Captain," yelled White.

"You little bastard," Landa bellowed. "I gave you a direct order."

"It's my boat, Captain. I'm responsible. I'm sorry." White looked aft and pulled his shift quadrant aft to the astern position. *PT-72*'s screws dug in and she started to ease away.

Landa's mouth dropped.

"Carl, quick!" Ingram yelled. Desperately, they reached out and grabbed Landa by the arms, jerking him across two feet of water as the PT Boat backed away. Seeing Landa safely aboard, Tubby White added more throttle just as a shell buried itself in the *Howell's* forward boiler room and exploded, sending debris high in the air. The forward stack toppled with a terrible screech.

Ingram and Offenbach relaxed their grip on Landa, letting him gain his footing on the PT's deck.

"Bastards," hissed Landa.

"Sorry, Captain, you would have been killed," Ingram said.

Landa, clutching flag and logbook to his chest, wrenched his arms free and gave Ingram a long, cold stare. "Maybe that's the way it should have been." Then he walked aft and sat by himself on a depth charge rack.

Tubby White, spun his helm, shifted all engines to ahead and firewalled the throttles. With a great roar, *Little Lulu* charged out, gained the step, and headed down The Slot; course one-one-zero degrees true.

18

8 March, 1943
   U.S.S. *Whitney* (AD 4)
   Tulagi Harbor, Solomon Islands

A ship's horn blasted, jolting Ingram awake. His eyes flipped open and he groped for the bunk light switch. Turning to the bedside stand, he found his watch: eight thirty two. Except...*damn*...that's eight in the evening. He'd slept over fifteen hours.

It was a two-man stateroom, but the upper bunk was empty. With a groan, he rose and sat on the bunk's edge, his head in his hands, stiff all over. Riding on *Little Lulu* had taxed his muscles,. The sea in The Slot had been up, and they'd bounced around. Ingram clutched number three torpedo tube for most of the three and a half hour trip just to keep from falling overboard.

He'd been so tired that he had turned in as soon as Tubby dropped them off at the *Whitney*. Now, he smelled like a goat and he was hungry. He untied his duffle and reached for his shaving gear. Just beneath was his eight by ten framed picture of Helen. He eased it out and said, "Evening, Hon." It was a recent shot by photographer Norman Howard of Hollywood --- a movie industry specialist recommended by Laura West -- catching Helen in just the right pose. He went to set it up on the little fold-down desk, but his hands began to shake and his skin turned clammy. Try as he might, he couldn't control the shaking, and he couldn't get the frame to stand upright. Finally, he stood and pushed the picture face-up against the bunk.

No wonder the photographer Howard did so many movie stars. He'd easily found Helen's essence: Her eyes. She could look right through you if she wanted. But here she smiled. In fact, both eyes and mouth smiled in this picture. It was as if her eyes still looked through you and held you fast to wherever you were standing.

God. She was all he ever wanted.

But...looking at her made the shaking worse.

"Damnit!" Tears ran, and he felt like he was going to throw up. So he gave up and walked for the head.

Fifteen minutes later, he returned from a long shower to find a note on his desk, Helen's picture propped on top:

Todd,

Stewards have saved chow in the wardroom. After that, we've a meeting in Rocko's office at 2130, Frank Ashton and Dexter Sands will be there, so bring your bullet-proof vest.

Jerry

Kelly and Offenbach wandered in just as Ingram and Landa sat. All rubbed sleep from their eyes and made little conversation as they wolfed their meal. The steak was tough and tasted like something between dried liver and genuine cowhide, but the potatoes, peas and Jell-O salad were wonderful.

Ingram was reaching for apple pie when Landa walked in and tugged on his shirt. "Time to go."

Ingram stood to find Landa's eyes hollow and dark. "You look like hell, Jerry. Have you slept?"

"Got pills from the doc. So I put in a few hours."

"How about chow?"

"Maybe later. Come on."

"Why don't you have some--"

Landa turned abruptly and walked out.

Ingram followed. "What is it, Jerry?" Landa was quick-pacing and it was hard to keep up.

"Puking, damnit. Can't keep anything down."

"What did the Doc say about that?"

Landa didn't answer as they clanged up a companionway to the 02 deck, finding a door marked:

THEODORE R. MYSZYNSKI. CAPTAIN, USN
COMMODORE DESRON 12

Landa hesitated, then knocked.

Myszynski's voice rumbled with "Enter."

Inside, they found Myszynski behind his desk, an unlighted cigar stub jammed in his mouth. Two portholes and a door to the 02 deck were open, while two rubber-bladed fans buzzed mightily, trying unsuccessfully to scour the dank, heat-laded humidity from the compartment. Moonlight filtered in from the outside, the only other light a sixty watt bulb on Myszynski's desk lamp.

Sitting to Myszynski's right was a thin, hawknosed, balding figure. The light was so dim, it was impossible to read his expression, but what Ingram did see were the twin gold stars of a rear admiral pinned on his collar. On the desk's other side was Frank Ashton.

Waving a hand to the two-star, Myszynski said, "Here. Say hello to Admiral Sands. I believe you've met Frank Ashton."

For a moment, it was the battle of the smiles as Ashton and Landa tried to out-grin each other while the others shook hands.

Ingram and Landa sat on a couch opposite the desk and Myszynski began, "Thanks for coming up on such short notice. Here," He passed over a clipboard. "My yeoman set up a roster for your crew. Can you sign it, please?"

Landa did so and handed back the clipboard.

Myszynski gave him a copy, then sat back and asked, "How are your boys doing, Jerry?"

The roster rattled in Landa's hand. After a deep breath he said, "Okay, as far as I know. My wounded are being well taken care of, and the rest are either sleeping it off or chowing down."

Myszynski picked up a box of cigars, opened, and offered it. Everyone declined, leaving Myszynski to select one of his own. He stripped the cellophane, and ran the cigar between thick lips, wetting it down.

Without looking up, Landa said, "I would like to have memorial services for the boys I left behind. And of course, for the ones down in the freezer." Absently, he began tearing off tiny pieces of the roster, letting them flutter to the deck.

Myszynski clipped the end of his cigar. "All set. Tomorrow morning, 0830." He pulled out a gold Ronson and lit his cigar, blue smoke swirling around his desk.

"Thank you ,Sir," Landa nodded.

"We've met before, Commander Landa." Sands fanned smoke from his face.

"Sir?" Landa said.

"Aren't you the one they call 'Boom Boom.'"

"Not to my face, Sir. I try to discourage it."

"I see. Well, my ship is the *Sioux Falls*. You nested to our port side last, hmmmm. September or October, I've forgotten, when was it?"

Landa's looked around Myszynski's office. With just the one light bulb, his eyes looked like dying embers on a charcoal fire. And the more Ingram tried to peer into them, the less he could see. At the same time, Landa looked gaunt, unwashed. And he smelled of sweat.

"Yes, Sir," Landa said. " Uhhh, last September, we'd just pulled in from Noumea."

There was an edge to Dexter Sands' voice that dug at Ingram. At the same time, Landa was poised almost like a rattlesnake making him think of *Don't Tread On Me*. More pieces of paper fluttered to the deck as Landa absently twisted them off the crew roster.

Sands said, "Tell us what you did."

"We moored in a nest outboard of you and rigged rat guards on our lines."

Ingram caught a gleam in Myszynski's eye. Rigging large, circular rat guards is done when mooring to shore. Rigging rat guards on mooring lines to a ship nested alongside is a serious insult, even more so when the ship has an admiral embarked.

Sands arched an eyebrow.

Landa responded with, "We tried to send a man over to the beach for guard mail. But your quarterdeck watch wouldn't let him pass because he wasn't suited out in dress whites."

"That's our policy."

"Even here? In a war zone?" Landa shot back.

"That's our policy."

Landa rubbed his chin. "Then, your chief machinist mate wouldn't pass over the fresh water hose until he had your captain's permission. Well, your captain made us wait while he took his evening meal--"

"---wait a minute." Sands held up his hands.

"---and had a cribbage game. We had to wait for two and a half hours for fresh water. Now our evaps weren't working at the time. We barely had enough water to run our boilers let alone cook our own chow, take showers and wash a suit of fresh whites."

"You can't--"

"Gentlemen, gentlemen," Rocko Myszynski interjected. "We're not here to discuss rat guards."

"Very well." Sands glanced at Ashton, then smiled thinly and sat back, his face masked in near-darkness.

"Jerry, I'm sorry about your ship..." Myszynski offered.

"Thank you. So am I, Commodore."

The three senior officers' eyes flicked to Landa as the tiny pieces of paper accumulated at his feet. Myszynski puffed smoke and said, "All right. Please tell us what happened."

Landa's voice shook as he relayed detail of the events leading to the *Howell*'s grounding on Mondo Mondo Island. At times, he lapsed into silence for ten or fifteen second intervals. Finally, he finished and sat back.

Myszynski held up a hand. "How much sleep have you had, Jerry?"

"Enough."

"Maybe we can do this later," Myszynski said gently. "Go. Hit the rack."

Landa puffed his cheeks then shook his head. "Now...Sir."

Dexter Sands picked it right up with, "And your ship?"

"What about it?" said Landa.

To Ingram, Landa's tone was insubordinate. And it must have seemed so to Admiral Sands, for he snapped right back, "I'm asking, Commander, what's the status of your ship?"

"Latest Dumbo report has her grounded on Mondo Mondo Island."

"I'm interested, Commander. Why didn't you set demolition charges?"

"I thought I just told you."

Myszynski, his face red, started to speak but Sands pressed, "Commander, I'm given to understand the weather this time of year is very pleasant at the Barstow Ammunition Depot in the California desert. Perhaps a little golf?" His eyebrows went up.

"I'll make you a deal Admiral. I'll tell you about the demolition charges, if you tell me why we didn't have air cover."

"Six Wildcats. That's all we had against fourteen Zeros." In the pale light, Admiral Sands face grew darker.

"And you couldn't carve out one or two Wildcats to send our way?"

"I resent that!" Sands fist slammed on the desk.

Myszynski shot to his feet. "Apologize, Commander Landa or by God, you *will* be counting empty shell casings in the California dessert."

"I...I...apologize, Admiral. It's that I've never had a ship shot out from under me. All those men in the aft end. They never had a chance." He took a deep breath and exhaled, his hands tearing more vigorously at the roster. Nearly half of the page lay in pieces between his feet. "I dream about them. I hear screams, I can't...can't..."

"Very well." Sands started to rise. "We can finish this later."

"Admiral, I'd like to get it done," said Landa. He added, "...Sir, please."

Sands looked to Myszynski who nodded. After sitting, he said, "Very well. And the demolition charges?"

Landa's fists bunched.

Ingram butt in, "Actually there's is something you should know, gentlemen,"

Landa turned, but Ingram pinched the top of his leg and said, "We set charges in the forward magazine and had them ready to go when the PTs showed up."

"Yes?" said Myszynski, sitting back, his arms folded.

"We finished loading the first three PTs, then sent them on their way. When the forth PT made our portside, we sent our gunner's mate forward to set fuses. That's when the Jap destroyer showed up and started shooting."

"What about your gunner?" asked Sands.

"Dead. A Jap sniper on Mondo Mondo got him." Ingram searched the faces of the three stone-faced men, unable to gauge their reactions.

The sound of aircraft rose in the distance. Instinctively, they looked to the overhead as general quarters was gonged throughout the ship.

"Shit," said Myszynski. Then he flipped off his lamp and muttered, "Sounds like a bunch of them tonight. Okay if we stay here? Admiral?"

In the darkness, they sensed, more then saw a curt nod from Sands. And in the dark, Ingram felt their eyes flick back to him as bombs rattled around Tulagi, *Finish it, you dope.*

"Okay Todd, I'll--" said Landa.

Ingram kicked Landa's leg. "Captain, please." Ingram plunged on, "Delmonico, our gunnery officer, ran forward, finding Hardy dead. As he ran back to tell us, he was seriously wounded, possibly by the same sniper."

"Yes?" asked Sands.

"Captain Landa asked Delmonico if Hardy had set the charges. Delmonico said he wasn't sure and then he passed out. So Captain Landa refused to leave the ship until--"

"Damnit, Todd. That's enough!" yelled Landa.

"No, it's not" Ingram shouted back.. "Lieutenant White told us, rightfully, to board; that his command, *PT-72*, was in jeopardy. Captain Landa refused to leave the ship until he determined the status of the demolition charges. Lieutenant White had actually started backing away. That's when Lieutenant Offenbach and I reached out and grabbed Captain Landa's arms. We yanked him aboard the PT boat at the last possible moment. A good thing too. Because the *Howell* took a direct hit in the forward boiler room just as we backed away. In my opinion, he would have been killed."

"Is that what happened, Jerry?" Myszynski asked.

Landa shrugged. He turned the roster and absently began tearing at the other end as bombs crunched in the outer harbor.

Quietly, Myszynski said, "Doesn't surprise me. From what I've heard, you all acted above and beyond the call of duty. Those flag saving sailors of yours; what a marvelous thing. You must be proud of them."

"I am. I'd like to put them in for a medal," said Landa.

"Okay, write them up. And Jerry."

"Yes, Sir?"

Myszynski nodded to the growing pile of paper at his feet. "Maybe you'd like your exec to have the crew roster for a while."

Sighs ranged through the office as Landa, his eyes unfocused, handed the page over to Ingram.

"Commodore, could I ask a question?" It was Ashton.

"Certainly."

"Commander Landa. Can you perhaps tell me about the performance of your proximity fuses?"

Landa looked up sharply, dampness glistening on his brow. "We didn't shoot proximity fuses."

Ashton's mouth dropped. "Why not?"

"I have my reasons." Landa returned Ashton's stare.

A curious Ingram turned to look at Landa with the rest of them.

"Would you care to share, your...reasons, with us, Commander?" asked Dexter Sands, the sarcasm evident in his voice.

"All I can tell you is that they're unreliable. Can't hit the broad side of a barn."

A bomb slammed into the ocean a scant one hundred yards away raising a hissing geyser. In spite of their professional sangfroid, they dropped to the deck and curled up. After a moment, they looked at one another, realizing they were okay. Then they took their chairs, dusting themselves off, trying to act as if nothing had happened. Ashton asked, "Don't you think that's rather foolish?"

Ashton's right hand shook, Ingram noticed. But then, both of his hands were shaking.

"Not at all," said Landa. Another bomb burst further away. Their eyes ran around the compartment again, wondering if they should fall to the deck again.

"The *Griffith* bagged a Val after you drifted into the squall, Jerry,"

Myszynski said. "Admiral Sands' cruisers and destroyers got seven of the twelve Vals that came after them. The wildcats got another three."

"Impossible," Landa said.

Ingram sat up straight. *Come on Jerry The Admiral can't be lying about that.* Another bomb flashed on Tulagi.

"They do work, Commander, I assure you." said Ashton. "And had you used proximity fuses, your ship might be here tonight, instead of beached and broken up in some New Georgia backwater."

An image of Edgerton, drinking soup at the other end of the *Howell's* wardroom table flashed through Ingram's mind. Then, the image changed to an open-eyed, hopelessly dead Redding, laying on the same table surrounded by blood-spattered medics who couldn't save him.

"Impossible!" Said Landa, his voice up several octaves.

Ashton shouted. "After we patiently instructed you on how to use them."

"Come on, you two," Myszynski growled.

The aircraft engines faded to the Northwest. Myszynski flipped on his desk lamp as the IMC blared, "*Secure from general quarters.*"

"Anything else?" Myszynski asked.

Ingram found his own fists bunched as he studied Landa in the pale light.

"I'm done," said Sands.

"That's it for me, Commodore," "Ashton said. "I have to get over to Cactus and catch a plane."

"You leaving us?" asked Myszynski.

"Back to the States," said Ashton.

Myszynski said, "Give my best to Dinah Shore."

Ashton stood. "I surely will. Good evening, Gentlemen." He walked out.

"Me too, gentlemen. Good night." Admiral Sands gave Landa a look, then followed Ashton through the door.

Myszynski waited just five seconds for Sands footsteps to fade. He pointed his cigar at Landa and said with a deep menace in his voice, "Damnit. You've lived ten out of nine lives. Why the hell do you have to be so insubordinate?"

"Ashton's a fop. Dexter Sands is--"

Myszynski smashed his fist on the desk, ashes tumbling off his cigar. "You're not going to last in this man's Navy pissing off captains and admirals.

And you've pissed me off. Your conduct is something I won't tolerate from any one in my outfit. Not even from one of my skippers!" His eyes glittered as he lowered his bald head, ready to charge, as if he were a 300 pound defensive guard, "Remember, Commander, there's only one *prima donna* around here. And that's me. No one else. Got it?" He jabbed his cigar at Landa.

"Yes, Sir."

"I've stuck my neck out, covering up for you. Now those days are over. Do I make myself clear?" He puffed blue smoke.

"Yes, Sir. " Landa said.

In the dark, it was impossible for Ingram to tell if Landa was contrite. Even if it were bright daylight, he knew that Landa's face would be, by this time, a hollow-eyed mask.

Myszynski continued, "All right, then. I want you to write up your action report and have it to me ASAP. I'm going to hold you here on my staff for a while just to muzzle and keep you out of sight. Then I'll figure out what the hell to do with you."

"At which time you'll flush me down the toilet?"

"No, no, damnit," Myszynski said. "But I do have to clarify this proximity fuse business for Captain Ashton."

"Ashton can go pound sand."

Ingram expected Myszynski to rise from his chair and rip Landa apart. Instead the Commodore said, "Come on, Jerry. You'll feel better after the doc gives you something."

"Already seen him."

Myszynski sat back, puffing.

"What now?" asked Landa.

"For starters, do an action report. And quit pissing off the brass, damnit. Rat guards, good God." Myszynski turned to Ingram. "Commander, perhaps you'd like to give your captain the ship's crew roster."

Ingram looked at the paper in his hands. It was almost all gone, a pile of tiny pieces lay on the deck between his feet. And his hands shook as he felt an anger building in his system. Ashton's admonition to Landa ranged through his mind; '...and had you used proximity fuses, your ship might be here tonight, instead of beached up in some New Georgia backwater.' *Edgerton. Redding.*

He hardly heard Myszynski say, "As for you, Commander, you're going Stateside."

"What?" Ingram's heart jumped.

"Stateside, I said. PCO training. After that, you'll be having your own ship."

"Ship? Where?"

"Right back here. So enjoy your time in the States. But remember, you still work for me."

19

---

8 March, 1943
    Fort MacArthur Dispensary
    San Pedro, California

Sergeant Thorpe stuck his head through the doorway to Room 312, a four-bed ward. Two beds were occupied: one, a pneumonia case, the other, a broken leg. Clacking gum loudly, Thorpe said, "Phone for you, Captain. I think it's a civilian, so I put it to your office."

Helen chuckled to herself. Thorpe referred to two desks crammed in a closet-sized vestibule down the hall as her office. "Okay, thanks."

The man with the broken leg, Corporal Jennings, had Helen worried. He'd fallen off a gun platform three days ago and broken his leg in two places. He looked pale, and she wondered if he was getting infected. She felt his forehead: clammy and hot. He was asleep and moaned.

She leaned close. "Jennings, do you hear me?"

Jennings opened his eyes, then focused on Helen. A corner of his mouth lifted and he muttered something.

"What?" she asked;

"I've died and gone to heaven."

"Nonsense. How do you feel?"

Jennings eyes ranged up and down her face. "Better."

"Open." She smiled and wielded the thermometer.

Jennings clenched his teeth. "You have ice water?"

"After we take your temperature."

"Please?"

"Open."

Jennings accepted the thermometer and sighed.

"Be right back." Helen checked the time.

Jennings moaned again, as she whisked out of 312 to her office. She walked in and picked up the phone. "Captain Ingram."

There was static on the line. Then, ice cubes clinked.

"Hello?"

"...Helen."

"Laura?" Helen flashed back to their dinner last Saturday night. She hoped she'd been decent company.

Laura gulped. "Helen. I have a letter from Todd."

Helen felt as if someone had shoved her in the basement morgue. Words hung in her throat; she couldn't get them out. "Wha---?"

"You knew, didn't you?"

"I...I haven't had a letter from Todd in four days." Which was the truth. But she did know. Ever since Shanghai Red's.

"Balls."

"Laura," she blurted. "I heard those two sailors in the men's room at Shanghai Red's. You had gone outside. Wha...what did Todd say?" She had almost said, is it true? Then she leaned forward, her body racked with tension. Her bare elbow brushed against a thick brown envelope, but she hardly noticed.

"You know damn well. Luther's dead." The glass clinked near the mouthpiece and Laura gulped again.

"My God,. Laura. I'm so sorry."

"A lot you can do about it."

Helen kept silent. Thirty seconds passed.

"You still there?"

"I'm here if you need me."

Another thirty seconds.

"I'm sorry," Laura's voice was little. "I'm not handling this well. It's not every day that one loses a husband, and I'm not quite used to it. I'm all cried out. I don't know what the hell to do."

"Why don't you come down here? I've a guest room. Stay with me for a few days."

"I could but..."

"But what?"

"NBC called. I start work tomorrow. We're doing the track for a film. A Navy documentary." She gave a hoarse chuckle. "Whoopie."

"Nonsense. You need someone to be with. Come on down here."

"Rain check, honey. Work's important to me now. Better than sitting around thinking about Lu...about it."

"I'll call tonight when I get home."

"Thanks."

"Thank you for calling. I really am sorry."

"I know. Forgive me for being such a brat." The glass rattled again.

"Tonight, then."

"His ship blew up. Todd said there was no pain. He went quickly-- hero-ically, Todd said."

Helen wiped her cheek.

"Todd, your husband," Laura said in a shaky voice. The bottle neck clanked on the glass. Liquid gurgled and she gulped. "Your husband is a hell of a writer."

"I know."

"He couldn't have put it any better. You take good care of that guy of yours, honey."

"I will. Do me a favor?"

"What?"

"Take it easy on whatever you have there."

"Okay...and Helen?"

"Yes?"

"Thanks."

"It's okay."

"Tonight." Laura hung up.

Helen lay her head in her hands and took a deep breath.

"Okay, Captain?" It was Thorpe, looking in the doorway, smacking his gum.

"Fine. Never better." She straightened up and blinked.

Thorpe waved at the large brown envelope on her desk. "Just came. Stamped 'Official Business.' Looks like you got a promotion or something."

"Couldn't be that. They just promoted me."

Sheila, the other nurse walked by. "I got Jennings' thermometer. He's up to 102."

"Jeepers!"

"I know

"Well, somebody has his sights on you." Thorpe walked off.

Wiping her eyes again, Helen grabbed scissors and slit one end of the envelope. A large sheaf of bound government mimeographed paper spilled out.

"No." She read it again, her eye racing across the page: Orders.

"No!" Her voice echoed. "They can't."

She put a hand to her chest and forced her breathing to slow. Then she read once again:

FROM:Commanding Officer, Seventh Army,

TO:Capt. Helen Z. Ingram, 712836, USA

DATE:6, March, 1943

SUBJ:Orders

INFO:Commanding Officer, Station Hospital, Fort MacArthur, San Pedro, Calif.

1. Upon receipt, you are hereby detached Station Hospital, Fort MacArthur.
2. You are ordered to report to Commanding Officer, 1st Medical Battalion, 1st Division, Seventh Army.
3. Upon receipt, you will proceed to USAAF Base, Long Beach, Calif. NLT 12 March, 1943 and report to Commanding Officer U.S. Army Air Force Air Station, for transportation.

4. Accounting data 6702211.3728 991 36/24700.331.

By Direction
  R. T. Bacon

"God. What is this?" She jumped from her desk and walked swiftly down the hall to the front office. A sign above the door read:

DR. RUTHERFORD T. MOORE, COLONEL USA, COMMANDING OFFICER

She swept past Sergeant Thorpe. "Is he in, Sergeant?"

Thorpe looked up from his typewriter. "Yes, but---"

Not bothering to listen, Helen ripped open the door and walked in, letting it slam behind her.

Moore looked up, then turned back to his desk. There was a pile of personal goods. He was sorting them into a box. "A patient died last night."

"What?"

"Went into cardiac arrest. We couldn't keep him. Just thirty-two years old." Moore stirred his fingers around the pile on his desk. "I guess I'll have to write the letter."

Moore looked seventeen. Helen had yet to see a trace of a beard on this round-faced, fair complected man. Gold rimmed glasses made him look even younger and professorial. Yet, she recalled, she'd never seen him smile. His medical certificates hung proudly on the wall behind: BA and MD from the University of Minnesota. Career Army, Moore was a pathologist by training.

"Oh, dear. I'm sorry," said Helen.

Moore went back to sorting the personal belongings on his desk. "I saw your orders five minutes ago."

"They promised." Her breathing became rapid again and she willed it to stop.

"Promised what?" Moore tossed a pack of cigarettes and a lighter in the box. A package of condoms went into the wastebasket.

"They promised not to...not to move me around."

"This is the Army." He waved casually. "This says you have until this Friday to report to Long Beach. You want to check out now?"

"Isn't that kind of swift?"

"Hell, I don't know, Helen. Like I said, this is the Army. Why can't you move around?"

Moore had transferred here last month. Apparently he didn't know. "I was on Corregidor. Then Mindanao with the resistance for six months. And I know things..."

Moore sat back and watched her, his glasses gleaming. "What do you know?"

"I can't." She couldn't tell Moore about stealing the Japanese Type 93 torpedo manual off Mindanao. In so many ways, they had said because of that alone, her duty was limited to CONUS: Continental limits of the United States. "They won't let me say."

"Have any idea where the Seventh Army is?"

She shook her head.

"I don't either." Moore pushed his intercom switch down: "Thorpe?"

Gum clacked. "Yes, Sir?"

"Call HQ and find out where Seventh Army is." Moore clicked off. "Don't worry, Helen. Probably better than this trash heap. Now tell me again. What's so secret that a little old girl like you can't tell her boss." The last was said with a *faux* Southern accent.

"You'll have to get that from Colonel Otis DeWitt."

"Who's that?"

"He's General Macarthur's aide for intelligence."

"How did you---?" The intercom buzzed. Moore reached over and snapped down the switch. "Yes?"

Thorpe announced himself with clacking chewing gum. "Seventh Army, Sir?"

"Yes?"

"HQ says it's a new outfit formed by General Patton."

"Well, where the hell is it?"

"Bizerte."

For the second time, Helen felt as if someone had tossed her into the morgue.

"Where's Bizerte?" demanded Moore.

"Tunisia, Colonel. North Africa. They're gearing up for the invasion of Sicily."

Helen sank back onto her couch, picked up the phone and dialed Laura West.

It rang ten times. Finally, the phone jiggled off the hook. "...Hello?"

"You okay?"

"...what time is it?"

"Almost eight-thirty."

"Day or night?"

In spite of her predicament, Helen rolled her eyes. Laura sounded lucid, a good sign. "Night. How do you feel?"

"Like a bulldozer ran through my mouth."

"Did you go to work?"

"No. I...jeez, it really is eight-thirty. I've been asleep ever since we talked."

"I promised to call back. I'm glad you took some time off."

Laura sighed. "I don't know. They get hot under the collar sometimes. How'd your day go?"

"It...it." Helen held her breath.

"What'd they do? Take away your movie privileges?"

"No, damnit!" she growled.

"What?"

She told her.

"But they can't do that. Didn't they promise you no more overseas duty?"

"More than that. But nobody seems to want to do anything about it."

"Listen. I know this congressman. He's fixed it for a couple of guys around here to go into the documentary film making corps. Navy or Army, it doesn't matter. They start as full lieutenants or captains or whatever, even get to wear a uniform and never leave home."

"That may not be necessary."

"Why not?"

"I've already put a call into a friend of mine."

"Does he have as much clout as a congressman?"

"I think so." She told her about Oliver Toliver, a Naval Lieutenant junior grade now with the 12th Naval District in San Francisco. Toliver had served with Todd on the U.S.S. *Pelican* in Manila Bay at the war's outbreak. The *Pelican* was sunk off Corregidor, and Todd, Helen, Toliver, and Otis DeWitt, made their break for freedom with six others in a thirty-six foot launch. DeWitt had since been promoted to Colonel and now worked for Colonel Charles Willoughby, Douglas MacArthur's Intelligence Chief in Australia. She finished with, "Otis DeWitt is in a very influential position. He has the authority to rescind the orders or at least figure out who issued them. So Ollie, that's Toliver, told me he would jump on the overseas line as soon as possible and talk to Otis."

"...I'd go with that. When do you have to go?"

"Friday."

"Good God! Isn't that short notice?"

"Sometimes they do that to you."

"Keep your chin up, toots."

Laura sounded good. "Okay. You, too."

20

9 March, 1943
   U.S.S. *Whitney* (AD 4)
   Tulagi Harbor, Solomon Islands

Someone knocked at Ingram's door.

"Enter."

Leo Seltzer walked in wearing dress blues and clean white hat. "Morning, Sir." He rolled his hat in his hands then said, "Shipping out and I wanted to say *adios*." He held out his hand and they shook.

"What are your orders?" asked Ingram.

"I'm over to Cactus to catch a noon C-47 for Noumea. Then it's Stateside for leave and refresher training then...who knows? Another can, I guess."

"Looks like I won't be able to pin that medal on you." Myszynski had endorsed and forwarded bronze star recommendations for Seltzer, Early, and Katsikas.

"Don't mean nothin,'" To an outsider, Seltzer's remark might have sounded ungrateful, even insubordinate. But Ingram took it the way Seltzer meant it. Others aboard the *Howell*, both living and dead, had been just as heroic and deserved medals as well.

Seltzer asked, "How 'bout you, Sir?"

"Prospective commanding officer training Stateside. Then I'm putting in for a twenty-one hundred." Ingram referred to a *Fletcher* class destroyer like the *Howell*.

"Holy smokes. Do you know where you'll be?"

"Not yet."

"Well, ain't that a pip?" Seltzer rubbed his jaw. "Tell you what, Mr. Ingram. You mind if I put in for your destroyer?"

"My honor, Leo. Wouldn't that be something? I might have a chance to pin that medal on you yet."

Someone knocked. Ingram opened it finding Landa not looking much better than the day before. "Hi, Captain."

Landa still looked like hell. "Rocko wants to see us. Oh. Hello, Seltzer. Where you headed?"

"Headed Stateside, Captain. Well, goodbye." He shook their hands then left. Landa said, "Rocko wants to see us again." They headed up two flights, knocked, and walked in Commodore Myszynski's office, finding him near a porthole, puffing his cigar and flipping through a file. He waved them to the leather couch and muttered, "Something's come to my attention."

Landa said nothing.

"Sir?" said Ingram.

Myszynski shifted his gaze to Ingram and raised his eyebrows, as if to say, *what the hell are you doing here*?

Something was happening that Ingram didn't understand. But he decided to press ahead, figuring he would be soon excused anyway. He blurted, "I thought I had orders Stateside, Commodore."

"Yes. Your PCO training will be aboard the *U.S.S. Hitchcock*."

"*The Hitchcock*?" asked Landa.

"One and the same," said Myszynski.

"What?" Ingram looked from one to the other.

"Rust bucket," Landa said. "She sits on coffee grounds at dockside."

"A rust bucket she may be, but Roland De Reuter will give Todd a fair shake," said Myszynski.

Landa nodded. "That's true. Old Roland is one of the best. He'll make a skipper out of you."

Ingram said, "I've already been a skipper."

"Not in the tin-can Navy. Here." Myszynski shoved a brown packet to Ingram and then checked his watch. "Your orders. A C-47 leaves Cactus at noon. Be on it. You're booked all the way through Stateside via air. Check my yeoman across the passageway. He'll fix you up with travel orders."

Ingram asked, "Where is the *Hitchcock*, Sir.?"

"Long Beach. You'll see your wife."

Helen! My God! Waves of joy flooded through him. It suddenly occurred that he wasn't going to be killed or maimed or terribly wounded. A great weight had been lifted off his chest. There would be a time of peace and quiet; Helen had suddenly surged into his life. "So much for Hemingway."

Landa nodded somberly. "You can start reading your mail, now."

"What the hell are you talking about," demanded Myszynski.

"My God!" The thought raced in Ingram's mind, how the hell do I let her know I'm on my way? I wonder if---.

"--Mr. Ingram? Hello?" Myszynski waved a hand.

Ingram smiled. "That's great news. Thank you, Sir."

Myszynski shifted his gaze. "Guess what, Jerry?"

Landa stared into space.

"Damnit! Are you still feeling sorry for yourself or do I have to check you into the loonie ward?"

That did something to Landa. He shifted his stance, his eyes darting quickly to Ingram. "Sorry, Rocko. What is it?" Landa raised a corner of his mouth and forced his tone to be more resonate.

Myszynski steepled his fingers. "Dexter Sands sent me a message this morning. He's requested you for his staff."

Landa sat up.

"You have any idea why he would want to do this?" Myszynski said.

Landa shook his head.

"You might as well hear this, Todd," Myszynski said. "But what I'm about to say goes no further than that bulkhead. Got it?"

Landa and Ingram nodded.

"Dexter Sands is not a forgiving soul. He plays favorites. And his staff has been with him a long time. Like a fraternity, they're tighter than a drum. Now, you, Commander Boom Boom Landa, have managed to ascend directly to the number one position on Dexter's shit list. First, you rig rat guards between your ships. Then, you embarrass him on the TBS. Then you mouth him in front of me, Ashton and your exec, which probably sealed your fate. He'd like nothing better than to get you over on the *Sioux Falls* and turn his people loose on you. They'd put you in a straight jacket and tie it shut with double bowline hitches. Then Dexter would shove you down a toilet, like," Myszynski snapped his fingers, "that."

"He wants to make an example of you in front of destroyer people, my people. He resents our independence. I can't let him do that to us."

"I didn't realize that, Commodore."

"Get used to the fact that you're on the ten most wanted list."

"Maybe I can make up for it."

"How?"

"I have an idea."

Myszynski slumped at his desk and puffed until his face disappeared in a cloud of smoke. "Balls."

"Commodore, may I?"

"Okay, shoot." Myszynski folded his arms.

"The *Howell*. I think we can salvage her."

"Balls."

"No, Sir. Basically, she's sound all the way back to her aft fireroom. If we send an ATF up there, she can be towed to Noumea, Australia maybe, even the States, where she can be mated to a new stern section. Look," Landa leaned forward, "I talked to Hank Kelly about it at breakfast. What we need to do is make sure she's secured. All watertight doors shut, the whole works. And then pick our time and send in the tug."

"What about the shell she took from the Jap destroyer?"

"Blew her stack off but Hank doesn't think it penetrated the boiler room. Even if it did, we still have a sound hull. So they replace two boilers. So what?"

Myszynski rubbed his chin.

"Look, Commodore. You want me to hang around here and scrub toilets? Okay. Count paper clips? Okay. But how about a real job? How 'bout letting me save the *Howell*? I know every bolt and nut in that ship and I can set up a salvage operation, chop-chop. It won't take much. Just the ATF when we're ready."

To Ingram, Landa's voice sounded plaintive; almost as if he were pleading for his life before a hanging judge. He talked fast and his words ran together.

Ingram caught a glance from Myszynski, both realizing Landa was trying to save a part of his soul in addition to saving the ship.

"Not a bad idea. Let me think about it. But there is another matter I just discovered." Myszynski leaned back in his chair peering directly at Landa.

"Sir?" asked Landa.

At length, Myszynski said, "Mr. Ingram. That'll be all. You better go pack and catch your airplane." A dark shadow crossed over Myszynski's face. Ingram knew he wasn't wanted.

"Yes, Sir. See you Jerry. Good luck." Ingram rose and shook hands with the two then headed for the door.

"Hot in here. Clip the door open would you please?" said Myszynski, fanning himself.

"Yes, Sir." Ingram walked out, clipping the office door open. A breeze wafted around him as he stepped in the passageway, cooling the office and pushing cigar smoke out the portholes. The yeoman's office was directly across. It was a Dutch door with a note pasted to the shelf. 'Back in five minutes.'

Head call, figured Ingram as he leaned against the bulkhead. The breeze became a bit stronger, cooling him. He sniffed at the clean, salty air, thinking of Helen.

"...what gives you the right to go against squadron doctrine?" said Myszynski.

"...I don't understand, Sir," replied Landa.

Myszynski's voice rose a notch. "Bullshit. A week ago, I sent the squadron specific written orders to use VT ammo. You refused to acknowledge it. Why couldn't you put your personal feelings aside, whatever the hell they are, and fire VT ammo like I told you? And don't tell me it's because Ashton is a jerk. I already know that. That's not the point. That ammo works, damnit!"

"Damnit Rocko. It's top secret. I could go to the brig."

"Nothing top secret about losing a ship and 128 men, is there? Look, the Griffith scored hits, and so did Dexter Sands' boys. They shot down Japs. Isn't that proof *enough? That's why Dexter wants your ass. I think he believes you were criminally negligent. And I'm not far behind him."*

"Yes, but you see, my brother--"

"Let me ask you. How many Japs did you shoot down?"

Silence.

"Well, Commander?" Myszynski's voice was icy.

"...one for sure."

"Pardon me, Sir." It was Upton, Myszynski's short, pudgy, redheaded yeoman. He stepped in front of Ingram, unlocked the Dutch door and walked in his office. "Can I help you, Mr. Ingram?"

"...you could have easily bagged three or four. Maybe the one that got you--"

Ingram cleared his throat. "Travel orders."

"--Shit," Landa yelled back. *"I didn't know it then. And you still don't know for sure."*

It was impossible not to hear. Avoiding Ingram's glance, Upton grabbed a manila envelope and handed it to him. "We have you booked on the noon plane out of Cactus."

"Right." Ingram couldn't get away fast enough. His bile rose as he walked out, slamming the little Dutch door behind him. Myszynski's voice trailed as he raced down the ladder, *"...the point is Commander. You disobeyed orders. Tell me why I shouldn't write you up for gross negligence and insubordination."*

Images of Edgerton, Redding and the *Howell's* capsizing stern section swirled through his mind. Vividly, he heard the screams of the dying. One hundred and twenty-eight of them. Todd Ingram stormed three decks back to his stateroom where he kicked the trash can; again and again. But like slamming Upton's Dutch door, it didn't give satisfaction. The difference was that Upton's Dutch door was, most likely, still serviceable; the trash can lay in a crumpled heap in the corner. As he packed, he debated if he should tell Kelly or Delmonico about Landa's refusal to use the VT shells that might have saved the *Howell*.

An hour later, he'd settled down and had finished packing when the quarterdeck messenger knocked. "All set, Sir. Boat just pulled up. Can I take that?" He nodded toward Ingram's duffle.

"Thanks, I'll be right there."

"Yes, Sir." The messenger threw the duffle strap around his back and with a grunt, walked off.

Ingram looked around the stateroom once, picked up his briefcase and walked toward the door.

Landa stepped in, his face dour, "Todd, before you go, I'd like to explain. You see, ---"

Ingram hauled off and socked Landa in the face. Cartilage crunched beneath his fist.

"Ooooff!" Landa stumbled back, and crashed into the bulkhead. With a groan, he sank to the deck, blood running from his nose. He looked up, "Wha...?"

"Good luck to you, too, Captain Boom Boom. And why don't you wish good luck to the 128 guys you left at the bottom of The Slot." Ingram picked up his briefcase and grabbed the door. With an afterthought, he turned, "Write me up if you want to, you sonofabitch." He walked out slamming the door. This time, it felt good.

PART II

...The race is not to the swift
or the battle to the strong,
nor does food come to the wise
or wealth to the brilliant
or favor to the learned;
but time and chance happen to them all

Ecclesiastes 9:11

...a ship doesn't have one voice, she has many.
You can hear them calling to each other out there, especially at night.

Jack Higgins,
Storm Warning

21

12 March, 1943
San Pedro, California

They call it 'Hurricane gulch: One side is formed by Santa Catalina Island, twenty-one miles off the coast of Southern California; the other side by the Palos Verdes Peninsula. When a weather front roars down California's Coast, the wind compresses between the two land masses and squirts through the 'gulch.' In so doing, the wind accelerates with a vengeance as it races inland, challenging those who walk the streets of San Pedro.

Especially uphill. Todd Ingram was dog tired. He'd been living in an airplane for the past four days. Even so, he was lucky to have made such a quick trip. They manifested him with twenty other officers and enlisted, Seltzer among them, on Admiral Halsey's palatial four-engined PB2Y-5 Coronado dead-heading to San Diego for installation of new command radio gear. The trip took sixty-one hours, and at each refueling stop, he tried, with no success, to call or wire Helen. At the Ford Island Naval Air Station in Hawaii, he got through to his home but the phone rang and rang.

They touched down on a sparkling San Diego Bay three hours ago. At

North Island Naval Air Station, a sympathetic scheduler gave Ingram a hop in a TBF flying to the Long Beach Naval Air Station at Terminal Island. After a half hour waiting for a nonexistent cab, he loaded his duffle on a Navy Bus which took him over the ferry to San Pedro where the driver, a seaman first class simply following orders, dropped Ingram unceremoniously at the corner of Seventeenth and Gaffey.

Three blocks to Alma Street. Uphill. For a moment, Ingram couldn't figure what he wanted more; his arms around Helen or twelve hours uninterrupted sleep. Maybe a little of both. Ruefully, he smiled to himself: It will be interesting finding out. Then it hit him that he hadn't showered since Noumea. His meals had consisted basically of sandwiches made from stale bread, lukewarm coffee, and an occasional apple or candy bar. Running a hand over his face, he felt the black stubble that had grown since his last shave at Ford Island. *How in the hell will she recognize me?*

With that, he started walking. The wind tugged at his dress blues as he trudged uphill. But it felt good and cooled him as he walked the steepening slope. And soon, he heard the school-ground noise of youngsters playing. He was suddenly washed over with a sense of guilt: it wasn't his privilege to hear the sweetness of that sound; the sound of peace and growth and the future of his country. Others deserved to hear this, to stand where he stood, not he: Others who lay at the bottom of The Slot.

Kids laughing. How wonderful.

He walked up to San Pedro High School and stopped at the athletic field letting his duffle drop. Through an eight-foot chain link fence, he looked out to see a number of young boys working out at hurdles, sprints, javelin, and shot-put. They wore uniform shirts and he realized it was a regular track meet. What better way to spend a Friday afternoon.

A gun barked.

Ingram jumped. Quickly, his eye caught the blue smoke puff from the starter's pistol. *Easy, you're home.*

Four boys sprang from the starting blocks and bent to the wind, their hair flying as they ran. One had freckles and long red hair. Two others had close-cropped dark-brown hair. The last was a blond; heavier and chunkier than the other three. Amazingly, it was this portly blond kid who led at the first turn. It must have been an important race, for many of the other events stopped, their participants turning to watch. A nearby coach working kids at the high jump, sat on his haunches, checking his stop watch from time to time. People yelled "Com' on, Blake."

Blake must have been the heavy blond kid, for he seemed to bend forward even more and go faster. Then, the red-headed kid started to catch up at the halfway mark. But Blake held his ground, two or three feet ahead of the red-head. Soon Blake was near Ingram at the three-quarter mark, his cheeks puffing and his face red.

Suddenly, Blake tripped on something and he fell headlong, his hands splayed before him. The others ran past as Blake rose to a sitting position and stared directly at...Ingram.

"Get up!" Ingram had no idea why he said it. He just did.

"Huh?" Blake eyes were watery and blood ran down his cheek where his face had smacked the track. Both knees were scraped with purple abrasions.

"Go, damnit!"

So Blake got up and started running, his hair flying as before. Ingram was amazed. The other three were a good half a track length ahead, yet Blake ran faster. He was catching up! Quickly.

Good God. The heart in that kid.

Blake passed Ingram a second and a third time and into the bell lap for the mile. Blake ran and ran, passing the two dark-haired boys on the final back stretch. He began closing on the red-head who made a mistake just as he passed Ingram. The red-head looked behind and spotted Blake only five feet behind. He stumbled a bit and Blake drew to within two feet. What the red-head didn't see was Blake's purple face, giving it his all.

By this time, everyone was yelling for Blake. Ingram couldn't help joining in, "Go Blake. Go! Come on Blake." He laughed to himself. He hadn't yelled so much since he'd seen Navy play Notre Dame two and a half years ago.

The red-headed kid broke the tape with Blake stumbling through a split-second later. Immediately, Blake caromed over to the pole-vault pit, teetered at the edge and fell face down into the sawdust. Two coaches ran to Blake and soon had him sitting up in the sawdust where he heaved great gulps of air. Eventually, Blake stood and started walking in ragged circles. People applauded as Blake shuffled about, his head down, hands on his hips.

Ingram drew a deep breath. There was something about Blake he wished he could put in a bottle. At the same time he felt a twinge of guilt for it was Blake, and men/boys like him, kids who could pick themselves up, that he would recruit for his ship, that he would take to into battle. He hoped he could bring them through in one piece, to resume the track meet, the competition of civilian life, which was difficult enough.

His eyes took in the track, as boys and coaches walked about. Mothers sat in the bleachers. The wind blew, dust swirled, paper and leaves floated on the wind, little white clouds darted overhead. The scent of eucalyptus wafted about, as birds chirped in the trees, and sun and wind gave heat and life-giving air to breath. Ingram stood there on this wonderful afternoon with crystal blue skies, luxuriating in this marvel of life. Compared to the place where he just came from, this all made sense.

The coach, a withered but nimble sixty year old, walked over. "Some race, huh?"

"You bet," said Ingram. "That kid really has heart."

"I'm glad you yelled at him. Sometimes, he gives up too easy. And he doesn't work out much. But he has lots of potential. If he does start working out, then Katy, bar the door."

"What is it that's in him do you suppose?"

"I think the answer is obvious." The coach glanced at the campaign ribbons on Ingram's blouse.

Ingram stepped back.

"You shipping out?" The coach looked at his duffle.

"Just got back."

"Welcome home, son." The coach looked to the top of the chain-link fence that separated them. "I wish I could shake your hand."

"Thanks, coach."

The coach grinned. "You know, these kids really are crazy. Guess what our football seniors did?"

"Shoot."

"Enlisted. The whole damn bunch walked into the Navy recruiting office as a group. They start boot camp in two months. Can you beat that?"

"That's great, coach." Ingram wondered if the coach realized what awaited some of those kids. Then it hit him. "Say, are you the football coach, too?"

"Yep."

"You have a great group of kids."

A whistle blew, and the coach looked over his shoulder. "Gotta go. Look, stop by sometime. I'd like you to meet my kids."

"Swell."

The coach tipped a finger to his hat and walked away.

Suddenly, Ingram felt tired. It was as if the whole trip had caught up with him. He looked up the block and a half, wondering if he could make it.

Helen.

You bet I can.

Five minutes later, he turned the corner and saw his house. *Is she home?* He checked his watch wondering what shift she was working at the dispensary. Maybe he would have time for a shower and a nap if she worked the day shift.

He straightened his cap, walked up the little brick path and mounted the steps. He tried the doorknob. Locked, damnit. Stepping back, he looked at the place, instinctively knowing she wasn't there. The blinds were down and the morning paper lay under one of the wicker porch chairs. He rang the doorbell and listened. Then he knocked. Nothing.

"Afternoon." It was a mailman. He had a nose that looked as if it had been through a meat grinder: a boxer's nose. But his eyes were lively and he wore a friendly smile. And the roadmaps in his eyes and on his cheeks belied that he killed a beer or two every afternoon. "Looking for someone?" he asked.

Ingram dropped his duffle and gave a sheepish grin. "My wife."

"You're Mister Ingrid?" The mailman pushed the mailbox flag down then reached inside.

"Ingram."

"Well..." He pulled out a letter, and stroked his chin.

There was something about the mailman's tone. "Well, what?" asked Ingram.

He seemed to make a decision. "You got ID?"

"What for?"

"'Cause this is from Mrs. Ingrid...er Ingram to you."

"Of course." Ingram pulled out his wallet and produced his Navy ID card.

With a nod, the postman handed over the letter along with two others from his mailbag, both bills. "Ain't supposed to do that, but what the heck. It gets to you quicker anyway. Right?"

"Right. Thanks."

The mailman walked off

Ingram stuffed the letters in his pocket then reached under the potted geranium finding the key. He let himself in, expecting a joyful, overwhelming feeling. Instead, he sensed dread. He walked to the bedroom finding everything neat and picked up. Same in the living and dinning rooms. Except...in the kitchen, the refrigerator door stood open. He peered inside. Nothing. It had been turned off. Then he punched a wall switch. No electricity!

"Jesus!"

He walked in the dining room and lifted the phone, finding a dial tone. Then he dashed to the garage. It was securely locked, but yes, the Plymouth was there.

Gone. Helen is gone. Hell, he figured, they must have sent her TAD somewhere. Maybe some sort of nursing course. He went back to the dining room, pulled out the address pad and looked up the Fort MacArthur dispensary number.

"Dispensary, Sergeant Thorpe speaking."

"Helen Ingram, please."

Gum clacked as Thorpe replied, "Ah ... whom may I say is calling?"

"Her husband. Lieutenant Commander Todd Ingram."

"Ah sh---, er, Yes, Sir. Could you hold on, please?"

"What for? All I want to do is speak to---"

The line went dead. Ingram drummed his fingers for forty-five seconds during which time he vowed that if the little goldbrick didn't come on the line shortly, he was going to jump in his Plymouth, drive out to the damned dispensary and personally throttle Thorpe, whoever--

"Colonel Moore, speaking."

What the hell? "I'm Commander Ingram looking for my wife."

"Where are you?"

None of your damned business! "At home. I just walked in."

"You haven't heard?"

The dread that had been lurking in shadows jumped out at him, almost as if it were a living, fire-breathing thing, shoving a hot poker in his stomach. He tried to ignore it, but it swept over him. "Is...is she all right?"

Moore gave a nervous laugh. "Oh, no, Commander. She's...she's just fine."

"May I speak to her, please?" He had to stop himself from saying *damnit.*

"I'm afraid that's impossible."

"What?"

"You see she's been transferred."

"Whaaaatt! To where?"

Another nervous laugh. "Oh, she'll do fine. She has plenty of experience with these things, er as you know. She should---"

"Where, damnit!"

"Seventh Army. I put her on the plane at Long Beach just this morning. She said she'd sent you a letter."

"What unit?"

"Combat Support Hospital, First Division, First Medical Battalion."

Where's that?"

"Ah, Bizerte, North Africa."

"What?" Ingram reached and pulled Helen's letter out of his coat pocket and slammed it on the table. Opening it, he saw Helen's near-perfect cursive. The date was yesterday. Then he said, "North Africa. They promised, no more combat. She's been though hell."

"Well, Commander, you must admit, she's in the Army. And it was so sudden. But I tried and tried."

"Tried to do what?" Ingram demanded.

"Well, first, we spoke with the Commanding Officer of the Third Coastal Armillary Headquarters. Then he referred us to the---"

"Where is she now?"

"On her way, I suppose."

"What route did she take?"

After an extended silence, Moore said, "You may call me, Sir."

"Damnit! What route did she take?"

"Mr. Ingram, You're being insubordinate."

"Listen, you mealy little backwater sonofabitch. Tell me where she lands next."

Colonel paused again and said, "Who is your commanding officer?"

"You're kidding."

"What unit are you attached to?"

"All I'm trying to do is find my wife and prevent a terrible injustice."

"I asked, Mr. Ingram, 'who is your commanding officer?' I'm going to report you."

"Donald Duck!" Ingram slammed the phone down.

At two in the morning, Ingram awakened on the bed, still clothed. Helen's aroma surrounded him as he lay there. The thought that she'd slept in this bed just a few hours ago was more than he could stand. By candlelight he rose, shaved, and took a long hot shower; his third since his return. After toweling off, he climbed between the sheets, almost sorry that he did. Her scent was there, she was there, and yet she wasn't. So near and yet Helen was gone. He re-lit the candle and read her letter again, finding no more clues than what Colonel Moore had relayed late this afternoon.

She finished with,

...I can't think of anything else, to do, hon. I've got to go and between you and me, I don't think Colonel Moore did his best to get me out of this jam. He's striking for Brigadier and doesn't want to shake the trees. The irony is that I'll probably eat better. The dispensary chow is terrible. And in a sense I'll be closer to you. Africa is closer to the Solomon Islands than California, isn't' it? I don't know for sure but it's nice to think so. Oh, I forgot to say that I called Ollie. Of course he was terribly indignant about the whole thing. He said he would put a call into Otis DeWill to see if he can get something moving from MacArthur's end. So there's still a chance.

I think of you forever. I know the Howell will keep you safe and bring you back to me healthy and happy. I'll bet I get home before you, so don't worry. My love to you again and again and again.

Many long and lingering kisses,

Helen

P.S. Say hello to Boom Boom.

P.P.S. I left Fred next door with Emma Peabody. She loves him and will take good care of him while I'm gone.

22

---

15 March, 1943
    U.S.S. *Hitchcock* (DD 357)
    Long Beach Naval Station
    Long Beach, California

It was a busy Monday morning as lumbering men-of-war, their radar antennae twirling atop their masts, maneuvered to clear the harbor and put to sea. Horns blasted under a slate-gray sky, while tugs and yard service craft darted through heavy traffic.

Ingram bent to check his watch: 0822. *Damn!* They were supposed have been underway twenty minutes ago. Instead, the *Hitchcock* was glued dockside, as yet another ship, an ancient four stack cruiser this time, sounded a mournful prolonged blast to back clear from the slip across the fairway.

The top of the *Hitchcock's* pilothouse was the best place from which to conn the ship, but it was the worst place as far as protection from bitter icy winds shooting off snow-capped mountains to the northeast. Her foredeck crew took refuge in the lee of the deckhouse, blowing on their hands, and stomping their feet. But up here, there was no hiding from the thirty-six degree temperature made far harsher by the twenty-five knot wind. Ingram stomped his feet and gripped the rail with his kid-skinned gloves. But he jerked his hands away, as the cold shimmered through the gloves like a messenger of Hades. The ubiquitous wind penetrated Ingram's Navy blue topcoat and he shivered anew with each gust wondering which was better: this or the sweltering, bug-infested heat of the Solomon Islands.

Roland De Reuter, *Hitchcock's* Captain, had requested tugs to stand by. But tugs were at a premium for the moment, shoving around the larger ships. Like this new one gliding past. Painted a menacing dark-gray, she was the brand-new U.S.S. *Essex*, a 33,000 ton aircraft carrier. The lead-ship of her class, she carried a deck-load of TBF Avengers and brand-new F6F Hellcats. The last time Ingram had seen a carrier was six months ago -- in the Battle of the Santa Cruz Islands. The *Howell* had tried to torpedo the mortally wounded aircraft carrier *Hornet* as she lay abandoned and dead in the water, the victim of a Japanese aerial attack. But she was tough. U.S. Navy torpedoes couldn't put her down. The *Howell* fled and later, the destroyers *Anderson* and *Musten* pumped more torpedoes into her, along with more than 400 rounds of five-inch ammunition. But still she wouldn't sink. Eventually, *Anderson* and *Musten* were forced to run when a Japanese task force hauled over the horizon. Their destroyers easily sank the white-hot steaming wreck with just four of their Type 93 torpedoes.

The *Essex's* visage gave Ingram a sense of calm. She was an answer to the Navy's war losses. And Ingram had heard there were twelve more in her class, right behind her. On top of that, there were yet another eleven repeat *Essex* class carriers ready, to be built.

Lurking in mid-channel behind the *Essex* were two new *Fletcher* class destroyers, also in dark gray paint, patiently waiting their chance to ease through the breakwater and crack open their throttles to assume escort duty. The sailors on the destroyer's foredecks stood braced as the wind whipped their peacoats and bellbottoms. Ingram's eyes darted around Long Beach Harbor, sensing a new vitality in the sailors and ships about him. Like the kid, Blake, at San Pedro High School: Young and untested, they nevertheless lent an aura of determination and were going to the front in larger numbers. Ingram had been locked in this bitter war since the first Japanese bombs fell in the Philippines on December 8, 1941. And now, sixteen months later, it hit him: *maybe we do have a chance.*

Ingram peered through a forest of masts, into the San Pedro Channel, where the wind churned the water like a child playing in a bathtub. Thirty, thirty-five knots of wind out in that mess, he thought. *Hitchcock* was a 381 foot, *Porter* class twin-stacked destroyer. She was narrow-beamed and rough riding in a seaway. Indeed, she seemed to buck and roll even if you looked at her cross-eyed with six lines doubled to the pier. The pencil-thin *Hitchcock's* foray into the San Pedro Channel today would be a challenge; like trying to make the Long Beach Pike's roller coaster feel like a ride in a Cadillac. Lots of kids seasick today, probably even me, he thought ruefully.

He hadn't paid too much attention to the men crowded on the bridge below until a familiar profile stepped into view. Freckled and thin, the sailor wore head phones over his white hat; sown on his pea coat were the chevrons of a second class boatswain's mate. "Leo?"

Seltzer's head snapped around. "Mr. Ingram? What are you doing here? I thought you and Mrs.---"

"---I thought you were on liberty." Ingram didn't want to be reminded of Helen. After some hard drinking on Saturday, Ingram had called a friend and was lucky enough to be attached to the *Hitchcock* now, rather than stand around for two weeks with nothing to do.

"Swapped with a buddy."

"What do they have you doing up here?"

"Captain's talker."

Seltzer must have pulled strings. He should be on leave, Ingram thought? "But how did you---"

Roland De Reuter stepped from the pilothouse and shoved his way among bridge watchstanders. He looked up to Ingram and asked in a thick, Dutch accent, "Meester Ingram. Are you aware of our engineering difficulties?"

"No, Captain." Ingram wondered if De Reuter knew his crew imitated him behind his back, holding a forefinger below the nose and goose-stepping.

"Hokay." The barrel chested commander checked his watch, then yanked a phone from a bracket and punched a button. Ingram guessed he spoke with the engineering officer in the forward engine room. At breakfast, he heard the two grumbling about a recalcitrant number two generator.

De Reuter shouted into the phone, then hung up. He cupped a hand to his mouth and called up to Ingram. "Number two generator hast fallen off the line. Ve are not certain if number one generator can carry the load."

"Your choice, Captain."

"*Ja, ja.* I let you know."

Two tugs pulled in from the main channel, halted and tooted.

Ingram wondered if De Reuter really wanted to use tugs. Destroyer sailors were a prideful bunch, where flamboyant captains conned their ships like hot-rods. With powerful twin-engines at their command, destroyer skippers took glory in muscling their ships in and out of tight spaces. But this Amsterdam-born man was different. He was a merchant skipper from the old school, who viewed things through the big lumbering ship, single-screw prospective. Rule one: in port, big ships need tugs. Naturalized at the age of eighteen, De Reuter sailed the Holland-America Line for years, while doing naval reserve duty in destroyers. At war's outbreak, he'd been called up and assigned as executive officer of the *Hitchcock*, a training and services ship, attached to the Long Beach Naval Station. A year later, they made him commanding officer. A ship without a squadron, the *Hitchcock's* only mission was to take student officers and enlisted to sea, giving them practical training in ship handling, gunnery, torpedo tactics and communication. For the next two weeks, Ingram was the senior of fifteen officers, mostly ensigns and jay gees, plus seventy-five new enlisted, headed out for intensive battle drills. As a prospective commanding officer, Ingram would lead the drills and do the ship's maneuvering, all under De Reuter's watchful eye.

A phone buzzed on the bridge. De Reuter picked it up, nodded, then shoved it back into the bracket. "Mister Ingram!"

"Yes, Sir."

"Number two generator is fixed. Are you prepared to get this ship undervay?"

"Yes, Sir."

" Do you wish to use these?" De Reuter's hand swept toward the tugs lying alongside, their powerful diesel engines calmly thumping.

"No, Sir."

"Hokay." De Reuter climbed the ladder to the pilot house and stood beside Ingram. "Fery well. Ve go now." He clamped a hand atop his hat, as a gust nearly blew it away. "How do you supposed to do this?"

Ingram thought he detected a gleam in De Reuter's eye. It was almost as if the Dutchman deliberately beat up his English to disarm his listeners. "Hold lines one and three, take in the others. Let the wind blow the stern out until we stick out into the channel. Then, cast off one and three and ring-up a one-third backing bell. That should give us proper sternway to back into the main channel."

"Anchor?"

"Port anchor ready for letting go."

De Reuter pursed his lips and rubbed his chin. "Worth a try. The tugs can pull us clear before you stick us in shit."

Ingram nodded. De Reuter, not Ingram, would be the one in trouble if the *Hitchcock* crashed into something, like the blazing-white16,000 ton hospital ship moored across the way. He decided to give his first order and turned to Seltzer. "Single up all lines."

While Seltzer relayed the order, De Reuter said, "You one of Boom Boom Landa's boys?"

"Yes, Sir. I have served with him." *What the hell? How did he know*?

"Boom Boom is a goot man. And I hear you had your own ship at Corregidor."

"Just a little mine sweeper, yes, Sir." De Reuter fell silent, so Ingram bent over to give his next order---"

"---chust tell me one thing, Mr. Ingram."

"Yes, Sir?"

"Why, you? Why all of this?" De Reuter waved a hand around him. "Navy cross. Philippine Campaign medal with battle stars? The Solomons? Purple Heart? You could have your pick of chuicy shore-side duty."

Ingram's mouth dropped open.

"You have a wife? Kids?"

"Uhh. Yes. No."

"One wife and no kids?"

Ingram nodded. "Only one wife."

A corner of De Reuter's mouth turned up for just a moment at the joke.

He's sharp as a tack.

"Where is she now?"

"I don't know."

De Reuter knit his eyebrows. "Yes?"

"An Army nurse. A captain, now. They tell me she's enroute to North Africa to join Patton's Seventh Army in a Field Hospital."

"What's her name?"

"Helen."

"A beautiful name. I'll have you for dinner. Helen too, when she comes back. My Hilda is a good cook. But you haven't' answered my question. Why go?"

Ingram took a deep breath. "I suppose we all have to go at one time or another."

"But you. Corregidor. That horrible fighting in the Solomons. Why don't you chust pack it up and...take a job like mine? I could talk to someone here. Fix something up?"

"Well, they're giving me a ship." Why was De Reuter talking like this, Ingram wondered? It was De Reuter's job to evaluate Ingram for command, not probe his personal life for the next ten days. But the truth was, Ingram's stomach didn't feel fit for command at the moment. More and more, the nightmares came: ships burning and sinking and men screaming from the darkness. Even during the day, feelings of fear and death and being trapped in a burning or flooding compartment gnawed at him. He turned away, pretending to examine the tugs standing by alongside. "It's...it's where I belong, Captain."

"Hokay. Let's go."

"Seltzer, tell main control to standby to answer all bells."

Seltzer punched his talk button and relayed the order.

"Fantail, take in lines four, five and six. Fo'c'sle, take in two, keep the slack out of one and three."

With lines one and three snugged to the pier, the wind easily pushed the *Hitchcock's* stern into the fairway.

Ingram called, "Take in one and three. All engines back one-third." "As soon as the orders were relayed, Ingram said, "Bo's'n mate of the watch; sound one long blast and three short blasts."

Conversation was impossible as the melancholy, baritone notes of *Hitch-*

cock's foghorn echoed loudly over Long Beach Harbor. Ingram and De Reuter faced aft as her screws bit the water, wind whipping their topcoats as she gained sternway. As soon as Sailors on the pier cast off lines one and three, the fo'c'sle Jack was lowered and the National Ensign quickly hoisted up the mast, where it snapped in the breeze.

De Reuter waved away the tugs, as they backed toward the main channel.

Ingram said, "Captain?"

"*Ja.*"

"Okay," said Ingram.

"Hokay, what?"

"Hilda's cooking sounds mighty nice."

"Goot. Now let's see you make this old girl do a polka."

23

25 March, 1943
  U.S.S. *Hitchc*ock (DD 357)
  Ten Miles South of San Clemente Island
  Coast of Southern California

The moon had yet to rise, but the water was calm, the air balmy with hardly a breath of wind. Under darken ship routine, the *Hitchcock* steamed at a lazy twelve knots, rolling easily through a star-laden night. It was a far cry from the mini-chubasco day when she had shoved off into rough seas, half the crew becoming seasick. Now, at ten in the evening, seasickness was farthest from their minds. After ten days of continual battle problems, they were dog-tired and had just turned in, the ship's somnolent motion acting like knockout drops.

They'd drilled non-stop at surface and anti-air gunfire drills, engineering drills, casualty drills, damage control drills, anti-submarine drills, communication drills, and replenishment at sea drills. De Reuter had driven Ingram hard and Ingram had driven the officers and men hard. Ingram had seen most of it before, but he was being evaluated on his ability to command, not simply do drills. This evening, after a hurried dinner, they plunged into another battle problem, firing their five-inch cannons at San Clemente Island, simulating a night shore bombardment. Promptly at nine thirty, De Reuter called 'secure,' left a wake up call for 0630, stepped into his sea cabin and snapped off his lights.

After two surface gunfire exercises early next morning, the rest of the day was to be given over to clean-up, while running at full power for Long Beach, eighty miles to the north. Scheduled to arrive at 1600, they planned to sound liberty call at 1630, letting the men head into the downtown gin mills.

Ingram looked forward to a quiet weekend at home, writing to Helen and scratching Fred's ears. All he wanted was to sit on the porch and watch and listen to the neighborhood. He also wanted to plant a victory garden in the back yard, now overgrown with weeds. Turning the soil would be honest back-breaking work. After that, he would hoe and rake, then put in seed: carrots, radishes and corn sounded good. If there was time, maybe he would try to get to know old Mrs. Peabody a little better.

The evening watch was set with Ingram's eyes feeling as if they were propped open with toothpicks. *Time to hit the hay.*

"Coffee Skipper?" It was Seltzer waving a steaming mug.

"Thanks." Ingram took the mug and wrapped his hands around it, hopping it would ease his nightmares.

Seltzer moved off, leaving Ingram alone on the starboard bridgewing. He looked around, seeing only the shadowy figure of the starboard lookout up on the pilot house. The pilot house's interior glowed softly with the red darken-ship lights. He gazed over the side, watching the bow wave churn small pools of plankton to a brilliant turquoise, oval-shaped luminescence. The ship rolled lazily, and Ingram wedged himself against the bulwark, letting her motion carry him back and forth. He felt himself relax, as if he were a child in a cradle, his mother rocking him from side to side. Above, the masthead swept across near-black skies, adorned with thousands of tiny beacons. At darkened ship, the view was unencumbered by running and deck lights, the spectacle brilliant, the stars overhead innumerable.

Taking a deep breath, he sipped his coffee thinking of Helen: her dark ebony hair; her skin; those eyes, so quick and full of mirth; loving eyes that grabbed you and took you in, only to let you go, feeling fulfilled and worthy. He wondered where she was now. He'd called that gum-clacking

Sergeant Thorpe a week ago Saturday, but the man was no help. Each time Ingram tried to pin him down, Thorpe became more evasive. Then Colonel Moore picked up the line. Once again, Ingram slammed the phone down.

God, he missed her. But how to find her?

Seltzer materialized from the darkness and asked, "More coffee, Skipper?"

Ingram looked down, surprised he had downed the whole mug. "No thanks. I better hit the rack." From his stance, Ingram knew something was on Seltzer's mind. "What is it, Leo?"

"Scuttlebutt has it that Captain Landa wants to salv*age* the *Howell*."

"Yes, he stayed in Tulagi to coordinate the operation." Ingram took a breath. It felt strange talking about Landa.

"Skipper, uh..."

"Yes?"

"Word has it, Sir, that you decked the skipper." His inflection said, 'What the hell did you do that for? Boom Boom Landa is a sailor's sailor.'

Actually, Ingram had been surprised that a squad of MPs wasn't there to arrest him each time the Coronado flying boat landed to refuel on its flight to the forty-eight states. Why hadn't Landa or Rocko Myszynski had him clapped in irons and pressed charges? What's Landa doing now? Does he have a black eye? He hit the deck pretty hard. Was anything else injured? "Maybe--"

"--Sir?" It was Peterson, an acne-faced young ensign standing one of his first officer of the deck watches.

"Yes?"

"There's a strange buzzing."

"What?"

"In the pilot house, Mr. Ingram. We can't figure out what the heck it means," said Peterson.

Seltzer shrugged.

"Okay." Ingram walked in the pilot house. Two quartermasters, stood over the chart table, their heads cocked toward the bulkhead, the red lights giving them a satanic aura.

"What is it?" Ingram demanded.

One of the quartermasters put a finger to his lips and bent lower. "It's coming from around here," he said.

Zzzzzt. Zzzzzt.

Now Ingram heard it.

"I think its underneath," said Seltzer.

Ingram stooped and peered under the table but it was too dark. He held out a hand. "Flashlight."

One plopped in his hand and he clicked it on finding a mish-mash of bulkhead mounted relays and devices that looked like the back door buzzers found in an average home. He crawled under the table and reached out to touch one.

Zzzzzt.

It's knocker intermittently whacked the bell. But the bell had been painted over so many times that its sound was softly muted. There was a brass label as well, but it too, had long ago been painted over. An ancient Navy maxim: *If it doesn't move, paint it.*

"Leo. It's that one. Scrape the label and see what it says," said Ingram.

"Sir." Seltzer flipped open his bosun's knife which was half buoy knife, half stiletto, and scraped on the label next to the ringing bell. "Can you hold that light closer, Sir?"

"Sure."

"Okay." Seltzer scraped, then drew a sharp breath.

"What?" barked Ingram. He was tired and irritable.

"Jesus, Sir. It says 'magazine fire and sprinkler alarm.'"

Good God! "Which one?"

Seltzer's scraped frantically. "Forward!"

Braced on his hands, Ensign Peterson peered under the chart table. "Does that mean there's a fire in the magazine? We could blow up!"

It could mean a number of things, young man, thought Ingram. None of them good. He whacked the ensign on the leg. "Sound General Quarters, Mr. Peterson."

Peterson hit the gong lever. Seltzer crawled out, stood at the 1 MC, flipped all the switches, and said sharply, "Now general quarters. General quarters. Man your Battle Stations. This is no drill."

As he stood, Ingram imagined the *Hitchcock's* sailors, incredulous after only a half-hour of desperate sleep, blinking open their red-rimmed eyes, rousing from their bunks, cursing, and pulling on their pants. But rouse they did, the ship coming alive as two hundred and fifty-five tired and grumbling men rushed about, manning their battle and damage control stations. Ingram moved out to starboard bridgewing as the general quarters team rushed in to relieve the regular watch. As soon as Seltzer took the sound powered phones and reported damage control central manned and ready, Ingram called for inspection of all magazines, particularly the forward one.

"...vat is it?" A hatless Roland De Reuter lumbered onto the bridgewing. Bare spindly legs and shower sandals stuck from underneath his heavy Navy topcoat.

Ingram waited for Peterson, the officer of the deck, to report to his Captain. But his mouth quivered and he was rooted to the spot.

"Vat?" Demanded de Reuter.

"Magazine sprinkler alarm, Captain, forward magazine," said Ingram.

De Reuter slapped his forehead. "Mine Gott."

Seltzer keyed his mike and said, "Bridge Aye." Then he turned to De Reuter and said, "Repair One is at the forward magazine, Captain. Starboard bulkhead is red-hot. They request permission to flood."

"Awww, shit," said Peterson.

Ingram growled through clenched teeth. "Stow it, Ensign." Then the visage of the *Barber* ripping apart jumped into his mind with a blinding flash. Men and five inch gun barrels and wreckage twirled hundreds of feet into the air over the Kula Gulf. His adrenalin thumped as if his bloodstream was under 3,000 pounds of pressure. A glance at De Reuter told him nothing; the man's face was cloaked in darkness.

Half-panicked men jostled around them, and Ingram found himself pressed against the bridge bulwark, facing outboard. Pools of brilliant turquoise luminescence bounced up and down the bow wake. The water looked inviting, safe, comforting; something he needed right now. He braced his foot on a bracket. *Go! Jump!* He pushed, knowing the sea would be a more friendly place than the white-hot explosion that would soon kill everyone aboard the *Hitchcock*.

His foot slipped.

Again!

He pushed once more. But something held him down.

"Mister Ingram. Do ve flood?" It was De Reuter, standing in the pilot-house hatchway. He was partially obscured by shocked sailors, their eyes darting in their sockets like half-panicked cows in the Chicago stockyards. It seemed they hoped for De Reuter to pass the word to abandon ship. Peterson hadn't helped things, and for the moment, Ingram would like to have wrung the little bastard's neck for getting the crew all worked up.

Ingram tried again to push off again but someone...it was Seltzer, held onto his shirt tail.

"How we doin' Skipper?" whispered Seltzer.

"Verdammit!" De Reuter shoved his way through to Ingram. "Vot should ve do? I want you to recommend something."

Too late now. Ingram eased his foot off the bracket. "Sir. Have the fire party enter and investigate the compartment. If there is a fire, then they should attempt to extinguish or suppress it with fire retardant. If it's really bad, then we should flood. If there is no fire, they should search for the cause of the red-hot bulkhead."

Seltzer stood close to Ingram, his vice-like grip still holding a handful of Ingram's khaki shirttail

"Let go, damnit," Ingram muttered to Seltzer.

"Vat?" said De Reuter.

Think. "Uhhh-the fire crew should be in asbestos suits, Sir," said Ingram.

"Goot." De Reuter nodded to Seltzer. "Make it so. Report as soon as possible."

Standing between the two, Seltzer pushed his talk button to relay the order while still holding onto Ingram's shirt with his other hand.

"Now, ve vait." De Reuter looked down and studied the deck, his hands on his hips. Peterson re-joined the group, sensing some sort of bizarre salvation among them. The rest of the chalk-faced bridge crew stared at the four men, their eyes focused on De Reuter and Ingram, as the U.S.S. *Hitchcock* steamed on a calm, blissful night off San Clemente Island.

Seltzer whipped a hand to his ear. The others watched closely, as the boatswain's mate listened and nodded. At length he said, "Repair One reports all secure, Sir. There was no fire. The bulkhead turned red-hot from an over-head power cable to the compartment light. The ammo handlers forgot to turn off the light after GQ. Apparently it was corroded and parted from the light fixture after they secured from tonight's shoot. It worked loose and swung down and grounded against the bulkhead, which made it turn red-hot. Power's been shut off, repairs to the cable are now underway." Seltzer gave a thin smile and stepped away saying, "Captain." Then he let go of Ingram's shirt.

De Reuter shook his head. "These old damned ships. Poof. We coulda gone up like the *Juneau*." Last October, the cruiser U.S.S. *Juneau* inexplicably exploded a day after retiring from fierce night fighting off Guadalcanal. All, except three of her crew of 700, perished, including the five Sullivan brothers. "This is cowshit, these old ships. This one shoulda been shot up for target practice years ago."

De Reuter punched Ingram lightly on the shoulder. "Not bad for the real thing. Not bad. Combat experience shows. Another of Boom Boom Landa's boys hast chust come through." Then he spun, walked back into his sea cabin and shut the door.

During the excitement, a half moon had risen, casting a silvery glow in the eastern sky. Ingram hardly noticed, while pleading with his heart to stop thumping wildly.

Seltzer, still standing by his side surrendered his sound powered phones to the regular watch-stander. After the man moved off, Seltzer said in a low voice, "Guess what, Sir?"

Ingram turned, to look at this man who had kept him from making a fool of himself. He almost asked, 'Why didn't you let me jump?' Instead, he said, "Yes?"

"Freddie Lang, the chief in charge of the repair party is an old friend, Sir."

"Come on, Leo, I'm tired."

"He let me in on it."

"On what?"

Seltzer looked from side to side then said quietly, "It's a set-up. They do it every time. Captain De Reuter has a hand-picked crew of fifteen trained guerillas. They worked like hell to empty the magazine in ten minutes flat. After that, they fire up the bulkhead."

It hit Ingram what Seltzer was telling him. No ammunition in the magazine meant the ship couldn't possibly have exploded. "De Reuter was pulling our chains?"

"Pretty slick, huh?" Seltzer's face glowed in the soft moonlight.

"I'll be damned." Ingram looked aft to the Hitchcock's wake. He would be about six or seven miles straight back if he'd had his way. Then he wondered if Seltzer knew about this before or after the drill. "Leo?"

Ingram turned but Seltzer was gone.

24

28 March, 1943
San Pedro, California

"He's a good boy, Mr. Ingram." Mrs. Peabody reached over to scratch the grey tabby cat behind its ears, "except..."

Ingram sat in a wicker chair on the front porch. It was still warm, and the Western sky flared with amazing reds and pinks as the sun dipped behind the hill. Fred lay stretched in his lap, sleeping. "Except what, Mrs. Peabody?"

Mrs. Peabody was a widow with grey-hair tied in a bun, She wore a polka-dot dress, was a bit portly, had rimless spectacles, and layer upon layer of laugh lines ranged around her thin lips and droopy eyes. She leaned down and whispered *sotto voce* for the second time -- the first time was to complain about old Mr. Templeton across the street and his organ music. As she did, Ingram swore he smelled beer on Mrs. Peabody's breath. He knew she canned preserves, and Ingram would have laid odds that she brewed her own beer.

She braced her hands on her knees, "Well, Fred snores...and...and..."

"And what?"

Her mouth spread into a wide grin. "He drinks from the toilet." She leaned back and gave a guffaw, which sounded like a hand-me-down from the now departed Mr. Peabody, a railroad engineer who had been with the Southern Pacific for thirty-five years. "I can't break him. Maybe you can figure something out?"

Ingram scratched. Fred raised his head, blinked, and fell back to sleep. "I'll do my best. Maybe set out a bowl of water..."

Mrs. Peabody looked up.

"Yes?" Ingram asked.

"Think I hear my phone. Excuse me." She hurried next door to her home. It was no wonder Ingram hadn't heard the phone's ringing. With five-inch guns cracking in his ears for two weeks, it was a miracle he could hear at all. Friday evening he had done some grocery shopping, cooked himself a meal, and sat in the living room, falling asleep with the radio going. He slept until ten on Saturday morning and, after a big breakfast, phoned his parents in Echo, Oregon, saying he would try to get up there before he shipped out. He wasn't sure if he could do it, but he vowed to try. Then he tromped into the back yard, dug the soil and planted his victory garden.

Mrs. Peabody didn't have to return Fred. He sort of delivered himself, ambling onto the Victory garden, as Ingram hoed a row for carrots. After watching for a while, Fred dug in the freshly cultivated soil and pooped while Ingram glowered.

With the exercise, Ingram easily collapsed Saturday night, sleeping eleven hours. He went to church Sunday morning, then came home, mowed the front lawn, trimmed the bushes, and watered. Now, in the early evening, he took a deep breath, leaned back, and languished in the chair. One could say, he had everything: a house, three square meals, Helen's cat, Helen's lingering perfume scent -- everything but Helen. In a way it was too much. Without Helen, it meant nothing. He wondered if he should just pack it up, head for the base, and stay in the BOQ until they gave him orders to a ship. Also. He felt guilty about not getting up to Oregon but the railroads were jammed. He wasn't sure if he could get back on time.

The horizon had turned a dark crimson, becoming a cobalt-blue as the first stars popped out. The Kraft Music Hall with Bing Crosby was on the radio tonight, Helen's favorite show. But that was in an hour or so. What to--

"Mr. Ingram! Mr. Ingram!" Mrs. Peabody shouted from her porch. Then she started running, almost tripping over her boxwood hedge. Her arms flailed in front of her as she waddled up the walk.

"What?"

Mrs. Peabody heaved great gulps of air and her face was flushed.

Ingram jumped to his feet.

"...telephone..." She pointed inside his house.

"Yes, telephone?"

After another gasp she managed, "...that was Mrs. Ingram on my phone. She's calling from some, place," she wheezed. "South America. She didn't know you were home. She..."

The phone rang in Ingram's house. He looked at her.

"Yes, yes. Go." She nodded quickly, her hand clamped to her chest.

Ingram dashed in the house and yanked the phone off the cradle. "Hello!"

Static ranged on the line. Then he heard a string of Spanish. No it wasn't Spanish. Portuguese?

He shouted, "Hello!"

"Todd. My God."

"Helen. You sound beautiful. Where are you?" He sat heavily on the couch.

"Todd, my God," she laughed.

"Helen, enough of the 'My Gods.' Where are you?"

"Natal, Brazil. Waiting for a hop over to Dakar."

"Dakar? That's Africa." Ingram felt as if the phone in his hand had turned to ice.

"Yes." They listened to static for a moment then she said, "What are you doing home?"

Ingram relayed a quick sanitized version of the *Howell*, then said, "So I just finished two weeks of prospective commanding officer training. They called yesterday saying I'm fully qualified for command. They're giving me a ship."

"...wonderful"

Todd sensed the connection going sour. Quickly, he said, "I love you so damned much, honey."

"...me too.. When do you..."

The line crackled loudly and he had to hold the phone from his ear. Then he heard a string of Portuguese. Suddenly, the line was clear. An operator said, "Hello Natal? This is the United States calling. Hello?"

Silence.

"Hello. California?"

"Yes."

"Sir, I'm sorry. The connection is lost."

"Can you try again?"

"Sorry. I don't have the number."

"Oh...thank you." Ingram hung up.

Fred jumped in his lap and Ingram scratched his ears. After a minute or so, he heard a foot scrape on the porch. He walked out to find Mrs. Peabody pacing. "Mrs. Peabody, I can't thank you enough."

"How did she sound?"

Rather than sugar-coat it, Ingram relayed what happened. "...so then the U.S. operator came on the line and that was it. The connection went dead. We really didn't get to talk that much."

"Oh, my. Did she say anymore about where she was."

"Natal, Brazil. That's a jumping off place for Dakar, Africa. What did she tell you?"

"Well, she told me she was still sending letters to you to," she swept a hand, "you know, out there. She asked about Fred and the house. I'm afraid I blurted something about the stranger last Thursday night. Then I told her about you and to call home. That's when---"

"Stranger? What stranger?"

"Didn't I tell you?"

"No." Ingram offered Mrs. Peabody a wicker chair.

"No, thank you. I have to go back. But yes, it was a little after ten. I swear I saw an officer, you know, a Navy officer, on your property."

"Doing what?"

"Well, Fred jumped up to my front window and started scratching up a storm. So I peeked out and there he was, ringing your doorbell. With your house being dark and all that, he walked around the side. After a few moments, I walked out to see what was going on. I'll tell you, I let the screen door squeak when I opened it. Then I slammed it behind me. Almost right away, he walked out the sideyard and down the street and around the corner."

"A Navy officer?"

"Well, I think so. He had a white officer's cap, a dark uniform and...you know...gold rings on his sleeves."

"How many?"

She rubbed her ample chin. "Don't know, two, maybe three."

"Did you see his face?"

"Dark hair. That's all I remember."

They talked for a while longer with Ingram promising to tell Mrs. Peabody if he heard again from Helen.

Fred jumped on his chest and started prancing up and down. "Wha...?" Ingram checked his alarm clock: It was ten after three.

Now the cat jumped off the bed, ran out to the living room then skittered back in, sliding under the bed.

Ingram sat on the bed's edge, scratched his head and yawned. Then he turned on the bedside light.

Tap. Tap.

He jumped. Looking out the window, he saw Mrs. Peabody's porch light flip on.

Tap. Tap. It came from the front porch. Ingram walked to the doorway and peeked around the door jam into the living room. A shadowy figure was framed in the front door window. He was clad in black with a white combination cap. Mrs. Peabody's Navy officer! The figure must have seen him, for now he knocked.

Ingram strode across the living room and flipped on the porch light. It was a Navy officer. The man looked up. Startled.

Landa!

"I'll be damned," said Ingram, a smile on his face. He undid the chain, flipped open the lock and opened the door. "Jerry?"

"Todd, mind if I come in?"

"Sure." Ingram opened the door and stood aside to let Landa pass. That's when Landa hauled off and threw a right cross, solidly connecting to Ingram's cheek. He fell backward against the door and sank to the floor...

He came to on the bathroom floor. After blinking at the ceiling for a moment, he heard voices. One said, "Are you sure he's okay?"

"He's fine." It was Landa. "He just went in the head for a moment." Then Landa and Mrs. Peabody started arguing.

"Uhhh." Ingram rose to a sitting position.

Heavy footsteps approached the bathroom door. Someone knocked and called, "Hello? Mr. Ingram?"

"Yes?" Ingram rose, his legs wobbly. After finding his balance, he felt his cheek, and looked in the mirror. Swollen. Maybe a black eye tomorrow.

"Open up, please." Footsteps shuffled at the door.

"Who's there?"

"Officer Bullard. San Pedro Police."

Good God! Ingram opened the door to find a police officer standing before him, wearing a leather jacket, and knee-high motorcycle boots, his cap tucked under his arm. Another motorcycle officer stood near the front door between a bug-eyed Mrs. Peabody and Jerry Landa. Ingram remembered he wore only skivvies and instinctively crossed his hands over his crotch.

"Dear me." Mrs. Peabody covered her eyes.

"Sorry." Ingram reached behind the bathroom door, lifted his bathrobe off the hook and quickly put it on. He walked out, pushing hair from his face.

Landa and Mrs. Peabody started talking at once. Bullard stepped between them, his palms straight out. "Awright. Awright. We can settle this easily right now." Bullard turned and said, "Mr. Ingram, do you know this man?" He nodded to Landa.

"Yes, Sir. He's my commanding officer."

"Well, then. What happened?"

Mrs. Peabody screeched, "It's the man from last Thursday night. He hit Mr. Ingram." Then she belched. Red-faced, she covered her mouth.

Ingram rubbed his cheek. "I heard something at the front door. I opened it and there was Commander Landa. Then I slipped. It was, er, dark."

"No lights?

"I hadn't turned them on."

Bullard turned to Landa. "Commander, you picked the damndest time to show up."

"Plane just got in from Brooklyn. Damned coast-to-coast flight; bouncing around. Tired." He lowered his eyes. "...emergency leave..."

"Why didn't you ring the bell?"

"I did. It doesn't work," said Landa.

Bullard nodded to the cop at the front door who reached outside and pushed the button. Nothing.

"I didn't know it was broken," said Ingram.

Bullard walked up and examined the red weal on Ingram's cheek. "Ummm. Nasty." He looked over his shoulder at Landa and said softly, "You sure you know this guy?"

"I know him very well. He was the captain of my ship. I was his executive officer. We just got back from overseas."

Bullard stepped back and scratched his head. "Wait a minute. Ingram, Ingram. Do you have a wife named Helen?"

"Yes! Why?" Ingram's hands went to his hips.

Bullard grinned and told the story about the night he steered Helen and Laura Dutton away from Shanghai-Red's to Olsen's restaurant. Then he put on his cap and walked for the door. "Welcome back, you guys. Where were you, anyway?"

Ingram and Landa looked at each other, then shrugged.

"Military secret, huh? Somewhere in the South Pacific, I'll bet. Well, you're okay in my book. Anything you want, just call. And I hope the Missus doesn't mind that I told the story. Say how is she?" He looked toward the bedroom to find Fred sitting in the doorway, blinking.

"On her way to Africa." Ingram quickly gave Bullard details. Behind, he saw Landa's shoulders sag as he relayed the story.

"Well, I'm sorry. Hope she returns soon. Okay, folks. That's it for us. Goodnight." Bullard and his partner walked out.

Ingram thanked a confused Mrs. Peabody for her vigilance. Finally, she beat a retreat.

After a long moment, Landa cleared his throat. "We even?"

"Yes, we're even. Sit, Jerry, sit." Ingram sat on the couch, massaging his cheek.

"Can I stay? The BOQ is jammed."

The whole issue of Landa's refusal to use proximity fuses flooded Ingram's mind. But he was so glad to see Landa, he decided to let it ride. "Promise to clean up after the cat?"

"If you're in a pinch."

"The guest room is yours. And your brother's trunk is in there."

"I'll go through it tomorrow." Landa opened the door, retrieved his B-4 bag off the front porch and shoved it into the middle of the floor. Then he sat heavily.

"How is...your brother?"

"Didn't make it. Infection set in."

"Oh, Jerry. God. I'm sorry."

Landa looked into space and nodded, his lips pressed together.

"Where did you bury him?

"...cemetery in Brooklyn." Landa sniffed.

"I wish I could say something."

"You don't have to."

"Coffee?"

"No, no, thanks. I'm ready for the sack. Except for one thing." He straightened up. "About this proximity fuse business."

"Yes," said Ingram, glad that Landa had brought it up.

"There are tin-can skippers out there who agree with me. They don't trust those things either. New, untested. High failure rates. Hell, Todd, we didn't know a damned thing about these VT's until good ole' Frank Ashton sashayed out there kissing everybody's butt."

"But Rocko ordered you to use them."

Landa thrust out his chin. "How did you find out?"

Ingram admitted to eavesdropping while he waited for travel orders across the companionway from Rocko's office.

"Hmff. So that's what set you off. Yes. Rocko did order me to use them. I didn't and I'm sorry about that. Sorry for not obeying an order, but not sorry about those damn VTs. I'll tell you, Todd. I've made peace with myself and I've made peace with Rocko." He sighed and went on. "Besides there's stuff I just can't tell anybody about this. What I can say is when I look up and see a

Jap diving right on me, I'd rather use something that's tried and tested like the Mark 18 fuse, rather than some Frank Ashton whiz-bang bullshit that has no performance back-up."

Ingram exhaled and couldn't help but reflect that it was a whiz-bang Jap dive-bomber that planted a bomb in the *Howell's* after engine room, blowing her in half. But then, he considered, VT fuse or not, that bomb would have found its way to the engine room, anyway. The Val had come from another direction and they just weren't ready. With no firing solution, he couldn't blame Landa, or fuses, or anyone else. More properly, he should have blamed himself for not being vigilant. In a way, the men being trapped in the after section was his fault, not Landa's. His shoulders slumped and he looked up, watery eyed. "I still think about Edgerton, hot lips, whatever the hell we called him. All those guys back there, screaming. All the time, I dream. All the time, I---"

"---Todd, damnit."

"No, you, damnit," he fairly yelled. "You don't know what it's like. You snapped out of it because you're strong. You're so damned strong you've muscles in your shit!" He stood and pointed. "You're not like me. It doesn't bother you. It--"

"---Shut up!"

Ingram sat, too tired to carry on.

"It still rips me up," Landa said, looking in the distance. "But bitching about it doesn't help. Yes, I am like you. I dream. But don't forget what we once agreed to."

"What?"

"*Let the dead bury the dead.*"

Ingram leaned forward and dropped his head in his hands. Quietly, he said, "I almost jumped overboard the other night. If it hadn't been for Seltzer, I would have."

"Bullshit."

"Scared the hell out of me." Ingram told him about De Reuter's red-hot magazine bulkhead stunt.

"Roland's still pulling that gag? Don't worry, you wouldn't have jumped."

"But I tried."

Landa picked up his B-4 bag and yawned. "Todd. Sometimes you really are a horse's ass."

"What?"

"If you really wanted to jump, you would have jumped, Leo Seltzer or not. Did you crap your pants?"

"No." Another phrase hit Ingram: Hemingway. *Don't look forward or back. Stay in neutral. Live for now and the time of your next meal.* "

"So how did you do?"

"Roland recommended me for command. They're giving me a ship."

Landa stuck out his hand. "That's swell, Todd. Congratulations. Which one?"

"*Pence.* Just about finished an overhaul in Melbourne. She'll be headed for Tulagi, soon. I'll be working for Rocko."

"Ralph Druckman's ship?"

"I think that's right."

"You lucky bastard, She's newer than the *Howell.* And Druckman's a hell of a skipper. You'll have a great crew."

Ingram gave a thin smile.

"We'll have to celebrate." Landa looked at his watch and rubbed his eyes. "Tomorrow."

"Right." Then it dawned on Ingram, "What's going on with the *Howell*? Can you really salvage her?"

"We've got Halsey sold. Now we're waiting for an ATF to haul her off the beach. In the meantime, there's something I have to do here."

"Yes?"

"I should go see Luther's widow. Laura? Was that her name?"

"Yes. But I wrote her a letter. I should be the one to go."

"No. He was one of my officers. I'll do it." He pulled out a rumpled piece of paper. "...NBC Studios in Hollywood. Woopie."

"Maybe you'll get discovered."

"Just my luck." Landa walked toward the guest bedroom. He stopped and said, "Your next door neighbor, Mrs. Peabody?"

Ingram yawned. "What a firecracker, huh?"

"Except she said I was the man from last Thursday night?"

"Yes?"

"Not me, buddy. Last Thursday night, I was in Brooklyn."

25

29 March, 1943
Hollywood, California

A soft spring rain had washed the city clean, and now it sparkled under a golden sun and rich blue skies. The trolley car merrily rattling down Hollywood Boulevard was jammed full of grinning soldiers, Sailors and Marines. Jerry Landa was lucky to have a seat. But he was uncomfortable in his dress blues, as the late morning grew warmer and warmer. It had been an arduous, two hour trolley car ride up from San Pedro, including a thirty minute wait in the downtown Pacific Electric terminal; but finally, he'd made it here and was anxious to get off. He stood, and his seat was instantly occupied by an Army Private who had trouble smoking a cigarette and chewing gum at the same time, a boy really. He joined his buddies at a window and they leaned out, waving at a pair of young girls sauntering down the sidewalk, their skirts billowing in a light breeze.

They whistled and howled. The cigarette-smoking, gum-chewing Private yelled, "Hi ya, toots."

The girls accepted it all nonchalantly, smiling and waving back.

The trolley picked up speed and swayed, its bell clanging mightily. Landa reached up and grabbed an overhead strap. *God love those kids. Looks like their first time on liberty. Have a good one boys, for in a couple of months, you're going to be men, and you're not going to quite understand why. Worse. Some of you won't be coming back.*

Landa caught himself. *Stop it. That's not why you're here.*

Two blocks later, the conductor shouted "Vine Street." The trolley slowed, then lurched to a stop. Landa jostled his way out with about twenty other servicemen and walked south. Two blocks later, he stood before his destination. A two story art deco building, it was the West Coast headquarters of NBC studios. Landa walked up the main steps and wove his way past a long line of people that ended at a theater window with a sign reading: RADIO SHOW TICKETS. He pushed through a pair of heavy glass doors, his heels clicking on the glossy black tile of a vast lobby. The only furniture was an empty large desk sitting before a bank of heavy plate glass windows. On the other side, stood an impressive array of floor to ceiling radio-transmitting equipment. Inside, men wearing white lab coats paced before the machines with clipboards, peering at gauges and taking readings.

Someone walked up behind him, "May I help you?"

Landa turned to find a balding uniformed guard with deep crevices in his face. A name tag read: JENKINS.

"Er, yes, I'm trying to find the NBC symphony orchestra."

"What in the world for?" Jenkins gave a dry smile and looked Landa up and down.

Landa removed his cap and said, "Well...er Dutton. Laura Dutton. I'm here to see her."

"I'm sorry, Sir. There's no Laura Dutton here. Now if you don't mind stepping---"

"---West. I forgot. You probably know her as Laura West. That's who I'm here to see."

Jenkins looked at Landa as he were a Nazi spy. "I'm sorry, Sir. The orchestra is in rehearsal and in any case, we can't allow any one back there to---"

Landa produced his best gleaming grin. "Hold on, Pal. I'm not here for autographs. Laura is married to a shipmate of mine. Actually, a guy in my crew." And then his face turned somber. "The guy was killed, and I'm here to pay my respects."

"Oh." Then he rubbed his chin. "Well, you should try her at home."

"I don't have the address. Everything is so private here in Hollywood, you know." Actually that wasn't quite the truth. Landa had tried many times to call Laura West, but the line was always busy.

"But if her husband lived with her..."

"This is where she works. Their real home is---was in Phoenix, Arizona."

"Well..."

"Look, Pal. I've got a ship to catch and a war to fight. All I want to do is give her my best wishes on behalf of the *Howell's* crew and see if there is anything I can do for her."

"Very well. Wait here."

"Thanks. Just tell her the *Howell's* Captain, Jerry Landa, is out here." The guard walked off and Landa strolled back to the plate glass to watch the radio engineers.

Three minutes later, Jenkins was back accompanied by another guard. "He said, "I'm sorry, Sir. The orchestra is in rehearsal and no one is permitted in or out. Now if you don't mind, please step outside. Perhaps you'd like a ticket to the Red Skelton show; the line just opened." Jenkins waved a palm at the front door and reached for Landa's elbow.

Landa said, "Hold on. I didn't come all the way up here just to take a load from two 4-F flunkies who can't even wipe their noses."

"You heard the man, Mac." The other guard stepped up and curled a lip.

"One moment, please."

It was a slender middle age woman with blond-silver hair pulled back into a bun. What amazed Landa was that she was over six feet. With grey-blue eyes, Landa figured she must have been a knock-out when she was young. She asked, "Is this man right? Were you Luther's commanding officer?"

Keeping his eye on the guards, Landa said, "Yes, 'mam.'"

"What ship?" she asked.

"*Howell.*"

"I'm Roberta Thatcher. Please come with me."

"But Mrs. Thatcher. This guy doesn't---" said Jenkins.

Roberta Thatcher spun and faced the guard. Actually, she looked down at him. "He's coming with me, Jenkins."

"Okay, okay. But don't blame me if..."

"If what?" she asked.

Jenkins shrugged and walked away. Soon, the other guard followed.

Roberta Thatcher turned and walked through a double door and into a rabbit-warren of wide corridors, vestibules and stairwells. She took a flight of stairs and walked toward the rear of the building, her heels clicking on the linoleum. Turning this way and that, Landa lost track of where they were. Mercifully, they drew up at a door simply marked: REHEARSAL 246.

Across the way, a door opened and a stout man with a thin moustache walked out. Landa recognized Xavier Cugat, who looked him up and down, smiled, and walked down the hall.

"Ahem." It was Roberta Thatcher.

"Yes?"

"There is a problem."

"Yes?"

"Mrs. West, er, Dutton is taking her husband's death rather hard."

Landa said dryly, "Well, she hasn't had a lot of practice."

Instantly, Mrs. Thatcher drew up to her full height and inhaled deeply.

"I'm sorry. That was below the belt." Landa really did regret saying what he did and wished he could take it back.

For the first time, her face softened. "I know. It must be terrible out there. You're very kind to stop by." She reached down and opened a door. "Go on inside. You'll see what I mean. I hope you can help her." She pushed the door a little wider and piano music drifted out.

"What?"

"Please. Go on in. And when you're ready, I'll get you a pass to the artist's cafeteria for lunch. If Mr. Cugat is still there, he might give you his autograph."

"Well, thanks." Landa walked in and the door was closed behind him. It was a large room, perhaps twenty by thirty. And dark. Only one floor lamp illuminated the ceiling. A few folding chairs and music racks were scattered about. In the far corner stood a gleaming black concert piano. An open window gave on to what Landa guessed was an alley. Outside, Landa could see the HOLLYWOODLAND sign in the hills greened by the recent rains. A woman was silhouetted before the window, playing something classical he realized. He felt at a loss, as the only music he knew anything about was Spike Jones.

Stepping closer, he found her hair was an uncombed sandy brown which jutted in every direction. In fact, it looked unwashed and ratted. Clear rimless glasses were fixed on her nose and she played with her eyes closed so he couldn't tell the color.

A half empty bottle of scotch sat on the piano. Beside that was a tumbler with about two fingers-worth. It's odor drifted about the room; the unbridled smell of the cheap stuff.

She was mashing her music, Landa could tell. On occasion, her finger often jabbed two keys at the same time. Once in a while she would stop and redo the passage and it would sound beautiful. The rest of the time, she went back to mashing it.

Landa slowly removed his cap, tucked it under his arm and stepped close. In spite of her hair, Luther's wife was...beautiful. Nobody had told him but, he mused, why should they? And she was good on the piano, he could see it was a Steinway when she put her mind to it.

Open your eyes, Laura.

She did, and they found him at once. Immediately, her playing became precise, beautiful, very professional, like many artists who made it look ridiculously easy.

She put her hand to her mouth and gave a petit belch.

Landa smiled.

"I've been expecting you."

"Who? Me?" Landa made a show of looking around.

"They always send somebody, don't they?"

Time to get serious. "No, not always."

'I see."

"I'm Jerry Landa, Captain of the U.S.S. *Howell*." He didn't add that his ship was beached on a godforsaken bug-infested island in the South Pacific.

She didn't offer a hand. "Luther's commanding officer."

"Ummm."

"He spoke highly of you."

The music was beautiful and her eyes were green.

"What are you playing?"

"Moonlight Sonata." She emptied the tumbler in two loud gulps. "Pour me another blast?"

"Okay." Landa poured three fingers, corked the bottle and then took it across the room and plopped it on a desk.

"That's mean."

"So is life."

She kept playing, her eyes closed.

"Who is Roberta Thatcher?"

"Orchestra Manager."

"So, that's it." Landa ambled over and sat on a folding chair right beside her little bench, " You know, she thinks the world of you."

Laura stopped and looked at him with blood-shot eyes. She swayed a bit and grabbed the side of the piano to steady herself. "How did he die?"

"Very bravely. He was--"

"--I didn't ask for platitudes, Mr. Landa. I want you to tell me exactly how my husband died."

Landa felt hot and unbuttoned his blouse as he matter-of-factly explained to Laura West how her husband's molecular structure was irrevocably unraveled in one gigantic bright flash. He finished with, "...the...*Barber*...it just blew up. He felt no pain. Nothing was left to feel."

Her mouth fell open. "Todd didn't tell me that."

"He wasn't supposed to. By the way," He reached in his pocket and produced a card. "I'm bunking at the Ingram's until I ship out." He wrote down a number. "If you want to call, please---" He handed it over.

She swatted it aside. "Bastard," she hissed.

"What?"

"You dirty bastards, " she yelled. She stood and threw the empty tumbler at him. "You're alive and walking around and having fun and hitting the bars. Where you going tonight? The Strip? Ciro's maybe? Earl Carrolls? But what about my husband?" She screamed, spittle flying from her mouth. "What about him. About us? Me?" Her head fell into her hands and she cried softly, her body shaking.

Landa felt drawn to her and stepped up to wrap an arm around her.

"Get out, you bastard. Out!" She pointed to the door.

Angry with himself for mishandling the situation, Landa buttoned his blouse and growled, "It's over, Mrs. Dutton or West or whoever the hell you are today. The time for self-pity is over. There is nothing anybody can do. In a manner of speaking, I'd say Luther is better off where he is than having to put up with your self-serving crap. Well okay, toots. You can bet nobody will bother you again. Of course, they wont have to, because you'll be atop the slag heap very, very soon. And that's one thing I'm glad I don't have to explain to Luther." Donning his cap, Landa walked over, uncorked the scotch bottle then walked to the window and poured it into the alley. He let the bottle drop. After it crashed, he said, "Good bye." Then he walked out, slamming the door.

26

29 March, 1943
    Building 42, Long Beach Naval Station
    Long Beach, California

Ingram took the steps two at a time, glad that he was on time for his appointment with Frank Ashton. The four striper had called early this morning, asking Ingram to stop by at 0900: Room 226. Ingram had gone into a panic trying to dig out his best set of dress blues. Even at that, the gold rings were tinged with the green envied by neophytes and worn with pride by the old salts. Recalling how everything around Ashton seemed to glitter, Ingram fretted about his uniform, realizing there was nothing he could do about it. He lost time shining his shoes, and to top that the San Pedro ferry had to wait ten minutes as a pair of tugs nudged a huge floating dry dock from the Bethlehem Steel Shipyards, down the channel.

No matter, I'm here. The pasty-cream clapboard two-story structure reminded him of a reform school he'd once seen in East Portland. Built in the early 1930s as an administration building, it had walls of a spongy plywood painted an off-yellow; the floors were covered with green linoleum polished to a bright sheen. Inside, he was assaulted by jangling phones, as officers and white hats dashed back and forth. Some doors were marked AUTHORIZED PERSONNEL ONLY, where Marine guards stood at parade rest, their eyes fixed in the distance. But it was hard to understand the fabricated sense of urgency as people dashed about, their eyebrows knit as if on a mission that would win both the Atlantic and Pacific Wars at a single stroke.

He walked up the staircase and onto the second deck, finding Room 226, the second door on the left. It had a frosted glass door marked:

ELEVENTH NAVAL DISTRICT COMBAT SUPPORT UNIT
AUTHORIZED PERSONNEL ONLY.

Two marine guards stood before the door: a sergeant and a corporal. Both were at parade rest; both wore sidearms. Ingram stepped up to the Sergeant, flipped out his ID and said, "Commander Ingram to see Captain Ashton."

The Marine Sergeant looked closely at the ID. Then his eyes ranged over Ingram as he verified the stats. The Sergeant's face became long with obvious disappointment that he hadn't nabbed a Nazi spy. Taking a deep breath, he said "Yes, Sir. One moment, please."

The sergeant knocked twice on the door, then stuck his head inside. There was some muttering, then a thumping of footsteps. The door flew open with Frank Ashton filling the entrance. He thrust out a hand, a broad smile on his face, "Todd. Great to see you. Welcome aboard." Taking Ingram's arm, Ashton ushered him inside, letting the Marine close the door.

Ashton's impeccably-tailored blue trousers were pressed to knife-edge seams. His shoes were polished to a spit-shine radiance and his shirt was bleached to a brilliant white and set-off with monogrammed gold cufflinks bearing a filigreed 'A.' "How have you been? Coffee?" Ashton walked over to a mahogany side table with a silver carafe. China cups rattled. "Cream? Sugar? Here, let me take your coat."

"Yes, Sir. Coffee black, please." Ingram was a bit red-faced as he gave Ashton his coat with the tarnished two and a half stripes on each sleeve. On the other hand, Ashton seemed to think nothing of it, as he carefully inserted a lacquered mahogany wooden hanger, then hung it on a tree beside his own coat with four dazzling gold rings on each sleeve.

While Ashton fiddled with the coffee service, Ingram took in the office. It was perhaps twelve by twelve. An ornate partner's desk with a forest green leather top, stood in the middle. Red-leather diamond-tufted executive swivel chairs were placed at each end. On the right side of each desk were three telephone sets. Except for portraits of President Roosevelt and Chief of Naval Operations Admiral Ernest J. King, there were no wall coverings. A bank of file cabinets ran along one wall. A large floor safe, its double doors yawning open, was on the opposite wall which also accommodated a seven foot leather couch. Three soot covered windows gave onto an alley, the torpedo and optics buildings across the way.

Ashton set a cup of coffee before Ingram and waved to the partner's desk. "Not bad, huh? Been in my family for 150 years."

"It's beautiful. Thank you, Sir." Ingram sat and tried the coffee. It was excellent: The best he'd tasted since...since before the war.

A phone rang on Ashton's side. He picked it up, and said, "No, I can't now. Please tell the Admiral I'll call back in..." he pulled a cuff to reveal a gleaming silver Whittnauer Chronograph, "in fifteen minutes. And hold all my other calls, please. Yes, thanks." He hung up.

Ashton gazed at Ingram for a moment then. "Thanks for coming on such short notice, I hope you're not inconvenienced."

"Not at all, Captain."

Ashton sat at his desk and flashed a smile. "In here please call me Frank."

"Thank you, Sir, uh, Frank."

There was a moment of awkward silence, then Ashton slapped both palms on the desk. "Well, I hear you have a ship."

"Yes, Sir, Frank. The U.S.S. *Pence.*"

"And what is she?"

"Destroyer. *Fletcher* class. Like the *Howell.*"

"I see." A shadow crossed Ashton's face. "I really didn't have a chance to tell you. I'm sorry about all that *Howell* business. She was a good ship."

"She may fight again." Ingram filled Ashton in on Landa's plans to salvage the destroyer.

"Yes." Ashton seemed preoccupied and looked out the window. Even with it closed, muffled sounds of the shipyard came through. Drilling and lathing machinery screeched. A long semi-truck laden with coils of wire and barrels of hydraulic oil rumbled down the alley. The massive forge down the way was really felt more than heard as it thumped intermittently, making the ground shake.

"Todd, there's something I want to explain to you. Something that could make a real difference in your life."

In the comfortable diamond tufted chair, Ingram tried to sit up and appear as if he were at attention. "Yes, Sir?"

"Frank."

"Frank."

"You are cleared for Top Secret?"

"Yes, Sir."

"The United States is in a position to exploit technological opportunities of an unprecedented magnitude." Ashton said. "You've seen just the tip of the ice-berg with the proximity fuse business. Other things will be soon coming down the pipe. More sophisticated radar, jet aircraft, acoustic torpedoes, frequency hopping, cryptographic analysis of the highest proportions. Why, with our code-breaking capabilities we can just about," Ashton dropped his voice to a low tone, "understand everything the Japs are broadcasting on the airways."

"No kidding?"

"Yes. For example, right now, and I mean right now," Ashton snapped his fingers, "we can tell whether Yamamoto is wiping his nose or changing his pants. Now mind you, you didn't hear this from me, but that's where the United States is going. By golly, we'll have this war won by 1947, 1948 tops."

Ingram sat back, staggered. New radars? What the hell is an acoustic torpedo? Frequency hopping? Jets? He thought the Brits were leading in that area, not the U.S. And what was that about Yamamoto's pants? Breaking Jap codes? He hadn't heard anything about that since his days in the Philippines, but then, they'd sworn him to secrecy. And all he could think of to say was, "I had no idea."

"We're involved in all sorts of things. Things that are just about ready for introduction to the fleet, like I did with the proximity fuse." He flashed a grin. "You with me so far?"

"Okay so far, Frank."

Ashton smiled at that. "It's too much for me now to introduce all this stuff to the fleet. I need help, a special kind of person. Someone with recent experience. Someone who has been out there and has instant credibility, an unquestionable reputation, a team player." Ashton's eyes bored into Ingram.

The guy is pitching me, thought Ingram. For a moment, he felt as if he were frozen in his chair. But then it swiveled on its base and for some reason that made him relax. "I see."

Ashton said, "You get the idea. I need someone with your experience. People will easily buy into the concepts when they see your chest of medals. It's a big effort and we'll eventually need a large staff."

"Okay. But let me ask." Ingram waved at the frosted glass door and its inverted black lettering. "What's a Combat Support Unit?"

"A fancy name. Actually, we're not connected with the Eleventh Naval District. It's just a cover for the fact that we're main interface to the fleet from the Department of Terrestrial Magnetism."

"Terrestrial what?"

Ashton explained the role played by the Department of Terrestrial Magnetism and its development of the proximity fuse. He finished with. "We did it, Todd. In just two years, we developed that fuse. Its reliability is fifty percent, soon on its way to eighty percent. And now, we've harnessed all that brain power to bigger, more spectacular projects.

Ashton's smile, his delivery, his manner, his dress; everything about Ashton said, 'Win.' Ingram sipped the wonderful coffee and sat forward. "Okay, but what about my---"

"---I know, I know. Having your own command is a big deal, Todd. But we need you." Another grin. "Hell, I need you. Someone with the Navy Cross who can stick it to the doubters, the nay-sayers, and, in some cases, I'm sad to say, the cowards." Silence reigned for a moment. The forge thumped outside. Ashton said, "I can promise you your own command within a year, probably sooner. But, right now, you're needed here. There is just too much technical material that must get to the fleet immediately." He drummed his fingers. "Do you have your orders, yet?"

"Yes, Sir."

"Well, I can fix that. In fact," Ashton grinned conspiratorially, "I can damn near fix any orders."

"I see."

"What do you think?"

A great wave of peace and relief swept over Ingram. *No combat.* He felt as if he were being elevated into clouds with vistas of golden streets and rambling, sun-drenched buildings with sidewalks inlaid with diamonds, rubies and emeralds. If he read Ashton right, it meant no more Japs. No more thundering cannon nor tearing bullets, nor screams in the night. No more blood-spattered compartments and men squirming on red-hot decks, their bodies burned to a crisp. "My God," he blurted.

Ashton's teeth flashed. "Your God what?"

"It sounds wonderful."

"Then what do you say?"

Yes, yes. Oh, hell yes, I want it so bad I'll do anything. Yes, yes. Of course, yes. Ingram drew a breath. He was surprised to hear his own voice say, "Can I think about it?"

"How about forty-eight hours?"

"Fair enough."

"You like golf?" Ashton gave an impish smile.

"Well, I haven't played since before the war."

"How 'bout the Virginia Country Club next Saturday? Say ten o'clock tee-off?"

"Sounds good to me, Frank." *Pretty snazzy. How did he swing the Virginia Country Club?*

Ashton stood and offered his hand. "I'll be proud to have you with me, Todd. You wont believe how much fun this is. And," Ashton winked, "...and I can promise your third stripe within sixty days."

They listened as another truck rattled down the alley, grinding its gears. Ashton said. "There's something else."

"Sir?"

Ashton's tone softened as he said, "It's no secret that I'm on the list for rear admiral. But also, I'm on the list to head BuOrd." He looked up and gave a coy smile.

Ingram said, "Congratulations, Sir."

"If that happens, they'll post me to Washington D.C. right away. That means you'll be running this office. And that means..." He shrugged.

"Means what, Sir?"

"The billet calls for a full captain. So you could have your fourth stripe in, say in six months."

Ingram knew there was something he should do. Yes. *Close your mouth.* His mind raced as he considered the possibilities. "Thank you, Sir. I don't know what to say." *Yes, yes. Oh, hell yes. Sonofabitch. A third stripe, maybe a fourth: Captain Alton C. Ingram, USN, stay-at-home warrior. Helen will be delirious with joy.*

Again, he said, 'Thank you, Sir." They shook.

"Frank."

"Frank."

27

---

29 March, 1943
  San Pedro, California

The phone rang stridently. Landa whipped and blinked at the harsh sunlight streaming in Ingram's little guest room. His watch said 9:32. But God, how his head throbbed, no doubt from the cheap beer he'd drunk last night at Shanghai Red's. The phone rang and rang." Okay, okay." With a groan, Landa got up and shuffled across the cold, hardwood floor finding the phone neatly placed in a living room niche.. "Hello?" he snapped.

"Todd?" It was a woman.

"Mrs. Ingram, er --- Helen?"

"No. Is this, uh, the Captain...?"

"Jerry Landa. Yes 'Mam."

"This is hard." Her voice sounded small.

It's Laura Dutton, or West, or whatever. She sounded sober. "Mrs. Dutton," Landa said, carrying the phone to the couch. The hardwood floor felt like ice and he put his feet up.

She exhaled. "Yes. Look, Roberta said I should talk to you."

"Who?"

"Roberta. Our manager."

The tall, thin woman who greeted Landa in the lobby. "I remember."

"I owe you an apology. I'm sorry. I acted terribly."

Landa sat heavily on the couch, at a loss for words.

"Hello?"

"I'm here."

"Well?"

Landa cleared his throat. "It's okay, Mrs. Dutton. I'd probably do the same thing. In fact I just about did last night."

"What?"

"Well. Todd and I went down to Shanghai Red's last night. It's sort of a dive down in San Pedro."

"I know."

"You do?"

She gave a small laugh.

To Landa, her laugh sounded good, and he wondered why. And he wondered why he was pressing the phone to his ear.

"I was there one night." She told him about her Saturday night on the town with Helen. "So you and Todd were out having fun?"

"Well. Todd and I hadn't really talked since we'd lost the *Howell*."

"Lost the *Howell*?"

Landa caught himself. He couldn't discuss that on the phone. "Well, not exactly. Anyway, it wasn't really about the ship."

"Go on."

"My younger brother died. That's why I'm here in the States -- emergency leave. I was back east with the funeral and taking care of things."

"Oh, my God." Her voice was high pitched. "Then you took personal time off and came all the way to Hollywood to...to..."

"It's okay. Really it is." Landa smacked his lips. He needed coffee. And it was cold in here. Todd must have left the heat off.

"Can I make it up to you?" she asked.

"It's not necessary."

"I got it. How would you like to see a radio show? Bing Crosby? Jack Benny? I can send a bunch of tickets. You can bring Todd and...and..."

"That's very nice, er Laura. Thank you. But I'm shipping out. I'm on stand-by for transportation to, well, you know, out there."

"Well then. How about a USO show? I'm doing another recital day after tomorrow right there on the base. You know, just like the one I did a while back..."

"Sorry, I wasn't there." Landa recognized the oblique reference to her piano recital at the base theater two months ago. Ingram had told him that Luther Dutton marched on stage and accompanied her on the violin. At the same time, Landa was at the officer's club, singing and shouting and pounding his mug for more beer.

"...well?"

He leaned forward. "Tell you what. If they haven't manifested me on a flight, then I'll show up."

"Good. I'll leave a ticket for you in will-call."

"You don't need to do that. I can buy general admission."

She chucked at his discomfort over having to sit in an area normally reserved for top brass. She said, "Front row center."

"I'll handle my own ticket. But thanks."

"Well. The ticket will be there if you want it. And thanks again for taking the trouble to come up yesterday. I was kind of crude. Please forgive me."

"Shock therapy."

"If you don't come tomorrow, how can I stay in touch with you?"

Landa sat up. It was the way she asked the question. Or was he inferring too much? Finally, he gave her his military address. "Thanks for calling. It's very nice of you."

"Yes. Goodbye." She hung up.

"She what?" Asked Ingram. They sat with drinks on the Officer's Club patio, watching the sun set over the Palos Verdes Peninsula.

"Drunk on the job. On the keyboard. Cheap scotch and all. But then she called back this morning and apologized."

"Wish I could do something," said Ingram.

"You can't. Nobody can. But she'll come out all right." The crushed ice in Landa's highball glass gave a comforting rattle. It was filled with scotch, a lemon twist perched on top: Scotch mist. He didn't want to talk about Laura, or his discomfort with the fact that he'd decided not to go to the USO concert tomorrow night. So he changed the subject. "I interrupted you. You were going to tell me about your day with Frank Ashton."

"He offered me a job." Ingram gave a crooked grin.

"He did what?"

Ingram's answer was obliterated by a pair of F6F hellcats roaring over the Officer's Club, heading for the NAS Terminal Island airstrip next door. Dropping their flaps and gear, they curved up and around, bleeding off speed to set up for their downwind leg. Watching them gave Ingram a good feeling. He'd seen a lot of the new fighters around Long Beach during the last couple of weeks. People praised them as the Zero buster. These, most likely, were joining the *Essex's* airgroup.

"Frank Ashton offered me a job this morning. Fleet Technical Liaison for a new Combat Support Unit."

"Frank Ashton offering you a job?" Landa stirred his drink with his index finger. "I'm surprised he isn't hiding in a cave somewhere."

"Jerry. Give the guy a chance, damnit."

"What about your ship? What about the *Pence*?"

"That will have to wait."

They looked up, as four more hellcats growled overhead in echelon. Soon the F6Fs peeled off into their landing patterns. Landa said, "So what was your answer?"

"I asked for a couple of days to mull it over." Ingram's stomach began to grind.

"You mean you really have to think about this?"

"I know how you feel about Frank Ashton and I'm sorry. But it's not clear to me why you two are at war. Probably, it's none of my business. All I know is that this seems to be an opportunity I should consider. Don't you?"

Landa downed his drink in one gulp, then carefully lowered the highball glass to the table and gently pushed it away. He leaned back and crossed his hands over his stomach. "Like you, Ashton's a ring knocker, huh?"

"That's a dumb thing to say." It just popped out. Ingram couldn't help it, and he couldn't dodge the fact that this had spun out of control. "This isn't an Academy Protection Society thing or whatever you want to call it. And it's not a question of shirking a command. He said I would get a ship soon. It seems a legitimate offer, and I believe I should really consider it."

"Umm." Landa nodded slowly. "I'm not talking about any Canoe U petty jealousy. What I am talking about is common sense. Here you are, fully qualified for command, and you have orders to your ship. All you have to do is hop on a plane and head for..."

"Tulagi."

"Yes. Tulagi. But Instead, you turn your back on it, when some sweet talking gold-brick offers you a cushy Stateside job."

Ingram felt his bile rising. "I don't like the inference, Jerry."

"What you going to do for an encore, Todd? Punch me in the snot locker, again?" Landa gave a demonic simile and waved at tables crowded with high ranking officers. "Right here in front of all this brass?"

Landa stood and straightened his blouse. "Well now, Mr. Ingram. Enjoy your tour with Frank Ashton. Next stop, CNO staff in Washington D.C. You'll like the Pentagon life. Plenty of south-ends to kiss on the north-bound ladder. For me, I'm on standby for a flight to you-know-where. So I'm moving out and staying at the BOQ. Good bye." Landa whisked his cap off the table and walked away.

28

31 March, 1943
San Pedro, California

The wind blew, waking Ingram up for the third time in the last hour. Early last evening, an unexpected cold front had snuck in bringing thirty knot winds and driving rain. And now, as he blinked at the darkness, it was stronger. He looked over to find the clock and telephone receiver missing from the night stand. Craning his neck over the edge of the bed he saw them scattered on the floor amidst a pile of magazines. He'd been tossing and turning so much during the night, he barely remembered knocking everything over. He reached down, hung the phone up with a clatter, then grabbed the clock and lifted it to his ear. It still ticked; the time read nearly two-thirty.

A gust roared and tugged at the little house, making him wonder if it could be torn off its foundation. The pressure built; the wind wailed and pounded. The garage door banged, and the branches of a Chinese Elm just outside scratched and thumped at the window. Fred lay at the foot of the bed, his head up, ears twitching. Ingram glanced at the window, its shade half drawn. For a moment, he expected to see Bela Lugosi peering in, black velvet cape and all. Then he turned over, glad in a convoluted way, that if he couldn't sleep, at least he had the storm for a bizarre form of entertainment.

Another gust roared; thick rain drops pounded the window. The garage door banged harder, and he realized he would have to crawl out of this warm bed, put on clothes, trudge out there and secure it, before it smashed itself to pieces. A light flipped on next door: Mrs. Peabody. Chances were the garage door was keeping her awake. *Damnit. I really have to go out there.*

After a while, Mrs. Peabody's light went off. He rolled to his back and laced his hands behind his head, staring at the ceiling. He'd heard nothing more from Landa, who had moved to the BOQ Monday night, taking everything except his brother's trunk. He'd already said goodbye to Leo Seltzer, who had finagled orders to the *Pence*. He'd been manifested aboard a flight which left Long Beach Airport at seven forty-five that morning for Honolulu. Strange when he shook Seltzer's hand, though. It was almost as if they were speaking for the last time. Seltzer didn't seem happy about Ingram's new appointment, and Ingram felt bad about that. And Landa would soon follow Seltzer back to the South Pacific.

He wished he'd called Jerry to say good-bye properly. He didn't like to leave things like that and realized, in many ways, they were too much alike: Impetuous, pig-headed. Quick to plunge ahead without considering all the consequences. Sometimes, such a quality was required for command, especially when fast, oftentimes intuitive, decisions had to be made. But it could get one into trouble, like last Monday at the officer's club.

Well, if Landa wants to keep risking his butt out there, fine. But Ingram had a chance to get away from all that and still make an important contribution; still hold his head up high. And, stay alive. In fact, Ashton had called yesterday morning, offering Ingram more time to consider. He finished with, "Let's talk it over Saturday after golf."

The wind roared, and the house shook and rumbled. The Elm scraped. Fred sat up now, looking from side to side. Mrs. Peabody's light flicked on again, as the wind screeched and twirled though cracks in the house. Something snapped like a shingle tearing from the roof. Fred rose to all fours, his eyes wide open. He looked at Ingram, then hopped off the bed, went to the window, stood on his hind legs and looked out.

"You've been watching too many Boris Karloff movies." Ingram rolled over and scrunched deep into the covers, mashing the pillow over his head in a vain attempt to muffle the noise. After a minute, he flipped to his back thinking of the intruder Mrs. Peabody had seen. A Navy officer. Lieutenant? Commander? Maybe it was the same person who had walked in on Helen?

The wind screamed again. But something was different. The garage door! The damned thing wasn't banging. Ingram sat up, finding Mrs. Peabody's light was still on. He felt like a heel. That hearty old widow had gone out there and done his job.

His feet had just hit the cold floor when he heard footsteps in the living room. A dark figure filled the doorway. "Ah!" he yelped.

He caught his breath as the figure walked toward him, raindrops running off a glistening overcoat.

"Todd!" she said.

"Helen?" In a second, he was out of bed his bare arms around her wet, raincoat. He found her mouth and covered it with his, kissing her deeply. "How did...?

"Change of orders. Why, I don't know. They turned me around and put me on a hospital plane flying directly to Long Beach."

"You should have called." He held her tight, kissing her eyes and cheeks.

"Phone was busy."

What a homecoming, he thought. Being tossed around an airplane in this storm must have been horrible. But then she couldn't get through from the Long Beach airport, he realized. "Damnit. Sorry. Off the hook...I knocked it over. Cab ride must have cost a fortune."

"Hmmmm. Bet you had a girl in here. What was her name?" She kissed him on the neck.

"Mrs. Peabody." He pulled off her scarf letting her silky black hair tumble out. He buried his face in that wonderful, sweet aroma. "God, I've missed you."

"Me, too, honey."

"You here for a while?"

"For Good. Back to fighting the battle of San Pedro."

"Fantastic." He took her face in both hands. There was enough light to see into her eyes. Raindrops ran down her face. Or were they tears? He kissed them away. "I love you."

"I Love you, too."

He kissed her again as she fumbled with her rain coat buckle. Finally, she tore it off, threw it aside, and wrapped her arms around his neck.

Wind blew through the house making papers tumble off the desk.

She said, "Umm. Your heart is jumping."

"Scared the hell out of me. Next time--"

"--Mrs. Peabody! You said Mrs. Peabody!"

"Yeah?" He sat back on the bed trying to pull her on him.

"Wait." She stepped back. "Mrs. Peabody."

"What about her?" Ingram stood and kissed her on the tip of her nose.

"Outside. She was doing something to the garage door when we pulled up. And my luggage is out there."

"She's out there now?"

"I think so."

"Good, God." Reluctantly, Ingram let her go. Then he walked to bathroom, grabbed his robe and put it on. "Don't go away."

"I don't think so."

Wind ruffled his hair as he walked into the living room. Sure enough. The front door stood open. He leaned outside just as a gust slammed against the house. He had to yell. "Hello? Mrs. Peabody?"

"Mr. Ingram?" She was huddled in a corner roosting like a mother hen on two large B-4 bags.

Ingram stepped out, shivering. "Thanks for taking care of Helen's bags," he shouted.

"She looks wonderful, doesn't she?"

"You bet."

"Isn't it a miracle?" She yelled.

"Miracle, what?"

"That she got to come home. I prayed and prayed."

"It sure is." Ingram tossed the bags inside. "Thanks for fixing the garage door."

"I'm afraid I had to nail it shut."

"I'll get to it tomorrow."

"It's that hinge. You should--"

"Good night, Mrs. Peabody. And thanks again." Ingram closed the door and locked it. The house was still dark as he padded through the living room. There was a pile of clothes on the bedroom floor. Helen lay in bed, waiting...

The aroma of coffee and bacon wafted in. Ingram's eyes flipped open. The rain was steady outside and the clock said: *Holy Smokes! Eleven fifteen.* Then he lay back and stretched, savoring the moment. Puttering in the kitchen was his just reward: Helen making breakfast. How much sleep had he had? He couldn't remember, and come to think of it, he didn't care.

Donning his robe, he walked into the kitchen. "Morning." He kissed her on the cheek.

"Almost good afternoon." She tossed a smile, grabbing toast as it popped up. "You hungry?" She wore a white satin night shirt that ran to mid-thigh.

"Depends what's on the menu." His arm went around her waist. "Ummm."

She chuckled, then pulled away to flip four sizzling eggs in the skillet. "About ready. Pour yourself some coffee and sit, mister."

Ingram did. It tasted wonderful. "Can you believe the time?"

She gave a sideways glance, "What, do you suppose happened?"

Ingram took a chair at the little breakfast table, waving his arms in the air. "Not my fault. No siree. Last night, I'm just laying there, fast asleep, minding my own business when this absolute, eye-popping, bombshell walks in my bedroom, disturbing the peace. What's a man to do?"

She set a plate of eggs, bacon and toast before him. "Eat, That's what a man's supposed to do."

Later, they sat back, sipping coffee and watching the rain. Both plates were on the floor with Fred happily licking the remains. Ingram finished his story of Ashton's offer by saying, "You'd like him. He's on a fast track. Next stop, the Pentagon."

She gave a quick smile, then held her cup with both hands and looked out the window. "It's only drizzling."

"Right. It's a great opportunity, honey."

"Yes." Helen rose and began to clear plates.

"What I really like about it is that I get to work in my specialty: Ordnance."

"Yes." Water ran. She scrubbed dishes, her back to him.

"All sorts of new stuff and technology. The Japs won't know what hit them." One of the many things Ingram loved about Helen was her eyes. They were beacons to her soul, reflecting so much of her. Just looking into her eyes told him so much, almost like speaking to her. But now, he couldn't see them. Why?

Helen shuddered.

"What's wrong?" Ingram walked over and spun her around, finding tears running down her cheeks. "Baby? What is it?"

"I'm fine," she said, "happy to be home." Wiping tears with the back of her hand, she said, "You want to have dinner at Olsen's tonight?"

"Olsen's? Well, yes. That's a good idea," He said with some sarcasm. "Why the hell don't we have dinner at Olsen's?" He held her tight then kissed her. Gently, he cupped her cheeks in his hands and tried to look into her eyes.

But she buried her face in his shoulder and said in a muffled voice, "Well, if you do, then you better fix the garage door so we can get the car out."

Near the corner of Ninth and Grand, Olsen's was a smallish, but upscale restaurant. A long bar dominated the right side of the room with several red-leather booths arranged against the opposite wall. A trio of sax, bass, and piano played softly in a far corner. The salad and prime rib were excellent. That was followed by a light dessert and coffee. Now, they sat back. Ingram fussed with his cup. "Did Ollie ever get back to you?"

"Just before I left. He said Otis was traveling with General Sutherland and would be inaccessible for three or four weeks."

"Ouch."

"There's nobody else we know that can work at that level is there?"

"No there isn't which means nobody ever got back to you about where those crazy orders to North Africa came from nor how they were rescinded."

"Not yet."

"Don't you think that's weird?"

"Weird...what?"

"Who issued them and why were they rescinded?" He grinned, "Not that I'm unhappy that they were rescinded. But, how did it happen?"

She shrugged. "...no idea."

"Well, let's try Ollie, tomorrow."

She toyed with the sugar bowl and nodded.

"Dinner all right?"

"Great."

"You feeling okay?"

"Yep."

The waiter walked over, bent over the table and said, "Commander, that gentleman over there has picked up your check."

"What?" They looked up to see an elderly couple walk by. The two waved, the white haired man saying, "Give 'em hell, Commander. And thanks for what you're doing for all of us."

Ingram tried to rise, but by then, the couple had walked out. He looked up to the waiter. "Who was that?"

"The Raffertys. Fine people. They're here often."

"Well, please tell them thanks for me the next time you see them." Ingram handed the waiter a two dollar bill.

"Of course, and thank you." The waiter walked off.

Helen's eyes glistened. "What marvelous people. I hope we're like that when we're that age."

"You ready?" He started to rise.

"Todd. What is it?" Her hand went to his forearm.

"It's you is what it is."

"We better go."

"You don't like Ashton's deal." It was a statement.

Her shoulders slumped.

"You think it's that bad?"

"How can you tell?"

"It's not as if I don't know you." He leaned over and brushed a tear from her cheek with the back of his index finger.

She doubled her fists. "God, I don't want this. I never have. Corregidor. Mindanao, the South Pacific, Brazil. All I want is a chance to live our lives."

"Me too, honey. And I thought this was it."

"No, it's not. " she said.

"What?"

"You know and I know that it'll rip you apart if you turn down the *Pence*. Your own command? You'd never get over it if you turned your back."

Ingram's face flushed. "But I told you Ashton said---"

"---I don't care what Ashton said," she hissed. "And don't argue. You think this is easy for me? Of course I don't want you to go. I just got here, remember? How do you think I feel. But I know you'll never forgive yourself."

"Honey..."

She took his hand in hers. "How much time do we have?"

"Time for what?"

"When do your orders say you have to shove off?"

He wished he smoked a pipe or a cigar, something that gave him time to think.

"Todd?"

"I love you, very much."

"Me too very much. Now, how long?"

"Two more days."

"What are we waiting for?"

They got up and walked out.

The next morning, Ingram was in the living room, sipping coffee. The phone rang and he picked it up. "Hello?"

"Ollie? Good God, how the hell are you?" Oliver Toliver III, a former shipmate of Ingram's aboard the *Pelican*, was now Ordnance Liaison Officer to the Fourteenth Naval District in San Francisco. Toliver, Ingram, Helen and Colonel Otis DeWitt, had escaped the horrors of Corregidor together in an open boat. After catching up with each other, Ingram broke the news.

"She's back?" Toliver's voice ranged over the line with incredulity.

"Walked in on me two nights ago," said Ingram. As in confirmation, he glanced out the front window, watching her talk to Mrs. Peabody.

"Where was she?" asked Toliver.

"Got as far as Natal, Brazil. Then she got new orders, rescinding the old ones."

"Well, I'm glad for you. But what a puzzler."

"Our words, exactly," said Ingram.

"Well, I called to tell Helen and you, that I got a message from Otis. He'll be in his office next week. He's been touring with General Sutherland. Then he'll grab a line and we can talk openly, rather than speak around all this gobbledegook."

"Well, you don't have to," said Ingram. "She's back now."

"You know, this is weird enough that I think I should follow through. Maybe it could happen again."

Ingram sat up at that. "You don't think so?"

"Well, let's put it this way," Toliver said. "Whoever tries that crap again will have to deal personally with General Douglas MacArthur. That's what Otis's message said."

"That's great Ollie."

"Yeah, but let's not stop there. Let's find the ghoul who did this in the first place."

"I'm for that. Say, you still have your Packard?"

"Nope, I sold it to a guy from Southern California. Got a brand new '42 Olds with hydramatic drive. Had to talk like hell to get the dealer to sell it to me."

"What the hell is hydramatic drive?"

"The coming thing."

"What's it do?"

"You drive along without shifting gears. But the damn thing craps out all the time. It's been in the shop ever since I bought it. No one knows how to fix it."

"That's progress. Why don't I feel sorry for you?"

"Come on Todd."

" Please let me know what Otis says."

"Will do."

29

31 March, 1943
 Base Theater, Long Beach Naval Station
 Long Beach, California

Sailors crowded the aisle forcing Landa to turn sideways so he could squeeze past. As he expected, the number of rings on the officer's sleeves rose the closer he drew to the stage. At last, he reached the first row finding three admirals standing about surrounded by a bevy of captains and commanders. They wore aviator's wings and cast icy stares, as Landa worked around to his seat. Checking his ticket number he found, *damnit, she'd done it*; his seat was right in the center of the front row.

No sooner had he sat then the lights flickered. Quickly, people took their seats and the place became dark, so much so that he had trouble reading his single-page blue mimeographed program:

By Popular Demand

Laura West

Featured Pianist with the NBC Symphony Orchestra

Returns with:

J. S. Bach - French Suite
Beethoven - Passionata
Chopin - Ballade
Brahms - Rhapsody Number 2

The seat to his left jiggled but, Landa didn't take notice until a blue sleeve with a rear admiral's brilliant gold rings flopped on the arm rest. Landa turned to look into steel grey eyes of a flag officer who nodded curtly. On the admiral's left was his aide, a full lieutenant with a wolfish face who gave a look as if Landa was already on his way to prison at Fort Leavenworth. To Landa's right was a close-cropped Marine bird colonel with more decorations than Macy's at Christmas time.

After a short, offstage announcement, a single spot light flicked on and Laura West stepped from behind the curtain with a radiant smile. Putting her palms together, she bowed deeply as the audience applauded. Landa was amazed. This was not the unkept, drunken Laura Dutton he'd met in Hollywood. This woman wore rimless glasses and her sandy, once messy hair was now meticulously pulled-back into a perfect French twist. She wore a long sapphire blue gown perfectly accented by a large rhinestone broach with matching earrings and bracelet. She looked a little thin, Landa thought, yet she brimmed with energy as she walked to her long, black, concert grand, sat and arranged herself.

She waited for the crowd to fall silent, then, with a smile, began Bach's *French Suite*.

This is what Landa had been dreading. He had no idea how he was going to pass the next hour, let alone stay awake. He reminded himself that he was surrounded by men who could decimate his career with the snap of a finger; thus he looked for something upon which to concentrate so he wouldn't fidget. Ahh, the Colonel's shoes. With glee, he noted something had spilled on the left toe of a pair of beautifully spit-shined shoes. And the Marine didn't seem to notice, as he stretched his feet out and laced his fingers over his belly, watching Laura.

And look at that! The Colonel's heel was scuffed and red chewing gum was stuck to his sole as...

...her playing seemed perfect. Landa's head was tilted, and he realized he hadn't heard anything like this before. But it made sense, as Laura leaned into the keyboard, almost becoming one with the piano; willing it to capture the sounds and nuances penned by Bach. Too soon, the Bach was done and Landa now had a far different idea of what Laura West was all about. Like the Admiral to his left and the Marine colonel to his right, he stood and applauded enthusiastically when the piece ended.

Then came the *Passionata...Ballade...2Rhapsody #2*; they all ended so quickly, the hour and twenty minutes having flown by. Landa, whose father was a stevedore, had never heard anything like it. This was on a level he'd never imagined. The tempo, the technique, the chords, everything blended; Laura West had done it all masterfully. And he wondered what it meant.

She stood, faced the audience with her left hand on the piano and took another bow, as a balding Navy lieutenant mounted the steps. With the audience cheering, cat-calling, and whistling, he handed her a large bouquet of red roses. She smiled, then stood on her tip toes and kissed him on the cheek, leaving the lieutenant with a broad grin.

Then Laura sat and waited as the lieutenant drew a floor mike to her side. Her voice seemed breathless as she said, "Well, boys, what a thrill to be back in Long Beach."

That got the crowd going again and she had to wait a full thirty seconds for the din to fade. "I told you I'd come back. Remember one of the pieces we did last time?" With that, she started playing *I'll be seeing you*. At a nod, the audience joined in the verse. Landa knew the melancholy words and found himself singing with everyone else. Then she played *Lili Marlene*, bringing moist eyes to the crowd. Even Landa felt a lump in his throat as she played and the crowd sang.

And, on the last note, Laura West looked directly at Landa. And smiled.

"How'd you work that one out, son?" It was the Admiral beside Landa.

"I hardly know her, Sir."

"You gotta be kidding." With a grin, the Admiral rose and clapped with the rest of the crowd.

With everyone standing, Laura had them sing *God Bless America*, and everyone's eyes went moist once more. The audience cheered, as she bowed, and bowed again. Finally, she stepped offstage for the last time, and the house lights came up.

Landa waited, as officers crowded up to the Admiral. The Marine colonel was gone; off to shine his shoes, Landa supposed. But he had to linger a few moments until things thinned out. Finally, he managed to step around the aviators and head into the aisle.

"Sir?" It was the flower-bearing Lieutenant.

"Yes?"

He handed Landa a small envelope. Inside was a heavy stock panel card with a handwritten note:

There's a party at the Villa Rivera, room 1600, the penthouse. There will be lots of uniforms and I think I need protection.
L

Built in 1921, the French gothic Villa Rivera Hotel had a steep-pitched copper roof, was sixteen stories high, and easily was the tallest structure in downtown Long Beach. Within yards of the Pacific Ocean, it had a commanding view down Ocean Boulevard west toward San Pedro and the Palos Verdes Peninsula. At the war's outbreak, the Navy had taken it over and converted it to officer housing.

It turned out the Rear Admiral who sat next to Landa was billeted in the penthouse which occupied the entire top floor. His name was Larry Dunnigan, and he greeted Landa like an old friend as he stepped off the elevator. Then Landa was handed off to Dunnigan's aide, the Lieutenant with the wolfish face who wore a Bakelite tag bearing the name: KLOSTERMAN. He shoved a drink in Landa's hand, then showed him around, his thick, beefy hand sweeping across the elegant foyer and high ceilings. Then Klosterman disappeared and Landa found himself alone among aviators, the decorated ones reliving dog-fights, and using their hands to once again, shoot down the enemy. Overhearing them, he learned Dunnigan commanded a carrier division.

Klosterman walked by and Landa asked, "Say Lieutenant, mind if I use a phone to check in with my transport in Long Beach? I'm on call for a flight to Pearl."

"Sure. It's in there." Klosterman pointed to an open door to what looked like a study. But just then, there was a commotion in the main foyer.

Laura West walked in on the arm of the broadly grinning bald Navy Lieutenant. Instantly, Admiral Dunnigan was at her side, with Klosterman rushing over to provide introductions.

Laura had taken off her glasses and undid the French twist, her hair now falling in long waves to her shoulders. A half dozen officers ranged around her, taking her hand and talking to her as Dunnigan stood by, nodding and smiling. At one point, the Admiral subtly eased a drink into her hand and Landa saw her mouth 'thank you.' As she raised her glass, she caught Landa's eye, nodded and gave a mock toast.

It was a tiny sip, a gesture really, Landa noted. He smiled and gave her a thumbs up. Laura nodded back. But then Landa's view was blocked by a tall Navy captain who stepped between them.

Landa sighed, walked in the study and closed the door. It was nearly pitch black but he couldn't find the wall switch. Finally, his eyes adjusted, and he found the phone on what looked to be an ornate desk by a heavily draped window. He dialed the number and while waiting, parted a drape with the back of his hand. A full moon brilliantly illuminated a blacked-out Long Beach against a cobalt blue sky. To seaward, a gentle wind stirred little wavelets in the harbor, their reflections dancing like jewels among the men-of-war darkly hulking at anchor.

Outside, the laughter and glass tinkling grew louder. Landa checked his watch. Damn, he'd been in here for five minutes while the numbskulls at Long Beach Airport tried to figure out if they had a spot for him on tomorrow's flight. Finally, someone came on the line. "Hello, Commander Landa? This is Chief Squire."

The door opened, letting in noise. He turned his back to it and plugged his ear.

"Yes, Chief?"

The door closed.

"We have a flight for you tomorrow. Actually there are two. You have a choice of the morning or late afternoon flight. Actually, the afternoon flight is far less crowded."

Laura West stepped right in front of him.

"Good God!"

"Commander Landa, Hello?...Hello?"

She said something.

Landa was dumbstruck. "What?"

"I don't know how else to say this." Laura ran her arms around his neck.

The phone was still pressed to Landa's ear as they kissed long and deeply. Then they broke and held each other for ten seconds.

"...hello, hello? Commander Landa? Are you there?"

Landa said, "The afternoon flight is fine, Chief. Thanks." Then he cradled the phone, put his arms around Laura's waist and pulled her a foot off the ground, kissing her slowly.

The door opened and Dunnigan's aide stood silhouetted against the light.

Landa growled, "Later, Klosterman."

Klosterman expelled breath and closed the door.

Landa eased her back to the floor. "Whew! Who would have ever thought?"

"I have a confession."

"So do I." He kissed her forehead, her hair. Her scent was Chanel Number 5, he thought.

"Me first. I've been thinking of you ever since you walked in on me in the...well, you know, the rehearsal studio."

It hit Landa. *She's on the rebound. Jerry. Get the hell out of here. Now!* But she felt so good, her voice sounding like velvet when she added, "I don't know why, except that I had to see you. Thanks for coming."

The hell with it. "Honey. I wouldn't have missed it for the world. Thanks for the front row ticket. The show was swell. You were swell." He kissed her again, and then again.

The door opened again and a figure stood in the doorway. "Ahem." It was Admiral Dunnigan.

Landa let her go. "Sorry, Sir."

Dunnigan reached over and snapped the wall switch flooding the room with light. "Just wanted to make sure you two hadn't jumped out the window." Then he snapped it off and started to close the door.

"Larry," said Laura.

"Yes?"

"Don't worry. I'll be right out."

"Well, you don't have to..."

"A promise is a promise, Larry. I said I'd do it."

"Okay, thanks." Dunnigan walked out, softly drawing the door shut, once again plunging the room into darkness.

And as the door swung, Landa realized a light was going out in his life.

"It's for his boys. They're about to ship out and Dunnigan wants me to give them a piece of...well...home."

"Right. You better get out there and I have to...hell, I have to ship out, too."

"No."

"Tomorrow morning, Early. Seven am flight," He lied. It was the toughest thing he'd ever done.

"Didn't you just say tomorrow afternoon's flight?"

"I have a DC-3 for San Diego tomorrow morning. Then I head out tomorrow afternoon." Another lie.

"To where?"

He tilted his head west.

"Oh God, I just found you. Can't you..." Her eyes bored in. "It's Luther, isn't it?"

Landa took a step back. "I don't know, Laura. Hell, I'm all mixed up, too. Yes, damnit, it's Luther. And I'm on an airplane, tomorrow. And it's about this damn war." He looked at her; grasping her arms he said, "Can't this wait, a little?"

"I only knew him thirteen short months. And yes, I loved him. But he's gone now. And I'm here. And you're...Oh God." She dropped her head in her hands.

The door opened and light streamed in.

"...ahem." It was Klosterman.

Landa had had all he could take. "Out of here, Lieutenant or I'll have your b--"

"--It's okay, Bruce. I'm coming." Laura looked up to Landa. "We'll talk after this. Twenty minutes, tops. Okay?" She kissed him on the nose.

"Okay."

"Stick around. Promise?"

"Promise."

"I'll play one for you." With a wink, Laura walked out with Klosterman holding the door for her.

Landa started to follow, but Klosterman closed the door. He drew up, ready to do battle. But then he waited in the dark, drumming his fingers on the wall near the light switch, counting to fifty. They applauded and soon, piano music drifted in. It was Laura playing something fancy. He didn't know what it was, but it was beautiful.

Shaking his head slowly, he muttered, "Jeremiah T. Landa, for what you are about to do, you are one stupid son of a bitch."

Then he opened the door and stepped in the hall. It was crowded; he couldn't see into the parlor. Her music followed him as he headed into the foyer, where he picked up his hat and walked out.

30

3 April, 1943
   IJN *Musashi*
   Truk Atoll, Caroline Islands

For the time being, the Imperial Japanese Navy didn't have a South Pacific force large enough to dislodge the Americans from Guadalcanal. A temporary, yet devastating maneuver was needed until ships could be repaired, a new Naval force assembled. Accordingly, Admiral Isoroku Yamamoto, Commander in Chief of the Combined Fleet, had been planning something new for the past month. Yamamoto had found another way to punish the U.S. Navy. As he did at Pearl Harbor, he would send massive airstrikes to Guadalcanal and the surrounding bases; not just one air-raid, but several, extending over a period of ten days or so. It had taken many days to scavenge aircraft off carriers and from land bases as far as 1,500 kilometers away. But now, they were assembled at Rabaul. Now they were ready. They dubbed it *Operation I*.

Today, the *Gensui* and his staff were fly to 600 miles south to Rabaul where, beginning tomorrow, the Admiral would personally direct the attacks.

Also, he planned to boost morale by participating in pilot briefings and touring local Army bases and hospitals.

Captain Yasuji Watanabe was a methodical man, one given to far more detail than even his spit-shined shoes and gleaming brass buttons on his crisp white uniform would indicate. As chief of staff, he was responsible to the *Gensui* to make sure his departure went off without a hitch. *Operation I* or this morning's itinerary; both had equal weight as far as Watanabe was concerned. He had just spoken to the Air Officer and was assured the eight plane fighter escort was taking off. There was one last detail he wanted to check before he went up to the *Gensui* and told him all was ready. Thus he quickly stepped down the ladder to the giant ship's second deck and walked to a hatch on the port side. A heavy-set second class petty officer stood at the door and offered to help him open it. Watanabe waved him off, then pushed. The door gave a little, but then slammed back in his face.

"What is this?"

"The Wind's up, Sir. Here, let me." The petty officer bent and put his shoulder to it. With some effort it opened, with the wind roaring and curling around the hatch, tugging at Watanabe's uniform.

He checked his watch: 0825. "It's blowing so soon?" *Unusual,* thought Watanabe, as he clamped his hand to his head. "I'll be right back."

"Yes, Sir! Just knock."

Watanabe stepped outside onto the *Musashi's* second deck, a promenade where official ceremonies were often held. Walking to the deck's edge he looked out. Yes, there they were. Fifty meters off the ship's port side sat the *Gensui's* dark green Kawanishi H8K2 Type-Two Flying Boat. Her four Mitsubishi-Kaesi fourteen cylinder engines were ticking over, with the pilot revving them occasionally to keep the amphibian in place. Fifty meters beyond that was another Kawanishi, her engines likewise throttling up and down to maintain her position.

Side buoys were lined up on the quarterdeck; the *Musashi's* Captain and many of her officers were gathered in ranks. Waiting inboard were the *Gensui's* staff, including the fleet medical officer, fleet paymaster, fleet codes officer and the fleet meteorological officer, who were to travel with him today.

Two admiral's barges stood off about ten meters, bouncing in chop, their engines rumbling, as they waited to transfer the entourage to the Kawanishis.

Wind shrieked in the rigging and Watanabe held his cap tight. He'd been up at first light watching a deep red sun ignite a herringbone sky to a fiery red. Now, dark clouds roiled to the northwest, where a bolt or two of lightning jabbed at the sea. Wind whipped the lagoon, as whitecaps slapped the *Musashi's* hull, sending spray over the maindeck. The two launches and the patiently-waiting Kawanishis were taking their share of wind-chop and spray, as well. Satisfied, Watanabe bent to the wind and walked back to the bulkhead and banged on the hatch.

It opened more swiftly this time. There were two sailors, the petty officer and a gorilla-like leading seaman who helped push as Watanabe stepped over the coaming. Once inside the comfort of the massive battleship, he said, "Thank you. Now, I want you to send up two men to carry the *Gensui's* personal gear. "All right?"

"*Hai!*" They bowed.

Watanabe moved quickly to the central passage-way, then up three companionways to the *Gensui's* deck. He strode past two sentries forward to an oak paneled door and knocked.

"Come."

Watanabe stepped in, finding the *Gensui*, resplendent in dress whites, pen in hand, sitting at his desk. Heijiro, the *Gensui's* orderly bowed quickly and backed out of the compartment to disappear into a vestibule where a door clicked softly. Yamamoto scratched a signature then carefully blotted it. That done, he stuffed the letter in an envelope, sealed it, and handed it over. "It's for Chiyoko. Could you..."

Watanabe took the envelope. "Of course *Gensui*. It will be on its way to Tokyo with this afternoon's guard mail. She'll have it no later than tomorrow evening."

Yamamoto looked as if a weight had been lifted from his shoulders. "Thank you, Watanabe."

"You're welcome, Sir." Automatically, Watanabe checked his watch: 0828. Today's schedule called for an eight-thirty departure, and he began to feel a tightness in his stomach. A tiny band of perspiration broke out on his upper lip. Watanabe wanted to dab at it with his handkerchief, but quickly decided against it. Besides, it looked like they would get off on time. But one never knew. The *Gensui* was punctual to a fault, and if something went wrong, Watanabe would hear of it.

Yamamoto cleared his throat. "Well, how does it look out there?" This was a polite way of saying he was ready to go.

Watanabe stood erect. "Trade winds are up early, Sir. I must tell you I don't think it's good for you to fly in this. It's blowing at least thirty knots out there."

The Admiral walked over to a porthole and opened it. Wind blasted in ruffling papers. "No, I don't mean that. Is everything ready for me to go?"

"Yes, Sir." He waited for a moment then said, "Is your gear ready?"

Yamamoto grunted and nodded to four bags standing in a corner. "That squarish one is a case of Johnnie Walker Black Label for Kusaka and his boys. So tell the lads to go easy. "Admiral Ryunosuke Kusaka was in charge of air operations at Rabaul.

Watanabe picked up a phone and dialed a number. "...yes, send in your men. The *Gensui*'s ready." Then he hung up. "I didn't tell you, there's a storm building off to the northwest. Are you sure---?"

Yamamoto gave a quick chuckle. "I keep forgetting, Watanabe. You're not a pilot." Like some of the American carrier admirals, Yamamoto earned his wings in 1923, when he was a full Captain: an old man among eager young aviation cadets. Besides poker and other games of chance, one of his passions was lively talk of flying.

"Sir?"

"Pilots love this kind of weather." Yamamoto slammed the porthole closed and twisted the dog tight. "First of all, thirty knots of wind helps you get airborne far more quickly."

"Oh."

"Second of all, with the water choppy like that, there's far less suction to hold the airplane." He held a hand out and raised it quickly. "Whoosh, off it goes. It's really quite an experience."

"Yes, Sir." Watanabe nodded. He'd been in flying boats many times and abhorred rough water take-offs. But he realized Yamamoto liked needling him about it.

There was a knock at the door.

"Come," barked Watanabe. Two petty officers walked in, bowed and headed for the luggage. He pointed to the square bag. "Be very careful with that one."

After they were gone, Watanabe said, "The Group PL-15 revisions to *Operation I* and last-minute dispatches are in your briefcase."

"Very good. Have you found any more land attack bombers for me?" Yamamoto glanced at his watch, grabbed his cap, and started for the door.

Watanabe let him pass. "Yes, Sir. Eleven in Batavia, in good mechanical order."

"Excellent. Order them to Rabaul. How many does that make altogether?" Yamamoto, the ex-gymnast, was light on his feet and skipped down the steps quickly. Watanabe, as always, was hard pressed to keep up. He panted as he said, "You should have 486 fighters, 114 carrier-based bombers, and now, 80 land-based attack bombers." They hit the main deck, where compartment hatchways opened as if by magic, with officers and men bowing, as the *Gensui* made his way to the battleship's port side. Finally, a double hatchway opened and bright daylight flooded the passageway. A lone bugle blew, as the *Gensui* stepped onto the main deck.

The *Musashi's* captain and over fifty officers and men snapped to rigid attention on the quarterdeck, the wind whipping at their clothes. Watanabe hung back as the *Gensui* walked down the line, shaking hands with senior officers. Finally, the entourage began its departure with people bottlenecked at the accommodation ladder, waiting to descend. Among them, Watanabe noticed Captain Kanji Takano, wearing whites like Yamamoto, while the others were in either greens or blues. *Where is his damned sword*, wondered Watanabe?

Takano spotted them, walked over, drew to attention, and saluted Yamamoto.

"Looking forward to our trip Takano?" said Yamamoto, returning the salute.

"Yes, Sir."

"We'll all learn a lot in the next few days. So will the Americans." Yamamoto gave a short laugh. "Say, Watanabe tells me you have a fuse off the American ship?" He looked to Watanabe who nodded in confirmation.

Inwardly, Watanabe seethed at how Takano brought it off so easily.

Signing Yamamoto's name to everything, Takano had dispatched the destroyer *Matukaze* to the American destroyer. Issuing stringent orders, he'd made Commander Ryozo Enomoto, the ship's commanding officer, personally responsible. Just today, Enomoto had radioed Fleet headquarters at Truk that he'd personally boarded the *Howell*, crawled into her forward magazine and brought up not one, but five samples of the secret American fuse. Now, Takano was flying to Rabaul in glory with the *Gensui* to meet the *Matukaze* and personally claim his prize.

"That's true, Sir," replied Takano.

"Excellent, Takano. Just Excellent."

Someone beckoned. Takano excused himself and walked back to the companionway to join his party and disembark

Yamamoto rolled his eyes at Watanabe, then started to speak, but his voice was drowned out by eight Mitsubishi A6M5 carrier fighters roaring overhead in tight formation. Carrying long-range belly tanks, they split into two four-plane groups and began to circle on each side of the ship.

Watanabe looked up, fighting a lump in his throat. Those lucky bastards, he thought. Those very lucky bastards. Were he to do it again, Watanabe would have become a fighter pilot. If only his eyesight was...

"We yearn to be young again," said Yamamoto.

"You have me there, Sir."

"No, I don't. You're two games up on me in mahjongg. When can you get down to Rabaul, so I have a chance to beat you?"

"There's a lot of work here, yet. Perhaps two more days."

Yamamoto lowered his voice. "Don't worry about Takano. We'll let him have his glory and I'll keep giving him useless tasks to keep him busy. Has he been in your way?"

"Not at all, Sir." Watanabe raised a hand to his mouth to cover a smile. "Does that mean this American fuse project is a hoax? There is no secret fuse?"

"I don't know. Who cares? As long as it keeps the little bastard busy and away from us." Yamamoto's eyes glinted.

"Of course, Sir." Watanabe smiled inwardly. *The little bastard* Takano was almost a head taller than Yamamoto.

The first boatload embarked and shoved off. It was time. The *Gensui* headed for the accommodation ladder, dragging Watanabe with him. "Very well, Watanabe. See you in two days."

Yamamoto saluted the officer of the deck, then the colors, and was gonged off the *Musashi*. Nimbly, he stepped in his barge and was soon aboard the Kawanishi with his staff. The boat pulled away and bounced clear of the amphibian. Almost immediately, the pilot gunned the engines. Propwash blasted mist past the tail, as the plane surged ahead, momentarily hobby-horsing. Then it skipped over a wave, ricocheted off another with an enormous splash, and was airborne by the time it was abreast of the *Musashi's* bow. Her right wing dipped, and she curved around and joined up with four of the fighters, the group circling the ship. With a roar, the other Kawanishi firewalled her engines and was soon off the water, the other four fighters protectively surrounding her.

The two groups joined side-by side, and passed directly over the *Musashi* at a hundred meters. The rumble of their engines was deafening. Spontaneously, the officers and men whipped off their caps and cheered, Watanabe waving as jubilantly as the rest, while the planes took up a southerly course for Rabaul.

Watanabe watched the planes recede in the distance, a cold tingling in his chest. The drone of their engines had long ago dwindled; finally they were lost to sight. When he looked around, he found he was alone. Everyone else had gone inside. Once again, he bent to the wind and headed for the hatch.

Then it hit him. How stupid. Tomorrow was April fourth, the *Gensui's* sixtieth birthday. Watanabe had forgotten to wish him happy birthday. And for that matter, so had the others.

31

4 April, 1943
   U.S.S. *Whitney* (AD 4)
   Tulagi Harbor, Solomon Islands

It was time to go. Landa wolfed a few more bites of his breakfast, then stood and said to Myszynski, "Excuse me please, Captain?" He was a bit surprised when Myszynski shoved his chair back from the wardroom table and said, "Hold on. I'm going with you."

In the passageway, Myszynski waited patiently while Landa buckled on a cartridge belt, holstered .45, bayonet and extra clips. Clouds roiled overhead as they walked to the *Whitney's* quarterdeck. Both wore pith helmets, and their khaki pants and short sleeved shirts were sweat-soaked by the time they ducked under the quarterdeck's canvas awning.

Myszynski planted his hands on his hips, jabbed an unlit cigar in his mouth, and looked Landa up and down.

"What?" said Landa.

Myszynski said, "If you don't look like Hoot Gibson or some such crap. I should have a picture of this. Scare the Japs to death."

"Better perfect my quick-draw, first."

"Blow off your damned toe."

"Million dollar wound."

"By the way, what should I do with that flag?" The flag Seltzer had rescued from the Howell was still in Myszynski's office. Landa had simply forgotten it.

"Save it for the ship when we re-commission her."

"Okay."

A lightning bolt zapped overhead, and thunder rumbled a second later. Landa stepped to the rail and held out a hand, as large droplets began spattering. "Damnit. Three days no-stop. When's it going to end?"

Myszynski said, "Might be just as well."

Landa's eyebrows went up.

"Word is, the Japs are up to something. Air attacks, we think. Intelligence is putting some stuff together, and it sounds like they're massing airplanes from Rabaul, as far down as Munda." Like Landa, he stuck out a hand, drew it back and wiped it on his trousers. "So maybe this weather has them grounded, which is why I'm sending you up today, instead of tonight."

"You sure they're coming?"

"Time will tell."

Just then *PT-94* rumbled up to the accommodation ladder and hovered close at an idle. Landa stood erect and saluted the Officer Of The Deck, a stout red-headed ensign. "Permission to leave the ship, Sir?"

The OOD returned the salute. "Granted."

Myszynski shook Landa's hand and then said, "I have other news for you."

"Sir?"

"Looks like your boy shaped up."

"Todd?"

"He's carrying out his orders. Just got a copy of his travel chit. He's on a PB2Y bound for Pearl. We should see him here in the next few days."

Landa nodded and looked at the deck.

"It worked," said Myszynski.

"I hit him pretty hard. I'll betcha Frank Ashton is pissed. Sorry about that."

Myszynski pointed a finger. "You stay away from him."

"Who, me?"

"Yes, you, damnit!"

"Yes, Sir."

"Let this old Pollock handle Frank Ashton. I'll level with you. Anybody who messes with my skippers better watch out."

Landa had a hard time not laughing at Myszynski's blasphemous statement of one of the Navy's fastest rising scions. Instead, he braced and saluted, "Permission to leave the ship, Sir?"

Myszynski returned the salute. "Granted. Carry out your orders. And remember what I said. Take all the pictures you want, but make no attempt to board the *Howell*. Don't get within five hundred yards of her. We're pretty sure there is a Jap garrison aboard her. If the weather shuts you down, too bad. Turn around and come right home."

"Commander Landa?" a yeoman stepped up, out of breath. Slung over his shoulder was a large leather bag, stuffed with envelopes.

"That's me," said Landa.

"Must have forgotten to check your mail, Sir. These have been in my office since yesterday." The yeoman reached in his pouch and handed over two envelopes.

"Thanks." Landa folded and stuffed them in his camera case. Then he turned to Myszynski. "See you later, Commodore."

"Remember. Pictures only."

Landa hoisted his camera case over his shoulder, took two steps down the accommodation ladder, then stopped. "The thought of those bastards running around on my ship---"

"---Jerry, don't. That's an order." Myszynski checked his watch. "Now let's see, four hours up, four hours back, you should be home in time for some late chow."

"What if I find---"

"---Jerry. I'm doing you a favor by letting you out of your cage. Just get up there, look over your ship, take your pictures, then get back here ASAP. Okay?"

"I'll do it, Commodore. By the way, any word on the ATF?" The ATF was a fleet tugboat. "Due in here tomorrow. Now git."

"Aye, aye, Sir." Landa scampered down the accommodation ladder. *PT-*

94 idled in, her engines rumbling. He jumped aboard, and the PT pulled clear of the 12,000 ton destroyer tender. As soon as she passed through the anti-submarine net, her skipper hit the throttles. With a roar from her three great Packards, the seventy-eight foot Higgins, rose on her step. A large plume of white spray spewed behind as she headed up The Slot at thirty-five knots.

They'd been running up The Slot for over three hours in the rain, navigating by radar, not seeing landmarks. Visibility was poor, but the seas were calm with long, low ground swells allowing *PT-94* to remain easily on the step, with hardly any of the bone-jarring crunching the PTs suffered in harsher weather. Landa stood next to Lieutenant junior grade Oscar Bollinger, a lanky, dark-headed officer with a shark-like overbite. On Landa's right was the boat's executive officer, a bespectacled young ensign named Ralph Thomas, who pulled a towel from around his neck to wipe rain from his glasses every two minutes or so. All three were bareheaded, rain whipping their faces.

During the trip, Bollinger often stepped into the chartroom to check radar fixes. There, a grinning, gum chomping, radarman was hunched over the receiver, "Gambino" stenciled on the back of his blue dungaree shirt. Everyone called him "Bambino," presumably because of his freckled baby-face. It didn't seem to bother the young sailor as he happily sat before his lightweight Army Air Corps SCR 517A radar, plotting fixes on the chart table. While below, Bollinger would turn the helm over to Ensign Thomas. But Thomas had to wipe his glasses every two minutes; so Bollinger gave the helm to Landa who settled in comfortably, keeping the PT on course 290 true.

After a while, Bollinger came up and stood beside Landa.

Landa shouted over the engine's roar, "Want your helm back?"

"You're doing fine, Sir," Bollinger shouted back.

Landa admitted to himself that he was enjoying steering this floating gas bomb. He waved at the chart house hatch. "How we doing?"

"Mondo Mondo is on the scope straight ahead about fifteen miles."

Landa nodded: Another twenty minutes or so.

A few seconds passed, then Bollinger yelled in Landa's ear, "How do you like PTs, Commander?"

"As long as it doesn't blow up."

PT-94 swooped over the top of a swell and eased gracefully into the trough. Bollinger asked, "What did you do in civilian life, Commander?"

"Career. Merchant Marine Academy, right into the Navy."

"Destroyers the whole time?"

"Haze gray and underway. How 'bout you?"

"Book store. I was headed to Harvard Business School when my dad died. I inherited his book store and that was it."

"Where?"

"Santa Barbara."

"Pretty town. You like it?"

"Love it. We have an apartment over the top. And it's lucky, too, having a place to live. It was tough in the depression. It killed my dad, I'm sure. After he was gone, we squeaked by. Then two years ago, we made a few bucks. Then zap! The Japs bomb Pearl Harbor and here I am."

"We?"

"Wife and a son." Bollinger reached for his wallet. "Here." He showed Landa a photo of the three of them, a blonde wife and a blond little toddler perched on her knee, with Bollinger hovering in back, his shark's teeth flashed a broad smile.

While Bollinger pocketed his wallet, Laura West popped into Landa's mind. He looked off into the mist, wondering if he had done the right thing at the Villa Rivera. No doubt, her reaction was just love on the rebound. If he had been able to stick around, they would have had a quick fling, probably a one night stand, then she would have dumped him like a hot tamale.

...but she felt so good in his arms. And her singing that night. Something had emerged from Laura that seemed to him so grand, so epic and all for the taking. It seemed so right. And she'd stopped drinking hadn't she? All because of him. Didn't he owe her something?

But then he saw the *Barber* blow up and Luther gone with it. "Awww, damnit."

"What?" It was Bollinger.

"I said, you have a nice family. What about---"

There was some commotion below. Gambino stuck his head out the hatch and said, "Captain?"

Bollinger ducked into the charthouse. A minute later, he came up, his lips pressed. "Mind if I take it now, Commander?"

"Of course. Everything all right?"

Bollinger shook his head slowly. "Damned radar. When you really need them, something always goes wrong."

"What?"

"Magnetron blew up. Gonna take a while to fix it. So we have to DR in..." he waved a hand at the rain, "in all this. But Bambino is one of the best. Let's keep your fingers crossed."

Landa bent over to unlimber his camera. As he did, it occurred to him that the visibility was, at best, one hundred yards. He rose and said, "Word is that there are Japs aboard the *Howell*."

"Doing what?" said Bollinger.

"Crapping in my shower," Landa said, an edge to his voice.

Bollinger laughed. "Time for everyone to wake up." He pushed a button. There was a loud screeching below and sailors poured out of hatches to the man machine guns and the aft-mounted forty millimeter cannon.

Thomas donned a pair of sound-powered phones and soon announced, "Manned and ready, Sir."

"Very well." He looked down to Landa and asked, "Well, Commander, how do you want to do this?"

"How about a quick pass from out of the mist? They won't know we were there until we're gone."

There was a whoop from below. A broadly grinning Gambino stuck out his head, "Radar's up, Sir. Mondo Mondo two miles, straight ahead."

Landa and Bollinger both gave an incredulous, "Two miles?"

"Yessir," Gambino said.

Bollinger quickly pulled the throttles back and the boat settled in the water, her wake catching up, lifting the transom and shoving the PT forward. He said, "Okay, Bambino. Keep on your scope."

"Yes, Sir." Gambino scrambled down the hatch.

"Damn," said Bollinger, we're a couple of miles ahead of our track."

"What happened?" asked Landa.

"Damned Army radars. Who knows? We had a fuzzy picture with the old magnetron. Maybe that's what threw us off." He paused then asked, "What now, Commander?"

Landa cocked an ear aft. The engines were much quieter, but still... "Think they can hear us?"

"Must have heard us before we chopped the throttles."

"How about now?"

Bollinger tipped his hand from side to side.

"How accurate is your radar?"

"Umm, should be plus or minus twenty five yards."

"Twenty-five yards?"

"When it's working right," said Bollinger.

"How is it now?"

Bollinger ducked in the pilot house then came out. "Resolution's good. I'd say it's okay."

"Can you put us on the step and make a quick pass. I figure I can get a few pictures, maybe a half dozen, before we duck back in the soup."

"Worth a try." Bollinger took out a towel and wiped rain off his face.

"We can't go closer than five hundred yards..."

"Suits me, Commander." Bollinger explained the plan to Thomas, who passed the word throughout the boat. Then he called down the chart room hatch. "Hey, Bambino. I want you to start calling ranges every one hundred yards once we get inside a thousand, Got it?"

"Yes, Sir."

Bollinger donned a steel helmet. "All set?"

Everyone nodded.

"Ralphy, your glasses dry?"

Thomas gave a broad grin and carefully arranged a steel helmet around his glasses. "All set, skipper."

"You ready, Commander?"

"Of course." Landa put on a helmet and buckled the strap.

"How about your lens cap?"

Landa flashed the uncovered lens to Bollinger. "Film is in the camera, too."

"Okay, boys, here we go." Bollinger advanced the throttles. With a thunderous blast, *PT-94* quickly gained the step and charged into the rain.

Gambino yelled up from the charthouse, "nine hundred, come right a bit...eight hundred, right on the money...seven...six..."

Suddenly, the *Howell* hove into sight.

"Five hundred yards," yelled Gambino.

"Close enough," Landa yelled.

Bollinger spun his rudder to parallel the ship. "She's all yours, Commander."

Even at five hundred yards it seemed as if they were right on top. Landa steadied his camera on the bulwark and began snapping pictures. That was when he saw a red flash, forward of the Howell's aft stack. "Sonofabitch! They've got the quad forties going. Go back!" He yelled.

Bollinger needed no encouragement and spun his helm to port as forty millimeter tracers arced overhead. "Ralph! Commence fire! Go for that forty millimeter."

Thomas relayed the command, and soon *PT-94*s port and starboard twin fifty caliber gun mounts began chattering, while the forty-millimeter methodically pumped out rounds.

PT-94 raced for the squall line. As Landa looked back, it seemed as if the Japanese had only two of the four forty-millimeter cannons going. But that was enough, each barrel capable of firing eighty rounds per minute. He was fairly certain the Japanese gun crew didn't have electrical power, so it would be difficult for them to track the PT manually. But they began to gather a rhythm, and plumes of water shot up off their starboard bow, then three more hit in rapid succession to port.

"Go! Go!" Landa yelled.

Bollinger jinked the boat right, then left, and tried to shove the throttles further forward even though they were already in the stops.

To port, a line of geysering plumes of water ate their way toward them, Bollinger whipped the rudder again, to the right this time and mercifully, *PT-94* whipped into the squall line, the visibility shutting down to fifty yards.

Landa was ready to cheer when he heard a loud metallic clang followed by a THUNK!

. . .

...rain dripped down his face and he blinked his eyes. Pain. Twenty-five thousand volts of electricity ran up his right leg. "Ahhhh!" Landa tried to rise.

"Easy, Commander." It was Gambino, putting a splint on his right leg.

"What the hell?" Landa's ankle throbbed horribly. And he had a goose egg on his head.

"Looks like you broke it, Commander," said Gambino. "But the skin ain't broken."

"You okay, Commander?" Bollinger stood over him.

"What happened?" Except for a pathetic gurgle, there was hardly any engine noise. And what ever was running in the engine room made the whole boat shake violently. Beside him, Ensign Thomas's lifeless eyes stared through his dripping spectacles into the rain. A pool of blood formed beneath his head and ran into the deck grating. "Oh my God."

Bollinger goosed one of the chokes, making the port engine backfire. Then it caught and the boat surged forward, as black smoke poured out the exhaust. Then the engine nearly quit with Bollinger having to do the whole process again. At length, he said, "Nips got in a lucky round just as we ducked in the soup. Hit the engine room, took out two engines and just about wiped out the port engine. Killed my Motor Mac down there." He nodded to his right. "...and Ralph,"

"I'm sorry."

"Me too. This was just his third ride. I was beginning to like the little jerk." Bollinger took off his helmet and dropped it on the grate. Rain dripped down his face and he ran a hand over his mouth. "We're taking on water faster than the pumps will hold us, so I'm going to have to beach us pretty soon."

Landa tried to rise. Pain shot up his leg. "Agghh."

"That's the bad news."

"Yeah?" Landa laid back, his leg on fire.

"The radar still works."

32

7 April, 1943
   IJN CinC Headquarters,
   Rabaul, New Britain Island
   Bismarck Archipelago

Yamamoto was quartered in the governor's mansion perched high on a hill where breezes were cool, the view of Rabaul's great natural harbor, breathtaking. The Germans had built the mansion in 1910; but ten years later, they lost it all. Rabaul and the Bismarck Archipelago were ceded to the Australians, part of Germany's World War I reparations: the end of their expansion in the Pacific.

Heijiro, the *Gensui's* orderly, awakened him at five o'clock with a cup of strong American coffee. He took a quick shower then dressed in a red housecoat. Stepping down the grand staircase and out the foyer, he walked outside onto the broad granite porch to watch the dawn break.

Twenty minutes later, a man on horseback materialized from the gloom. With a grunt, Isoroku Yamamoto walked down the steps to greet him.

"Good Morning *Gensui*." Vice Admiral Ryunosuke Kusaka was perched aboard a shimmering black horse; but he looked like a scarecrow silhouetted against the broad expanse of Rabaul Harbor, 1000 feet below. Dressed in green utilities, the officer in charge of Southeast Area Fleet operations in Rabaul had insisted on eating his men's rations. And his body looked like it. Yamamoto estimated he weighed no more than fifty kilos.

The Eastern horizon glowed with the new day, making Yamamoto's housecoat seem to radiate. "Come on up, my friend. Have some breakfast."

Kusaka leaned back a bit, swung a leg over the saddle, then let his weight ease him off the horse. "No stomach for it, *Gensui*. Too much Johnnie Walker last night." Silently, Kusaka's aid, a full Navy captain, stepped forward, caught the horse's reins and led it away, its hooves clopping into the murk.

Yamamoto nodded with a chuckle. Kusaka had him there. They had drunk a lot last night. After a final *Operation I* planning session, lasting until 9:30,Yamamoto, Kusaka, Vice Admiral Matome Ugaki, his Chief of Staff and Third Fleet Vice Admiral Jisaburo Ozawa had done quite a bit of damage to the case of scotch Yamamoto had brought from the *Musashi*.

Yamamoto said, "Well then, come on in. We have green tea, sea bream and cold beer to wash away last night's tremors."

The blast of a whistle echoed up from Rabaul Harbor. Then an anchor chain rattled in a hawsepipe. They stopped to listen and watch, as the sun rose above the hills to the east.

They'd been friends for over three decades and Yamamoto knew Kusaka had something to say. "What?"

"Good news. Ozawa has agreed to give us the last of his eight dive bombers."

Yamamoto raised his eyebrows.

"From the *Zuikaku*," Kusaka offered.

"And?"

"And they're taking off now and will be here in three hours. After refueling and arming, they can be ready to go at, say, ten-thirty or eleven."

The corners of Yamamoto's mouth turned up. He raised his arms momentarily and dropped them to his side. "Good work, Kusaka. How did you ever convince him?"

"After you went to bed, I threatened not to refuel his carriers."

"Excellent. We'll hold off the attack until those planes are ready. I don't want them to go unescorted."

"I agree *Gensui*. It's only a two hour delay at the worst."

Yamamoto took Kusaka's elbow and led him through massive double doors. Aids and attendants stood about, but Yamamoto dismissed them all with a wave of his hand. He said, "At last, we have fine weather today." It had rained heavily the past three days causing Yamamoto to postpone *Operation I*.

"Yes, *Gensui*. And it's reported to be clear over Guadalcanal."

"Excellent." Yamamoto sniffed, as the odor of fresh breakfast wafted from the kitchen. "We have eggs."

Kusaka grimaced.

Yamamoto slapped Kusaka on the back. "First some Bromide. Then the eggs." Yamamoto led him into a well appointed, high ceilinged dinning room. The long mahogany table was huge, and could easily accommodate twenty diners in splendor. He dragged one of the heavy chairs out and said, "Here, sit, Kusaka, sit."

"But, I'm not hungry."

Suddenly, Yamamoto's face turned stone-cold. "Damn you." He pushed Kusaka into a chair.

"What?"

"You'll eat."

"But I just--"

Yamamoto leaned over and grabbed Kusaka's lapel, his voice rumbling. "Why do you think I had to come up here?"

"But *Gensui*..."

"I need every bit of you. Healthy. Not on some sort of fast, making the men look up to you. Now, there's food for you in the larder. And I want you to eat, damn it." He leaned closer. "These strikes are our last chance to hold onto the Solomons. If they fail, we fail. To bring this off, my pilots need a healthy air officer. One they can look up to; one who can properly lead them."

Yamamoto released Kusaka' lapel and stood.

"Yes *Gensui*..."

"That's why I had you up here this morning. To eat, damnit!"

"Yes G---"

"--We'll have a proper American breakfast." He clapped his hands. Stewards poured into the dining room, carrying gleaming silver trays laden with steaming food. "You'll need every calorie throughout these ten days."

Kusaka's stomach knotted in protest. "Yes, *Gensui*."

The attack force began their takeoffs from Lakunai Airfield at exactly ten-thirty. Commander In Chief Isoroku Yamamoto stood at mid-runway, resplendent in dress whites, with full medals and sword, waving at his planes as they roared past. He was by himself, purposefully away from his entourage. He wanted his pilots to see him.

Each time a plane thundered down the runway, Yamamoto saluted, then grabbed his cap by the bill and waved it in the air. Since he was the only one in dress whites at the air briefing earlier this morning, most of his pilots managed to wave back, while coaxing their bomb-laden aircraft off the ground.

The last plane took off, a twin engine land attack bomber. Yamamoto turned and watched it race to join its squadron. The rumbling engines from the orbiting attack force of nearly one hundred planes were almost deafening. Another seventy planes would join them along the way, rising from airfields on the outer Bismarck's, Buka, and Bougainville making this raid 170 planes in all, about the same size as the Pearl Harbor attack force. Except this time, Yamamoto thought ruefully, there targets were not a peacetime U.S. Navy, lolling about on antiquated battleships, nursing hangovers on an early Sunday morning.

"We'll soon find out," Yamamoto muttered. Under a warm sun, he walked to the shade of a scraggly palm, joining Admirals Kusaka and Ugaki. Hovering behind them was Captain Takano who had been waiting four days for the *Matukaze*. Due in today, the destroyer had been delayed in Vila, having wiped a starboard drive shaft bearing.

Ugaki swatted a fly off his cheek. "The fleet meteorologist says the weather looks good for the next week or so."

"Which means we can do at least four raids before we return Ozawa's planes," said Yamamoto.

The strike force steadied on a course toward the lower Solomon Islands, the sound of their engines fading. More to himself than anybody else,

Yamamoto said again, "We'll soon find out."

A leading seaman walked up and tapped Takano on the shoulder. "Sir, the base operations officer sends his complements."

"Yes?"

"I'm to tell you that the *Matukaze* dropped anchor fifteen minutes ago."

"Good!" exclaimed Takano. "Tell---"

"---good news Takano?" Yamamoto asked.

"The best, *Gensui*. The *Matukaze* has just arrived," said Takano.

"The secret ammunition is finally here?" asked Yamamoto with mock incredulity.

"Yes, Sir. Now at the harbor."

"Well, then," said Yamamoto. " Don't let us keep you waiting. Best not to keep the good Captain Enomoto waiting, either. "Take my car." Yamamoto waved to his midnight-blue Packard super 8 touring limousine, a war prize from the American embassy in Batavia.

"You mean..."

Yamamoto's eyes were bright. "Please, please, go ahead. I won't be needing it. I'm going to wait here for my lads to come back."

Takano was so excited he didn't notice that Kusaka and Ugaki's eyes were dark and malevolent. He bowed deeply. "Thank you, *Gensui*. Thank you." He ran for the Packard like a teenager released from home on a Saturday night.

"Bring me one," Yamamoto shouted after him.

"Yes, Sir," Takano blurted over his shoulder.

He didn't hear the three admirals laughing as he went.

The *Matukaze* was an old *Udaki* class destroyer built in 1924. With two Parsons turbines powered by four Kanpon boilers, she was still swift and capable of thirty-four knots. Her armament consisted of four 4.7 deck canons and six twenty-one inch torpedo tubes in two triple mounts. Long and narrow, she had a high forecastle and raked mast and stacks, giving her a low and graceful silhouette. Even now, while swinging at anchor, she looked to Takano as if she were racing along at thirty knots.

The shore boat pulled alongside with Takano surprised to find a glossy varnished boarding ladder waiting for him. A bugle blew as he climbed up to the main deck where Commander Ryozo Enomoto, a short, balding man of 190 pounds, saluted smartly. Gathered in ranks behind Enomoto were the ships officers.

"How nice, Enomoto. Thank you very much" Takano returned the salutes and shook Endnote's hand warmly.

Smiling broadly, Enomoto introduced Takano to his officers then said, "would you care to?"

"Lead the way, Captain," said Takano pedantically, as if he were waiting for a high school student to demonstrate a term project.

"They're right over here in the machine shop." Enomoto walked across the deck to a hatchway.

Two sentries stood aside as Enomoto, Takano and the ship's executive and gunnery officers, stepped in the small space where they were engulfed by the odors of hydraulic fluid and cutting oil. Perhaps two by three meters, it was tight, but efficient, Takano noticed, with lathe, drill press, and grinder arranged neatly on one bulkhead, a gleaming stainless workbench on the opposite. Securely strapped on the workbench were five five-inch shells, their tops covered with a canvas.

Enomoto looked perplexed.

"What?" said Takano.

"I told them to leave one out." Enomoto glared at his gunnery officer.

The red-faced lieutenant stepped forward, yanked open a tool-drawer, and produced a web wrench. "*Hai!*" With a bow, he handed it to Enomoto and stepped back.

Enomoto proudly held up the web wrench. "Do you wish..?" Pointing to the canvas-covered projectiles, he was asking if Takano wanted to personally unscrew the fuses.

Takano's heart raced. He would have liked nothing better and it was all he could do maintain his decorum before the other three men. Suppressing the urge to rip the canvas off was a supreme effort. Mustering all his calm, he waved casually. "Please, go ahead."

"Yes." Enomoto untied the line, the canvas falling to the deck. "Here you are, Sir."

Takano's heart plunged into an abyss. "Is this some kind of a joke?"

"Sir?" Enomoto's face turned white,

"You dolt!" Takano yelled.

Panic stricken, the executive and gunnery officers beat a hasty retreat.

"I don't understand," said Enomoto.

Takano screamed. "These projectiles are capped with Mark 18 mechanical time fuses."

"Isn't that what you wanted?"

"No," screeched Takano. It occurred to him that the *Gensui*'s Packard limousine waited patiently at dockside -- and that he would have to return it soon -- empty handed.

"What do I say to him?" he yelled.

"Wh --- who? asked Enomoto.

"What am I supposed to tell the *Gensui*?" he screamed again.

33

Enroute -- Noumea to Tulagi
  7 April, 1943

Ingram ran a hand over his thick stubble. He'd been flying for the past three days. He hadn't bathed and his meals consisted of cellophane-wrapped peanut butter sandwiches accompanied by innumerable cups of lukewarm coffee poured from thermoses that had flown more miles than Jimmy Doolittle. Occasionally, he was able to grab a shave and stretch his legs when they stopped for fuel.

And now, he was headed for Tulagi in a beat up PBY, the last nine hundred mile leg of a laborious trip from the States. Loose rivets rattled as they droned along, the pilot picking his way through clouds shimmering in bright moonlight. At 8,000 feet, the air was cold, smooth, stable, and somnolent, a marvelous relief from the rough weather they'd been through the last two days.

The pilot was a twenty-two year old j.g, by the name of Elmer Nephron, a kid with a lop-sided grin from Kentucky who spoke with a drawl and answered to "Neff."

Jumping aboard the PBY, Ingram admitted that he was more than a little excited about the prospect of seeing the *Pence*. Ralph Druckman, her commanding officer had been a year ahead of Ingram at the Naval Academy. His recollection was that Druckman was a good man, and thus Ingram had reasonable expectations to find the destroyer in decent shape when he boarded her in -- he checked his watch -- in another five hours.

He looked out the PBY's big blister window, watching moonlit clouds scoot by. His body was dog-tired, but with the coffee, his mind raced. Not only over the anxiety of seeing his first command, but the events on the first leg of the flight kept Ingram's thoughts churning.

They had taken off from Long Beach aboard a lumbering four-engined PB2Y Coronado when he introduced himself to the man sitting beside him. He was a tall, lanky, three striper named Mike Novak, who was on a return trip to Hawaii with a briefcase chained to his wrist. Novak had long, sandy hair and a burnt freckled nose that made him look as if he'd just stepped from the Waikiki surf. Naturally, he had a bright, disarming smile, and as the Coronado climbed out from the California coast, they got to talking; Novak taking in Ingram's Navy cross, Ingram spotting Novak's gold submarine pin. After five minutes, they discovered they had a common acquaintance: Frank Ashton, Novak's cousin on his mother's side.

Their conversation dwindled when it grew dark. Novak flipped on his little overhead light, opened his briefcase and pulled out papers. Soon, he was scrunched far in the corner, his shoulder raised, making sure no one could see what lay before him. Over the next hour, he had a lot of material scattered on his lap; so much so, that he undid his seat belt to make room.

That's when they hit the downdraft. The Coronado plummeted like a lead brick. Men screamed, and the odor of vomit raced through the stricken plane. The engines roared and Novak hit the ceiling with a 'thunk,' his papers scattering. Ingram was half asleep, but had left his belt buckled. He flipped open his eyes to see Novak's feet wiggling beside his head. The cabin lights blinked off and passengers screamed again.

Then the Coronado caught itself and Novak plummeted. Ingram was barely able to guide him into his seat, where Novak sat sprawled, woozy and rubbing his head. After a while, the Coronado flew into clear air and the cabin lights blinked back into life. Ingram's heart thumped and his face broke into a cold sweat. About him, people cursed and moaned.

Do something.

Looking about, he spotted the mess of papers on the deck beneath a semi-conscious Novak. The briefcase had fallen to the floor stretching the Commander's arm to full scope. Ingram bent over, picked up the briefcase and eased it back into Novak's lap, the lid still open. Then, he scooped papers off the floor.

That was when he noticed a series of messages marked TOP SECRET. As much as he tried to tear his eyes away, he couldn't help but read the subject of one: YAMAMOTO DEPARTS TRUK LAGOON. Another message read: YAMAMOTO GARRISONED RABAUL. Then he found folders under his seat with broad red stripes marked 'TOP SECRET ULTRA.' Quickly, he stuffed all the papers in the briefcase as Novak's head flopped back and forth with the turbulence.

In twenty minutes, Novak was fully awake. With a sheepish grin, he mumbled his thanks, drank a Dixie cup of water, and soon was exploring his briefcase as Ingram dropped off to sleep.

Ingram felt a nudge.

"Mr. Ingram?" Novak flipped off his seatbelt and leaned close.

"Yes?"

"Was it you who returned the material to my briefcase?"

"Yes, Sir."

Novak bit a fingernail for a minute. "What did you see?"

Ingram knew what was coming and made a show of smacking his lips. "Nothing Commander. I just shoved a bunch of stuff back in your briefcase without looking."

Novak asked, "What made you think you had to do that?" Novak's face may have looked like a Waikiki a surfing idol, but his eyes were like Count Dracula.

"Do what?"

Novak gave a shallow smile. "To not look. See here, Mr. Ingram...Todd. I have to ask this. There was classified material in there."

The possibilities unfolded: Novak would radio ahead. Military police would be waiting in at Hickam Field. Interrogations. Signed Statements.

Ingram had no desire to be delayed in Honolulu while security goons reviewed his background, questioned him incessantly, and then maybe had his orders changed, sending him to supervise a fuel dump in Peru. "Couldn't see a thing," he said, yawning.

"What?"

"Lights went out."

"Oh, yes?"

"Yeah, when the plane leveled out I strapped you in. Then, like I said, I shoved your stuff in the briefcase, put it on your seat and zipped it up."

"But when did the lights--"

"---you should be more careful, commander."

"What?"

"Turbulence. You know. Happens all the time. Like right now." Ingram pointed. "You should fasten your seatbelt."

As if to reinforce his point, the plane jiggled a bit with some turbulence. Novak quickly buckled his seat belt. Later, he stood and spoke in low tones with other passengers. Then he returned to his seat with a sigh, and started talking about surfing on the Island's North side. Suddenly, he began reminiscing about Ashton, and at one point talked about his great-grandfather's accomplishments with Dewey in Manila Bay.

With the most innocent look he could conjure, Ingram said, "I thought it was Farragut at Mobil Bay."

Novak looked in the distance, grunted, returned to his reading and eventually fell asleep. They rode the remaining four and a half hours to Hawaii in silence.

Ingram checked his watch: Tulagi in ten minutes. The PBY's engines droned effortlessly in clear, stable air. It was late morning with bright sunshine and crisp, white, clouds rolling easily on the western horizon. Nephron had invited Ingram forward and he had been sitting in the right seat for the past hour. The co-pilot, a young acne-ridden ensign named Bailey, was in the radio compartment fiddling with the radio receiver. It had gone sour two hours ago and now Bailey, a genius with electronics, sat on the deck with the flight engineer: tubes, wires and screws, scattered all over the floor.

They were at 5,000 feet when Nephron pulled back on the throttles and eased into a shallow left bank for their decent into Tulagi Harbor. Peering out his window, he said, "Lookie here."

Ingram craned his neck to look out the port side. The activity seemed more pronounced than usual. Ships at anchor belched black smoke while others headed out to sea, large wakes churning behind. He nodded and said, "Something's going on, all right."

Nephron leaned around his seat and shouted aft, "How ya coming, fellas? I gotta have landing instructions. And I gotta call the Commander's ship, so he can get a ride."

Bailey clacked gum and said, "Drive the plane, Neff. I'll let you know."

Nephron muttered, looked out the window and pointed over to Guadalcanal, where many black dots swirled about. "Damn, look at all the planes coming up from Cactus. Must be going after something." Then he tapped his fuel gauge and shouted back to Bailey. "I'm down to 120 gallons, with no place to go, except Jap country."

Bailey yelled back, "What the hell do you want me to do? Fix this damn radio or come up there and help you drive?"

Nephron said, "Keep your shirt on. I'll land this thing. You fix that radio."

"Couple more minutes," said Bailey.

"I ain't got two minutes. We're going in." Nephron pulled further back on the throttles letting the twin engine amphibian descend more steeply.

Ingram offered, "You want me to head aft?"

Nephron waved a hand, "Naw, naw, Commander. Keep your seat and buckle up tight. You're in for some fun."

Five minutes later, they were 200 feet off the ocean, zipping over the fairway. Near the end, Ingram saw an anchored *Fletcher* class destroyer whip past. As Nephron turned to ease into their downwind leg, Ingram grabbed a pair of binoculars and focused on the destroyer's little white numbers near the bow: 452. "Hey, that's my ship!"

"You sure?" Nephron reached behind his head to flip a switch. Soon, the wing tip floats eased down and locked into position.

"No mistake. That's the *Pence* all right."

Nephron grinned and said, "Well, maybe we can fix you up after all. Looks like they have their whale boat alongside. We'll give you curb service."

He leaned back to his engineer. "Smiley, try and raise that ship on the signal lamp. Tell 'em we have their next commanding officer aboard and to please send the whaleboat."

"Yes, Sir." The flight engineer scrambled aft to signal through the port blister window.

By the time Nephron advanced the PBY's fuel setting to AUTO RICH, opened the cowl flaps and set the props in the flat pitch position, Smiley was back, patting Ingram on the shoulder, "All set Commander. They're waitin' for you."

Nephron turned the plane again and lined up on the fairway for their final approach. Then he eased back on his throttles and the plane glided down. "See? We aim to please, Commander. After all, this is strictly against regulations. But what the heck, you're so tired you look like Frankenstein warmed over. Figure I'm doing the Navy a favor just keeping you alive." Nephron quickly looked around to his co-pilot and flight engineer. "You guys buckled up?"

Bailey said dryly, "Try not to crash into a ship, Neff." Earlier, Nephron had turned white telling Ingram about landing here a week ago. It was foggy; they nearly hit a ship illegally anchored in this same fairway. Nephron said he goosed the throttles and barely bounced the PBY over the errant vessel which turned out to be an ammunition ship.

"Soooo, solly, Choley" Said Nephron in a passable Richard Loo accent. "No honorable filahwoks this morning."

Ingram cinched his seat belt as tight as it could go. Sometimes water landings could be bumpy. Instead, the water sparkled as an eight-knot wind stirred little waves making it an amphib pilot's dream. Nephron eased off the throttles then pulled slightly back on the yoke. The twin Pratt & Whitney R1830 engines backfired softly as the PBY sank the last few feet, its step kissing the waters of Tulagi Harbor. Easily, she settled, a tumult of white mist trailing behind her. Within ten seconds she wallowed at taxi speed, heading for the *Pence* just two hundred yards away. "How's that, Commander?" Nephron asked.

"Smooth. You want to switch jobs?"

"No thanks, Sir. I get seasick." He pointed to the *Pence's* whale boat, which had just shoved off. "Here's your taxi."

"That was quick," Ingram said, looking at his ship. She wore a dapple pattern camouflage that gave her a determined, business-like appearance. But nothing could detract from her clean, flush-deck lines, her raked stacks and mast, her five single five-inch gun mounts defiantly pointing at the sky.

Smoke belched from her stacks. And men were perched at the bow peering down at her anchor chain which stood straight up and down. Ingram muttered, "Damn, they're hauling in the anchor." Then, he leaned over and shook Nephron's hand. "Thanks Neff."

" See you in the next war, Commander."

Ingram rose from his seat and pat him on the shoulder, " Let's hope not."

34

---

7 April, 1943
Tulagi Harbor, Solomon Islands

Ingram jumped into the whale boat, stumbled, and held on.

"Better hurry up, Commander. They like to write you up for missing movement." It was Leo Seltzer, standing at the tiller. And he wasn't wasting time, ringing his bell, backing clear of the PBY.

"I'll be damned!" Ingram walked aft and shook the boatswain's mate's hand. "Good to see you, Leo."

The whaleboat's engine roared as she gained sternway. Seltzer said, "Welcome to the *Pence*, Sir."

Seltzer's voice had a sarcastic edge. Ingram asked. "Were you worried?"

"I knew you'd see the light." Seltzer shifted his rudder, rang four bells, and headed for the destroyer.

Seltzer was busy approaching the destroyer's port side, so Ingram let the remark go. Besides, she looked as if she were underway. The *Pence*'s anchor had cleared the water and her fo'c'sle crew was hosing the mud off.

As if reading his mind, Seltzer said. "Another five minutes and we would have been gone, Sir."

"What's up?"

"Jap raid, so we've been told. Coastwatchers say lots of Nips headed down The Slot."

A small wave curled at the *Pence's* bow. She had headway now, perhaps three or four knots; but Seltzer expertly drove the whaleboat directly under the port boat davits, where the falls were lowered and waiting. The hooks were soon snapped into place and a strain taken. The moment the whale boat was hauled clear of the water, the *Pense* picked up speed. By the time the boat was even with the maindeck bulwarks, a considerable wake gushed down her sides.

"Welcome to the S.S. *Luriline*, Commander Ingram. We offer group rates, Dungeness crab, and our special today will be is a self-guided tour of Iron Bottom Sound, courtesy of the Imperial Japanese Naval Travel Agency," said Seltzer.

"Besides all that, how do you like her?"

"Great ship. She's been through the mill a couple of times, but the skipper's brought her through in good shape."

"How's the chow?"

"Lousy."

"Okay, thanks, Leo." Ingram climbed out and stepped on the main deck,

Seltzer pitched Ingram's duffle over. "We do accept tips." He gave a thumbs up and the deck crew began hoisting the whaleboat all the way to the davit tops. Then he added, "See you on the bridge. I'm GQ helmsman."

"Okay."

Ingram stood by himself for a moment, taking in his ship. Wind was at his face and the destroyer rolled slightly as she gathered way. Through the forward engineroom hatch, he heard the engine-telegraph clang. Immediately, the uptakes whined, as more air and fuel oil was fed to her hungry boilers, allowing more steam to flow to the turbines for more speed. For all he had been through, it felt good. The *Pence* was a living, breathing thing of muscle and bone, with over 300 souls bringing her to life. As if someone had turned on a gleaming spotlight, Ingram realized it all made sense. This was where he belonged. He hadn't felt like this since he'd commanded the minesweeper *Pelican*. *Yes, you made the right decision. Landa was right. So was Helen.*

"Todd!" someone shouted.

Ingram looked up to see a helmeted figure leaning over the signal bridge. He recognized the silhouette as Commander Ralph Druckman, the man he was relieving. Ingram saluted and shouted back, "Permission to come aboard, Captain?"

"You bet. Now dump your gear in my day cabin and get up here, pronto."

"Aye, aye, Sir."

By now, Ingram reckoned the ship was cutting through the water at twenty knots, heading south into Iron Bottom Sound. Behind him, the boatswains' mates had gripped in the whaleboat in record time and dashed off to their general quarters stations, Seltzer among them. Quickly, he walked through the midships passageway, found the captain's day cabin, and changed to working khakis. Then he dashed two flights up to the bridge.

Ralph Druckman had been a 3.9 student at the Naval Academy. Many were put off by his rather permanent scowl, but Ingram discovered in his sophomore year that Druckman had a great sense of humor. But he never smiled. Never. Thus he acquired the nickname 'Deadpan Druckman' which sometimes became 'Deadman Druckman' behind his back. Ingram walked up to the thin, sandy-haired full commander. "Good morning, Captain."

Binoculars were pressed to Druckman's eyes. He swept the sky, then looked aside quickly and shook Ingram's hand. "Welcome aboard, Todd. Heard they pinned a Navy cross on you. Congratulations."

"That was a while back, Sir."

"Hell of a time for a change of command ceremony."

"I guess someone forgot to invite the Japs."

"They must have found out somehow." Druckman's binoculars went back to his eyes.

"What do you want me to do?"

"No time to bring you up to speed." He pointed to the starboard bridge wing. "Stand there and look intelligent."

"Okay, but can somebody tell me what's up?"

Druckman again searched the sky. "Jap planes. Bunch of them. Coming down The Slot. So many pips the radar looks like it has the measles."

"How far out?"

"Twenty miles was the last range. The information isn't clear." He stepped into the pilothouse and said, "Find out from Greenhorn if they want us to form up, damnit." Then he stepped back outside., "Best you put on a helmet, Todd. It's gonna be a long day."

Ingram found one in a rack in the pilot house. As he buckled it on, he spotted Seltzer at the helm. The sailors on either side of him gazed open-mouthed at Ingram, as if he'd just stepped off another planet.

The boatswain's mate winked at Ingram and said from the side of his mouth, "Buck up, you guys. He ain't no used car salesman." He grinned. "Some welcoming party, huh, Mr. Ingram?"

Ingram's response was cut-off by the TBS screeching, "*Greenhorn, this is Socrates...*" An unintelligible series of phonetic letters followed.

Ingram stepped out to the bridgewing and found Druckman, "Who's Socrates?"

"DESDIV Eleven." He pointed to the low outline of four destroyers about five miles ahead, white froth kicking from their transoms.

"*Griffith* and *Isaacs*?"

AUmm, plus two new ones, the *Haake* and *Lindsay*. We were late getting underway because we had to refuel. And then---"

Suddenly, a great volley rose from the ships of DESDIV Eleven, the sky peppered with black smoke puffs, as twenty or so menacing black dots orbited overhead. To the northwest, Ingram spotted a pair of Lockheed P-38 Light-nings, following a twin-engine Mitsubishi G4M1 "Betty" bomber down to the sea, fire and smoke trailing from one of its engines. The Betty went in with a great splash and the P-38s eased from their dives heading for the *Pence*. At full throttle, they whined overhead, then pulled up into the sky. The men on the Pence's bridge shoved their fists in the air, cheering as the P-38 did a victory roll.

Druckman pointed to the Plexiglas status board. Ingram quickly scanned it finding at least twenty bogies listed. But the data was confusing. No targets were designated. And with the shooting, the noise from all around was deaf-ening; Ingram couldn't understand what Druckman was saying.

Atop the pilot house, the gunnery officer shouted and pointed. Ingram squinted as others raised their binoculars, finding five Val dive bombers flying toward them in a tight vee formation at 10,000 feet. They were close, only about three miles away. But it was a perfect fire-control solution because the planes were directly abeam of the ship, unmasking all of the *Pence's* guns.

"Bearing clear, batteries released," barked Druckman.

The gunboss yelled "Commence fire," and in unison, the *Pence's* five five-inch guns roared at the dive bombers. Soon, black puffs blossomed beside one of the planes. It jiggled for a moment, then drifted off to the left, smoke trailing from its engine. The guns roared, and another plane virtually exploded in a bright, red flash, bringing more cheers from the men on the bridge. But the other three dive bombers plodded on, holding formation. Finally the lead Val pushed over, screaming down at the *Pence*.

Guns roared. Cordite laden smoke tore at Ingram's nostrils. Five-inch brass cartridges spewed out from behind the gun-mounts, clanging on the deck. His gut wrenched and his heart pounded and the sides of his head seemed to close in. In spite of the powerful volley racing skyward, a remote voice urged him to find a hole and crawl in. Through it all, he heard Druckman call for flank speed and left full rudder.

Another Val, the trailing one, lost a wing and began insanely spinning, parts tumbling through the sky. The remaining two Vals released their bombs, pulled up, and clawed for altitude.

Druckman shouted over the din, "Shift your rudder!"

Seltzer spun his wheel clockwise, the ship leaning to port as she whipped in a turn to starboard.

The bombs straddled the *Pence*, one going off twenty yards to starboard, the other, thirty yards to port. Twin columns of foaming white water rocketed into the sky, as the explosions ripped at the destroyer with two strident WHACKs! But the *Pence* kept going, her five-inch guns firing at the Vals as they tried to escape. One shot erupted near the lead Val. A light haze suddenly trailed from her engine. She wobbled a bit, but kept on, disappearing in haze.

"Cease Fire," called Druckman. He said to his talker, "Report damage aft." Then he caught Ingram's eye, "How about that?"

Ingram's ears rang from the gunfire. He shouted, "Damn fine shooting, Captain."

Druckman yelled back, "Notice the dead time? Three, maybe four seconds, each gun?"

"Very rapid. You have great gun crews."

"The loaders have arms like tree stumps. And the proximity fuses help a lot."

"VTs? You're using VTs?" Ingram blurted.

"Of course. Wouldn't be caught without them." He waved at a smudge on the ocean where a Val had hit the water. "There's your proof."

Suddenly, Druckman looked over the side. "What the hell? We're losing speed."

The talker turned to Druckman and said, "Captain, the forward fireroom has a split seam ten feet beneath the waterline at frame eighty-six, Sir. Water is pouring in and the snipes have wrapped-up numbers one and two boilers."

"Good God!" said Druckman.

The talker's face was like chalk.

"There's more?"

The talker gulped. "Split seam in the aft fireroom. Uhhh, frame one-thirty-three, right at the waterline. They had to wrap up boiler number four."

"Number four?" Druckman was incredulous.

"Ye...yes, Sir. And the burners went out on boiler three. But they have it going again. Mr. Lissenger says our best speed is twelve knots."

"Jesus!" Druckman looked at Ingram, his mouth working. Then he nodded at the pilot house. "See if you can raise Rocko on the *Whitney*. Ask him to send a tug." Then he turned to his talker. Get Mr. Lissinger on the---"

"--- Captain!" The gunnery officer leaned out and pointed. Another twin-engined "Betty" bomber was about four miles out, no more than thirty feet off the deck; headed right at them.

Ingram grabbed the bulwark, his hands frozen.

"Do you have a solution?" Druckman yelled to the gunnery officer.

"On target and tracking," shouted the gunboss.

Druckman roared, "Bearing clear. Batteries released!"

The Gun Boss's voice echoed, "All mounts commence fire!"

Within three seconds, all gun mounts blazed: Five inch, forty millimeter, and twenty millimeter. The smoke was so great that at first that it seemed to envelop the ship. When it cleared, the Betty had halved the distance, her starboard engine trailing smoke. Ingram started to cheer. But it caught in his throat when he saw a long black torpedo slung beneath the Betty's belly.

On the Betty flew, straight for the *Pence*, still trailing smoke, thick and black now. The plane was pretty well ripped up, Ingram reckoned. But he had to admire the man at the controls. Most likely he was terribly wounded and knew he was about to die. Yet he held an iron grip, piloting his plane in with shells bursting all around, great spouts of water kicking up before him from the five-inch guns.

One thousand yards.

Suddenly the Betty exploded. Parts and flaming debris splattered over the ocean. Men pounded each other's back. They yelled. Druckman punched Ingram's arm.

But Ingram grabbed the bulwark, his mouth, open, an icy fire raging in his stomach.

"What is it, Todd?" asked Druckman.

Ingram pointed. A deadly, white wake trailed from the Betty's funeral pyre. It gained speed, arrowing straight for the *Pence*.

"Torpedo!" Druckman shouted, "Hard right rudder."

Seltzer need no urging as he twirled his helm.

Druckman was trying to "comb the torpedo's wake." But the *Pence* had lost power and was slow to answer her helm.

The 1,760 pound aerial torpedo smacked into the *Pence's* bow, just forward of her five-inch gun. The wallop was terrific, throwing Ingram two feet off the deck. Feeling heat and fire and abject terror, Ingram landed in a jumble of arms and legs of semi-conscious men, some groaning, others cursing. Miraculously, they sorted themselves out and stood, none seriously injured. But they shouted at one another. Ingram realized they had been deafened. After a minute, there was a high-pitched ringing in his ears and he began to hear the bellows and cries of desperation from up forward.

Ingram found Druckman leaning against the forward bulwark. He shouted in Druckman's ear. "Are you all right?"

Druckman shook his head; his eyes unfocused, "...give me a minute."

Ingram peered over the bulwark forward to see smoke clearing from the ship's foredeck. There was no bow. The nose of the ship was blown open like a loaded cigar. It hit Ingram. They still had way on. "All stop!" he shouted. He looked in the pilot house to see the leehelmsman staring at him dumbly, still in shock.

Ingram ran in the pilothouse and rang up 'stop' on both engines, then dashed outside to see if it took affect. But it was too late, as he heard the unmistakable sound of a bulkhead giving way. Then the ship began to yaw, listing to port as she did. Druckman's hard right rudder was still on. He looked in the pilot house and shouted at Seltzer. The boatswain was on his knees, both hands clutching the helm for support. His helmet had fallen off with blood soaking his hair and running down the side of his face.

"Leo. Rudder Amidships!" Ingram shouted. "Seltzer! Are you okay?"

Seltzer blinked and his eyes lit up. "Rudder amidships, aye, aye, Sir." He pulled himself to his feet and turned the wheel.

But the ship listed drunkenly to starboard and didn't recover. At the same time, there was a great hiss of steam followed by a loud crack and a roar as another bulkhead gave way.

"She's going, Todd." It was Druckman. Blood ran from his ears as he grasped Ingram's arms.

"How can you be sure?" Ingram yelled.

"Huh?"

The *Pence* slipped another five degrees to starboard. Gear tumbled off the decks into the water. Screams drifted up to him from back aft. Then it hit him. Druckman was right.

She is going.

He yelled at the captain. "Do you want to abandon?"

Druckman stared dumbly.

"Ralph?"

Druckman nodded, his lips pressed.

"Abandon ship!" Ingram shouted. He grabbed Druckman's talker. "Pass the word."

"What?"

"I said 'abandon ship,' damnit! Now pass the word."

"Y--yes, Sir."

Ingram dashed in the pilot house, flipped the 1MC switch, and announced "Abandon ship," three times. He was surprised to hear the metallic echo of his voice ranging about the ship. Strange, he thought. My own voice telling these fine men to get away from something I've worked all my life to achieve.

Seltzer yanked off his headphones and said, "Your abandon ship station is the port whaleboat, Mr. Ingram."

"You the cox'n?"

"Yep."

They ran for the signal bridge and zipped down to the 02 deck where a confused Druckman stood aimlessly, having been shoved down the ladder by two of his officers. Men cursed and milled around the boat davits, as the deck force frantically ungripped the whaleboat. But, it was impossible; the ship's list was nearing thirty degrees to starboard.

An explosion aft knocked Ingram on the deck. Steam and smoke shot out the deck hatches as scalded men emerged on the weather decks writhing in pain and screaming for mercy.

"After fireroom," someone yelled. They struggled to their feet, their faces dazed, minds numbed. It was cold salt water hitting number three or four boilers, maybe both, causing the catastrophic rupture. A crazed realization hit Ingram that one of the boilers in the forward fireroom could go off as well. "Jump!" he shouted. The men about him needed no urging. Two sailors grabbed an incoherent Druckman, steered him to the starboard side and pushed him into the water now awash to the main deck.

"Not long, now, Leo. Let's go." Ingram turned to see a shadow dash back up the bridge companionway. "Seltzer, damnit! Get back here."

Seltzer stood a deck above him, undoing a halyard. "Be right there." Quickly he un-belayed it and began hauling down the U.S. flag.

"Leo! No time."

"It's okay. I'll have this thing---"

Another explosion erupted beneath Ingram, tossing him in the air. A cold shock hit him and he found himself in the water, amongst flaming wreckage and clamoring men. Someone yelled; he looked up to see the main mast coming down on him as the ship began to roll. Ingram frantically swam clear of the mast, as it capsized toward him. Just before it smacked the water, he spotted Seltzer's form on the signal bridge, tangled in halyards and shrouds.

"Leo!"

The mast smacked the water, taking four shrieking sailors with it.

"Leo, for crying..." Ingram started swimming toward the capsized wreck. But a hand grabbed him and pulled him back. "Let go!"

"It's okay, Sir." It was one of the sailors from the *Pence's* bridge crew.

Ingram struggled for a moment, then finally let it go. "Okay."

They kicked their way out of a patch of burning fuel oil and wiggled toward a life raft. Two hands grabbed his shirt; he slithered aboard, joining seven other wet, oil-soaked, exhausted men. He lay on his back for a moment then turned to his side, looking into the eyes of Ralph Druckman. The captain's face was almost completely black, smeared with fuel oil. He coughed and spat; blood ran from a corner of his mouth. Finally Druckman gasped. "Todd. I'm sorry. I really wanted to give you a fine ship."

"It's okay."

Druckman rolled to his back and spoke to the smoke-filled sky. "I'm really sorry. Those were my boys." He clasped his palms to his chest. His mouth quivered, "God, I'm so sorry."

Ingram sat up. He reached over and clapped Druckman's shoulder. "Not your fault, Ralph. You did all you could."

"I'm really sorry." Was it sea water or were tears at the corners of Druckman's eyes. He struggled to a sitting position. "Damn ship wouldn't come around. Shoulda missed that torpedo."

"It's okay, Ralph."

The raft pitched suddenly, and Druckman fell into Ingram's arms.

Both looked up as the *Pence* gave a mighty groan. Fully capsized, her dull red bottom glistened just as her forward section slid under, leaving her stern canted high at an impossible angle. Amongst hissing steam, collapsing bulkheads and the tortuous grinding of metal, she began her final plunge, ten or so men frantically swimming to get clear.

Druckman gave a loud groan as the *Pence* slipped under the waves, rumbling and erupting as she headed for the depths of Iron Bottom Sound. Great air bubbles vomited skyward, leaving a pool of fuel oil, her life blood, glistening on the surface. while dunnage of the living and dead bobbed about in stunned silence.

Still holding onto Druckman, Ingram darted about the swirling, oil-soaked wreckage. "Leo, you damned fool." He urged. "Come on, Leo."

PART III

There is nothing that gives a
man consequence, and
renders him fit for command,
like a support that renders
him independent of
everybody but the state
he serves.

George Washington

For is it not true that the furious intensity of searching for something is often
merely a mask for our fear of actually finding it?

James Webb
The Emperor's General

35

9 April, 1943
  Intelligence Center for the Pacific Ocean Area (ICPOA)
  Pearl Harbor Naval Base, Hawaii

Mike Novak hung up the phone. Captain Roland Ferguson, Commanding Officer of the U.S.S. *Santa Barbara* had just confirmed his suspicions. *Damnit!* Now he had a major security problem. Looking out his window into a bullpen of cryptographers, he drummed his fingers for a moment, then dialed Major Robert St. Clair who, in addition to his duties as brig commander, was now director of FRUPAC security.

A sleepy voice answered, "Hello?"

"Bob. It's Mike."

St. Clair coughed spasmodically. At length, he managed. "It's late."

In the background, Novak heard St. Clair's Zippo click, then his exhale. "Bob, do you remember me telling you about that two and a half striper who rode with me on the PB4Y out from Long Beach?"

There was a moment of silence. "You mean the guy you think saw your, ahem" St. Clair cleared his throat in respect for an unsecure line, "ah, *stuff* while you were unconscious?"

"Precisely. I just rang off with a cruiser captain who was sitting in the seat behind. He not only told me the lights came on right away, but he saw Ingram reach in the aisle and pick up my...*stuff*."

"That was nice of him to help you out."

"Damnit. The sonofabitch lied to me, Bob. It wasn't dark like he said. The lights were on. He could have read all that material without anyone the wiser."

"So what can you do about it?" Taking another drag, St. Clair picked tobacco bits off his tongue.

"Well, I'm wondering if we should bring him back here, so we can find out what he knows. After all, he could pop off to someone."

"Isn't this guy a destroyer skipper? The one with the Navy Cross?"

"...yes."

"Don't you think that's overkill?"

Novak drummed his fingers.

St. Clair came back with, "I'd be glad to help you out, but we should be sure."

"If I am sure, what can you do?"

"Well, I would send someone to bring him back."

"Bring him back? Why do we need someone to bring him back? Can't we just send him orders?"

"Well, I would suggest Augustine Rivera."

"Who's he?"

"You've met him."

"I have?"

"Yes," St. Clair exhaled. "That day with Sujiyama."

The Japanese torpedo officer off the ill-fated *I-1*. A cold tremor ran down Novak's spine. "I thought he was just a jailer."

"Far more than that. He's a very talented man."

"How is Sujiyama?" Novak hadn't interviewed the coke-drinking, cigarette-puffing officer for weeks.

"He'll be okay."

"Okay from what?"

"Well...he fell down and broke his jaw."

"Did Rivera do that?" blurted Novak.

"Of course not. But I must say, Rivera does enjoy interviewing our little friends. But his real specialty is war-zone security. You send a guy like him down there to make sure your boy does come back. To make sure your orders aren't overridden."

"You send a Marine Major to do that?"

"Actually, he's a specialist warrant officer from Naval CID. So I can make him anything I like. Right now, he wears a Navy lieutenant's bars. We use him to track down AWOLs in SOWESPAC. You know, some kids get scared. They hide out with natives. Marry a fat old native wahine and lay low. That sort of thing. Augustine Rivera knows how to dig 'em out."

"That's a drastic step. Almost like bringing back a prisoner."

"Well, you're the one who's on edge. And that puts me on edge. I'm only doing my job, here."

"I don't know..."

"Consider what's at risk, Mike."

"I got it." Novak snapped his fingers.

"Got what?"

"My cousin. Frank Ashton. He knows Ingram. Let me call him first. Check on Ingram's reliability. Then I'll get back to you. Is this Rivera available right away if we need him?"

"He just brought a guy back and is enroute to Noumea."

"Let me think about it. I'll get back to you."

"When?"

"Five, six hours."

"Don't let it drag out." St. Clair gave a long exhale and ground out his cigarette.

With a shudder, Novak hung up.

Novak pulled every trick to get an overseas line. It took two hours and fifteen minutes before one was available: near one a.m. mainland time. First, the operator connected him to Ashton's rental in Belmont Shore. No answer. She dialed Ashton's office at the Long Beach Naval Shipyard. It rang once, then, "Ashton."

"Frank, it's Mike." The line swirled with static.

"Who?"

"Mike Novak," he shouted.

"Cousin Mike? All the way from Hawaii? What are you doing up so late?"

Novak grinned at the irony. It was two hours later in Long Beach. "Working, damnit, just like you. Look. I need some help. I...uh met a fellow on my trip back to Pearl and, without going into this too deeply, I ran into a bit of a security problem."

As bad as the connection was, Novak heard Ashton's chair squeak as he sat up. "Yes?"

"I believe you know this man."

"Yes?"

"And I need your opinion on his reliability."

"Okay."

Novak ran the precautions through his mind. The line was not secure. But then there was no specific project to discuss. No highly classified subject. *The hell with it.* He leaned back, plopped his feet on the desk and said, "His name is Todd Ingram."

Novak heard Ashton exhale. But he knew his cousin didn't smoke. Unlike St. Clair, Ashton was too neat and fastidious. Sound modulated terribly on the phone line, but Novak clearly heard, "You mean Lieutenant Commander Todd Ingram? The one with the Navy Cross?"

"That's him, all right."

The line clicked, but Novak heard noises on the other end, indicating Ashton was still there. Or was he? "Frank? Hello? Frank"?

"Yes, yes. Don't forget, this is an open line."

"I know that."

"Okay. Yes, I considered having Ingram work for me."

"And?"

"Well, I met him in the South Pacific and thought he was a pretty squared away guy. Then I heard his ship was damaged, or something, and that he was here in Long Beach for prospective CO training. So, I looked him up."

"Yes?" Novak dropped his feet to the floor and carefully placed both elbows on his desk. "In what capacity?"

"Basically, I wanted him to run a Combat Support Unit here, as part of the Eleventh Naval District."

Novak scratched his head. "What's a Combat Support Unit?"

"The main interface from the fleet to the Department of Terrestrial Magnetism."

"Good God." Novak decided to let that one rest. He hadn't heard of the Department of Terrestrial Magnetism and wondered if it had anything to do with Buck Rogers and Buster Crabbe.

Ashton continued, "I needed to know more about him and did some checking."

"And?"

"He's been known to bully senior officers."

"What?"

"I discovered a charge has been filed by an Army Colonel over at Fort MacArthur that Ingram was using his Navy Cross to throw his weight around."

"I don't get it."

"Something about trying to obtain preferential treatment for his wife, who was a nurse there. Trying to go over the heads of senior officers, just to get her orders changed."

"Why would he do that?"

"...I don't know. Because he thinks he's God. So, if you ask me, Mike. The man's not reliable."

"You think he would lie?"

"In a flash. Anyone as disrespectful as that is capable of anything."

"What about his character?"

Ashton seemed to think it over. Then he said, "I thought that's what we were talking about."

"Overall, I mean."

"Like I said. The man's not reliable."

Novak drummed his fingers.

Now it was Ashton's turn. "Mike? Mike?"

"I got it. Thanks, Frank." Novak hung up.

In Long Beach, Frank Ashton hung up and his chair squeaked as he sat back. He cupped his hands and held them over his nose for ten long seconds, inhaling and exhaling. He looked down seeing his trousers wrinkled. And his shirt had turned a putrid gray-whiteish; in fact, this one, he'd worn for the last three days.

"God." He muttered. He hated to do that to Ingram but the man had turned him down, hadn't he? And that damned Army Colonel from Australia, Otis DeWitt had been sending messages asking questions. Ashton had ignored them but now, he picked up the flimsy on his desk, here was one from Colonel Charles Willoughby, Douglas MacArthur's Intelligence Chief. In Brisbane Australia. How the hell did she finagle that?

Slow them down, that's all he could do. Even the selection committee; they were asking questions, now.

Ashton pressed his hands to his temples, trying to understand why things were closing in so quickly. A fog horn blew in the harbor; the forge thumped down the alley signaling to Ashton the round-the-clock ferocity of the Long beach Naval Shipyard's dedication to defeating the enemy. With all of his being, he wanted to be a part of it. And yet...

He looked down to his shoes.

Scuffed.

Strange. That gave Ashton some solace. Scuffed shoes were something he could take care of. He opened the bottom drawer of his desk, pulled out his shine kit and methodically laid everything out on his desk. He took off his shoes and thought for five long minutes about which one he should do first.

The left one, he decided. Like they taught him as a plebe in the Naval Academy, always start off with your left foot. At one ten in the morning, Ashton soaked the cotton in water, dabbed it in the shoe polish and began his spit shine.

The morning was clear, the ocean blue, sparkling, as the twin-engined R4D lined up for the main runway at Noumea. Having just graduated from flight training, Ensign Julian Carruthers had been in the fleet for two months. Instead of going on to fighter pilot training as he wanted, he'd been assigned to multi-engined aircraft, and now was attached to the Naval Air Transport Service. He only had thirty-five hours in "Gooney Birds" and now, he had just been ordered to land this thing.

"Don't you think we should make another pass, Lieutenant?" Carruthers pointed to the ocean. "Look at the white caps."

All Carruthers knew was that the pilot's name was Lieutenant Gilbert. Carruthers had never met him before. Gilbert, a slim, sinewy, dark man with a pockmarked face just nodded and said, "It's all yours, Ensign. Like I said, pretend you're in command. Now go ahead and land this airplane. In one piece, I might add. And don't forget, I'll be watching every move.

"Y...Yes, Sir." Gilbert eased the Gooney Bird down to 2,500 feet and flew over the runway. What he saw made him feel as if his stomach were full of cement. The wind sock stood straight out, almost perpendicular to the runway. And the radio had pooped out long ago, so they couldn't obtain wind and barometer conditions. Carruthers, a short stocky high school math teacher in civilian life, said, "'Scuse me, Lieutenant, but that sock is straight out."

"So?" Gilbert's eyes were dark, almost malevolent.

Carruthers gulped. "Looks like a twenty knot cross-wind from the north."

Gilbert slouched back in his seat and folded his arms. "Like I said, you land this bucket, Ensign. And you're being rated, so it better be good."

The tower flashed them a green signal light. They were low on gas, and there were no other aircraft in the area.

Time to go.

Sweat stood on Carruthers' forehead as he eased the R4D into a downwind leg and headed back out to sea, going through the check list. On a couple of occasions, he had to show Lieutenant Gilbert where things were, like the landing gear and flap levers. But things were moving faster and faster. They were soon lined up on final at 1,000 feet. And the Gooney Bird bucked and yawed in the gusts.

One of Caruthers's check pilots had been a Texan who often yelled, 'Yeeehaw' or 'Ride 'em Cowboy,' when they hit turbulence.

What the hell? Carruthers figured, so he pulled back more throttle and screeched, "Ride 'em cowboy."

His grin to Gilbert earned him another icy stare.

A hundred feet. The plane bounced on the gusts as if it were a ping pong ball.

Shiiiit. What did that crazy Texan say about cross wind landings?

Lining up with the upwind side of the runway, he again stole a glance at Gilbert, seeing a bit of moisture on his brow as well. *Hope the sonofabitch can save our ass if I screw up.*

Fifty feet. With ailerons, Carruthers dropped the right wing and kicked in left rudder, sideslipping the Gooney Bird over the runway threshold.

You can do it...

He yanked the throttles all the way back, letting the plane settle. With satisfaction, he heard the right wheel squeak as it kissed the runway. *Ahhh, just like the book says.*

Just then, a gust hit and the plane bucked. A spasm of terror shot up his spine, as he realized the plane was trying to fly.

"Ahhh!" Carruthers heard his own voice as he kicked in more opposite rudder to keep the plane lined on the runway. And then the right wing lifted and the wheel broke free. They were airborne!

"Shit!" yelled Carruthers. "Flaps up!"

Gilbert's hand rummaged on the pedestal. "What the hell?"

Carruthers took a hand off the yoke for a moment and pointed. "There!"

Gilbert shoved the lever up, raising the flaps, killing the lift. Soon, the plane settled on both wheels and began to slow. The tailwheel dropped to the runway stabilizing their rollout. Soon, they were heading for a jeep that waited to lead them to their parking area.

Carruthers looked over. "Sorry about that, Lieutenant. I'm kind of new at this."

Gilbert pushed his garrison cap back on his head and gave a twisted grin. "That's okay, Ensign. You did okay."

"Really?"

"Only thing I would have done differently was to raise the flaps a little sooner."

"Does that mean..."

"Yes, you pass. You did well."

"Thank you, Sir."

.   .   .

Augustine Rivera waited until Carruthers stepped into the operations hut. Then he walked in the opposite direction and found an unattended jeep near the base fuel dump. But it had no keys.

It took him ten seconds to hot-wire it. In another forty-five seconds, he was off the base and headed for the waterfront. Better not do that again he thought, as he unpinned the pilot's wings from his khaki shirt. He loved impersonations. Once, he'd impersonated a doctor up in Espiritu Santo and had caught an AWOL kid who wandered in, wanting treatment for crabs. But today, he knew he'd gone too far. And yet, he'd done it, flying all the way from Pearl Harbor in the guise of a pilot. Everyone had bought it, even Carruthers who he had picked for the leg from Palmyra. And yet...that landing. He hadn't figured on poor flying conditions.

He liked impersonating Marines better. They were close to the earth and elements. They knew how to fight. They knew how to kill. And Augustine Rivera whose father was a Chicago meat-packer had taught him about that. Growing up in Cicero had completed his education.

Rivera could have traveled on regular orders. But people had habits of radioing ahead, with senior officers helping their people out, issuing warnings, allowing his prey to hide out.

He'd learned the hard way.

Do it to them before they do it to you.

36

12 April, 1943
   Kotukuriana Island,
   Solomon Islands

"...where the hell are they?" muttered Bollinger.

"Still must have their hands full," said Landa, referring to the mind-numbing number of Japanese aircraft that had flown down The Slot five days ago. The skies had filled ominously with the sound of Japanese aircraft engines. Hundreds, so many the noise was overwhelming. Gambino picked his way through the muck to the other side of the island to watch them fly down the Strait. Then he came back wide-eyed, reporting breathlessly that the whole damn Jap air force was on its way to Guadalcanal.

Two hours later, the planes were back. But this time, Gambino reported that American fighters jumped them from time to time. He'd seen two Japanese planes fall from the sky, in flames, far out into the Strait.

Landa's mind snapped back to the present. "Don't worry Oscar. They'll find us."

Bollinger said, "Yeah, but that PBY yesterday. He has to have been looking for us. They just don't know where we are."

"And they'll try again," said Landa.

"Maybe the Japs hit them so hard they wiped the place out. Maybe they counter attacked, you know, re-invaded Guadalcanal," said Bollinger.

Landa rolled in his make-shift hammock to look at Bollinger. He was senior in rank, but he'd stepped aside to let Bollinger stay in command since it was his crew. Besides, Landa's foot was mangled. He couldn't walk. His ankle was swollen like a balloon and hurt like hell. Now he wondered if he'd made the right decision. "Come on, Oscar. Go read the Sunday paper and shut up, for crying out loud."

"Today's Monday."

"Sorry, I lost track." Landa rolled to his back, put his hands behind his head and tried not to think of his foot.

"Let's hope we can use the signal mirrors."

"Wouldn't that be nice?" replied Landa. Yesterday, when the dumbo flew over, they'd had their signal mirrors ready, but it was overcast. No chance to reflect sunlight at the searching rescue plane. It had been rainy off and on the entire eight days they'd been trapped here, which is one reason they hadn't been found. Landa didn't know which was worse, sitting here and slowly rotting or having the sun come out, with the mosquitoes eating them to death. As it was, they had leaches, bats, land crabs, stingrays and jungle grunge.

Eight days, it may as well have been eight decades. It seemed so long ago that they'd been shot up by cannon fire from his ship. Damn, that made Landa mad. Those bastards were on *his* ship, eating whatever was left in *his* store rooms, smoking *his* American cigarettes, while sitting back and plopping *their* split-toed sandals up on *his* ward-room table. Shit!

A couple of lucky shots had wiped out *PT 94's* starboard and center engines. And the port engine wasn't long for the world. So rather than struggle exposed in the New Georgia Strait, Bollinger whipped his wheel and steered through the Lingutu passage, separating Mondo Mondo and Kotukuriana Islands. Belching smoke, *PT-94's* port engine took them southeast along the passage between Kotukuriana and the New Georgia Islands. Things went well for five hundred yards, but then the engine threw a rod, giving out entirely. With the boat holed and sinking, Bollinger had no choice but to nose into a mangrove swamp. *PT-94's* bottom ground on rocks and tree stumps until she lurched to a pathetic, mind-numbing halt. With Ensign Thomas's lifeless body lying on the cockpit grating, Bollinger and Landa looked at one another, stupefied, refusing to believe the collective 4,000 horsepower that the throttles once summoned was no longer available.

An armed Japanese barge appeared almost immediately, raking *PT-94,* killing one of her men and wounding another. But Bollinger's men rallied with their fifty caliber machine guns and forty millimeter canon, driving them off. But not before a fire started. They barely had time to grab small arms, a few parcels of food, an emergency radio and dash off the boat which exploded with a great roar, the 100 octane gas sending a roiling red-black mushroom cloud up into the rain.

Oddly, the Japanese left them alone after that. It seemed strange. The enemy occupied what they called Fort Mondo Mondo leaving Landa, Bollinger and his crew holed up next door on Kotukuriana Island, living alongside the Japanese in an unsettled peace. With the boat burned out under a thick jungle canopy, there seemed no way to draw attention from rescuers. And now, their food was nearly gone, another man had died, and it was still raining.

If only the damned emergency radio worked. The receiver was shot, but Gambino, the radar genius, was working on it. So they kept grinding the hand-cranked generator, transmitting every four hours, hoping against hope.

Landa lay back in his hammock. Bollinger and Gambino had made it for him from jungle vines and strung it between trees so Landa could keep the weight off his foot and keep away from the land crabs. It started raining again and he held his hand over his face as water dripped though the trees. It turned to a downpour, and he tried to think of home, of New York, of Brooklyn---

Someone yanked at his sleeve. "Huh?"

"Bambino re-wired the receiver. Now we're hearing something," said Bollinger.

"No kidding?"

"A faint signal. Can't tell if they hear us or not."

"Shit!" Gambino shouted from across the clearing.

"What?" yelled Bollinger.

"Connection broke. I gotta do it again."

Bollinger yelled from the corner of his mouth, "So what are you waiting, for, Baby face? Hurry up. I have a date Saturday night, so I'd like to get back if you don't mind."

"...yes, Sir."

Bollinger looked at Landa. The corner of his mouth turned up.

He's doing better, thought Landa.

Bollinger said, "That kid has talent. Someday he'll put us all to shame, after he invents some new electronic whiz-bang shit and becomes a millionaire."

Fire raged through Landa's swollen foot. "Ahhh...must be infected." Both looked at the foot for a moment, then averted their glance. The pain finally subsided, but the foot kept throbbing. He didn't know if that was good or bad. Supposing, he said to himself, the damn thing is so badly infected it's ready to fall off. Would I feel pain? Or maybe, it's getting better and the pain is just letting me know that--- "What?"

"---said, 'looks like these are yours.'" Bollinger handed over two crumpled envelopes. "Bambino was scrounging for parts and found them in your camera case."

Landa remembered the mail clerk aboard the *Whitney* had handed him a couple of letters just before leaving. He'd forgotten all about them. "Thanks."

Bollinger made to walk away.

"Oscar."

"Yes?"

"Keep on grinding."

"Thanks, Jerry."

"For what?"

"You know." Bollinger walked off.

The rain had let up, and there was enough afternoon light to read. One letter was an invoice from an attorney for settling Josh's estate. The second letter was stamped AIR MAIL -- SPECIAL DELIVERY and was from, "My God, Laura." He was amazed to see the postmark was dated March 31, just thirteen days ago

Quickly, he ripped it open, trying to keep errant rain-drops off the paper.

. . .

March 31, 1943

Dear Jerry,

Three things:

First: I want to again thank you again for taking time from your bereavement leave to see me and try and help me when I was in the dumps. Please accept my deepest apologies for my behavior. I have no excuse. It just seemed the thing to do. A violinist in our orchestra lost a son over Europe and swallowed a bottle of sleeping pills. But they pumped her stomach and now, she seems back on the road. She's divorced and her son was her life so I know how it must have hit her

Sometimes I wonder. Was she really trying to kill herself when she did that? Or was she trying to kill it someone else? If so, who? Her son for walking out on her? Her ex-husband who left so long ago? It makes me I wonder, who was I trying to kill with all the drinking? Me? Luther, for having the temerity to get killed? Maybe it's just as well that I don't know.

Second: I have a confession. Luther was my life, I'm sure, except I really didn't know him that well. I know that now. I think most marriages must be that way; a process of glorious discovery and evolution over a long period of time. Luther and I had only known each other for thirteen months. Of that, we were married five months. Much of the time, he'd been at sea. I wish I'd known him better. Mrs. Thatcher tells me in marriage, that comes with time. And now, my time for Luther is gone. Of course, his time is now infinite and besides, he's with God. In death, we did part. In the interim, I feel guilty and dirty. And I don't know why. I think that is what makes me want to drink. The damn guilt --It's a vicious circle.

Third: About last night. I suppose you're gone now so whatever happens, happens. Maybe we won't see each other, but then again, maybe so. The rational part of me says you did the intelligent thing by walking out. On the surface it all seems right; proper for Luther's memory. So I'll not bore you with how I felt later. But you should have seen Larry Dunnigan. He was really angry when he found out you had left. He nearly fired Klosterman on the spot. (That man is such a fop isn't he?)

Forget the guilt, Jerry. It will rip you up, wherever you go. Now I'll make you a deal. You write to me and I'll stay off the booze. I'll give you until tomorrow night to receive your letter. Then I get knee-walking, commode hugging drunk again. Just kidding. I'll try, I hope you do too. Until then,

.   .   .

Love

Laura

Landa lay back, clutching the envelope to his chest.

Guilt.

Landa thought, There I was, hugging and kissing Luther Dutton's widow in some posh Long Beach hotel. What a bastard you are, Landa. But then, she is a living, caring intelligent, good looking woman, so warm, so accomplished. Just the sound of her voice gave him a tingling in the nape of his neck.

Guilt.

Damnit! She's Luther's widow, and I'm thinking like a fraternity boy on a Saturday night.

Guilt.

Carefully, he folded the letter and tucked it under his shirt, the driest spot he could think of. "Arrrgh" Pain shot up his leg as he rolled to his side. Then it started raining. In the day's dimming light he watched the tiny droplets hit the water, making perfectly symmetrical little craters far out in Marovo Lagoon. It built to a cloudburst and roared. The only sign of civilization was Bollinger's pathetic Sterno fire about ten feet away, where men huddled, taking solace more from the light than what little heat it offered.

Guilt.

After a while, he smiled and his foot stopped hurting. He turned his face to the sky and said, "Not guilty, your Honor."

37

13 April, 1943
  Imperial Japanese Navy Eighth Air Fleet Headquarters
  Rabaul, New Britain island
  Bismarck Archipelago

Dusk fell; the last of the planes had returned two hours ago. Still wearing dress whites, Yamamoto sat at a table in the pilot's briefing hut beside an old friend, Vice Admiral Jisaburo Ozawa, Commander in Chief of the Imperial Third Fleet. Sitting at the end of the table was the ever-present Captain Yasuji Watanabe. Across the room sat Captain Kanji Takano, a non-smoker, keeping a respectful distance from blue clouds swirling about.

In the waning light, the last air crew shuffled out and climbed onto a stake truck, its gears clanking sharply as it pulled away. The three senior officers scanned their notes while birds squawked and monkeys screeched outside, the night re-capturing the jungle.

They had just finished the last of four massive air-raids and were summing up the results of *Operation I*: First, they had hit Tulagi in the Lower Solomons on the 7th, then New Guinea in three places; Oro Bay on the 11th; Port Moresby on the 12^{th;} and today, Milne Bay.

A monkey whooped in the distance, as Watanabe lit a cigarette and meticulously added up columns. At length, he coughed politely and said, "*Gensui*, with these four missions, the enemy has lost one cruiser, one destroyer, twenty-five transports, and 134 airplanes."

Takano waved a hand at Watanabe's smoke. "It looks as if we sunk two, not one destroyer, *Gensui*."

Watanabe sighed.

Yamamoto overlooked the intrusion and said to Ozawa, "Excellent, just excellent."

"Congratulations, Sir." Watanabe bowed.

Ozawa nodded his approval.

"Four missions is all we can do for now. We have had these planes on loan too long. It's time." To Watanabe Yamamoto said, "Give the order. Send them all back." He turned to Ozawa and said, "Thank you for your patience."

"An honor, Sir," said Ozawa. Most of the planes used on *Operation I* had belonged to Ozawa who was reluctant to bring up the fact that fifty-one planes had not returned. The worst was the loss of his irreplaceable pilots.

Takano said, "If I may suggest, Gensui, that we stage another raid on Tulagi. Perhaps even the Russells. The Americans have a PT base there that is---"

"Takano!" said Yamamoto.

All eyes snapped to Yamamoto. They were surprised to hear him speak sharply.

"Sir!" Takano fairly sat at attention.

"I have a job for you."

"You do?" A sense of hope rushed through Takano. Quickly, he added, "Sir." After the bollix last week with the fuse off the *Matukaze*, he'd been completely ignored. Everyone knew Yamamoto was looking for a way to diplomatically get rid of him.

"The *Matukaze*," said Yamamoto. "I want you to board her and return to that American destroyer."

"Return, Sir? But we--"

"--You don't know for sure. Perhaps Enomoto overlooked something. Try again, damnit! I want *you* there this time."

"I, uh yes, Sir. But the *Matukaze* is laid up. It's her starboard shaft. They're waiting for a--"

"I don't give a damn about the *Matukaze*'s shaft. You go aboard her and have it fixed. Use my name, damnit. If it's not fixed within two days then you have just one shaft to get you down there and back. Is that clear?"

Watanabe felt almost sorry for Takano. The man's lip quivered and a silence descended, the sound of guttural voices giving over to the penetrating screeching of New Britain's jungle.

"Yes, Sir," said Takano.

"Then go," said Yamamoto. "Watanabe will cut your orders."

"Yes, Sir." Takano walked out.

Watanabe bit his fingernails as Ozawa looked serenely out the window.

"Where's Ugaki?" demanded Yamamoto.

"Dengue fever. The doctor put him to bed," said Watanabe.

"Ahh."

"What is it *Gensui*?" asked Ozawa.

"I'm about done here. I'll be returning to Truk, soon."

"Yes?" said Ozawa.

"Before I go, I'd like to tour some installations and see those lads up close."

"Good idea," said Ozawa. "They would appreciate it."

"Where would you like to go?" asked Watanabe.

"I'd like to see the people at Buin, Bellale, and Shortland Islands," said Yamamoto.

Watanabe and Ozawa exchanged glances.

"Is there something wrong?" asked Yamamoto.

"Do you think that's wise, Sir?" asked Ozawa.

Yamamoto fixed him with a gaze.

Ozawa said, "I mean Bellale and Shortland are at the lower tip of Bougainville, only a little over three hundred air miles from the Americans on Guadalcanal."

"Yes?"

Ozawa stood his ground. "I mean, they could shoot you down, *Gensui*."

"How would they ever know I was there in the first place?"

"Coast watchers, perhaps?"

"Nonsense." Yamamoto turned to Watanabe, "Schedule it for me. Make it on the eighteenth, weather permitting. I'll return to Truk the following day."

"Sir, I beg you to re-consider," Ozawa said in a tight voice..

"I really must do this. Our boys need it." Yamamoto clapped a hand on Ozawa's shoulder.

"Perhaps, Sir, if you spoke with Ugaki." Watanabe interjected,

"Whatever for? You just told me he's in bed with dengue fever. He needs his rest." Yamamoto's eyes narrowed. "Now set up the schedule."

"Yes, Sir," said Watanabe.

"I'll be going back up the hill, now. Please send for my car." He turned to Ozawa. "Would you care to join me for dinner?"

"Yes, Sir. If you don't mind, give me five minutes to finish a few details here," said Ozawa.

"You, too, Watanabe?"

"Thank you, Sir. That sounds very nice."

"All right. But before you go, get the message out. I want them to have time to prepare. I'll wait outside. The sunset is beautiful." Yamamoto walked out.

Ten seconds after Yamamoto left, Ozawa snatched off his hat and threw it against the wall, "This is asinine! Doesn't that fool realize how dangerous that is?"

Watanabe drew his breath in sharply at hearing the *Gensui* referred to as a 'fool.'

"Well? He is endangering his life. What if he's shot down? What would we do without him?" Ozawa growled,

"What choice do I have, Sir?"

Ozawa looked in the distance for a moment, then said more to himself than to Watanabe, "Go ahead. Send the message. But we have to figure a way to stop this nonsense." He walked out.

On his way to Yamamoto's for dinner, Watanabe pulled into the command compound and hand delivered his message to Vice Admiral Tomoshiga Sajejima, the new commander of the Eighth Air Fleet. After signing for it, Sajejima sent it down the hall for encryption into the Naval cipher. Thirty minutes after that, it was given to First Class Radioman Matome Tayama, one of the Eighth Air Fleet's most skilled radio operators. With the last glimmer of twilight, the surrounding jungle turned once again to its full nocturnal disarray, as Tayama started transmitting his message. It was 1755, local time.

At 2155 local time, the moon had drifted past its zenith above Diamond Head, bathing Oahu in a shimmering, travel-poster splendor. The headquarters of the Fleet Radio Unit -- Pacific (FRUPAC) had moved up the hill two weeks ago near the rim of the Makalapa crater. It was a large, two-story wooden building near Admiral Nimitz' headquarters. At daytime, onlookers enjoyed the majesty of Oahu in one sweeping glance. But the view was marred by the carnage below in Pearl Harbor, still covered with oil slicks, the blood of battleships sunk on the December 7, 1941 Japanese sneak attack. But now, at almost 10:00 p.m., only vague outlines could be seen below, the whole area blacked out.

Radioman First Class Jesus Alfonso Ramirez was one of about two hundred radio operators in the second floor bullpen on duty that night. He was a highly skilled member of about one thousand radiomen, fondly called the "On the Roof Gang." Suddenly, the chirping of a radio signal filled his ear phones. Ramirez jabbed a foot pedal, starting his wire recorder; then went to work on his typewriter, taking down five digit groups. By 2212, Ramirez was finished. After carefully sealing the message in a red-banded envelope marked TOP SECRET ULTRA, he raised his hand for two things. The first was for a messenger, who immediately signed for the message then headed out the door. The next was for a cup of coffee. Ramirez needed a refill, especially after that message. That Jap operator was good, a professional, he could tell. His key was crisp and clear; almost as good as Ramirez, who had to concentrate hard to keep up.

The messenger took Ramirez's message down to "the basement," a series of sub-divided air-conditioned rooms, which housed the Intelligence Center for the Pacific Ocean Area (ICPOA). There, the envelope was logged in by Lieutenant Thomas B. Ketchum, the duty officer, who every day, handled hundreds of Japanese messages. Ketchum scanned the message finding it was from the Commander of the Imperial Japanese Eighth Air Fleet, a naval unit near the top of Ketchum's "watch list." He picked up his phone and dialed a number on the intercom.

A man in a window office across the room answered, "Novak."

"Sir, it's Lieutenant Ketchum." Ketchum saw him look up sharply. "We have an interesting message here."

"Yes?"

Ketchum swallowed. Novak had been almost living here for the past two weeks. It seemed he was becoming more irritable every day. "It's from Commander Eighth Air Fleet." Ketchum read off the addressees.

Through the window Ketchum saw Novak swivel in his chair and drum his fingers. Finally, he said, "Top priority. Have Plummer run the robot. Then give it to Burnside. I want to see it as soon as possible." Novak's phone crashed on the hook.

"Aye, aye, Sir," Ketchum said to a dead line.

Ketchum walked over and handed the message to Howard Demergian, Yeoman Second Class and said, "As fast as you can, Demergian."

"Yes, Sir." Demergian took the message and fastened it to a clipboard beside his key punch machine, which was manufactured by International Business Machines of Armonk, New York. Demergian hummed, as his machine clacked away. He'd been a musician, most recently, a trombone player in the band aboard the U.S.S. *Pennsylvania*, the Flagship of the Pacific Fleet until she'd been bombed in drydock on December 7, 1941. With no place to go, Demergian and many of the other musicians off sunken battleships, were assigned to cryptographic duties, because of their acuity at reading music. In effect, they read a form of cipher which was similar to the skills required for cracking codes.

Ten minutes later, Demergian was done. He stuffed the cards in an envelope, labeled them, entered his log, then walked to Lieutenant Ketchum and handed the envelope over, along with the original message.

"Thanks," said Ketchum, who entered both items in his log. From there, Ketchum walked through a curtain into the next room and handed the punch cards to Jackie Plummer, an ex- tuba player off the U.S.S. *California*, turned cryptographer first class. Plummer and his crew of three third-class cryptographers, were acknowledged as the best on the IBM equipment which surrounded them: tabulators, collators, printers, and a monstrous hybrid called a comparer, built just for FRUPAC. After signing for the envelope, Jackie and his crew ran the tab cards through a "robot routine," which stripped out the additives: these were numerical codes added to numbers in the five letter group to throw off eavesdroppers. A new set of punch cards was produced, which Jackie carefully ran through the main program for decrypting messages in JN-25, the Japanese Imperial Navy code. Since last summer, they had a lot of trouble with JN-25. The Japanese had changed their codes, and FRUPAC had only been able to recover twenty to thirty percent of the average message, whereas before, they could recover almost 100 percent. But now, they had captured the code books off the Japanese submarine I-1. Working with Commander Novak, Plummer had written a new decrypting program for JN-25, and this was one of the first times they were going to try it.

Two hours later, the machine groaned to a stop.

Jackie examined the cards. "It's friggin' mish-mash."

They slurped coffee and thought for five minutes. "Wait a minute," said Jackie. "Let's run 'em through backwards."

Nobody objected, so the machines once again clacked, ground and rattled. An hour later, it was done. Jackie Plummer examined the cards and grinned broadly. "Take the rest of yesterday off, you guys."

Then he ran the cards through a printer. The message came out in code groups translatable to Japanese. He pushed a button at his desk, and Lieutenant Ketchum was there in fifteen seconds.

Ketchum examined the print-out for a moment and said, "Okay." Taking the message, he walked into another curtained area containing small cubicle offices, each with closed glass doors. One was labeled , "Lt. Colonel, Gerald L. Burnside, USMCR." Ketchum knocked, then walked into a smoke filled, closet-sized cubicle

Burnside, a lanky, sandy-haired Japanese language expert, was one of ICPOA's best language officers. He had spent three years in Tokyo as an attaché from 1936 to 1939. He could read, write and speak the language perfectly. Now he was tilted back in his chair with his feet on his desk, scratching his head and studying a list of encoded values from the recently broken four digit 'Maru Code,' a code used by the Japanese merchant fleet.

Since they were golfing buddies, Ketchum dropped the honorifics. "Got one for you, Jerry. Novak says to drop everything and hop to it."

Burnside chain-lit a cigarette and said, "Screw Novak. I've got a least another four hours to go on this before it's cleaned up." Burnside and Ketchum shared the same opinion over Commander Novak's oftentimes bullying methods.

Ketchum waved a hand, "No, no, I got a feeling about this one, Jerry. I think Novak may be right. Here, look at the sender and addressees." He handed the print-out to Burnside.

Burnside scanned the addresses, then raised his eyebrows. "Give me ten minutes."

Ketchum smiled inwardly. Burnside had said that many times in the past, not emerging from his smoke-filled office until hours later, with a completely broken message.

Six hours and twenty minutes later, Ketchum was passing by Burnside's cubicle when the door burst open. The Marine's face was pale; his shirt was unbuttoned, the knot on his tie was slipped and his shirt sleeves were rolled up.

"What?" Asked Ketchum.

Burnside reached back in his office, grabbed a pack of cigarettes, lit one and slipped the pack in his top pocket. "Incredible. Just damned incredible. Come on." He blasted through curtains toward Novak's office.

Ketchum could hardly keep up, as Burnside burst into Novak's office. Novak was on the phone and gave them an irritated glance. He turned and continued his conversation in low tones with his back turned.

Burnside said softly to a gawking Ketchum. "Shut the door, Tom."

Ketchum did so, just as Novak wound up his call. Slamming down the receiver, he hissed, "Just what the hell do you mean by---"

Burnside held up a hand. "---Mike. For once, just shut up."

Novak started to say something, but then fell silent.

Burnside handed over the message.

With a glance toward Ketchum, Novak said, "Is it that big of a deal?"

Burnside said, "Just read it."

Novak quickly read the message. Then he laid it down. "Good God." Then he read it again and laid it on his desk.

"We've got the sonofabitch," grinned Burnside. "We've really got him."

Ketchum asked, "Is it okay if I..."

Novak nodded.

Ketchum picked up the message and read:

FROM: COMMANDER EIGHTH AIR FLEET

TO: FIRST BASE FORCE 26TH AIR FLOTILLA

ALL COMMANDING OFFICERS 11TH AIR FLOTILLA

COMMANDER, 958TH AIR UNIT

CHIEF, BALLALE DEFENSE UNIT

1.THE COMMANDER IN CHIEF COMBINED FLEET WILL INSPECT BALLALE, SHORTLAND, AND BUIN IN ACCORDANCE WITH THE FOLLOWING:

2. 0600 DEPART RABAUL ON BOARD MEDIUM ATTACK PLANE (ESCORTED BY 6 FIGHTERS);

3. 0800 ARRIVE BALLALE.

4. IMMEDIATELY DEPART FOR SHORTLAND ON BOARD SUBCHASER (1ST BASE FORCE TO READY ONE BOAT)

5. ARRIVING AT 0840. DEPART SHORTLAND 0945 ABOARD SAID SUBCHASER

6. ARRIVING BALLALE AT 1030. (FOR TRANSPORTATION PURPOSES, HAVE READY AN ASSAULT BOAT AT SHORTLAND AND A MOTOR LAUNCH AT BALLALE.)

7 1100 DEPART BALLALE ON BOARD MEDIUM ATTACK PLANE, ARRIVING BUIN 1110.

8. LUNCH AT 1ST BASE FORCE HEADQUARTERS (SENIOR STAFF
OFFICER OF AIR FLOTILLA 26 TO BE PRESENT).

9. 1400 DEPART BUIN ABOARD MEDIUM ATTACK PLANE

10 ARRIVE RABAUL 1540.

11. INSPECTION PROCEDURES: AFTER BEING BRIEFED ON PRESENT
STATUS, THE TROOPS (PATIENTS AT 1ST BASE FORCE HOSPITAL)
WILL BE VISITED. HOWEVER, THERE WILL BE NO INTERRUPTIONS
IN THE ROUTINE DUTIES OF THE DAY.

12. UNIFORMS WILL BE UNIFORM OF THE DAY EXCEPT THAT THE
COMMANDING OFFICERS OF THE VARIOUS UNITS WILL BE IN
COMBAT ATTIRE WITH DECORATIONS.

IN THE EVENT OF INCLEMENT WEATHER, THE TOUR WILL BE POST-
PONED ONE DAY.

MESSAGE ENDS

Novak asked, "What can we hit him with?"

Burnside said, "Guadalcanal. Marine Corsairs. They have the range and
the firepower. If not them, Army P-38s."

"You sure?"

"Positive." Burnside lit a cigarette and blew smoke across Novak's desk.

Novak read the message again. "Okay. I'd better tell Layton." Commander
Edwin T. Layton was Fleet Admiral Chester Nimitz' Fleet Intelligence Officer.
"But then---"

"What?"

Novak stared into the distance. "What if it's a trap?"

Burnside puffed his cigarette for a moment. Then his jaw dropped.
"What? You mean they know we've broken their code?"

"That's what I'm trying to say. What if someone on our side shot his mouth off that we know all about what Yamamoto's doing? What if that got back to the Japs? And they laid a trap."

Burnside glanced at Ketchum. "Sounds far fetched. Can you prove it?"

Novak began, "I may be acting super cautious, but there's a Lieutenant Commander down in the Solomons that may have let everything slip."

"You're shitting me." Burnside sat heavily into a side chair.

"What's crazy about this is that this Lieutenant Commander is probably dead. But even so, it's imperative we find out what he knew and what he told others before he died."

"This is insane."

Novak leaned forward, his elbows on his knees and said, "Luckily, I have someone out there to check it all out. Let me explain."

The phone rang, startling the men. "Damnit. Novak snatched the receiver from the cradle. "Commander Novak."

"Mike. It's Bob St. Clair."

"Uh, I'm in a meeting. But I do have to talk to you."

"Get back when you can. I'll be here."

"Tell you what, Bob," Novak looked at the others who averted his glance. "I'll just listen."

"Okay. Do you recall your two and a half striper friend?"

Novak leaned forward and tapped his pencil eraser on the desk. "Of course."

"Well. I have very bad news for you." St. Clair's Zippo lighter clicked in the background.

"Yes?" Without realizing it, Novak bit into the eraser.

After a long exhale, St. Clair said, "His wife will be receiving a telegram, soon."

"No!" Novak spat the eraser out and leaned back, relief flooding over him.

"Killed in action, I'm afraid."

"Oh. This is such terrible news." Novak plopped his feet on the desk and sipped coffee. Burnside and Ketchum began to rise. He waved them back into their chairs.

"Yes. It's very sad. You'll have a full report via regular channels," said St. Clair.

"He was a very brave man." There was a lengthy silence, so Novak continued, "Thank you for calling."

"You're welcome." Novak hung up. Looking at the others he said. "Our security problem is moot. There is no problem."

Burnside said, "Well, that's something."

"I'll get this to Layton right away. Thanks. That's a great job."

Realizing they had been dismissed, Burnside and Ketchum walked out.

Novak tilted way back in his chair, his thoughts lingering on the dead lieutenant commander. The happenstance sinking of the U.S.S. *Pence* had, after all, turned out to be a stroke of luck. Ingram's death helped to nullify the possibility that the ULTRA code system would be compromised. With a pang of guilt, he recalled the man and their ride together on the PB2Y. In reality, Ingram was a decent man, married, soon to be skipper of his own destroyer. Later, Novak had learned Ingram had been at Corregidor, escaping the night it fell to the Japanese. That was how he earned the Navy Cross. On the long flight to Hawaii, he'd seen Ingram take a furtive swig from a bottle of Paregoric: Tincture of Camphor Opium; good for upset stomach and diarrhea; a mixture he'd secretly resorted to in his submarining days, when things went bad. Novak knew that as scared as Ingram was about returning to action, he was one of the Navy's finest. A man who would step up, no matter what was raging around him, or through his mind. Too bad. And now he was gone.

In a way, Lieutenant Commander Ingram was everything Novak wanted to be. Yet Ingram lay somewhere in the bottom of Iron Bottom Sound, trapped in the twisted hulk of the U.S.S. *Pence*. Novak had learned of the destroyer's loss within thirty minutes of when it happened. But it had taken seven gut-wrenching days for St. Clair's man to confirm Ingram was dead.

With a sigh, Novak picked up the phone. Time to call Layton who would, no doubt, pass it on to Nimitz. But no doubt, this would go all the way to the top.

38

14 April, 1943
  Headquarters, Commander In Chief, Pacific Fleet
  Makalapa Crater, Pearl Harbor, Hawaii

It was eight a.m. when Commander Edwin T. Layton walked into the Admiral's outer office, a worn manila folder under his arm. Over the doorway, a sign read:

NATIONS, LIKE MEN, SHOULD GRASP TIME BY THE FORELOCK,
INSTEAD OF THE FETLOCK.

The tall, thin, dark haired commander whipped off his hat and nodded to Lieutenant Arthur C. Lamar, the Admiral's Flag Lieutenant.
  "Zero Zero is in and will see you now," said Lamar.
  "Thanks." Layton walked past Lamar's desk into the office of Admiral Chester W. Nimitz, Commander in Chief, Pacific Fleet and Pacific Ocean Areas. The room was tastefully decorated with rattan furniture. Hawaiian flowered drapes framed a pair of windows which gave onto a spectacular view of Pearl Harbor. Nimitz glass-topped desk was cluttered with brass

ashtrays cut from gun shell casings. Beneath the glass were stringent slogans and an autographed picture of Douglas MacArthur.

Nimitz smiled up at Layton and said in his Texas drawl, "Morning Ed." As always, in these daily briefings, he bade him to sit in a chair to his left.

The Admiral looked fit, Layton noticed. He'd been up for his two mile hike at six this morning, had breakfast, then spent another half hour on the pistol range before stepping across a passageway to his office. Only Layton, and a handful of others knew that the pistol range was not there through whimsy. It had been prescribed by Captain Elphege Alfred M. Gendreau, Pacific Fleet Surgeon and Nimitz' housemate. Nimitz' hands had began to shake, but after just three weeks on the range, it had all but gone away.

The white-haired, tanned Admiral caught Layton staring at his left hand. "Anything new, this morning?"

Layton couldn't help but note the irony: Both admirals had fingers missing from their left hands. The ring finger of Nimitz' left hand was missing, lost in a 1916 accident, while demonstrating a new diesel engine prototype. His counterpart, Isoroku Yamamoto had lost the index and middle fingers of his left hand in battle. And that's why Layton was here this morning: Yamamoto. He opened his manila folder and passed over the message Novak had given him just an hour ago. "Our old friend Yamamoto."

A ship's whistle blasted up from Pearl Harbor as Nimitz read. Layton glanced out the window, still repulsed by remnants of the Japanese sneak attack.

Silently Nimitz rose, his crystal blue eyes glimmering, and walked to a large wall-mounted chart. With his fingers he stepped off the distance from Guadalcanal to Bougainville's southern tip. "About 300 miles, I'd say."

"Yes Sir, three hundred twenty, actually."

"Yamamoto is very punctual, isn't he? Insists on being on time everywhere. Right?"

Layton realized that Nimitz was asking for his personal view of the situation. A Japanese language expert, Layton had spent several years in Japan as a Naval attaché and knew Yamamoto far better. He'd seen Yamamoto many times formally and on occasion, informally. Once was just six years ago during a hunt, when Yamamoto entertained officers from the U.S., British, Dutch and Japanese Navies at the Emperor's hunting preserve. They'd chased ducks with long-handled nets, with Yamamoto laughing and cheering the men on as they ensnared the terrified, quacking birds. Later, their catch had been cooked and served up amidst odors of ginger and teriyaki sauce, complimented by Asahi Beer and Johnnie Walker Black Label Scotch. Yamamoto had been a wonderful host, making sure every guest ate his fill, drank to his heart's content, and left with a warm handshake and one of the Emperor's ducks. Layton said, "Yes, Sir. That's true. On the occasions I met him he was always there at the exact hour. And we were cautioned to prepare by being fifteen minutes early. Tardiness was not tolerated by the *Gensui*."

"Okay, what do we have?"

"We have F4Us at Henderson Field, but their long-range tanks have been removed and the brackets disabled. So they're out of the picture. But we also have Army P-38s at Henderson which have the range to reach Bougainville. Already, they're escorting bombers up there."

"But they haven't done fighter sweeps."

"No, not yet. There's a shortage of long range tanks. Once they get a good supply in there, they'll do that on a daily occurrence."

"So it is feasible?"

"I believe so Admiral. But we'd need confirmation from the Army boys down there to make sure."

"Okay." Nimitz sat and drummed his fingers for a moment. Then he steepled them and said. "Assassination. Political assassination."

"This is war, not politics," Layton shrugged.

"Even so, we'd need FDR's approval."

Yes, Sir."

Nimitz looked up. "What do you say? Do we try to get him?"

"He's unique among their people," said Layton. "Their officers, their enlisted rank and file, all idolize Yamamoto. Aside from the Emperor, probably no man in Japan is so important to civilian morale. And if he's shot down, it would demoralize the fighting navy. You know the Japanese psychology; it would stun the nation."

Nimitz starred into space. "...he's done wonders for their Navy. A great leader; a forward thinker, not afraid to take chances, aggressive, not intimidated by politics. And he gets one hundred five percent from his men.

"But you know, Yamamoto does have one weakness. A small one but noticeable."

Layton loved it when Nimitz went off like this. The sessions were terribly one-sided but it always showed the best part of the Admiral. "What's that, Sir?"

"It's the way he plans; in fact, the way they all plan." Nimitz smacked a palm on his desktop. "Tsushima Straits, 1905. Pearl Harbor, 1941. These massive air-raids in the Solomons just a few days ago." He looked Layton dead center in the eye. "What do they all mean to you?"

Layton was hard pressed to keep up. "Knock out punch?"

"Exactly. What they're really trying to do is to wipe out everything in one, decisive stroke. Look back at what they did to the Russians at Tsushima. Surprise attack. The war was over for the Czar before it began. A decisive, bold stroke. " Nimitz threw a hand toward the window and Pearl Harbor beyond. "Same thing there. Sink our battleships in a surprise attack without declaring war. A decisive, bold stroke. And now the business in the Solomons. Close to two hundred planes, right?"

"Yes, Sir."

"Just like at Pearl Harbor. And what were the damages they claimed?"

Layton opened his manila folder and shuffled among his intercepted dispatches. "Yes, Sir, here it is. The Japanese claimed one cruiser two destroyers, twenty-five transports, sunk and 134 airplanes either shot down or wrecked on the ground."

"A decisive bold stroke. See what I mean? They think they really scored big."

"Well, yes Sir. But the Japs only sunk the destroyer *Pence*, a gasoline tanker, the *Kanawha*, one New Zealand corvette, the *Moa,* two Dutch merchant ships, and twenty-five airplanes."

"All well and good. But my point is Yamamoto's approach to things. He thinks he sunk all that tonnage, and that's the way he'll continue to plan. Just like he did at Midway, I might add. There he was trying to draw out the remainder of the U.S. fleet and sink it in one decisive, bold stroke."

Layton nodded, not about to argue with Nimitz' logic.

Nimitz stood, walked to the window and looked out, his arms folded.

"The one thing that concerns me is whether they could find a more effective fleet commander."

"Yamamoto is head and shoulders above them all." After a pause, Layton continued, "You know, Admiral Nimitz, it would be just as if they shot you down. There isn't anybody to replace you."

"Okay." The Admiral turned. "It's down in Halsey's bailiwick. If there's a way, he'll find it. All right, we'll try it."

Layton made to rise, but Nimitz waved him down with a palm. Pointing to the Yamamoto message on his desk, he said, "You know, this ULTRA stuff is getting better and better."

"What helped were those code books we salvaged off the *I-1* last January. That allowed us crack the latest revision to JN-25."

"Interesting. We just lost the *Moa*. Wasn't she one of the two New Zealand corvettes that helped sink that Jap? Where was it?"

"The *Moa*. That's right, Sir." Layton opened a large manila folder. "Off the northwestern tip of Guadalcanal, let's see," he ran a finger down a column of dates, "January twenty-ninth."

"Ironic, isn't it?"

"Yes, sir."

Nimitz pressed his lips. "Well, we have cause for concern, here."

"Admiral?"

"The Japs putting two and two together and figuring out we've broken their code, especially if this mission is successful."

"We'll have to keep mum."

"More than that." Nimitz took out a message pad and began writing. "This goes to Halsey. I'm recommending he should leak it afterwards that we got the dope from coastwatchers." He finished and read the last line aloud, "'If forces in your command have capability shoot down Yamamoto and staff, you are hereby authorized initiate preliminary planning.' How does that sound?"

"That'll work, Sir."

"Okay." Nimitz tore off the message and handed the draft to Layton. "Send that on to Halsey with one copy to Frank Knox, another to Bill Leahy, suggesting he forward it to the President."

"Will do, Sir."

"Make sure the message to Leahy stresses the importance of the timing. And God, don't forget to send a copy to Ernie King."

Layton debated in his mind whether or not to tell the admiral that Novak had warned him about an errant lieutenant commander in Tulagi. A loud-mouth insubordinate officer who could tip off the whole operation to the Japanese. Novak had said the problem was being taken care of. But Layton made a mental note to check with Novak before asking the Admiral for the final go-ahead.

Well, there were several layers here: King, Leahy, Knox and Roosevelt, in that order. Layton could afford to wait while allowing the machinery to get up to speed. He said absently, "Four days, Sir."

"The clock is ticking, Ed." Nimitz lifted a thick, red-stripped folder from his in-basket.

Layton made a mental note to check with Novak at least twice a day. Once committed, it would be hard to stop Halsey and his crew. "Yes, Sir."

A half hour after sunset, the Imperial Japanese Navy destroyer *Matukaze* weighed anchor from Rabaul Harbor, cleared the minefield and stood into the St. George Channel. From there, she headed south, shaping a course for the Solomon Sea, Bougainville and Kolombangara. As the *Matukaze* worked up to speed, Captain Kanji Takano sat alone in her wardroom, the table piled with ordnance data and the latest information on American combatants.

The wardroom lights clicked to red, as Commander Enomoto, walked through the light lock. He dogged the hatch, and the lights returned to white fluorescent. "Good evening," said Enomoto, evenly.

Takano looked up, "How are we doing?"

Enomoto tossed aside his duffle coat, then sat heavily. "Fifteen knots. Best we can do without the starboard shaft." They had decided to get under way for Vila and wait there for the specially-made shaft bearing being flown down from the Uraga Shipyards in Japan. Unlike Takano, Enomoto's reputation hadn't suffered much, despite the mix-up from his last trip. Indeed, his overweight jowly face belied a keen mind and he was still regarded as one of the best destroyer skippers in the South-East Command. He continued,

"Then we must zig-zag, lest a submarine catch us with our pants down. We should be in Vila by noon tomorrow."

Takano said, "How long to fix the shaft?"

"Four hours. If the bearing is there."

"Well, if it's not there, we'll just continue."

"Captain. With respect, Sir." It had been hard for Enomoto to add the latter. "We're in a war zone. We got underway against my better judgment with only one shaft. I'll not take my ship into the New Georgia Sound without her full capabilities -- without both shafts. It would be suicide."

"That's insubordination!"

"Then relieve me."

They glared at one another. A life-long ordnance specialist, Takano had virtually no experience at sea nor in command. As much as he wanted, relieving Enomoto was an impossibility. He offered a meager compromise, "we pray that the bearing is there."

39

14 April, 1943
    U.S.S. *Sands* (APD 13)
    Tulagi Harbor, Solomon Islands

Someone shook Ingram's shoulder. His eyes snapped open.

A voice resonated in the dark. "Sir. Your wake-up call."

"What time is it?"

"0630, Sir. We embark troops at 0730; underway at 0800."

In the dim light, Ingram recognized the face of one of the *Sand's* third class quartermasters, who was politely reminding him it was time to get off the ship. They needed the space for a contingent of Marines scheduled to arrive in an hour. A half an hour after that, they would be shoving off, for a raid on a Rendova airfield.

Ingram and the *Pence's* crew had been rescued the previous Wednesday evening by PT boats, then returned to the destroyer tender *Whitney* in Tulagi Harbor. Since the *Whitney* was already full of shipwrecked sailors, the DESRONTWELVE staff officer billeted Ingram, Druckman and two other *Pence* officers in the embarked officer's quarters aboard the *Sands,* an old four-stacker converted to a high speed troop transport now nested alongside the *Whitney*. She was On the second day, a hollow-eyed Ralph Druckman was ordered to the States to join the CNO's staff; the rest of the *Pence's* officers and men were quickly distributed to other ships. So Ingram had been by himself, sleeping fitfully between air attacks, writing to Helen, and waiting for orders.

They'd recovered Seltzer's body the next day, and Ingram had to identify it. And now, the boatswain lay in one of the *Whitney's* overcrowded freezers, waiting for the next refrigeration ship to come in to offload food for the living, then carry home the dead.

There was a bizarre twist to Ingram's situation. He was not officially viewed as a member of the *Pence's* crew, especially since his orders and records hadn't been validated on the *Pence*. In fact, he hadn't even been logged aboard. There hadn't been time. Worse, his orders, personnel folder and pay records were in his duffle bag, laying on Ralph Druckman's bunk, which was now at the bottom of Iron Bottom Sound. So, in a matter of speaking, he was a man without a country, or at least a man without a duty station. The only person who could provide new orders was Rocko Myszynski who, until last night, had been at sea with Dexter Sands' battle group.

With a sigh, Ingram heaved himself off the bunk and padded down the companionway to take a shower. When he returned, he found a note on his bunk:

Todd,
I'm back in town, so let's talk. Now.
Rocko

After dressing, Ingram picked up his ditty bag, containing his only possessions, and left, just as the Marines began stepping aboard. He quickly mounted the *Whitney's* gangway and headed for the wardroom for breakfast.

"Sssst!"

Ingram looked up to see Myszynski beckoning from the deck above.

Ingram saluted. "Good morning Commodore. Have you had chow, yet?"

Rocko said sotto voce, "No. Now get up here, quick." Then he walked forward and disappeared around a corner.

Ingram stepped up the ladder and was soon in Myszynski's office.

Puffing on a glistening, black stoggie, Myszynski closed the door softly and flipped on a light. He gestured for Ingram to take a chair, then moved around his desk.

"Something wrong, Sir?" asked Ingram.

"In a moment. What do you want for breakfast?" Myszynski picked up a phone.

Ingram sputtered out a breakfast order. Myszynski did the same, calling for a pot of coffee, and hung up. He stared at Ingram for a long moment.

"I'm sorry, I don't get it, Commodore." Ingram held out his palms.

"Okay, first things first. I'm sorry about the *Pence*."

"Not your fault, Commodore."

"You going to be okay?"

Ingram nodded slowly. Outside of a stilted conversation with Ralph Druckman, he hadn't talked to anyone since the *Pence* went down.

"You've been alone, haven't you?"

"I'm fine...but..."

"But what?" Myszynski asked gently.

"...a lot of people got ripped up."

"Who?"

"Well, aside from the guys who were killed outright, Ralph Druckman, for instance. I'd say he's a broken man, now. A zombie." *What's Rocko getting at?*

Myszynski blew smoke at the overhead. "I'd say you're right. That's why we sent him back to CNO's staff. To give him time to get back on his feet."

"*Pence* was a great ship. You should have seen his gunners."

"I've read the reports."

"In fact..."

"What?"

"I've been thinking about it. Those damned proximity fuses really work."

"You noticed."

"We shot down two, maybe three Vals. One bomb was a near miss and opened up seams in the engineering spaces. We could have handled that, but it was that damned Betty, low on the water; that's what did us in."

"I see."

"And we even splashed that Betty; unfortunately, it was a split second after he released his torpedo."

Myszynski looked into space and said, "You know, timing is everything. Arleigh Burke was talking about it the other day at Tulagi -- in that pig-sty we call an 'O' Club." Arleigh Burke was commodore of Destroyer Division Forty-Three.

"Sir?"

"Arleigh was talking about decision-making. He said, 'The difference between a good officer and a poor officer is about ten seconds.'" Myszynski cocked his head.

It sunk in; Myszynski was fishing. "If you're asking about Ralph Druckman Commodore, I don't think that's the case. He was decisive and did things right the first time. Well before ten seconds passed."

"Okay."

"Seeing his people being killed and maimed is what did him in."

"I was sorry to hear about Leo Seltzer."

"...did Ralph tell you what he did?"

"Outside of a sketchy battle report, Ralph didn't have a lot to say."

"We were abandoning; you could tell she was going to capsize. This...that crazy Leo ran back up to the signal bridge and started to take down the flag."

"Again?"

"Again. Then, a boiler blew and the ship rolled suddenly and took...took him...I" Ingram ran the back of his hand against his cheek, surprised to find tears running down. He caught his breath and blurted, "I'm not the skipper, but I'd like to nominate him for another medal. The Silver Star this time."

"I'll endorse it."

"...posthumously, of course. He never..." Ingram shot to his feet, "Excuse me." Then he ran out of Myszynski's office.

Some primordial guide sent Ingram down, ending up in the engine room, where he sat behind a huge turbo-generator, crying like a baby. But no one heard, he was sure, the thing made so much noise. Until---

"---Sir?" It was an engineman looking down at him. He wore sweaty, oil stained coveralls, and had a clipboard under his arm.

"Huh? I'm fine. Just looking the place over." Ingram rose and ran a hand through his hair.

The engineman eyes clicked over to a bracketed telephone on the main control board.

The one hundred plus degree heat and the humidity pressed in on Ingram. "Thanks for the tour, Sailor." He headed for the ladder and climbed quickly, gaining the main deck. Resigned to returning to Myszynski's office, Ingram took his time climbing to the 02 level.

"Todd? Todd Ingram? Is that you?"

Ingram looked up. "Good God. Tubby. How are you?" He shook hands warmly with Tubby White. "You still pouring steel marbles in vent ducts?"

White ignored the remark. "Say Todd. You look kind of flushed. Are you okay?"

"Been down in the engine room. So, tell me, how's the PT boat business?"

"PT's are fine, Todd. Actually, it's a lot different. I like the work but..." he looked down. "...it gets intense at times."

"What brings you here?" Ingram sensed Tubby wasn't happy.

"Just saw Commodore Myszynski. In fact, he's looking for you." His eyebrows went up.

"I know."

"Talk about marbles in the overhead; things have come full circle." He told Ingram about Landa and *PT 94* being trapped on Kotukuriana Island.

Quickly, Ingram drew in a breath. "What? Jerry?" He stepped close. "What happened?"

"Yeah. Oscar Bollinger, Commander Landa, and *PT 94*'s crew were gone. Disappeared. We had no idea what happened. Air search and rescue didn't turn up a thing, except a bunch of pissed off Japs aboard the *Howell*. Then they picked up some week radio signals yesterday over at CACTUS which we picked up later at the PT base. It sounds like Jerry Landa, Oscar Bollinger and the rest of *PT 94*'s crew are stranded somewhere south of Mondo Mondo. So guess what? They've selected yours truly to go up and find him. Plus we have another job."

"What?"

"Blow up the *Howell*. Halsey ordered it. Doesn't want the proximity fuse to fall in the Jap's hands. That's why it has to be a demo party, rather than airplanes. We have to wire the magazines and make sure everything blows up."

"Don't forget we set charges in the forward magazine."

"Yeah, but we figure the Japs have disarmed all that."

"Speaking about the Japs, what are you going to do about them?"

"They're sending two other PT-boats loaded with Marines to clean them out while we pick up Oscar."

"Did you step forward and volunteer?"

"Somebody goosed me at officer's call." White waved a folder. "Well, I better get down there. Collect some jarheads and join with the other skippers. See you later." White saluted and walked off.

No wonder Tubby looked on edge. Ingram called after him, "Good luck."

White turned and waved, then disappeared around the midships passageway.

Ingram knocked on Myszynski's door.

"Come!"

Ingram walked in. "Commodore, I'm sorry. I---"

There was a plate of eggs on Myszynski's desk. He waved a fork at Ingram and said, "Where'd you go?"

"Walked around the main deck, Sir. Ran into Tubby White. In fact he told me about---"

"---sit. Your breakfast is getting cold. And fresh eggs, too. Just in from the States. Dig in while they last." He waved his fork at a plate covered with a silver cloche and a steaming mug of coffee nearby.

"Thank you, Sir."

They ate in silence. Finally Myszynski sat back and lit a cigar. "You okay now?"

"Never better. Just needed a breath of fresh air," Ingram lied. Waving a hand at the door he said, "I just ran into Tubby White. He told me about Jerry Landa."

"It's good news. I thought we'd lost him." Myszynski blew smoke.

"I sure hope it works."

"It's a dicey operation. We're not quite sure what the Japs have going up there." Myszynski asked, "You want another ship, I suppose."

'*I suppose*?' "You bet."

"You must be losing count of the ships that have been blown out from under you."

Ingram sighed. *Penguin, Howell, Pence.* "I'm ready, Commodore."

"Why do I have the feeling I'm not convinced?" said Myszynski.

"Damnit! I really want this."

"I think you do want it but I think another part of you says 'no.'"

"Commodore, I--"

"Here's the deal, Todd. I want you to stand down for a while. Just to get you off the edge, so to speak. Plus, I don't have another ship for you at this time."

Ingram opened his mouth to speak but then thought better of it.

"So where do we send you? Back to the States? Under normal circumstances, yes."

Ingram raised his eyebrows.

"But I have a problem here."

"Sir?"

"It's the reason you're up here, instead of the wardroom..."

"Yes, Sir?"

"What do you know about a guy named Augustine Rivera?"

"Who?"

"Lieutenant Augustine Rivera, United States Navy Reserve. Sometimes he's Major Augustine Rivera, U.S. Marine Corps Reserve."

"I haven't heard of him."

Myszynski pushed back in his chair and knocked ashes off his cigar. Plopping his feet on the desk, he said, "He's sort of a bounty hunter who tracks down flamboyant AWOL cases."

"Okay."

"He has a set of TAD orders for you to accompany him to Pearl."

Ingram jumped up. "What?"

"I've not had the pleasure of meeting this guy, yet. He was waiting for me when we moored last night and did I get an earful. This morning he was down in the wardroom, eating chow, waiting for you. That's why we're dining up here."

"What the hell for?"

"Keep your shirt on." Myszynski pointed at the chair.

Ingram sat. "Why would someone want to," he paused, "'accompany' me to Pearl. And how could orders like that originate in the first place?"

"I don't know. Have you had any serious run-ins of any kind lately?"

Ingram racked his brain. "Can't think of anything. Did he indicate what sort of TAD I'm supposed to do?"

"No. Just Pearl Harbor. Think, Todd," Myszynski urged, "There has to be something that brings this guy out from under his rock."

"I can't. What the hell would an AWOL specialist want with me?"

"I don't know. I hear this guy is really good. He could find Judge Crater if they paid him enough. Come on, Todd, think. Anything. San Pedro? The *Hitchcock*? Maybe you misplaced a registered pub off the *Howell*? You know. Some guys get chickenshit about that kind of thing."

"...no."

"Corregidor maybe. All that gold?"

"I don't think so."

"Nasipit?

"Uh, uh."

"Jap torpedoes?"

Ingram shook his head.

"Damn. Hawaii?"

"No. IBwait."

Myszynski took out another cigar and lit it.

"It's not much."

"Try me."

Ingram told Myszynski about the trip from Long Beach to Hawaii aboard the PB2Y amphibian, the air-pocket, and Novak, the FRUPAC commander being knocked unconscious.

"Yeah?"

"Well, I sort of told a fib."

"What sort of fib?"

"The stuff in the guy's briefcase spilled on the desk. I picked up a bunch of papers, much of it message flimsies for him while he was still woozy. I figured I was doing him a favor. But, yes. Some of the stuff was classified TOP SECRET. And there was a few marked TOP SECRET ULTRA. It was---"

Myszynski slammed down a fist. "Jesus, Todd! You're not supposed to know that ULTRA even exists." He sat back for a moment and finally said, "go on."

"Novak came to. After a while, he asked if I saw any of the stuff that went into his briefcase."

"And?"

"And I said, 'no.' I lied, saying the lights were off when I re-packed his briefcase. But the lights were really on. The reason I fibbed is that I just didn't want to go through a security ringer in Pearl, be delayed, even have my orders changed." He added, "Nor get my ship."

"So this Rivera could be working for someone from FRUPAC, maybe even your Commander Novak, who is worried about what you may or may not know."

"That's all I can think of."

"Did you actually read the messages?"

"Well...I."

"Todd! Damnit!"

"Okay. Yes, Sir. Just two. There were so damned many. Big print, too. I couldn't help it. One was about---"

"---Don't." Myszynski held up a hand.

Ingram stood and jammed his fists on the top of Myszynski's desk. "All right, Rocko, I looked at the traffic. I couldn't help it. The messages meant nothing to me, I can guarantee you that."

"Take a seat, Todd."

Ingram sat.

Myszynski leaned forward. "I've never liked what I heard about this goon Rivera. Every time he delivers someone, they always seem to have a broken arm or something."

"Jeez."

"Guess what I told him last night?"

Ingram shook his head.

"I said that you were missing in action aboard the *Pence* and are presumed lost."

"You..." Ingram felt cold.

"Officially, you're dead."

"Don't tell my wife. I've been writing her."

"This guy is good. Maybe check with someone off the *Pence*. Or maybe around here. He knows the ropes. He'll probably check with your wife at which point the cat will be out of the bag and some dark brown smelly stuff will collapse directly onto the fan. So, all we're doing is buying time. I don't know what his plans are. He may stick around here. He may go back to Pearl. Somehow, you have to disappear until I get rid of Rivera; maybe talk to some boys at FRUPAC. Find out what the hell's going on. But unless you say differently, I don't think you ought to stay out here until this thing sorts itself out.

"Doing what?""

Myszynski leaned forward. "Jerry Landa is in trouble."

"Go with Tubby?"

"I think you'd be a great help."

"Tubby and a bunch of crazy Marines?"

"Well, there's three PT Boats and that's going to take some coordination. Or, I can send you on your way to the States where Rivera can catch up to you and break your arms."

Ingram's mouth turned dry. Suddenly, he thought about his bottle of paregoric. But that was at the bottom of Iron Bottom Sound. "Do I have a choice?"

"I knew you'd be pleased."

40

16 April, 1943
Fighter Strip Number Two
Guadalcanal, Solomon Islands

In 1936, the Army Air Corps issued stringent specifications for a new long-range interceptor. The aircraft was to have two engines and a minimum speed of 360 mph at 20,000 feet. Lockheed Aircraft Corporation of Burbank, California, submitted its first military design with their newly appointed Chief Research Engineer, Clarence L. "Kelly" Johnson as one of the contributors. The revolutionary twin-boom, twin-tail design was accepted on June 23, 1937 and designated XP-38 by the Army Air Corps. The XP-38 prototype was delivered in January 1939 and made its first flight on January 27th of that month. Tragically, the XP-38 crashed on February 11, 1939 at the end of a record-breaking cross-country flight from Burbank to New York. But the crash was logged to pilot error; the program pushed on.

Kelly Johnson could have perhaps described his new fighter plane to the War Department officials in the following terms:

. . .

The P-38 is a mid-wing cantilever monoplane powered by two 1,520 h.p. Allison 1710 twelve-cylinder vee liquid-cooled engines, driving counter-rotating Curtis Electric constant-speed full-feathering airscrews, each 11 feet, 6 inches in diameter. With a wing-span of fifty-two feet, the aircraft weighs 15,500 pounds fully loaded and has a service ceiling of over 35,000 feet with a maximum speed of 414 miles per hour. A gondola is located between the engines, which provides a spacious cockpit housing a pilot. Featured also are a tricycle landing gear and fowler flaps. Armament consists of a twenty millimeter cannon surrounded by four fifty caliber machine guns, all straight-ahead [non-converging] firing from a compartment located in front of the pilot. Later models can be modified to carry rockets, bombs, and photographic reconnaissance equipment.

The late morning on Guadalcanal's Fighter Two airstrip was brilliant. Two miles west of Henderson Field, the air had been washed clean by an early morning thunderstorm. The man paused in the shade of a coconut palm to watch a pair of P-38 *Lightnings*, wearing their olive drab paint schemes, lunge into their take-off runs. Behind the P-38s waited four Bell P-39 Aircobras, three Marine F4F Wildcats, and then five more P-38s. Marc Mitscher whipped off his long-billed ball cap and wiped sweat off his face watching the P-38s roar down the runway. Trailing great clouds of dust, they lifted off and headed west, not bothering to form up; a sure sign something was brewing up The Slot.

The palm's shade didn't help offset Guadalcanal's dank, oppressive humidity; nor was there any relief from the ever present, malaria-carrying mosquitoes. That's why Mitscher wore cumbersome long-sleeve khaki shirts and trousers. It was for protection. He didn't want to take any more chances than he had to with mosquito bites. Admiral Nimitz, after a visit to Guadalcanal six months ago, had contracted malaria and was in the hospital for a month. *The hell with that.*

Known for a crisp temper, hard work, and a lean staff, Mitscher preferred to walk by himself or drive his own jeep. He hated committees and indecisiveness. His sweat-soaked shirt and cap were devoid of campaign ribbons, trappings of office, or other paraphernalia, save two: his collar-mounted rear admiral's twin stars and gold aviator wings proudly pinned over his left-breast pocket. A passerby might have mistaken the fifty-six year old Mitscher as a retread chief warrant officer, having just been called away from his civilian job as a night manager at a bowling alley. Instead, Mitscher had been appointed as Air Commander, Solomons, just two weeks ago by Admiral Halsey. A thirty-seven year Navy veteran, Mitscher had spent half the time at sea. A flier since before America's involvement in the great war, he set up the first aircraft catapult aboard the cruiser *Huntington*. Later, he flew one of the Navy's four NC-1s in a pioneering transatlantic flight, making it to the Azores before his plane sunk. He'd been the first air officer aboard the Navy's first true carrier, the U.S.S. *Saratoga*, landing the first plane on her deck. Mitscher breathed, ate, and slept aviation; and his deeply tanned, wrinkled face, dominated by piercing blue eyes, stood in evidence. About a year ago, he'd been the skipper of the U.S.S. *Hornet,* which delivered Jimmy Doolittle and his sixteen B-25s to raid Japan almost one year ago.

Two P-39s bounced and jiggled onto the pierced steel-planked airstrip, revved up their engines, and jumped into their take-off runs. Mitscher watched them rise, his mind going over the latter part of the message Halsey had forwarded from Nimitz last night:

...IF FORCES YOUR COMMAND HAVE CAPABILITY SHOOT DOWN YAMAMOTO AND STAFF, YOU ARE HEREBY AUTHORIZED INITIATE PRELIMINARY PLANNING.
   NIMITZ

Halsey had added parenthetically, that he would remain in Noumea until tomorrow, Friday. Then he was committed to fly to Brisbane, Australia for his first face-to-face meeting with that "...self-advertising son-of-a-bitch," as he referred to General Douglas MacArthur. Thus Halsey wished his fellow aviator and friend, "Pete" Mitscher all the fun in shooting down Yamamoto.

Time to get to it. They're waiting. In the morning's full heat, Mitscher turned to complete the trip from his command headquarters to the "Opium Den," as the fighter operations hut was called. As he walked, he looked over to the P-38 Lightnings, quietly waiting, their engines ticking over, dark, menacing. It was hard to believe that twenty to twenty-five year old kids, sat in those cockpits, chomping gum and looking into the sky, oblivious to what would happen tomorrow. Only today counted...

...the P-38s normal range of 460 miles wasn't enough, he knew. But with drop tanks, the range increased to over 800 miles, enough to do the job, thought Mitscher as he reviewed Nimitz' message for the third time. The big question was, would the drop tanks arrive on time?

As much as he wanted to watch the other P-38s take off, he reluctantly quick-paced to the Ops hut, gratified it was surrounded by a large number of jeeps and trucks.

The first P-38 roared over his head as he gained the sparse shade of the control tower. By the time he walked into the Ops hut, numbers two and three had gone.

"Ten-hut!" called Marine Brigadier Field Harris, his chief of staff.

Mitscher was amazed. There were forty, maybe fifty officers from all the armed services in the impossibly hot room. Army, Navy, Marines, even a couple of Coastguardsmen. But his quick eyes caught the one unifying element; most wore aviator's wings.

Harris kept talking as Mitscher walked up to the front, "...that's about all. He'll arrive off Bougainville at eight in the morning. That's what we're counting on. That this Nip is as punctual as he's supposed to be. If he is, we'll be there to jump him. But don't forget, that'll be our ten o'clock, since the Japs keep their own time two hours ahead of us. Anyway, we figure that's the best place to jump him. Surprise is of the essence for this to work right. Also, secrecy is of the utmost importance. Nobody is supposed to know we have this dope. So keep your mouths shut, before and after. Now, any questions?"

No hands went in the air. All eyes flicked to Mitscher.

"Maybe security can suffer just a bit." The Admiral made a signal. Instantly the sides of the tent were rolled up, providing natural circulation and a bit of relief from the sweltering atmosphere.

He turned and faced them just as Lightings number four and five blasted overhead. After a long look, Mitscher nodded approvingly, "So many of you. Word gets out fast when there's a Jap on the block."

They chuckled and Mitscher began. "Thank you for coming on such short notice, gentlemen. I wish we had deep theater seats for you all but, hell, this is Cactus base, and what I have to add wont take long.

"First of all, I want to thank you for your interest. It's going to take all our help to get this bastard. And from that aspect its all of our show; not Army or Navy or Marine, but all of us. Is that clear?"

The men, ranging in rank from second lieutenant to brigadier general, nodded as one.

"Okay. For example, we're going to need some welding specialists to modify the P-38's wing tank brackets. Who can help us with that?"

A bald bare-chested man with a bright-red full beard wearing mud-caked trousers and boots raised his hand.

"Yes, Curley?"

A set of dog-tags dangled around his neck, and the man's deep voice resonated with, "Admiral. I've got two master welders and the equipment to go with them." A full commander, John W. "Curley" Summers had a masters in civil engineering from the University of California and ran the U.S. Navy's Construction Battalion unit on Guadalcanal.

"Okay, thanks, Curley. Please report to Colonel Viccellio and---yes, what is it?"

A scarecrow thin Marine Major, named Victor L. Stafford had raised his hand. In a drawl that was almost impossible to understand, he said. "Beggin' your pardon Admiral, but mah men and our Corsairs would love to have a crack at this Jap. You sure we can't go?" Most in the hut knew Stafford had lost a younger brother at Pearl Harbor, trapped in the engine room of the U.S.S. *Oklahoma* when she capsized. For Stafford, shooting down Yamamoto was personal.

Mitscher said quietly, "Major Stafford, I would like to say yes, but isn't it true a maintenance tech hacked off your drop-tank brackets and threw them away?"

"Well, yes, Sair. But all ah needs is a few days and we'll be ready."

"Sorry, Major. We don't have a few days."

"...Yas, Sair."

"What that means is this is to be an Army Air Corps show. All the way. Their P-38s have better long-range capabilities, anyway. So I meant what I said. We're all together in this. We must help the Army boys as much as possible."

Another Major, this one from the Army Air Corps in the back of the room raised his hand. "Excuse me, Admiral, but the last time I checked on this Island, there *were* no long-range drop tanks to be found."

Mitscher said, "That's why I was late. Jumping around on the radio all morning. We just found a bunch of 310 gallon drop tanks in Port Moresby. The Ninetieth Bombardment Group has agreed to help out. They're loading them in B-24s and they're supposed to be here by late this afternoon."

"Are you sure those gas-jockeys can find Guadalcanal?" someone catcalled.

Mitscher had been on Guadalcanal for two weeks. But it had taken him just two days to master the "death's head" grimace prevalent there. He gave it now and held up crossed fingers. Silence descended suddenly.

"So the way we figure is that each plane will go out with one 165 gallon tank and one 310 gallon tank. That should do it for range."

Using a white kerchief to mop sweat from his brow, a Navy captain asked, "Is this mission on for sure, Admiral?"

"We're supposed to plan as if it were on. But yes, we are awaiting final approval."

"By whom?" The captain, a non-aviator, folded his arms.

"It'll be coming from pretty high up, I understand; maybe even Navy Secretary Frank Knox or the President himself."

Someone gave a low whistle.

Mitscher responded with another death's head grimace.

Silence.

"Okay. Now, are our P-38 boys here?"

A voice called from the back of the hut. "Here Admiral." It was the Army Air Corps Major who had spoken earlier. The crowd parted, and two men walked forward: one, a solidly built Air Corps major, the other, a tall, lanky Army Air Corps captain. The major stepped up and saluted. "John Mitchell, Sir, 339th Fighter Squadron." He nodded to the Captain beside him, "This is Tom Lanphier, one of my senior pilots."

Mitscher shook their hands, "Okay. Has Intelligence given you the dope you need?"

"Enough to get started, Admiral, " said Mitchell.

"I want you to plan your routes out of sight of land; low on the water to avoid Jap radar and coast spotters. That's going to take some doing."

"Can do, Admiral," said Mitchell. "We'll go all the way up there fifty feet off the deck."

Mitscher took in the two men before him. He'd heard of the 339th and knew it was one of the best in the South Pacific. And these two had fine records. So did the rest of the squadron, for that matter. Mitscher had no complaints with these pilots. If anything, they were too serious. But then that's what it took to stay alive these days. Even so, he wished he were going with them. He said, "Good. How many planes can you take?"

Mitchell and Lanphier exchanged glances and shrugged. Finally Mitchell said, "All eighteen, Sir. I figure four planes to take out the Betty. The rest to oppose the six-Jap CAP and any Zeros that may sortie from Kahili."

"How many Zeros can we expect in Kahili?" asked Mitscher.

Field Harris flipped pages on a clipboard. "Seventy-five, Admiral."

"Seventy-five Zeros. That's a handful for just fourteen P-38s, Son," said Mitscher.

The left corner of Mitchell's mouth turned up slightly. "About the right odds for us, Admiral."

There was a collective sigh in the hut and Mitscher's death's head grimace became a warm smile..

Harris asked, "What do you think about jumping him while he's aboard the subchaser? Blast him with all eighteen planes?"

A fly landed on Lanphier's ear. He swatted it away and said, "Sir, I wouldn't know a sub-chaser from a toilet seat."

"That's right, Sir. He could jump overboard or any number of things, and you'd never really know if we got him," said Mitchell.

"So you think we should get him in the air, Major?" asked Mitscher.

"Yes, Sir." It's our only chance," said Mitchell.

A jeep pulled up outside, it's tires crunching in the gravel. Wearing a garrison cap and side arm, a young, tow-headed ensign, shouldered his way through the crowd, leaving a wake of grumbling officers. The ensign walked right up to Mitscher, saluted and said, "Sorry about the intrusion, Admiral, but the ops officer said you would want to see this."

Silence fell in the room, as Mitscher opened the envelop and read the message. The flimsy rattled in his hand as he said absently to Mitchell, "Where do you think we should hit him, Major?"

Mitchell walked up to a blackboard-mounted map. "Probably best catch him here, Admiral." He pointed to Bougainville's Southern tip. "Just west of Kahili when he's setting up to land." Then Mitchell turned to Lanphier. "What do you think, Tom? Can you lead the shooters?"

Lanphier nodded, "You bet. We'll give it all we've got. Give us a little cover and watch us go."

Mitscher looked up and said, "Okay. Kahili. We'll go with that." He turned to the two Air Corps aviators and held out his hand. "God speed. Let me know what we can do. Any questions?"

They shook hands with Lanphier asking, "Just one, Admiral."

"Yes?"

With a sidelong glance at Mitchell, Lanphier looked at the message in Mitscher's hand. "Is that what we think it is?"

"Good question, Captain." Mitscher handed over the flimsy.

With Mitchell looking over his shoulder, Lanphier whistled as he read:

SQUADRON 339 P-38 MUST ALL COSTS REACH AND DESTROY. PRESI-DENT ATTACHES EXTREME IMPORTANCE THIS OPERATION.
   KNOX

Novak's afternoon meeting with Howard O'Grady had gone well. O'Grady passed along high praise from Admiral Lockwood about the effectiveness of Novak's predictions of Japanese Fleet movements. Emerging from SUBPAC headquarters, a smiling Novak was given a message from Bob St. Clair requesting that he stop by. So he drove his Jeep under a golden sun and pulled up next to the base brig's front door. St. Clair, his head surrounded by a blue-grey cloud of cigarette smoke, met him in the lobby. Accustomed to Novak's penchant for cleanliness, St. Clair automatically waved him through the security checkpoint and into the lavatory where Novak went through his ritual of washing incriminating scribblings off the palm of his hand

He emerged into the lobby where St, Clair pointed to the front door and said, "I could do with a little sunshine."

"Sounds good to me," said Novak, just as glad to confer outside, rather than in one of St. Clair's dinghy holding rooms.

Once outdoors, St. Clair said, "I have word from Rivera."

"I thought we were done with him." Novak leaned against his jeep, his arms folded.

"Not exactly. It looks like Ingram is alive."

"What?" Novak's mouth dropped open. "But you said..."

"I know. Commodore Myszynski told us Ingram was dead. But it looks like the deceased Mr. Ingram had the temerity to continue writing letters to his wife *after* the *Pence* went down. So draw your own conclusions."

"Myszynski lied?"

"We're not sure, but that's a possibility." Taking a final puff, St. Clair field-stripped his cigarette and carefully pocketed the tiny wad of paper. "What do you want to do?"

It swept over Novak. ULTRA was again in jeopardy. The Yamamoto operation could be in jeopardy. But it was too late to warn Layton. Approvals had gone all the way up to FDR and out to Halsey and Mitscher. He turned to St. Clair, "The man's a security risk. I want him...what do you say...?

"Neutralized?" asked St. Clair, lighting another cigarette.

Novak climbed into his Jeep and pondered for a moment. "Yes, Neutralized. But what does that mean?"

"We'll take care of it."

Kicking the Jeep's starter, Novak ground the gears into reverse. He started to release the clutch, then had an afterthought, "Jesus! Don't kill him."

St. Clair blew a smoke ring, "Oh, we'll be nice to him."

It began misting as St. Clair ducked inside. He walked to his office., closed the door, drew the blinds and lit up a cigarette. Sitting back, he plopped his feet on the table and smoked in the dark, mulling options in his mind. On the one hand, Ingram could be all he was cracked up to be: Navy hero, Corregidor survivor, Spruance protégé, soon-to-be destroyer captain. That is if ships weren't always being blown out from under him, he smirked.

The Chesterfield burned down to his fingers and he butt-lit another, not bothering to crush out the first.

On the other hand, Ingram could be a Section 8 case, a dumb blabber-mouth or worse, a spy. Novak had told him about the insubordination charges on the mainland filed against Ingram. And then there was this lying business.

There was just too much at risk here. ULTRA could be compromised. And Novak was too much of a nice guy to do the right thing. This is war and somebody has to step in and take control, St. Clair decided. Dropping his feet to the floor, he grabbed a pad and scrawled out a message in neat block lettering.

NEUTRALIZE INGRAM

Rivera would know what that meant; they'd worked together long enough.

Outside, a drizzle grew to a downpour as he buzzed for the duty corporal. After the man left for the radioroom he reached for his Chesterfields.

Gone.

"Shit." He wadded up the package and tossed it in the trashcan.

The cigarette machine was across the courtyard, he would have to run through all that damned rain. He didn't want to do that and he wasn't going to lower himself, bumming cigarettes from an enlisted man. St. Clair drummed his fingers, becoming desperate.

Of course! That Jap, Sugiyama. Upon Novak's instructions, St. Clair had kept the little bastard in cigarettes by the carton. *Time for a little peaceful exchange.* St. Clair rose and headed for the second floor, humming the mournful strains of the *Kimigayo*.

41

16 April, 1943
PT -72
New Georgia Sound, (The Slot), Solomon Islands

The night was near pitch-black under a heavy overcast. But it was warm with the humidity so thick, Ingram wondered if they breathing or drowning. The waves were steep, slowing *PT-72* to a laborious ten knots as she climbed a swell, pitched over the top, and slammed down into a trough. Shaking green water off her snout, she fought her way up the peak of another mountainous wave, where a twenty knot wind whipped water aft, drenching the men in her cockpit. On the left was a hatless Tubby White, wiping water off his face and spinning his helm to maintain a semblance of course. Ingram stood alongside while Tubby's exec, Winston Fuller, a young chunky ensign, stood in the chartroom hatchway, calling radar ranges. Fuller, with thin sandy hair, was a Churchill look-alike; so much so that they called him Sir Winston or Winnie for short. With a deep baritone voice, Fuller oftentimes lived up to his nickname. Even now he rumbled, "Ten point two miles to Mondo Mondo, Tubby."

Peering into the gloom, Tubby flipped his wheel, trying to guess the peak of the next swell. Finally, they crested and smashed their way down into another trough. When they hit bottom and flattened out, he asked, "How's our SOA?"

Fuller looked into the chartroom, then poked his head out. "Not bad, we're a little ahead of our track. Looks like fifty minutes to go."

"Okay. Anything from Bollinger?"

"Not a peep."

That wasn't good news. And there had been worse news earlier. They had shoved off with *PT-88* and *PT-60*, the latter two boats embarking a squad of Marines each, for a total of twenty-six men. To distribute the weight, the Marine's inflatable assault boats and demolition gear was secured around the 40 millimeter canon on *PT-72's* after-deck. An hour out of Tulagi, PT 60 hit a half-submerged oil drum, leaving a four foot gash just above her water-line at the bow. Her only recourse was to leave it on the step in order to keep the gash out of the water and reverse course for Tulagi, the embarked Marines frantically bailing water. Later, *PT 88,* with her remaining thirteen Marines, developed trouble when the storm hit. First, her starboard engine conked; she pressed on for thirty more minutes, then the center engine died. So *PT-88* was obliged to head for the small, advance PT base in the Russell Islands, which meant the raid on the *Howell* would have to be postponed. Tubby White had thought of turning around and accompanying *PT-88*, but Ingram argued against it; that Landa and the men of *PT-92* needed to be picked up.

"Anymore from PT-60?" Asked Tubby White.

Fuller looked down and checked a clipboard. "Last I heard they were within sight of Tulagi, and the Jarheads were keeping even with the water." The radio squealed and he ducked down the passageway. A minute later, he was up. "Just got a report from PT Base Command in the Russell Islands. *PT-88* put in there and found parts to fix her engines almost immediately. Her Marines were disembarked but she's on her way up here to support us."

"How far behind?"

"Only about a half hour. She's running at full speed over smooth water in the lee of New Georgia. Said she'd check in by TBS when she got within range."

"That's something, anyway." Tubby turned to Ingram, "I guess we keep going."

"Those guys have been rotting up there for eight days."

"Okay." Tubby turned and called toward the hatch, "Winnie, get down there and listen up for Tommy." Tommy Madison was *PT-88*'s skipper. "And keep trying to raise Bollinger."

"Aye, aye, Sir," said Fuller, scrambling back into his chartroom.

Cascades of seventy degree water flew back from the bow and drenched them. Tubby wiped off his face. "I've had time to think this over."

"Think what over?"

"I've always felt bad about the way I left the *Howell*," said Tubby. "You're an okay guy, and so is Jerry Landa. I acted like, well, you know, a sap."

"Tubby. This isn't the time---"

"---Sir. Please let me finish." After a moment he said, "This war is a bunch of shit. Losing buddies is a bunch of shit. Fighting Japs is a bunch of shit." He shook his head and pursed his lips. "You know? Maybe I'm gonna eat it some day, and I don't want to go out with hard feelings."

"There's no hard feelings."

Tubby worked his boat up a wave where she crashed over the peak, then nearly slid sideways into a broach. "Whoa, Trigger, whoa!" Tubby yelled, spinning his wheel. Finally *PT-72* slithered into the trough and began her inexorable climb to the top of the next wave. When the boat settled down, Tubby asked, "You sure?"

"Yes. No hard feelings."

"How 'bout the caper with the marbles?"

Ingram gave a short laugh. "Hah! Jerry blew his stack. Really pissed. You should have seen him. He didn't get a wink of sleep that night."

"See what I mean?"

"Forget it. It was a great stunt. He knows he was had. Down deep, he likes that kind of stuff."

"Really?"

"You're not going to eat it, Tubby."

A minute passed, then Tubby said, "How 'bout the last guy who stood here?"

That brought Ingram up short. He had forgotten about Tubby's predecessor. Until a few minutes ago, all he thought about were his own shaky nerves. Tubby was talking about something that happened when *PT-72* was trying to rescue them off the *Howell*. Tubby was exec that night, but became captain very quickly when Tommy Kellogg took a bullet through his head. They promoted Tubby to skipper right away, and during the ensuing weeks, he acquired a reputation for ruthlessness and cunning. Completely changed, Tubby's boyish grin and college pranks were gone. Now, Tubby was all business: serious, methodical, calculating, deadly at his controls.

But Tubby needed an answer, before the specter of Tommy Kellogg ate at him like a pig's carcass dipped in hydrochloric acid.

Ingram closed his eyes. *Think of something, Captain.*

Finally, it came to him. "There's no today or yesterday, Tubby."

"What?"

"It means the toughest thing for you to do is to forget what happened in the past. There's nothing you can do to bring back Tommy Kellogg, Luther Dutton, Leo Seltzer or---"

"---Seltzer bought it?" Tubby's mouth was aghast.

"Leo is gone." Ingram told him about the *Pence's* sinking then continued, "...Leo or anybody else for that matter. You have to put your mind in neutral. Think of nothing before or after. Think just of today or yesterday. And forget about home."

Tubby nodded slowly and rubbed his chin.

"You have a girlfriend?"

"Yes."

"You close to her?"

"Well, we're getting kind of serious."

"What's her name?"

"Janet."

"Well, it's time to forget Janet. Just put her out of your mind. Don't think of her. That way, you wont be so on edge out here."

"Hell. I write to her. And what about the letters she sends me?"

"Don't open them. Tie them in a bundle. Don't answer anything until you're about ready to go home. Then, when you have orders stateside, answer Janet's letters as fast as you can and zip on home to her."

As Tubby thought that over, *PT-72* headed down a wave. Suddenly her transom whipped to starboard and she began sliding sideways. "Whoa!" He twirled the helm to starboard just in time. The boat straightened out at the last moment, hit the flat, then began to trudge up the front of another wave.

Spray flew past and a forty-knot gust howled in their ears. Then the wind eased and Tubby said, "Wisdom, I guess, comes with the Navy Cross."

"That's not the Navy Cross talking. That's Ernest Hemingway." Ingram decided not to tell Tubby about hearing it from Landa.

"No shit?"

"No sh---Look out!"

The wave was so big Ingram lost sight of the horizon. At least forty feet he guessed.

Tubby added power, then more power. Soon, they were climbing at a forty five degree angle. In desperation, Tubby added full power.

Ingram held on. All he could see was the mountain before them and, strangely, Winston Fuller's chalk-white face in the hatchway where he death-gripped a grabrail. *PT-72* pitched over the top with Tubby chopping the power just as they slid into the trough, great sheets of water whipping into their faces.

Tubby laughed and it made Ingram angry. Angry that he was so scared; angry at Tubby's impertinence; angry at his nonchalance about the wave. And why the hell wasn't Tubby scared?

"What about you?" Tubby yelled.

"What about me?" Ingram sputtered. "What about that damned wave?"

"Leave the driving to me."

"Okay." Ingram didn't have a choice and so far, he admitted, they were still alive.

"Now what your wife? What's her name?"

"Helen."

"Yeah. Helen. I've seen your stacks of mail. You mean to tell me you don't read her stuff, or write to her?"

Ingram thought that one over. He yelled into a gust, "honest answer?"

"Please."

"I devour her letters and write every damned moment I can."

In spite of the wind and rain and wildly pitching boat, Tubby turned to Ingram. They locked eyes for a full two seconds, an eternity.

Ensign Fuller popped his head out of the hatch. "How's it going?

Ingram and Tubby White began giggling, then laughing, louder and louder.

"What did I say?" said Fuller.

Ingram and Tubby laughed into the wind, the sound yanked from their throats and mingling with the spray.

At two in the morning, the storm abated and a pale half moon sifted through the clouds. They crept within the lee of New Georgia and soon were a mile off the coast cruising at ten knots with the engines muffled, battle stations manned.

Suddenly Fuller whooped from the chart room.

"What?" said Tubby White.

Fuller's deep voice caromed up the hatchway, "It's Mr. Bollinger. We have him weak, but clear, on CW."

"Where is he?"

"Kotukuriana Island. Inside. All we do is take the Lingutu passage into Marovo Lagoon. They're about a five hundred yards southeast."

"So how do I get there?" asked Tubby.

"Come left about three degrees. That should put us on course for the entrance."

"Got it." Tubby eased his wheel.

"Also, Mr. Bollinger says to watch out," said Fuller. "A Nip DD has been patrolling out here. And he says there may be Japs on the Mondo Mondo side of the entrance."

Quickly Ingram and Tubby scanned the horizon with binoculars. Ingram looked at Tubby who shook his head. Then they scanned Mondo Mondo Island.

Nothing.

Tubby called down the hatch, "We can't see anything. How about radar?"

"No contacts, Sir. Clean as a whistle."

"There's the entrance. What do you think?" Tubby nodded toward where little white wavelets cascaded over rocks.

"Looks clear back there. Let's try it --- hold it." Ingram did another one-hundred eighty degree sweep aft with his binoculars.

"What?"

Ingram scanned forward, toward Mondo Mondo. *Damn!* "Look. See that?"

"Yeah, there's something." Tubby twirled his lens knob. "Yeah, there's a barge moored right alongside the *Howell*."

"Right." Ingram's heart sank. "We have to do something right now."

"It's a damned work party." Tubby's voice rose a notch. "Japs are offloading the ship's ammo onto a barge." His eyes were wide as he looked into Ingram's eyes. "That's five-inch stuff. What the hell would they want with that?"

"That's five inch ammo, all right. Worse, it's five-inch proximity-fuse ammo they're offloading."

"Shit! They're going to haul it off and...and...copy it and shoot it back at us." Tubby pounded a fist. "Hell! We gotta do something. Winnie. Get Tulagi on the horn. Get some airplanes up here and bomb the crap out of them."

Ingram lay a hand on Tubby's arm. "I don't think so." He pointed at the *Howell*. "See that?"

Tubby hunkered down behind his binoculars. "A tug?"

"Yeah. That barge will be long gone before daybreak. Planes may not find them. They could pull into shallows under trees somewhere and hide until the following night. And it's not far to their airfields at Vila or Buin or Munda. A few hours ride. Then they fly the stuff out."

"Aw, shit!"

"Yes. Shit."

"Okay, then. I'll lob a fish into them. Hell, I'll let them have all four fish."

"Can they run that shallow?"

"Don't know. We can try."

Ingram pressed, "And what happens if a torpedo hits the barge or the ship. Chances are it wont detonate the ammo."

Tubby stared into the darkness. "There has to be something."

"There is."

"Well, fill me in, would you please?"

"Okay, Tubby. Here's what we have to do."

. . .

Augustine Rivera wished he were back in airplanes. Anything but these stinking, pounding, tooth-jarring PT boats. He'd been seasick when they pushed off into rough weather out of Tulagi. For the first time in his life, he was thankful for the intervention of a Supreme Being when the engines gave out. From what he'd overheard, he suspected that they having gas filter problems.

But *PT-88s* skipper, Tommy "Hubba Hubba," Madison, a grinning, solidly built ex-USC quarterback had radioed ahead to the Russell Islands PT base. Parts were waiting on the pier. Miraculously, the engines were quickly fixed, the Marines disembarked, *PT-88* underway again.

And now, they were growling up The Slot at full speed, occasionally jumping a wave, making Rivera's stomach feel as it were a piñata ready to burst.

"How you feeling, Major?" Madison stood easily at his wheel, steering with just the index finger of his right hand.

"Like shit."

"Well, don't go below, You'll loose it all."

The PT jumped the top of a wave its engines racing as the screws came out of the water. Rivera quickly braced himself.

WHACK!

The sonofabitch is enjoying this, Rivera realized. Madison isn't trying to steer around the waves. Swallowing his pride, he asked, "Got any Dramamine?"

"That'll put you to sleep, Major." Tommy Madison yelled into the chart house. "Hey Waterman. "Anything new?"

Over the engine's throaty roar, Rivera heard, "Yeah, we just raised Tubby."

"What's he have to say?"

"Waiting for us. Wants us to rendezvous and do something."

"Not one of his stunts," said Tommy.

"Whose Tubby White?" asked Rivera.

"Football buddy."

"Where did you guys go?"

"USC."

"No kidding. So did I," grinned Rivera who never went to college. He racked his brain. *What the hell were they called? The Centurions? Spartans? Athenians?*

"You were a Trojan?"

"Yeah, I tried out for football but they said I was too small," said Rivera.

"I'll be damned." Tommy Madison yelled down the companionway, "Hey Waterman. Pass up some crackers. On the double."

"...Sir."

A package flew though the hatch. Madison's hand leaped out, catching it in mid-air. "Here. Best thing for you."

"Thanks." Rivera laid a cracker on his tongue and forced himself to munch.

"Still can't figure why you didn't stay with your Marines, Sir."

Actually, it was a blessing in disguise when the Marines disembarked. After receiving St. Clair's message, he'd fast-talked himself aboard *PT-88*. But the sergeant became edgy and began asking pointed questions. Rivera was having trouble putting him off. "Reconnaissance, Lieutenant. We need information on the Jap garrison and I got stuck with the job."

"I see. Uh. Do you mind, Major?" Madison pointed at the crackers.

Rivera handed over the package, noticing Tommy Madison was driving with both hands, steering around the waves, the boat crashing less and less.

Madison shoved three crackers in his mouth. "Fight on, Trojans."

What the hell is he talking about? "Fight on."

42

15 April, 1943
  PT-72
  Off Mondo Mondo Island
  New Georgia Sound, Solomon Islands

The Higgins built PT Boat was rated in excess of forty knots. But *Little Lulu* had three things going against her: her three engines were sadly in need of overhaul; she carried hundreds of pounds of extra ammo and fuel; and worse, she'd been on the run so much, her bottom was covered with cancerous-looking tubers and barnacles.

Tubby White made a show of shoving the throttles against the stops. He waved a hand toward the knotmeter with a sheepish grin and yelled over the Packard's growl, "Thirty-four knots, that's it for poor old *Lulu*." He waved to *PT-88*, keeping station 200 yards aft and slightly to port. Even Tommy Madison is faster than us. "And I used to beat him all the time."

With the boat soon to engage the enemy, they were all jumpy. Ingram checked his watch. Less than three minutes to go; then they would dash past the *Howell* with all guns blazing. "Okay, Tubby, Give it all you got. See you in ...how long?"

"Ninety minutes?"

"Okay. Ninety minutes. Ingram checked his watch, "It's now 1127, so let's say at 0100."

"Right, 0100."

"But if I'm not there, I want you to take off. That's an order. Okay?"

Tubby touched his helmet brim with his forefinger. "Yes, Sir."

"Okay." Ingram turned and walked aft.

Tubby stepped from his helm and said, "Take it, Winnie." He followed Ingram into the gloom, finding him near the transom. "Todd, hold on."

Ingram spun. "What?"

"Let me go with you. I mean, by yourself, this is a suicide mission."

Ingram knew that if he talked to anyone right now he'd probably cry like a baby. So he bent over and made a show of checking the items he'd transferred from the Marine's demolition kit. Aloud, he said, "Five TNT blocks, fifty feet of detonating cord, hmmm, let's see, okay; one block of Composition C-4; and here's the five blasting caps; 100 feet of time fuse and four, no five M-60 fuse lighters. Best we can do." He sealed the water-tight pouch, then nudged it toward the port rail where it lay alongside a one-man liferaft pack. As an afterthought, he reached in another satchel, pulled out six hand grenades and tossed them in his pouch. "Insurance," he muttered.

Tubby moved closer. "I said, 'Let me go with you,' damnit. You're doing a Hari-Kari."

"If I can't get the *Howell* to blow, Tubby, it's you who'll do the suicide mission with *Little Lulu*." Ingram looked out to sea for a moment massaging his belly, willing away the rising bile. For some reason, he'd forgotten to draw paregoric when he prepared for this mission earlier in the day. Actually, he wasn't supposed to need any. This was to be a cake-walk. Pick up Landa and *PT-94*'s crew, let the Marines blow up the *Howell* and waltz on home. But now, the specter of single-handedly facing the enemy staggered him.

His stomach surged and he gagged, turning from White to cover his mouth.

"You okay, skipper?"

"Never better." Just then his stomach surged and he let out a tortured croak that mingled with the Packard's roar.

"Then how 'bout letting me go with you?"

Trying his best to look casual, Ingram made a show of cinching the .45 automatic pistol in his shoulder holster. *Take my place, you idiot. I'd be glad to drive your boat.* Fire raged in his belly, but he managed to hold it down. He sat on the aft torpedo mount, kicked off his boots and began lacing on a pair of sneakers. "You know, Tubby, sometimes you can't see the forest from the cactus bushes."

"What?"

"In case you don't realize it, you're captain of this vessel and you're not going to abandon her. And damnit, you're going to carry out your mission."

"What I meant was---"

"---The U.S.S. *Howell,* a ship of the United States Navy, will be off the starboard beam in about sixty seconds. I'll need cover so you better hop to it."

"But you got Tommy Madison." Tubby jabbed a thumb over his shoulder at *PT-88.*

"For crying out loud, Tubby. This is your boat. Act like it."

Tubby's shoulders sagged. He held out his hand. "Good luck."

"Give 'em everything you got, Captain." Ingram shook.

"You do the same, Todd, and come back to us. We'll be waiting. Okay?"

"Okay. 0100."

"0100." Tubby clapped Ingram on the shoulder and walked forward.

Ingram turned to the 40 millimeter gun-crew and asked the pointer, "I need someone to toss my gear when I jump."

"You bet, Sir." The trainer nodded to a loader. "Hey Blake. Throw that stuff over when the Commander takes his dive." The tone of his voice said, 'this son-of-a-bitch is crazy but we gotta do what he sez.' Then gun trainer hunkered down to his sight, working his hand wheel, training the gun a bit forward.

A thin, barechested sailor, wearing just boots and a helmet, emerged from behind the mount, clutching a clip of 40 millimeter ammunition. He was a wide-eyed seaman apprentice, no more than nineteen years of age. "Sir?"

"I go as soon as the shooting starts." In spite of the warm night, Ingram's teeth chattered.

"Yes, Sir."

Twenty seconds later, they curved around a spit of land, and the *Howell's* ghostly hulk hove into view, no more than 500 yards distant.

The talker yelled, "Commence fire!"

Forward, the twin fifty calibers began chattering, joined by the foredeck-mounted twenty millimeter canon. Seconds later, the 40 millimeter pointer hit his foot treadle and the gun roared into the darkness. Aft, *PT-88's* guns opened up, flashes spitting from their barrels.

Ingram shouted over the din, "Ever volunteer for anything, son?"

Blake shook his head.

"Me neither. So let this be a lesson to you." He jumped into the night.

Ingram was still churning and tumbling underwater when *PT-88* roared past. He didn't see a dark figure jump off her transom.

The wake tore at him and he held his breath, flipping over and over. Finally, the water smoothed a bit. He clawed for the surface, gasping for air, the water still frothing as *Little Lulu* blazed away at the *Howell*. The two bundles bobbed less than ten feet away. He grabbed their straps and swam for the beach, a hundred yards distant. Soon, he felt the gentle swell of the surf and knew he was about to touch bottom. A last glance to his left proved that *Little Lulu* had disappeared into the night and by now, was most likely slowing for the Lingutu Passage.

Suddenly, an eerie feeling washed over Ingram. He looked to his right. "What the hell?"

To the northwest, a Japanese destroyer glided around the cape, slowly, deliberately, with very little way on.

"Oh, God, no."

Knife drawn, Rivera tread water just five yards behind his prey. He turned and ducked holding his position underwater for thirty full seconds. Finally, he rose, poking just the top of his head above water.

Shit! Ingram had already made it ashore and into the jungle. Rivera had intended to take Ingram on the swim in and then simply run down the beach and swim out to PT-88, now laying off the Lingutu Passage, covering *PT-72's* rescue efforts. But all that damned tumbling in *PT-88s* wake had cost him precious seconds. And then Ingram had suddenly turned around, nearly spotting him. Now the tables were turned. Ingram could see him more easily from shore.

Wait.

Rivera tread water for five minutes with just his face out. Exasperated and out of options, he dog paddled for some rocks, pulling his .45 from his shoulder holster as he rose from the water. His training took over. *What would I do if I were Ingram. St. Clair hadn't said so but with all this, the guy could be a Jap spy.* But then, Rivera hesitated. *Could Ingram really be a Jap spy?* A look at the *Howell* and a look at the Japanese destroyer slowly approaching seemed to be a rendezvous of some sort. *Maybe.* But the more he thought about it, the more he came up with riddles rather than answers.

Augustine Rivera crawled over some rocks, and found Ingram's footsteps, leading directly to the *Howell*. *Is he really here to talk to Japs?* Better find out. Better put a stop to this shit.

Rivera started walking.

With *PT-88* cruising in figure eight's outside, Tubby took *Little Lulu* straight in the Lingutu Channel at ten knots, Fuller calling radar ranges and bearings. A minute later, they turned left into Morovo Lagoon. Almost at once, a thin beam of light winked at them from just off the port bow. "Gotta be them," said Tubby. He called to his crew, "Keep a sharp eye, you guys. Winnie. Get up here."

Fuller scrambled topside, strapped on his helmet, and stood by the searchlight.

The light winked again, closer, its beam glittering across the water. "Getting close," said Tubby.

They were near shore and Tubby reversed engines, bringing the PT to a stop. A match flared, and a cigarette glowed close off their port bow. Tubby pointed, "Over there, Winnie."

Fuller flipped on his searchlight, illuminating a group of perhaps ten men, sloshing under the mangroves. Beside them, lay the burnt-out carcass of *PT-94*, her blackened ribs sticking in the air like the skeleton of a beached whale. A man yelled in a horse voice, "Turn that thing off you dumb bastards. Trying to get us all killed?

"It's Bollinger, all right," Tubby chuckled. "Secure the light, Winnie." Then he put the center engine in gear and eased the *Little Lulu* toward the beach. The bottom was sandy mud, and with a boatswain on the foredeck swinging a leadline to call depths, Tubby nudged *PT-72*'s nose right into the shore.

Tubby stepped up to the foredeck. "Quick, get them aboard."

Little Lulu had a good eight feet of freeboard off the beach and they had trouble reaching down to haul the men up.

"Blake, Roberts, Templeton, get down there," barked Tubby. The three jumped down and finally, debilitated *PT 94* survivors were passed up to flop onto the foredeck like dead fish. A voice called from below. "These guys didn't make it." With grunts and soft curses, two inert forms were hauled up and quickly covered with tarps. Then the rest of the shipwrecked sailors were manhandled aboard where they lay sprawled on the foredeck panting, staring up into the night.

Tubby stepped among the forms finding a heavily bearded supine figure propped up against the charthouse. "Commander Landa? Is that you? Welcome aboard."

"Ah, it's Tubby White," Landa said in a raspy voice. "The ball-bearing king of the South Pacific. Pulled any more stunts lately? Did they have to order you out of the Purvis Bay Officer's Club just to come up here and torment me?"

"Where are you hit, Commander?" White propped a life jacket behind Landa.

"Foot's broken. All swollen up."

"We'll get you fixed up soon."

"What took so long?"

"Jap air raids." White explained about the Yamamoto raids and Ingram losing his ship.

"Rotten deal for Todd."

"Yeah, rotten deal for a lot of guys. Leo Seltzer didn't make it."

"No!"

"We'll take good care of you, Commander." Tubby pat Landa on the shoulder and started to rise.

"Got any morphine?"

"Not much. And it looks like a couple of your guys are hurt worse than you."

"Listen. My damned leg's on fire," Landa hissed. For days and days and days, it's been on fire. They'll probably have to hack it off when I get back. The least you can do is to---"

"---As soon as I can, Commander." Tubby checked his watch. "Right now, I've got Todd Ingram to worry about."

"Ingram? What the hell does he have to do with this?"

"No time, Sir."

"Shit! Why are you and I always arguing?"

"I seriously don't know." White moved back toward his cockpit.

Intent on cursing at White, Landa sat up to call after him. But bolts of lighting-swift pain ran up his leg and he flopped back against the chart-house, exhausted.

Oscar Bollinger kneeled beside him. "Easy, Jerry." Maneuvering a mug into Landa's hand, he held out a thermos and poured.

Landa sipped piping hot liquid, its warmth coursing through his system. "Wow. Who would have ever thought rotgut Navy coffee could ever taste so good." Taking another sip, he grabbed Bollinger's sleeve. "Say, what does Tubby mean about Ingram? Is Todd aboard?"

"I don't think so."

"Then where the hell is he?"

Ingram checked his watch: Just thirty-five minutes had passed since he'd jumped off *Little Lulu*'s transom. Without incident, he'd swum ashore and made the *Howell*'s starboard side. Then he primed the five TNT blocks with det cord, blasting cap and fifty feet of time fuse. Holding his breath, he dove and managed to dig beneath the *Howell*'s keel where he wedged the TNT bundle in the sand. Directly above was the 40 millimeter magazine; four feet above that, the magazine containing over three hundred five-inch projectiles for Mount 51.

Carefully, he raised the time fuse from the water, blew off the end to make sure it was dry. Then he slowly twisted on an M-60 fuse lighter until it seated. Satisfied, he looked up to the ship looming over him. Nobody peered down, taking aim at him. Which made sense. All the activity was on the ship's opposite side, the port side where the ammo barge was moored. There hadn't been any sentries and the ammunition off-loading party had resumed work shortly after Tubby White's diversionary raid.

Piece of cake; it's gone as planned. All that remains is to dash cross the island, jump in the raft and paddle like hell for PT-72. Time to yank the safety pin, then pull the ring on the fuse lighter and run.

No.

The ship was ruggedly built by San Francisco's Bethlehem Steel Company from her solid keel to her longitudinal framing system. There was just no guarantee that the dynamite was going to penetrate enough to touch-off the projectiles in the magazine.

It'll work; it has to. Ingram fished for the fuse lighter under the rock. He found it and groped for the safety pin and---

--- *No. Damnit.* He let the fuse drop. In resignation, shook his head. *I must do this.*

Helen, I love you.

With a glance up to the main deck, he half-dog paddled, half-walked forward to where the anchor's flukes stuck out of the water. The starboard anchor chain was still taut so he knew it wouldn't rattle. He listened, hearing only an occasional guttural shout or thump of equipment.

Oh, God be with me.

Looping his pouch strap over his shoulder, he heaved himself up the chain, hand-over-handing until he reached the hawse pipe, just below the main deck. With a foot, he braced himself on the chain, reached up to the main deck and grabbed the base of a stanchion. He lifted himself up and peeked over, fully expecting a rifle barrel to be jabbed between his eyes, the muzzle flash the last thing he'd ever see. *I hope it's painless.*

Clear. There were no sentries. And from the muffled noises, he could tell the Japanese hadn't figured out how to manually cycle the ship's ammo hoist, which would have allowed them to raise the fifty-four pound projectiles directly up from the magazines to Mount 51. Instead, they had to hand- pass the cumbersome rounds up several decks, a slow and laborious process.

Carefully, he crawled up to the main deck, eased over the lifeline and dashed for the fo'c'sle hatch. Clawing at it, he found it undogged, quickly raised it, and stepped down the ladder where he softly lowered the hatch over his head. Inside, he felt as if he were crawling inside a gigantic carcass. Without blowers and exhaust fans, the *Howell* couldn't breathe. She was a dead ship, and her atmosphere reeked of corruption, and fuel oil, hydraulic fluid, stopped-up drains, spoiled food and body odor. Worse was the scent of raw feces, the enemy no doubt issuing their contempt in the un-serviceable washrooms. He stepped down a ladder into the *Howell's* moribund bowels and found the first deck. Aft, the hatch to the chief's mess deck was closed, nevertheless a pungent odor of teriyaki odor swept over him. *Damn, they've been cooking up here.*

He opened the door slowly. Except for thumping aft and an occasional rasping command, it was quiet. Pale light bled from somewhere in officer's country. Someone could be ransacking back there; who knows?

He quickly dashed through the chief's messdecks and into mount 51's ammunition handling room. *Now, for the Hope Diamond.* Ingram stooped over the projectile hoist and eased the cover open. There! Right before him was a five-inch/38 anti-aircraft projectile. This one, he knew, was capped with a mechanical time fuse which explained why the Japanese hadn't taken it. They were, no doubt, hunting for the revolutionary variable time-fused projectiles, the ones Landa had ordered buried at the bottom of the magazine. It could take them a while, he realized.

He put his foot on the pedal and, looking both ways, eased the round out of the projectile hoist.

Footsteps.

From back aft, someone walked up the passageway through officer's country. Quickly, Ingram looped the pouch over his shoulder, grabbed the projectile in both hands and ducked through a darkened hatchway into the chief's portside bunkroom.

Feet thumped in the handling room and someone called, "Kashima?" Kashima!"

Ingram backed against a bunk.

"Kashima!" The man's voice echoed.

The shell grew heavy in his hands, so he turned and laid it in a berth.

"Huh?" A figure stirred beneath him.

Ingram froze. A man was laying here. Most likely Kashima, taking a few unauthorized winks.

Kashima jerked upright just as Ingram hit him in the nose as hard as he could. Cartilage crunched and, with a low groan, Kashima slumped back into the berth, a glistening wetness gathering around his mouth and jaw.

"Kashima," the man said. Footsteps again. A flashlight clicked with Ingram hurriedly ducking behind a locker. A blazing beam of light swept over the compartment, miraculously missing Kashima's unconscious figure. He was deeply sunk in a mattress once occupied by a much heavier man. The light flicked away and with a grunt, the man walked across the handling room and searched the starboard berthing compartment, calling out and swinging his light back and forth. Cursing and stomping his feet, he finally disappeared aft.

Ingram didn't realize he'd been holding his breath. And his heart was thumping so loud, he was surprised the man hadn't heard him. *Breathe you stupid bastard, breathe*, Ingram challenged himself. Three times he willed his lungs to move and he blinked his eyes just to make sure he was alive.

Do it! Quick!

Ingram was about to walk when--

"Uhhhh..."

Kashima!

Quickly, Ingram drew a length of line and tied the sailor to the bunk. Kashima groaned again and Ingram slapped tape over his mouth.

Hurry, damnit. Tubby can't wait forever.

He stepped out to the five-inch ammunition handling room, making sure it was clear. Then he ducked back into the bunkroom and retrieved the five-inch projectile. Working carefully with a wrench, he unscrewed the nose-fuse, then sat the projectile on its base. Taking the one and a quarter pound block of C-4 from the pouch, he tore off the cellophane wrapper and began molding the C-4. Strange, this stuff, he thought, as he rolled it back and forth. For such a small, pliant mass, its destructive power was unimaginable. Yet here it was in his hands, as elastic as child's putty. Soon, he'd rolled it into a long, cigar shape. Inserting it into the projectile, he mashed the C-4 into the cavity where the mechanical time fuse had been. Next, he stuck in a blasting cap, then connected that to one end of the remaining fifty foot section of time-fuse.

Noise topside. He looked up. Feet thumped on the foredeck above him. Someone was climbing into the five-inch gunmount. *Get going!*

Ingram ran numbers through his mind. The fifty feet of time fuse burned at forty seconds per foot: That gave him a little over a half hour.

Enough.

With the pouch strap looped over his shoulder, he carried the five-inch round back into the handling room. Flipping open the hoist door, he eased the projectile in the hoist, then coiled the time-fuse on top. Patting his pockets, he found an M-60 fuse lighter and twisted it on the time-fuse cord until it seated. There! He pulled the safety pin. *Now, damnit!* With a quick jerk, he tugged the pull-ring and dropped it into the projectile hoist. And almost immediately, he was rewarded with a scent of smoking cordite. *It's cooking. At about one a.m., this place goes sky-high.* He dropped the projectile hoist lid and turned to run. *Okay.* His watch read 1226 am.

Wait. There is something else. What if someone finds this thing before it goes off? Ingram rubbed his chin. Soon the answered came to him. The projectile hoists were padlocked when the ship wasn't at general quarters. *Where the hell is the damned lock?* In the gloom, Ingram fumbled around the shelves and structural ribs. *Damnit!* Frantically he reached. Then, he saw the padlock dangling off the side of the projectile hoist cover. Snap! Done.

He turned to run forward and--

"Hai?" A stout figure, almost a head shorter, blocked his way. He'd come through the chief's messdeck, the same way as Ingram. The man ran off a string of Japanese, not realizing Ingram's identity in the shadows.

Ingram faced him and bowed slowly, his heart racing.

The figure jammed his hands on his hips as Ingram turned and walked aft.

"*Tomare!*" The man yelled.

Ingram broke into a run and, "---oof!"

--plowed into a surprised Japanese sailor who had just stepped from a stateroom. Somehow, Ingram kept his balance as the sailor careened to the deck, causing the other man to trip and fall. As Ingram dashed on, the other man quickly regained his feet and, fully enraged, charged after Ingram, yelling and cursing. Swiftly, Ingram dashed up the companionway to the main deck finding--

--Three open-mouthed officers blocking his exit to the weatherdecks.

Up! Ingram grabbed the companionway rail and raced up to the 01 deck, charging past two incredulous sailors. One made a half-hearted grab at his shirt, but Ingram batted his hand away, swung on the next companionway rail and rocketed up to the bridge deck.

Japanese stood before him. An officer. And this one was ready, crouched. Ingram lowered his head and crashed into the man's chest. But the Japanese was solid and didn't fall over like the man below. Nevertheless the man staggered aside but held his ground, blocking Ingram's exit to the safety of the open bridge.

Nowhere to go.

Strident curses roiled from below as men charged up the ladder. The Japanese officer was poised to jump. Ingram spun on his foot, ran into the captain's sea cabin and slammed and bolted the door before the officer could react.

Outside, the officer bellowed and kicked at the door, then it thumped as the man put a shoulder to it. Someone new shouted outside and a bolt clacked home. Ingram jumped to the side as an automatic weapon thundered. Bullets ricocheted and zinged about, one shattering the porcelain toilet at Ingram's feet. But he wasn't hurt and miraculously, the door held; leaving a fist-sized hole.

A wheezing, sobbing Ingram looked wildly around the compartment. There was no exit. Only a porthole which he slammed and dogged shut. From desperation, he pulled his .45, chambered a round and pumped four rounds through the door. He wasn't rewarded with screams of pain but he heard men scramble for cover. He'd bought a minute or two of time.

After a minute, someone called. "Hey, Joe. You here for cigarettes? Food? Maybe things aren't so hot over on New Georgia. You a fly-fly boy, Joe? Shot down? Or maybe you one of those PT Boat guys?"

Ingram leaned against the bunk, Landa's bunk, desperately trying to think.

"You understand me, Joe? Hey! I went to the University of Washington, Go Wolves, huh?"

Ingram's eyes dashed to the vent piping in the overhead, making him think of Tubby's marbles. Tubby! He checked his watch. 12:32. Less than a half hour.

"By the way, Joe. We found your little present down in the projectile hoist. A sledge hammer took care of the lock. Too bad. C-4. Good stuff, huh? Come to think of it, where the hell did you get that?"

Ingram felt as if a cold, Atlantic wave had picked him off a jetty and swept him out to sea. *They've found the C-4 packed shell. Everything a waste. All that time, Oh, God.*

He looked at the pistol. Four rounds left. *Three for them; the last for me.* He stood. *Helen, goodbye my love, my darling. I'll always love you. Always.*

He raised the .45 at the door.

"---So how you doing Joe? You want to come out? We take good care of you."

His finger curled around the trigger and reached for the door lock.

"Or we can toss a grenade in or toast you with a flame-thrower. What's it going to be, Joe? We're running out of time."

Ingram realized the pouch was still over his shoulder. He lowered his pistol and said, "University of Washington Wolves, huh."

"You bet."

"Okay, Washington, I'm coming out."

43

17 April, 1943
PT-72
Marovo Lagoon, Kotukuriana Island
New Georgia Sound, Solomon Islands

Little Lulu's engines idled at a low rumble as they drifted in Marovo Lagoon. To the west, a pale, quarter moon settled over one of New Georgia Island's sharp, volcanic peaks. Tubby White checked his watch for the fifth time in the last two minutes:1238. Oscar Bollinger stayed on deck but the rest of *PT 94's* sailors, two of them in serious condition, were arranged comfortably below. Jerry Landa had refused to be taken down, so they propped him against the deck house on the port side near the forward torpedo mount, his leg splayed before him.

Tubby checked his watch again: 1239. *Damn.*

"You said 0100?" muttered Bollinger.

"Yes. We agreed: no later than 0100."

"And then?"

"We didn't discuss that," Tubby lied.

"Well, we still have twenty minutes."

"Yep."

"Mr. White?" It was Landa.

"Sir?"

"Perhaps if you killed your engines, you might hear something; paddling, a voice, maybe."

Tubby exchanged glances with Bollinger. "Worth a try, Commander." He reached to the instrument panel and flipped switches, stopping the engines. A tension-filled quiet grew among them that was as thick as the ground-fog forming on the shore of Kotukuriana Island. Tubby leaned to the charthouse hatchway and said softly, "Watch our drift Winney. Best we don't end up on rocks." *Why the hell am I whispering?*

"You bet," Fuller whispered from the charthouse.

"How much time left?" asked Landa.

"Twenty minutes, give or take, Commander" said Tubby.

"...uh, you got any more morphine?" asked Landa in a soft tone.

They'd given Landa some a half hour ago although Tubby knew it wasn't enough. He looked down the hatch to Fuller who drew a thumb across his throat. Then he whispered over to Landa, "Sorry, commander. The rest went into the guys below."

Landa's teeth gleamed in a grimace.

"Soon, Commander. Once we power up, I'll have you aboard the *Whitney* in no time."

"Okay," groaned Landa.

The moon was gone, the darkness nearly complete, except for the panoply of stars overhead silently screaming in hoary brilliance.

Captain Kanji Takano felt victory. He'd done it! He'd talked the American out. And just minutes before, he'd received his greatest reward. He'd been in the forward magazine, shining his flashlight way in back. He'd spotted some curious looking projectiles back there. It was almost as if someone had deliberately hidden them; they were stuffed all the way against the far bulkhead. It had taken five minutes to crawl over the other rounds. But he'd made it. Yes! Before him was a projectile tipped with a fuse he'd never seen before. It must be! The Soviets were right! Takano was delirious with joy. Finally, he would please the *Gensui*.

Taking out his web wrench, Takano carefully unscrewed one of the fuses and shoved it in his valise. He'd intended to remove at least four more but he heard commotion. Lieutenant Abe, *Matukaze's* gunnery officer had summoned him to the bridge where they'd trapped an American stow-away. And Takano was the only one among them who spoke English.

Now, at the door to the captain's sea cabin, Takano sighed with relief when the American announced he was coming out. 'Get ready to shoot the bastard,' he mouthed to the men behind them. Hands on his knees, he turned back to the door. "Good choice, Joe," he said. "So come on out and have a tall cool one. San Miguel. All you want."

The latch clicked and Takano raised his pistol, a Nambu 8 millimeter.

From behind the door, a voice bellowed, "It's the Washington *Huskies*, you son-of-a-bitch!"

A hand grenade sailed through the hole in the door and plopped on the deck at Takano's feet, its fuse hissing.

"Aiyeeeeee." Someone screamed.

Takano dove onto the open bridge just as the grenade went off, the explosion driving him against the bulwark.

Coughing, Takano tried to rise to his feet as smoke roiled out of the barbette room.

Someone fired a shot up the companion way.

"All you want Buddy," a voice growled. Something thumped and rattled and soon, three more grenade explosions pounded Takano in rapid succession: one in the pilot house; one down the companion way; and a third back in the barbette room. With smoke thicker than ever, Takano strained to rise upright. Coughing, and stumbling, he braced himself against the bulwark and tried wiping his eyes. Opening, them again what?

An apparition from hell emerged before him. Teeth clenched, face riddled with cuts and smeared with smoke. Hair plastered to a sweaty forehead. An American.

With a growl, the man splayed his left hand over Takano's face and drove a fist into his stomach.

Bent over and gasping in pain, Takano was conscious enough to realize the man had climbed the bulwark and leaped over the side. Holding up his hand, he was astonished to see he still held his Nambu but hadn't fired a shot.

What else can go wrong?

Wheezing horribly, Takano struggled to his feet, pain in his stomach thumping and pounding. Aft, flames licked from the deck below. Somehow, the American's grenades had started a fire.

The smoke cleared and he looked over the side, seeing a man's head break the surface.

"Light!" He called. "Someone get me a light!"

Holding his feet together, Ingram let himself plunge deep. Surprised he didn't hit bottom, he kicked for the surface aiming for the ship's starboard side., He put out a hand and touched the hull about the same time he broke the water's surface. Gasping for air and trying not to splash, he looked up, expecting a vast row of machine guns ready to blaze away at him. But there was nothing except shouts and mayhem amidships. He remained still for twenty seconds realizing his ears rang loudly. He looked up again, seeing a fire had broken out on the 01 deck, the flames illuminating wisps of smoke that drifted into the night.

Ingram dove and stroked for shallow water, searching for his rock. He rose again, standing in hip deep water, groping for the time fuse. Ah! There it is. Gently pulling, toward shallower water, he followed its length until--

---a figure rose before him and pointed a .45 right at his chest. "Hold it right there."

In that moment, Ingram discovered what it meant to jump out of one's skin. After the initial jolt, all he could think of to say was, "God! Don't shoot!"

"Raise your hands and shut up."

"American," Ingram gasped.

"More than you know. Now put up your---"

A spotlight flicked on washing the man in a white, glittering light. "What the--"

Gun shots rang out; three splotches ranged across the man's chest. Exhaling sharply, his mouth formed an 'O' as he flew back.

Ingram ducked, but not before a bullet clipped his right ear. He held his breath, hearing bullets punch the water above him. Opening his eyes he looked up, seeing the man's body, splayed face-down on the surface, back-lighted by the spotlight above him. They must have found a battle lantern, Ingram figured. More bullets chopped the water around the body, great wisps of blood slowly curling around as a bullet occasionally hit home, making the body jerk spasmodically.

Go!

With thumb and forefinger circling the time-fuse, he kicked hard and pulled with his free hand. After swimming twenty feet, he rolled on his back, let his face break the surface, and allowed himself just one gasping, desperate breath. Down again, he swam another twenty feet trailing the time-fuse. *Okay.* Breaking the surface he looked up. The spotlights were concentrated about forty feet away. Japanese soldiers were on the fo'c'sle shining battle lanterns on the dead man, not looking in his direction.

One more thing to do.

Ingram dove and, still trailing the time fuse, found the rock. Reaching beneath, he fumbled at the stubby, cylinder-shaped M-60 fuse-lighter. He raised his head above the surface, gasping for air and ducked again. Cursing to himself, his mind reeled with the fact that his real opportunity to blow up the ship had been stifled. That University of Washington Japanese Wolf-Husky had discovered his booby-trap in the projectile hoist. He didn't give a chance of one in ten for this TNT package. *But it's all I got.*

Now, damnit. Easing out the safety pin, he yanked the fuse-ring. He was rewarded with the tiny gurgle of burning fuse which began its deadly journey to the five-block TNT bundle wedged beneath the *Howell's* keel. Quickly, he checked his watch:1244. *Time to scram.* Swimming underwater, he furiously breast-stroked away from the ship, paralleling the coast.

After two hundred yards, Ingram struck for the beach, rising from the water among a large outcrop of rocks. Gasping, wheezing, he fell to his knees, content to catch his breath and watch the commotion aboard the *Howell.* The Japanese had a brought around a small skiff and three men were aboard, hauling the body from the water.

Aboard the *Howell,* the fire had grown larger. Men dashed about her decks, throwing buckets of water at the orange-red flames. Ingram leaned against a rock, for another moment. *My God. That was an American back there. What the hell for? And why point a gun at him and tell him to put up his hands like in some gangster movie?*

A glance out to sea told him the Japanese destroyer had eased in close; as did the tug, both intent on shooting water on the flames. *Oh, God, that destroyer.* Ingram checked his watch. 1253. *Detonation time is 0114. Get moving!*

Quickly, he rummaged among the rocks, finding the one-man life-raft pack he'd dropped off earlier. He plunged into the trees, dragging the rig behind him hoping Mondo Mondo Island was as narrow as he thought it was; hoping that he could reach the lagoon quickly and start paddling; hoping he wouldn't run into Japanese soldiers; hoping that Tubby White would hang around just a little longer.

Takano leaned over to examine the bullet-riddled body. The man's eyes were open in surprise. He said to Lieutenant Abe, "...can't tell if this is him for sure. I only saw the American for a moment and his face was streaked with soot. This man seems to me free of soot." Takano didn't really want to think of the man he saw on the bridge. He hoped he never saw anything like it again.

Lieutenant Abe thumbed the man's collar devices. "This one is a Marine major."

"And I'm almost sure the man I saw was a Lieutenant Commander. Two gold leaves," said Takano.

"As does this man," said Abe. "A Major."

"But my man's leafs were shiny. He was Navy, I tell you. There were two of them."

"Well, Sir. If you insist. We'll start searching." *Wait,* Takano remembered. *You have what you want.!* "Hold on, Abe."

Sir?"

"Call away the life boat. We're going back."

"Now? But Sir, what about---" Abe gestured to the body.

"Damn all that. We're going back. Now." For assurance, Takano pat his valise. Yes. The fuse was still there.

. . .

They stared wide-eyed at the tree line where the *Howell* was supposed to be, arguing about the explosions.

"Maybe they're fishing with dynamite," said Landa.

"At this time of night?" said Bollinger.

Tubby checked his watch: 1257. He shrugged then said, "He had a half dozen grenades in his pouch."

"Too loud for grenades," said Landa.

"Do you suppose it was his TNT misfiring?" offered Bollinger.

"Don't think so. When TNT goes, you know it," said Landa.

Tubby called down the hatch, "Anything at all?" The radio had gone on the fritz and they had lost contact with *PT-88*.

"Can't hear a thing," said Fuller He had the front panel open and was checking a schematic. "Seems all right. Maybe it's this damned lagoon."

"Keep trying."

"Yes, Sir."

They fell silent until 0100.

"Let's wait five more minutes," said Tubby.

No one argued with that and they waited another ten minutes, with Landa fidgeting loudly. Then suddenly, a ship's whistle ripped the night, blasting six times. "What the hell?" said White.

"Must be that Jap tin can." Bollinger said.

"You mean a Jap tin can is standing off the entrance?" asked White, incredulously.

"She was there a couple of days ago," said Bollinger.

"Jeez," said Tubby. "You mean we're bottled up in here?"

"Maybe exit the other way," Bollinger proposed.

Tubby's head whipped aft. "We may have to, but it's uncharted back there. We could run aground."

"May be our only chance," said Bollinger.

"Can't we just take off now, then come back and pick Mr. Ingram up tomorrow night?" asked Fuller.

"We wait," rasped Landa. His face screwed up in pain.

"Tha's right," said Tubby.

"Tubby, what about Jenkins and Fliegerman?" Bollinger spoke of *PT-94's* two burn victims laying in the bunks below. "They need immediate attention. I don't think Jenkins can make it through---"

"Oscar. Five more minutes," said Tubby.

"I could order you."

"It's my boat damnit. And I---"

"---Sir, over there." In the gloom, a sailor pointed off the port bow.

They all moved to the port side, just as a yellow one-man life raft emerged from the night.

"Todd?" called Tubby.

The raft bumped into *Little Lulu*'s side. Ingram hissed, "Damnit, Mr. White. I gave you orders to shove off at 0100."

Tubby turned and called aft. "Wind 'em up!"

Two sailors reached down to haul Ingram over the gunnel, as the three great Packards coughed into life.

Scrambling aboard, Ingram rose to his knees and came face to face with Landa. "I'll be damned."

"What do you say, Lunkhead?"

I'm afraid I screwed up our ship."

"You been playing with matches again?" said Landa, extending a hand. "Good to see you." They shook.

"Let's hope the matches work. How was jungle life?" Asked Ingram.

"Travel posters aren't all they're cracked up to be."

"Well, let's get you home." Ingram stood and said to Tubby, "Some Japs on the south end of the Island. Might give us trouble on the way out."

"What happened to the TNT?" asked Tubby, shifting the engines into gear.

Ingram checked his watch. "Maybe another minute or so, but I don't think it will set off the---

---an enormous blast lit the night, spewing flames and smoke hundreds of feet into the air. Ingram was knocked to his hands and knees. The shock wave swept past rolling *Little Lulu* twenty degrees onto her starboard beam. Trees, bushes, enormous chunks of rock and pieces of the *Howell* splashed around them. The blast seemed to echo in Ingram's ears forever and ever, as more debris rained about, including small rocks and a fine coat of dirt.

Finally, it was over. Ingram rose, seeing sailors splayed on the deck, shaking their heads. The worse off seemed to be the twenty-millimeter gun crew on the fo'c'sle.

"You guys okay?" gasped Tubby.

One by one, they rose shakily and looked back, nodding dumbly.

Landa sat up, blinking dirt from his eyes. An un-helmeted Bollinger lay unconscious on the cockpit grate, a gash across the top of his head. Tubby knelt beside him. Bollinger groaned. Tubby palmed a large flat rock then threw it overboard. "He looks okay, concussion maybe. Damn, I should have given him a helmet.

"What were you saying about the TNT?" Tubby asked, an eyebrow raised.

"I honestly didn't think it would work," replied Ingram, watching flames roil over Mondo Mondo Island.

"You gotta think they're off balance right now," said Landa.

"Yeah! Let's go while the getting's good," said Ingram.

"Right." Tubby eased the throttles forward and headed for the gap between Mondo Mondo and Kotukuriana Islands. He called down the hatchway, "Winnie. I need a bearing to Lingutu Entrance."

Fortunately, Ensign Fuller had been below and had not been hammered as severely as the sailors topside. He said almost immediately, "Zero-two-six, Tubby. About three hundred yards."

"Zero-two-six, it is," said White, easing in right rudder to settle on the recommended course.

Just then, something cracked overhead; lighting up the Lingutu Entrance as bright as day.

"Starshell!" shouted Ingram.

Simultaneously, gunfire barked at them from the Mondo Mondo side of the channel.

Another starshell popped open, sizzling beneath its parachute, lighting the sky.

44

17 April, 1943
PT-72
Kotukuriana Island, Lingutu Entrance
New Georgia Sound, Solomon Islands

"For God's sake, hit it, Tubby," shouted Ingram.

White shoved the throttles to the stops and hollered, "commence fire."

PT-72's gunners began raking Mondo Mondo Island to port. Japanese bullets plinked around the deck with Ingram and two other sailors hauling the semi-unconscious Bollinger into the relative safety of the pilot house's starboard side. *PT 72* soon gained her step and thundered through the Lingutu Entrance into New Georgia Sound.

"Cease fire," yelled Tubby.

Ingram jumped in the cockpit, and grabbed binoculars. Adjusting the lenses, he spotted the Japanese destroyer standing about 4,000 yards off their port beam. "Jap tin can. That's what the horn blasts were about. She backed off. Way off. Must have realized the *Howell* was going to blow." He looked to where the *Howell* had been. All that remained was twisted wreckage and an orange-red ball of fire licking the sky.

Tubby cranked in right rudder to present the Japanese a smaller silhouette. "I'll bet a month's pay that fire is lighting us up like a Christmas tree."

As if in confirmation, two 4.7-inch rounds hurtled at them: one exploded a hundred yards behind them; the other screamed overhead and blew-up a hundred yards in front, both shells raising tall, white, water columns.

"Damn, we're bracketed," yelled Ingram.

An open-mouthed Landa gasped, "How the hell did that bastard learn to shoot that well?"

Fuller's head popped out the hatch. "I have Tommy, er Lieutenant Madison on the TBS. He's two miles out and is attacking right now."

"That's something," said Tubby.

Two more rounds smacked the water fifty yards before them.

"Screw this. He's got our range. Next one is on us." Tubby shouted, winding in left rudder. "We'll hit the sonofabitch from both sides Winnie, come on up here."

Donning sound powered phones, Fuller joined them, his face white and eyes wide open.

PT-72 reversed course and steadied up on the Japanese destroyer. Shells whistled overhead as *Little Lulu* quickly ate up the range.

"Anyone see Tommy?" asked Tubby.

"That him?" Ingram pointed into the darkness forward of the starboard beam.

Fuller raised his binoculars. "You bet. Go gettum Tommy!"

Tubby raised his hand over his head. "Call the range at 2,000."

Fuller sighted on the stadimeter and soon yelled, "2,000 yards!".

Tubby slashed down his arm . "Fire one!"

Nothing.

"Fire three!" he yelled.

PT 72's torpedo tubes were silent.

"What is it?" Ingram jumped to the cockpit.

A shell whistled overhead, raising a giant plume a hundred yards to starboard.

"What are you waiting for, Tubby?" yelled Landa.

Tubby jabbed the firing panel. "Something's wrong. Damn buttons won't work." He hollered over his shoulder. "Winnie, get over here."

Fuller was there in an instant and began fiddling with the panel. "Everything's dead. Must be a circuit breaker."

"Go!" yelled Tubby. "Damn jinx boat," he yelled as Fuller dashed down the hatch.

Another shell splashed astern.

"How 'bout firing manually?" Ingram shouted.

"Right---awww shit!" Tubby pointed.

On deck, Kramer his torpedoman, lay in a crumpled heap by number one torpedo tube. Ingram figured he was a casualty of the fire fight exiting Lingutu Passage,

Tubby looked at Ingram.

I don't want to go out there. Ingram gulped, "How do I do it?"

Tubby pointed. "Impulse charge on top of the tube. Smack the firing pin with this." He reached in a cabinet and handed over a claw hammer.

Ingram looked around wildly for a moment, trying to find Fuller. But the Ensign was absorbed in the chart house with his circuit breakers.

"Todd?" said Tubby.

Cursing under his breath, Ingram grabbed the hammer and ran forward just as another 4.7 inch round hit, raising a fifty foot plume of white gleaming water right off the port bow. The concussion drove him against the pilot house. He caromed off and nearly tumbled overboard, only keeping himself on the boat with a frantic grab at a life ring-mount.

He was still shaking his head when another shell landed before them with *PT-72* jumping though the water column and out the other side. Ingram looked up, wiping water from his eyes. They were close to the destroyer. No more than fifteen hundred yards: three-quarters of a nautical mile; a fair distance to a man in peacetime; but here, it looked as if they were right on top of the death-spitting silhouette.

He found himself on the deck beside the torpedo tube. The torpedoman beside him groaning, holding his shoulder and rolling on the deck.

Suddenly, Ingram was caught in a hoary brilliance. The destroyer's search light had found them, locking them in a stygian light no matter how hard *Little Lulu's* 50 caliber machine gunners tried to smash it.

"Todd!" Tubby bellowed.

Ingram looked up to see Tubby's silhouetted outline.

"The firing pin!"

Looking down, Ingram saw the glint of the impulse canister's brass firing pin mechanism atop the torpedo tube. "Got it."

Sitting up, he swung the hammer at it -- and missed! Worse, his hand hit the tube. Blue-white bolts of pain quick-pulsed up his arm and he let go. Incredulously, he watched the hammer fly overboard as if it were in slow motion. "Son-of-a-bitch!"

Another shell screeched overhead and landed fifty yards on the starboard quarter. The explosion rang so loud that Ingram couldn't hear. He looked aft, watching Tubby's mouth open with, "Todd!"

His face contorted with pain, Landa crawled to Ingram's feet and extended something. "Here! Damnit. Take it!" Landa screamed, his teeth glittering.

"What?" Then it hit Ingram. Landa was holding out...his shoe! Of course. A wheezing, desperate Ingram reached down and grabbed Landa's dirt-encrusted shoe. With a savage swing, he smacked the firing pin housing with the heel. The tube coughed. Smoke wisped past his face. Something flashed into the searchlight's beam.

PT-72 then whipped into a violent left turn to head back toward the beach, another shell exploding in their track. Ingram rose and stumbled back to the cockpit, expecting at any moment, for a white-hot 4.7 inch shell to cut him in half.

But then suddenly, the searchlight went out and they were plunged into complete darkness. But something had flashed and it wasn't a Japanese shell.

Ingram stood and took stock. *I'm alive.*

"Look at that," Tubby whooped.

"What?" said Ingram, peering into the gloom, his night vision razed by the searchlight's brightness. "What the hell is it?"

Tubby said, "They put their damned rudder over hard when they saw the torpedo. So they're in a tight turn and the torpedo misses but, for some reason, it prematured right alongside him. It must have really scared the Jap, because he's heading in the opposite direction."

"You're kidding." Ingram fumbled for binoculars. His hands shook so much that he couldn't focus. Finally, he jammed his body against the bulwark to steady his hands and gradually, the image swam into view. With a final twist of the knob, he made out the destroyer's stern silhouette, her wake churning a blue-white phosphorescence as she boiled away at high speed. "Why did he do that?"

"I don't know, but he had us cold," said Tubby. He kicked in a bit of rudder to hug the shoreline.

"Lousy shot." Ingram shook his head.

"I'll say."

Ingram's right hand began to shake. In fact, it shook so much he had to lower his binoculars. "Tubby?"

"What?"

"See? I told you. You're not going to eat it."

"I've used up so many lives, I've lost count. I just don't give a damn, anymore."

"I admire your optimism." Ingram's teeth began to chatter.

"You okay, Skipper?"

"Just tired, that's all." Ingram clamped his right wrist with his left hand, willing the shaking to stop. Fortunately, Tubby didn't see it, for his attention was distracted by Fuller, passing up a mug of coffee.

But Tubby's mug shook when he raised it to his lips. Coffee splattered on the deck grate and he said with a sidelong glance, "You know what? I thought I peed in my pants back there."

"I wouldn't have blamed you," said Ingram. Now his left hand shook.

"Actually, Bollinger's coffee hit my crotch when the *Howell* went up."

"Your secret's safe with me." Both hands were shaking. Ingram grabbed the bulwark and held on as if he were being tugged by a 100 mile an hour typhoon. Noticing Tubby watching, he asked, "How's your coffee?"

Tubby looked away for a moment, then said, "Too hot right now. Say, you want some?"

"I'll wait for a while, thanks." They locked eyes for a moment then looked away.

"By the way, you're not going to put me on report, are you?"

"For what?" Ingram had to bite his lip keep his teeth from chattering.

"For disobeying orders. You know... waiting after 0100?" Tubby's hands were around the helm in a death-grip so tight, his knuckles were white.

"I'll think about it."

. . .

The IJN *Matukaze* steamed northwest at thirty-three knots, her brilliant wake trailing into the night. On the bridge, a fuming Commander Tyozo Enomoto faced aft, watching the flames of the beached American destroyer recede over the horizon.

"I only have one of these." Takano was trying to explain. With clothes blackened by grenade smoke, soot was smeared over a face bloodied by a number of cuts. Takano dug the fuse from his bag and held it out. "Just one," he nearly sobbed. "The rest went up with," he nodded aft. "I must get to Vila."

"Why?"

"To catch a plane for Rabaul."

"Why?"

"I must report to the *Gensui!*" Takano nearly yelled.

Ass kisser. Summoning reserves to control his rage, Enomoto said, "we had him in our sights, Captain. Thirty more seconds and he would have been blown to pieces."

"But that torpedo---"

"---doesn't matter which direction we were going. We had already dodged torpedoes from the boat to seaward and were combing the wake of this one. We," Enomoto repeated this for the third time so his sailors could hear, "didn't have to reverse course, Captain Takano." Enomoto was worried his crew would blame him for the cowardly about-face before the little PT Boats.

"I don't care about those boats, you fool. Just get me to the Vila airfield," said Takano.

Enomoto became rigid. He didn't like being called a fool before his men. Getting a grip on himself, he decided to play it by the book. Vila was only two hours away. Then he'd be rid of this piece of dog shit. "Yes, Sir. We're bending on our best speed."

"As fast as you can. It's extremely important."

Enomoto counted to five. "Yes, Sir."

45

18 April, 1943
   PT-72
   New Georgia Sound, (The SLOT)

PT-88 trailed in *Little Lulu*'s wake as they hugged New Georgia's coast, the water far calmer than what they endured on the trip up. A woozy and bandaged Oscar Bollinger was below with his crew, some eating ravenously, others curled up, asleep in bunks

Ingram leaned against the cockpit drinking a cup of coffee, his hands calm now. The quarter moon was descending over New Georgia as Fuller called from the charthouse, "Tommy, er Lieutenant Madison for you, Tubby."

"What's he want now?" muttered Tubby. They'd already talked for five minutes, updating one another on the night's action. Both boats had miraculously come out in good shape. "Patch it to the bridge," he said, picking up a microphone.

'*Seven-two, this is eight-eight.*"

Tubby adjusted the squelch knob. "Seven-two, *over*," he replied.

"*Interrogative, Marine major. Over.*"

"*What Marine major? Over.*" asked Tubby.

Ingram was nearly asleep, the cup slipping from his hand. Now he snapped to full consciousness. *How the hell could I have forgotten?*

The speaker squealed with, "*Er, we carried a Major that launched over the side about the same time as your man. He was supposed to join up with him and return with you. Over.*"

"*No idea, Tommy. Where did--*"

"Tubby, do you mind?" Ingram reached for the mic.

"Not at all." He handed it over.

"*Eighty-eight. Where did you pick up this Major and what was his name. Over?*"

With a new voice on the line, Madison's tone became formal "*Ah, roger seven-two. His name is Major Rivera with orders to recon the Jap garrison aboard the Howell. We picked him up from Fishbait. Over.*" Fishbait was the radio code name for *Whitney*.

"*He didn't make it. Over,*" said Ingram

Tubby's eyebrows went up.

"*No?*" A surprised Madison forgot radio procedure.

"*Eight-eight. Be advised the Japs got him. We'll amend our SITREP. Seven-two, out.*" Ingram hung up the mic.

"What the hell?" asked Tubby.

Ingram explained. Then he called into the chartroom telling Fuller to incorporate the change into the situation report about to be broadcast to Rocko Myszynski That done, he knelt beside Landa. "How's it going?"

Little Lulu jumped the top of the crest and plowed into the next wave, making them surge forward. Landa groaned, "It's okay. Tell Tubby to punch it up. The sooner we make Tulagi the better."

"Tubby says this is our most economical speed, " Ingram lied. They were holding down the speed to keep the boat from bouncing. "How 'bout some coffee?"

"Stomach's upset."

Fuller walked up, grinning.

"Send your SITREP, Ensign?" asked Ingram.

"Yes, Sir."

"Well, what the hell are you smiling about?" demanded Landa.

"I just remembered there was some morphine in the aft-liferaft emergency pack," said Fuller, beaming like a tail-wagging golden retriever trotting up to its master with a pheasant in its mouth. "Here."

"I'll be damned." Landa displayed a long row of even white teeth.

"I'll do it," said Ingram, taking the kit from Fuller. He tore open the cellophane wrapper, then pulled out a syringe and ampoule. "Get you higher than a kite."

"Try me."

Ingram stuck the needle in the ampoule, drew ten milligrams then jabbed it into Landa's thigh. Soon, Landa sighed and closed his eyes.

"How's that?"

"Great. Ready for a beer."

The boat smacked a wave, but Landa didn't flinch. Ingram looked at Tubby and pumped his fist up and down. With a nod, Tubby fed in more throttle until they were going full speed, the wind blowing harder, spray whipping back, *PT-88* steadfast in their wake..

Landa didn't seem to mind as *Little Lulu* bounced and jiggled. In fact, it looked as if he were drifting off.

Ingram rose.

"Todd?" Landa's voice was surprisingly calm.

"Yeah?" Ingram dropped back to his knees.

"Sorry to hear about the *Pence*. She was a good ship."

"Yeah...one of these days, maybe."

"You'll do fine. And Rocko will give you another can."

"That's what he said."

"How did Ralph do?" Landa smacked his lips.

"It really ripped him up." Ingram explained about Druckman. "They've parked him Stateside for a while."

"And Leo?"

"Leo was trying to haul down the flag when the boiler blew. She capsized and dragged him down with her."

"...one flag too many." Landa ran a hand over his face. His eyes blinked. "What happened?"

"Jap air attack. But I have to tell you, those proximity fuses really did work. We took out two Vals, and damaged another before a low-flying Betty launched her torpedo. And we got that one, too."

Landa's eyes unfocused for a moment. Then he looked at Ingram. "...I'm sorry."

"For what?"

"My fault. That damned proximity fuse mess."

"Come on, Jerry."

Landa opened his eyes. Absent the creases of pain, he again looked like the old barroom hound, Jerry *Boom Boom* Landa, shouting for beer and singing rotten songs.

Tubby gave the helm to Fuller and walked over. "How you doin,' Commander?"

"Better." He looked at Tubby. "There's something I've been meaning to say. My apologies for giving you a rough time aboard the *Howell*."

"Water under the bridge, Commander. Don't worry about it," Said Tubby. "Er, while we're at it, Sir, sorry about the marbles."

"Shit, that was a great stunt. You were smart to clear out. I would have killed you."

"I'm not that dumb, Commander," said Tubby.

"No, I suppose you're not." Landa scrunched around, rearranging himself and flashing his Pepsodent smile. "Now, I'm feeling great."

"And now you're soused," said Ingram.

Landa flashed a grin. "That I may be, but I have Mr. Fuller to thank for an hour or so of bliss. Then it's back into the pit."

"You'll be home soon. The doctors will give you all the morphine you want," said Tubby. He rose and looked at his watch. "I have to check in with headquarters." He walked away.

"I want to explain my problem with the VT fuses," said Landa.

"You don't need to."

"Yes, I do. Now listen," Landa hissed, "before the pain comes back. It's about my kid brother."

Ingram's eyebrows went up.

"Josh and I were very close. We grew up in Brooklyn. Hell, I beat up on kids who beat on him. Then those kids sent their older brothers to beat up on me."

"Ummm."

"One happy family. Then I joined the Navy, and Josh grew up to become a hell of a scientist. An MIT Ph.D. whiz-kid. Here's my point. He helped develop proximity fuses in a secret lab in Washington D.C."

"No fooling?"

"And guess who his boss was?"

Ingram shook his head.

"Frank Ashton."

"You're kidding!"

"I thought the damned fuses were bad, because my brother had been mortally injured by one. I saw red, couldn't think straight. I condemned the program because of what happened to him. His problem was that he thought the fuses were defective. That they could blow up if hit by another radar beam."

"Can that happen?"

"No."

"So what did happen?"

"One blew up in his face. That put him into a coma for several months. Then he got that infection and died."

"Why did the fuse blow up in his face?"

"I got there just before Josh died. He came out of his coma but he was rambling, almost deranged. He recognized me enough to say that it wasn't the proximity fuse that was screwed up. It was Frank Ashton who prescribed the wrong test procedures. Josh said he followed Ashton's procedures to the letter and that made the damned thing blew up."

"No!"

"Yeah. But keep in mind, this is all top secret stuff. I mean you and I haven't talked. Got it?"

"Sure."

Landa laid his head back. "I just wanted you to know why I acted like I did. That's all." His eyelids fluttered.

"It's okay, Jerry. Say, do you think you should tell Rocko about this?"

"Rocko doesn't trust my opinion about Ashton, and he'll think I'm being sour grapes, so I'm going to sit on it for a while. But I do have proof."

"You do?"

"...yeah. In your house. That damned crate in the guest room...Josh's journal...so he told me anyway..." Landa's eyes closed and he drifted off.

Ingram pat him on the shoulder, then stood to join Tubby and Winston Fuller in the cockpit.

Rocko Myszynski had been up since midnight, drinking brackish coffee and pacing the deck of the *Whitney*'s commodious radio-room. Her third-deck radio-central compartment was an area of about twenty by forty, where the temperature hovered at a blessed, air-conditioned, sixty-eight degrees. Many tried sneaking in to cool off, but were eventually kicked out by Marine sentries. There were twelve radio operators on duty, with twice as many messengers, technicians and cryptanalysts moving about to the sound of bleeping radio-receivers and clacking teletypes.

"All done, Sir." Bailey a radio operator yanked a message from the typewriter, its platen buzzing furiously.

"Thanks, sailor." Myszynski walked over to a stool and sat. He smiled at the irony of message's beginning:

FINAL: NOTRE DAME 21; JAPS 0

Great news! He was surprised to see the *Howell* was destroyed and that PT-96's crew had been rescued. Damn, a full sweep. And without the Marines. *How the hell did they do that?*

They'd even shot it out with a Jap destroyer and lived to tell about it. But then came the last part.

REGRET TO REPORT AUGUSTINE RIVERA, MAJOR USMC, KIA.

"Sonofabitch!" Myszynski jumped off the stool. How the hell did Rivera get aboard PT-88? He'd specifically told Rivera to stay away.

First things first. He leaned over to Baily and said, "Radio PT-72 to head straight for CACTUS to MEDVAC their wounded out. I'll confirm the orders to Henderson Field in a few minutes."

"Yes, Sir," said Baily.

Myszynski drummed his fingers. *Now, it's time to find out what the hell's going on with this Rivera crap.* He sat down to compose a message to Admiral Halsey.

46

18 April, 1943
   IJN C in C Headquarters,
   Rabaul, New Britain Island
   Bismarck Archipelago

Standing before the full-length mirror, Yamamoto waited, as his orderly knelt at his side, adjusting his sword belt. He lifted a cuff on his wrist and looked at his watch: 0529. Today, he would mingle with fighting men: ground troops, artillery personnel, tankers and worse, the wounded. Thus he chose not to wear dress whites, as he'd done while cheering on his pilots. Instead, he was outfitted in greens, a uniform compatible with his ground forces. Another quick look: 0530: *Yes.*

He nodded to Heijiro who handed him his cap, bowed and stepped back. Yamamoto carefully fixed the cap on his head and, after a final look in the mirror, headed for the door. Yamamoto's footsteps echoed as he walked out of his suite, down the stairs to the foyer and out the mansion's front door into a new dawn. Breathing deeply, he stood for a moment, taking in the golden-red splendor of the sunrise, giving life to the jungle abounding on New Britain. With his eyes closed, he let the early morning soak in; and listening intently, heard his own heartbeat mingling with the cacophony of life about him. An image of Chiyoko materialized before him; she was so close, he could almost reach out and touch her. And then she...

There is work to do. Opening his eyes and raising his chin, he walked briskly down the steps, finding his midnight-blue Packard limousine waiting, its rear door held open by his aide, Commander Noboru Fukusaki. Proudly, it stood before a caravan of five staff cars and three trucks. Four motorcycles were in front of the Packard, their engines ticking over, ready to lead the way. To Yamamoto's consternation, the entourage had grown to the point where they needed not one, but two land attack bombers for transportation to Bougainville. Traveling in his plane would be Rear Admiral Rokuro Takata, the Combined Fleet's Chief Surgeon, Fukusaki, and another staff officer. His Chief of Staff, Vice Admiral Matome Ugaki, would be in the second plane, along with the Combined Fleet's Meteorology officer, two staff officers, and of all people to travel to a combat zone, Captain Motoharu Kitamura, the Chief Paymaster.

Yamamoto stepped in the limousine, finding Ugaki perched in the back seat.

"Good Morning," said Yamamoto settling beside Ugaki.

His Chief of Staff grunted a reply, but Rear Admiral Takata nodded with a wan smile and said, "Good Morning, Sir." Raising a fist to his mouth, he stifled a low belch.

Yamamoto, Watanabe, and Takata had drunk saki until ten last night. Then they switched to scotch, going to one in the morning. Now, Yamamoto could tell, the doctor was feeling the effects. Ugaki would have been with them too, but he was still under the weather with dengue fever and hadn't joined them last night.

Folding his body, Fukusaki got in and pulling the door behind him, reached over his shoulder and rapped the divider window separating the driver's compartment from the back. The driver waved a hand out his window, then put the Packard in gear and started out behind the motorcycles, their sirens screaming.

"Are the hospitals visits lined up?" asked Yamamoto, grabbing an overhead strap as they swayed around a curve.

"Yes, Sir. We start at Shortland," said Fleet Surgeon Takata.

"We're going to Balle, first," Ugaki corrected.

"Well, yes Sir," said Takata. "But that's too small and there's no hospital. Our first hospital will be at our second stop, which is Shortland Island."

"Any Guadalcanal veterans there?" asked Yamamoto.

"Yes, Sir. Quite a few," said Takata. "Most of the Guadalcanal casualties have healed and returned to duty. The ones you will see today are the more difficult ones, burn victims, amputees and so forth."

They rode in silence as Yamamoto mulled over what he wanted to accomplish today: mainly, buck his boys up, wherever they were; in a foxhole; behind a machine gun; or sprawled in a hospital bed. Give them confidence and convince them to take the fight to the Americans. If we don't, he planned to say, they will surely bring it to us.

Presently, they descended onto level ground and skirted Rabaul, driving right to Lakunai Airfield, headquarters for the Eighth Air Fleet. The main gate barrier was raised and they drove through, four sentries at attention. The caravan snaked along a road paralleling the main runway and soon drove up to the operations hut, pulling to a stop in a swirl of dust and pebbles.

Parked before the operations hut were two Mitsubishi G4M2, twin-engine land attack bombers. Painted dark-green on the top and duck-egg-white on the bottom, the only difference between the two planes were their tail numbers: closest to the operations hut was aircraft number 323, the other, 326. Standing at attention before each G4M2 were seven men wearing flying suits: Pilot, co-pilot, radio operator/top turret gunner, observer/side gunner, mechanic/side gunner, and tail gunner.

Yamamoto stepped from his Packard and said to his companions, "We have a moment. Some tea, perhaps?"

"No thank you, *Gensui*. Excuse me, please; I think I'll board, now." Ugaki bowed and walked toward G4M2 number 326.

At a glance from Yamamoto, Takata stifled another belch. "Sir, I think I'll wait until we're airborne."

Tiny lines crinkled around Yamamoto's eyes. "You can't be ill, Takata. That was the best scotch last night. How could you---"

---His gaze shifted to one side, where he recognized Flight Warrant

Officer Takeo Kotani, his pilot. Looking back to Takata, he said, "Some bi-carb, maybe?"

"I've already had two portions, *Gensui*."

"I'm sure you'll be fine, Takata." He clapped the man on the shoulder then walked over and shook hands with a bowing Kotani. "Good to see you, Kotani. How's the leg?" Kotani had suffered a terrible wound to his left leg while on a night mission over Guadalcanal five months ago. Yamamoto felt guilty about keeping him on as his pilot. Kotani was one of the best. Nearly healed, he belonged back in combat.

"The leg is doing very well, thank you, Admiral. And for today," Kotani waved a hand across the sky, "we have beautiful weather forecast all the way down to Balle. It will be a nice, smooth trip."

Yamamoto stepped close and said in a conspiratorial voice, "Would you mind if I did the take-off?"

"Of course, Sir. And you shall do it from the left seat."

"Well that's nice of you Kotani. But the left seat, that's---"

"---Excuse me *Gensui*." It was Watanabe. After waiting a respectable moment, he said, "Captain Takano is here, just arrived from Vila."

"He's back already?"

"As much as I hate to say this, Sir, I believe you should speak with him."

"You're joking."

"Just for a moment, Sir. See what he has."

"Very well."

"He's back here, Sir," said Watnabe, leading the way.

Checking his watch, Yamamoto looked at Kotani and twirled his index finger over his head. *Start Engines.*

With a sharp command to his crew, Kotani dashed for his G4M2. Other members of the Admiral's entourage took the cue and walked for their respective aircraft.

Watanabe lead Yamamoto around the side of the operations hut, where Takano sat on a bench in deep shade. His eyes were closed; a mug of tea was clutched in his hands, and he seemed on the brink of toppling over into the dust.

Watanabe barked.

Takano's eyes snapped open and he jumped up. Recognizing Yamamoto, he braced to attention and saluted.

Yamamoto stepped before him and, returning the salute, looked him up and down. "Takano, you look as if you've been dragged through a Kanpon boiler fired up to 650 degrees superheat."

"I'm sorry, Sir."

"So what do you have?"

"The new American fuse, *Gensui*. It's amazing."

"What's amazing?"

"I've been up all night, taking this fuse apart. It's...it's...astonishing."

The four-bladed Mitsubishi-Hamilton propeller on Kotani's left engine rolled. After three revolutions, the engine caught, the nacelle shaking and spewing dark-blue smoke, the prop wash stirring dust and papers.

"How did you get here so quickly?"

"The *Matukaze* took me to Vila Air Base then I commandeered a plane and flew here. I took apart the fuse on the way up. You should see---"

"---You disassembled a fuse while airborne?" demanded Yamamoto.

"All of my career, Sir, ordnance has been my trade. It wasn't difficult, and the fuse is harmless now. And I was curious, I had to know." Takano nodded to a valise on the ground. "It's all here. So neat, so...elegant."

Mitsubishi G4M2 number 326 started up, with the last of Ugaki's group scrambling aboard. Yamamoto spun to look at the two planes, their engines ticking over, waiting patiently. Turning back to Takano he looked at his watch and said, "We're out of time."

"I'm sorry, Sir." Takano bowed deeply.

Grabbing Takano's elbow, Yamamoto waved to his G4M2 and said. "All right. You have my curiosity up. You will ride with me and explain this fuse. We have the Fleet Surgeon to fix you up and you'll have food fit for the Emperor himself."

Takano looked down at his tattered uniform. "But Sir. I don't have---"

"Nonsense, let's go. I want to see how the damn thing works." Yamamoto picked up the valise and handed it to Takano. Then he looked back and said. "You sure you can't come, Watanabe?"

"Thank you Sir. But I'm swamped." Watanabe gave a helpless shrug.

"Very well. I'll see you this evening. Perhaps we can have dinner again?"

To others, it might have been a command. To Watanabe, it was pure pleasure to be in the *Gensui's* company. "Yes, Sir. I look forward to it. Have a good trip."

Yamamoto lead Takano to the G4M2 and, following Naval custom, was the last to board as senior officer. Handing up Takano's valise, he stepped inside and the hatch was closed.

Watanabe watched the two G4M2s waddle onto the taxi-way and draw to a halt to run up their engines. Then, bomber 323 taxied onto the active runway, lined up and braked to a stop, its engines rumbling. Shading his eyes against a brilliant rising sun, he spotted Admiral Isoroku Yamamoto, Commander-in-Chief of the Combined Fleet, sitting in the pilot's seat. Standing on the brakes, Yamamoto fire-walled the two Kasai fourteen-cylinder radial engines. They quickly gained full rpm, thundering in their mounts. Then Yamamoto released the brakes and 323 rolled. In moments, her tail was up, and seconds later, she was airborne, arcing to the right. Almost immediately, 326 lumbered onto the runway and lunged into her take-off. Watanabe glanced at his watch: exactly 0600. It never ceased to amaze him how the *Gensui* managed to handle things so punctually.

"...and there are ten fuel tanks, five starboard, five to port." Kotani proudly explained the G4M2's fuel management system from the copilot's seat. He pointed out the window, "The oil reservoirs are there, in the leading edges inboard of the nacelles..."

Yamamoto smiled indulgently, not wanting to dampen Kotani's enthusiasm, as they flew in clear skies at 700 meters. Bougainville's coast loomed off their left wingtip, with the Emperor Mountain Range forming a verdant spine down the island's axis. Mount Bali, an active volcano, trailed ashen-grey smoke from its 3,000 meter peak, while rivers and mangrove swamps splotched an ill-defined shoreline. Ugaki's plane was tucked abreast of the right wingtip at no more then ten meters. Three hundred meters above and slightly behind were six A6M Zero fighters flying cover. As Kotani predicted, the day was beautiful with Bougainville so clear, Yamamoto felt as if he could step out and walk on the Island's thriving carpet of primordial jungle.

Yamamoto had been fascinated for the past hour and fifteen minutes, as

Kotani explained the features of this newer version of the G4M2, It was a model 22, he said, with more speed and longer range than the earlier version. But, Yamamoto and Kotani averted their eyes to avoid the fact that the G4M2's increased range was achieved by sacrificing armor-plate protection. Kotani was explaining the plane's four twenty-millimeter canons when Yamamoto checked his watch: 0735. *Damnit! I've forgotten about Takano.* Looking up, he said, "Kotani, can you wait a moment?"

"Of course, Sir."

Taking care not to brush against the throttles, Yamamoto slid out of the pilot's seat.

"Balle in twenty-five minutes, Sir," Kotani said. "Would you like to do the landing, too?"

"You really think so?"

"Well, I'll be right here." He leaned back and winked to the co-pilot seated right behind in a jump-seat.

"I'd like that. I wont be long." Yamamoto made his way through the crawlway to the G4M2's commodious midsection.

The two gunners tried to rise from their positions at the twenty millimeter canons, but Yamamoto waved them down. The others, except for Admiral Takata gazing out a porthole, were asleep. Also asleep with his head back and mouth open was Captain Takano sprawled in the right side of a set of double seats.

Yamamoto's sword lay cross the left seat cushion. Carefully, he laid it on the deck and sat, swearing softly as he unsuccessfully fumbled with the seat belt buckle.

Takano must have sensed the movement for his eyes popped open. He sat up and began to rise. "Sir, I'm sorry. I didn't---"

Yamamoto pushed against his knee, "---Stay, Takano, stay."

"I didn't mean to fall asleep."

"Nonsense. Now tell me what you have there." He pointed to the valise between Takano's feet.

Takano reached down and picked it up. Carefully draping a rag across his lap, he began pulling parts from the Valise. "This appears to be a production fuse for the U.S. Navy's five inch cannon."

"Yes?" Yamamoto stared, fascinated at the components accumulating in

Takano's lap. Tiny wires dangled from one or two of them. "It looks like a radio set."

"Yes, Sir. Actually more than a radio set."

"More?"

"I believe it's a radar set. It can sense the distance to a target then, at an optimum moment, trigger a detonator which fires the main charge."

"What can that do to a ship?"

"A ship is not the problem, Sir. This fuse is an anti-aircraft weapon."

"What? No!" Yamamoto shook his head. "Impossible." He dashed an angry glance at Takano.

Takano bit his upper lip and plunged ahead. "With respect, Sir. This is how they do it. Here is the transmitter; this is the receiving antennae. And see this?" He lifted a glass tube. "This is what's called a thyratron. It fires the detonator."

"So?"

"The glass is extremely hard, Sir." He handed it to Yamamoto.

Yamamoto tapped it with a fingernail, his days in a gun turret coming back to mind. "You're aware of the ballistic forces on a projectile?"

"With respect, Sir. It's my career."

"An influence-fuse that is set off when it reaches an optimum distance to the target?"

"Yes, Sir."

Suddenly the light went on, for Yamamoto exclaimed, "It *is* amazing. But how do they overcome set-back?"

"Super-hardened glass, Sir." Katano tapped the thyratron with a small screw-driver.

Yamamoto picked up the little transmitter. "I wonder how long it would take us to--"

Both looked up to a sound like rocks bouncing off the aircraft. Then the plane swerved to the left and nosed down, quickly. "What the hell?" shouted Yamamoto.

"We're under attack!" the left gunner yelled.

Fukusaki ran over and, muttering *"Gensui,"* fished out Yamamoto's seat-belt. He clicked it home and yanked it tight as it would go. Yamamoto nodded as the G4M2 dove more steeply, it's engines screaming. The only thing he could think of doing was to grab his sword off the floor.

A hot missile whizzed by his head and punched out through the plane's thin skin. With his heart pounding wildly, Yamamoto clutched his sword to his chest and looked frantically from side to side, feeling helpless, wishing there was something he could do.

The sound of rocks clanged again. Except now, a bullet penetrated the roof and blasted a one centimeter hole in the forward bulkhead.

"No target," screeched the right gunner.

The left gunner shouted, "My side. P-38," and yanked the cocking lever of his twenty millimeter cannon. He pulled the trigger and nothing happened. "What?"

"The safety's on, you idiot!" Takano bellowed at the man.

"Ah." The gunner flicked the switch, just as a shell ripped through his chest. A fountain of red blossomed over a smoking hole in his flight suit as he tumbled back.

A shadow flashed overhead. Yamamoto looked out the porthole. They were low, perhaps twenty meters off the ground; trees whipped past in a blur.

"Fire!" someone screamed.

Through the porthole, Yamamoto watched in horror as orange-red flames erupted from the right wingroot and licked at the fuselage. More shells ripped into the plane's hull, one blowing off Fukusaki's left arm at the elbow.

The plane jinked to the left. But the whole right side was immolated in flames. Fukusaki screamed. Takano shrieked also as smoke poured into the cabin. The G4M2 shuddered as cannon fire methodically punched into the plane. Suddenly, the right wing folded up into the fuselage as if on hinges. His eyes wide open, Yamamoto clutched his sword as the G4M2 plunged into the jungle.

47

17 April, 1943
   Headquarters, Commander In Chief, Pacific Fleet
   Pearl Harbor Naval Base, Hawaii

An early afternoon storm gathered, bringing a sudden cloudburst. Commander Michael Novak leaped from his jeep and was soaked thoroughly during a frantic fifteen second dash to CINCPAC headquarters' front door. Once in the lobby, water ran into his eyes. His damned ID was wet. But there was no alternative but to present himself to smirking Marine guards and push on. With squishing shoes, he turned down a long hall, finding a signboard marked:

EDWIN T. LAYTON, CDR USN
PAC FLT INTELLIGENCE

The door stood open. Layton sat at his desk, cigarette clamped between his fingers, studying a sheaf of papers splayed before him. His desk was a jumble of papers, messages, manuals and thick books, many spilling onto the floor and across the room.

Novak rapped twice, "Here I am."

Layton stood. "My God, Mike. I didn't mean for you to come by submarine."

"Ha, ha. Very funny." Novak made a show of shaking water on Layton's carpet. Pushing aside a pile of books, he sat on a leather couch,

Layton rose and closed the door. "Coffee?"

"If that's the best you can do."

"You hear the news?" Layton's tone was dark.

Novak sat up.

"Frank Ashton committed suicide."

"You're kidding."

"You were related. What was it..."

"Cousins. We weren't close. What happened?"

"Shot himself in his office. Apparently the Admiral's selection board discovered he'd lied about his being in combat in World War I. And then, of all things, the San Pedro Police filed a breaking and entering charge against him."

"Holy Cow!"

"Apparently his life was full of lies. He gun-decked his record to show a lot of time at sea but it wasn't true. He couldn't do it. Got seasick all the time. Worse, the Department of Terrestrial Magnetism in Washington D.C. discovered that Ashton covered up the fact that his fuse testing procedures were erroneous and sloppy, causing the death of at least one high-level civilian-scientist."

"I'll be damned." Novak was truly amazed.

"Well, I thought you should know. And now for better news." Layton dropped an envelope on the couch armrest "Read that. There's something there that has me confused. " It was a double red-stripped envelope marked TOP SECRET. Inside was a flimsy, its date-time group announcing that it had been transmitted -- Novak checked his watch hoping the rain hadn't ruined it -- just twenty minutes ago:

TO: COMSOPACAREA
FM:COMAIRSOLOMONS
INFO:CINCPACFLT

POP GOES THE WEASEL. P-38S LED BY MAJOR JOHN W. MITCHELL
USA VISITED KAHILI AREA ABOUT 0930. SHOT DOWN TWO
BOMBERS ESCORTED BY ZEROS FLYING CLOSE FORMATION. ONE
SHOT DOWN BELIEVED TO BE TEST FLIGHT. THREE ZEROS ADDED
TO THE SCORE. SUM TOTAL SIX. ONE P-38 FAILED RETURN. APRIL 18
SEEMS TO BE OUR DAY.

BT

Novak sipped his coffee and said, "So they brought it off. Congratulations, Ed."

"Thanks."

"I like the part about April 18." Mitscher (COMAIRSOLOMONS) was referring to Jimmy Doolittle's B-25 raid on Tokyo exactly one year before. The irony was that Mitscher was commanding officer of the carrier, U.S.S. *Hornet*, which launched the B-25s. Halsey (COMSOPACAREA) was also along as commander of the entire task group. Novak handed back the message with, "What's the problem?"

"Mitscher is telling Halsey there were two bombers. We were only expecting one. Zero Zero wants to know; does that mean we really got Yamamoto? Or, better yet, what or who did we shoot down?"

Novak knit his eyebrows. *Hell, I can't tramp into some Bougainville jungle and find out who those fly-boys shot down.*

"Do you have any traffic?" Layton must have been reading his mind.

"Ah." It clicked in Novak's mind. "Actually, we do. We're working on a long one right now. Let me get over there and see how they're doing."

"I'd appreciate it."

Novak stood up and without warning, sneezed.

"And while you're at it, find a dry uniform."

Novak made a show of wiping his nose with a wet sleeve "I'll do my best." Then he stomped out.

Novak was back forty-five minutes later, rapping on Layton's door. His hair was combed but it was wet, and he still wore the same damp uniform. His shoes even squished as he walked in Layton's office, a briefcase tucked under his arm.

"Did I give you permission to enter?" Layton said caustically.

Novak opened his briefcase and pulled out a red-stripped envelope marked TOP SECRET. "Shut up and read."

Layton shot a questioning glance at Novak.

"The Jap intercept."

"Okay." Layton sat back to read the message while Novak walked to the side-table and poured coffee.

SECRET TELEGRAM: No. 181430, [1943-4-18]
FROM: THE COMMANDER, SOUTH EASTERN AREA FLEET AND
AIR ARM

TO: THE MINISTER OF THE NAVY
THE COMMANDER IN CHIEF

1.THE TWO RIKU-KO AND SIX CHOKE-AN FIGHTER PLANES
CARRYING THE COMBINED FLEET HEADQUARTERS ENCOUNTERED
ENEMY FIGHTER PLANES, TEN PLUS IN NUMBER AT 0740 OVER BUIN
TODAY AND ENGAGED THEM IN AIR BATTLE. THE NO. 1 RIKU-KO
CARRYING THE DIRECTOR, SURGEON COMMANDER, STAFF
OFFICER OKEZUMI, AND EIGHTH AIR FLEET ORDNANCE CAPTAIN
TAKANO, ON FIRE FELL INTO THE MIDST OF A JUNGLE 11 MILES
WEST OF BUIN IN A SHALLOW ANGLE. THE NO. 2 RIKU-KO
CARRYING THE CHIEF STAFF OFFICER, THE CHIEF PAYMASTER, THE
CHIEF METEOROLOGICAL AND OPERATIONAL OFFICER AND STAFF
OFFICER MUROI MADE A FORCED LANDING INTO THE SEA, SOUTH
OF MOILA. IT IS KNOWN, AT PRESENT, THAT ONLY THE CHIEF STAFF
OFFICER AND CHIEF PAYMASTER WERE RESCUED. THE RESCUE
FORCES ARE AT WORK AT PRESENT.

2. AMERICAN RADAR FUSE LOST ON NO. 1 RIKU-KO. ADVISE
FURTHER INTELLIGENCE ACTIVITIES TO FIND ANOTHER.

MESSAGE ENDS

Layton grinned and smacked his fist into his palm. "We *did* get him. We got Yamamoto. Looks like we got a bunch of others in the bargain, too."

"I'd say so," said Novak. "Except it looks like Ugaki lived."

"Ummm." Layton went to hand back the message but then re-read a section. "Say, who's this fellow Takano? I haven't heard of him before."

Novak sat heavily. "We dodged a bullet on that one."

Layton looked up, handing back the message.

Novak had hoped Layton wouldn't pick up on the reference to Takano. Now, he was forced to explain, "Takano was an ordnance expert. And a friend of the Royal Family. Apparently, he got a proximity fuse off the *Howell* before they blew her up. Now it looks like Takano and that fuse went down with Yamamoto. So they're back to square one as far as understanding what we really have."

"How was the *Howell* blown up?

Novak explained.

"You mean it came down to just one man, the ship's exec, to wire the thing up, to keep our stuff out of the Jap's hands?"

"Yes." Novak tried to smile. So much for a case against Ingram, he thought. The man not only had the temerity to survive the *Pence* sinking, he also had saved the Navy's bacon by single-handedly blowing up the *Howell*. In a way, Novak was glad Ingram had survived. But the ramifications against Novak could be dark.

Be careful, very careful.

"Who is this guy?" asked Layton.

"Todd Ingram," Novak muttered.

Layton snapped his fingers. "Ingram. Ingram. That's it! Isn't he the guy who got out of Corregidor? Navy Cross? A Spruance protégé?"

"That's him."

"Ummm." Layton scrawled notes on a pad and checked his watch. "Zero Zero breaks from a meeting with Spruance in ten minutes. I'm next to go up there and brief him. What do you think about recommending that he give Ingram a Silver Star?"

"Of course."

"Right." Layton wrote furiously. Nodding at the Japanese message, he continued. "Hell, without clearance, nobody could put the story together. We can't show the world that Jap message, can we? Zero Zero will figure a way to take care of Ingram. He loves to honor heroes. We'll catch him when he comes through Pearl. Right?" Layton's eyes narrowed. "Jeez, Mike. You're shaking. You should have got into dry clothing like I said. Go on home. Take a hot shower. Have a shot of whiskey."

Novak would have liked nothing better, but he was five minutes overdue for a meeting at Admiral Lockwood's office. He stood, unable to stifle a prolonged sneeze. Then, he sneezed again. And again.

"Just about time." Layton stood and gathered papers into a folder. Holding up a message flimsy, he said, "You know anything about a Marine Major by the name of Augustine Rivera?"

Novak felt as if he'd been shot in the back. "What?"

"Rivera," Layton said absently. "Got a message here from Halsey to Zero Zero about a renegade Marine Major down in the Solomons using phony names. Guy could be CID. Guess we'll have to check."

"Never heard of him." Blood rushed to Novak's temples.

"Ummm." Layton stuffed his papers in his briefcase and looked up. "Damn, Mike. Maybe you should go see the doc. You look like hell."

Taking out a wet handkerchief, Novak pat his face, finding it flushed and clammy, almost as if he were in cold, damp, Chicago rather than balmy Hawaii. He turned to walk out.

"You did a good job, Mike. Will you pass that onto your boys from me?"

Novak sneezed again. "Sure will. Thanks."

EPILOGUE

The sadness of evil men is that they believe no truth that does not paint the world in their colours.

Eric Ambler
The Schirmer Inheritance

He also said to the multitudes, "when you see a cloud rising in the west, you say at once, 'a shower is coming'; and so it happens. And when you see the south wind blowing, you say, ' There will be scorching heat'; and it happens. You hypocrites! You know how to interpret the appearance of earth and sky; but why do you not know how to interpret the present time?

Luke 12: 54-56

There are no atheists in foxholes.

Anonymous

A cab emerged from swirling fog, pulled up and honked. Four figures walked from the little house on Alma Street. Todd and Helen Ingram scrambled in the back seat.

"Jerry," Helen said. "It was Frank Ashton who did it."

"Hold on a sec, hon." With an arm around Mrs. Peabody, Landa hobbled to the cab's front door. His leg was in a cast from foot to mid-thigh and it took a while for him to turn around. With a grunt, he sat gingerly in the front seat, then muttered as he heaved the cast off the curb and inside the cab.

Mrs. Peabody bent to hand over his crutches. Standing back up, she belched involuntarily and clamped a hand over her mouth

Pretending not to notice, Landa said, "Thanks, dear. Sure you don't want to go to dinner with us?"

"Brrrr. Too cold for me. I'm going to sit by the fire and listen to *The Whistler*." Mrs. Peabody hugged her arms around her waist.

"But, I need a date tonight," protested Landa.

"You'll do just fine." She leaned down, pecked him on the cheek. "You know what, Commander Landa?"

"To you Mrs. Peabody, it's Jerry," said Landa.

"You have the prettiest teeth." Mrs. Peabody walked off, giggling.

The cabbie, a thin, balding man with wire-rim glasses, rolled his eyes. His nametag read, 'Louie.'

When she was gone, Landa said to no one in particular, "Smell that? I swear she brews her own stuff." With a grunt, he closed the front door and popped his crutches against the taxi meter, jamming the flag. "Er, sorry," he said.

"Forget it. Where to?" said Louie.

Landa half-turned to the back seat. "Where we going, kids?" When no one replied, he looked over his shoulder, seeing Ingram locked in an embrace with Helen, kissing her deeply. "Hey, you guys. You want to go back inside? I don't mind going on alone. You know. Give old Jerry the slip. Nobody cares." In an aside, he whispered to Louie, "He just got in last night."

Louie whispered back, "Ohhh. Maybe we should just take 'em downtown and charge a nickel a peek." He eyed Landa. "You must have some clue of where we're going, otherwise," he jazzed the accelerator a couple of times, "we're just burning up precious gas off my ration card. You must see what I mean."

Landa waved at the fog. "What's it matter? How can you go anywhere in this?"

"Try me."

Landa grinned. "Brooklyn?"

"You bet. Then I married this little Italian girl from California and look at me now."

Landa leaned forward and looked at Louie's belly. "Looks like she's feeding you well."

"Ehhh."

Ingram came up for air. "Olsen's Café. West Ninth Street at Grand."

"You don't have to tell me where Olsen's is," Louie muttered. He jammed the cab roughly into gear and popped the clutch.

Ingram tossed a paper-wrapped package over the seat into Landa's lap. "Almost forgot. This is for you. Greetings from Rocko Myszynski. Air Mail -- Special Delivery."

Paper rattled as Landa undid the twine. "Hey, thanks. Gift wrapped from Macy's, I see. New pair of pants? Hawaiian shirt? What you been up to...aw." Landa pulled back a corner to find a United States flag. Slowly, he undid the rest of the wrapping and held it up. Instinctively, he knew it was the flag Leo Seltzer rescued from the wreckage aboard the *Howell*. He turned and said, "Is this the one?"

"Rocko wanted to make sure you got it."

"Damn."

"Rocko told me to remind you about that job," said Ingram. Three weeks previously, Rocko Myszynski had sent Landa a letter saying he needed a new Commander of Destroyer Division Eleven. The job was his for the asking but Landa had dragged his feet in accepting.

Landa re-wrapped the flag. "...just not sure."

"All you have to do is say yes, Jerry."

"Nice cab you have here," Landa said to Louie.

"Thanks. Say, I can't help but notice. Looks like you were, you know...out there." Louie waved at the decorations on Landa's blouse,

"I've been back for six weeks." Landa turned to the back seat. "Which reminds me, Mr. Ingram? You're out of uniform."

"What now?"

"Where's that medal?"

"...what medal?

"You think I'm stupid? That I don't read ALNAVs? The Silver Star Nimitz hung on you last week."

"You didn't tell me last night," said Helen.

"Well, we had other business to take care of," Ingram gave a grin.

"Todd!"

Louie whistled. "Silver Star. Hey, that's pretty good."

"He's got a Navy Cross, too, " said Landa. Ingram kept silent, so Landa turned to Helen. "So what was that you were saying about Frank Ashton?"

"It *was* him," she said.

"You're telling me that Frank Ashton cut those orders?" asked Ingram.

"Exactly," she said. "Otis told me that Frank Ashton pulled strings in the Pentagon to have me transferred just so he could break in our house without anyone around and ransack that trunk and...and..."

"...snag Josh's journal."

Helen propped her arms on the front seat, her perfume teasing Landa's nostrils: *Chanel number 5.* "It was that motorcycle cop that figured it out. Bullard. They found a fingerprint on the garage door hasp. The FBI matched that to Frank Ashton. In the meantime, Otis DeWitt, with all his Army contacts, discovered it was Ashton who issued my orders for Africa. He relayed the word to the selection board through Ollie."

"You would think he would dream up something less radical," asked Ingram.

"Apparently he thought so, too," shrugged Helen. "Because he had my orders rescinded. And then there was a selection board inquiry, then the San Pedro Police department investigation all at once. So he shot himself."

"My kid brother would be alive if it weren't for him," said Landa.

"Jerry, let it go." Ingram reached and clapped a hand on Landa's shoulder.

"...damned kid." Landa took a deep breath and said, "So, I hear you're getting a ship?"

"Yeah, the *Maxwell*. A new tin can built by Bethlehem Steel right here in Pedro. They launched her last week."

"And Todd's going to be working for you?" asked Helen.

"Yes, Boom Boom. So what do I tell Rocko? Are you my new boss or what?" said Ingram.

"You keep calling me 'Boom Boom' and I'll bust you to ensign."

Ingram shot back, "You can only bust me to ensign, Boom Boom, if you're my boss."

"Okay, okay. I'll take the job." Landa sighed.

"Good. It's settled," said Ingram. "So I guess I won't call you," he enunciated clearly, "Boom Boom, anymore."

"You crack me up, Ingram," muttered Landa.

Louie blurted, "Hey, the papers said they shot down that guy Yamato."

"Yamamoto," said Landa.

"Yeah, P-38s shot down Yamato. Bzzzt." Louie flew a hand toward the windshield. "That's out where you were?"

"Maybe," said Landa.

The cab took a sharp right from Gaffey onto Ninth, its tires squealing.

"You mean we set the guy up for a hit? Louie asked. "Like in New York or Chicago?"

"Well, coastwatchers spotted him and we shot him down, if that's what you're asking," said Ingram.

Louie looked up to the rear-view mirror and asked, "Ain't that political?"

"Maybe you should ask Leo," said Ingram.

"Who's Leo?" asked Louie.

"Forget it," growled Landa, rattling the package in his lap.

After a dark moment, Louie said, "Look you guys, I'm sorry if--Whoa!" A red neon sign loomed out of the fog; an eerie beacon blinking: OLSEN'S. He made a great show of jamming on the brakes and lurching to a stop. "So how's that for navigatin'?"

"Eh." Landa tilted his hand from side to side.

"So get out. You swabbies are stinking up my cab."

"That's it." Ingram threw his hands in the air. "Let's go." He and Helen climbed out.

Landa reached for his wallet.

"Your money's no good here."

"You serious?"

"You bet."

"Thanks."

Louie nodded to Todd and Helen, "Those kids are tops in my book. I hope your leg gets well real soon. And thanks to you and all you guys out there." His head dropped for a moment. "Me and Loretta have three kids. But I tried. I got a busted eardrum. The Navy turned me down three times, the Marines twice." He held out his hand.

Landa shook and flashed a thirty-two tooth grin, "You just keep doing what you're doing. That's why we're out there. For you and Loretta and your kids."

"Okay, Boom Boom."

"Get out of here." Landa handed his package to Ingram, hobbled out, and pulled his crutches clear. Louie peeled out just as the door slammed, disappearing into the fog.

"Sorehead," muttered Landa. He hadn't noticed a car parked before him, --- a light green Cadillac convertible with its top down. A lone woman sat at the wheel, a scarf over her head. She turned to him, clacking her mouth, as if it were full of chewing gum and said, "Hi ya, toots. Wanna ride?"

"Well, how do you like that?"

Laura West got out and walked up to Landa, threw her arms around him and kissed him. "You're walking much better. I'm proud of you, hon."

"It ain't easy."

"Baloney. You're just looking for sympathy."

Ingram's mouth hung open. Finally, he managed, "You and Laura?"

"Do I need your permission?" asked Landa.

"No, I meant... Aw, hell." Ingram reached for Laura and hugged her. "Good to see you, Laura."

"You too, except," she stepped back, "you're looking kind of thin."

"It goes with the job."

She waved toward the restaurant's front door. "Well, I guess that's why we're here."

"You still offering piano lessons?" Helen hugged Laura.

"Anytime, hon." She cocked her head as a cumbersome melody drifted out from the restaurant. "Sounds like the guy in there needs 'em, too."

"Let's go see," said Helen.

"Okay, Toots," said Laura, clacking her gums. She slipped an arm through Landa's.

A ship's horn echoed loudly through the basin: one long blast was followed by three shorts. The fog rolling up Ninth Street made Olsen's seem close, obliterating everything else, as if this was the only refuge on the planet. Ingram turned to Helen finding a tear running down her cheek. "Brrrr. Must be the damp air," he said kissing the tear away.

"Must be," she replied.

Both of Landa's eyes were misted, too. He caught the others looking and said, "Damn fog."

The ship's horn bleated again.

Ingram said, "Come on, Boom Boom. Let's go have a steak."

THE NEPTUNE STRATEGY

"An undeniably seaworthy tale for military-action buffs...fortunately, Ingram has much of WWII yet to serve." —**Booklist**

**Four Japanese bombers dive out of the clouds.
Their target is the USS Maxwell.**

As the ship is rocked by massive explosions, Commander Todd Ingram is thrown overboard...where he watches in horror as his embattled ship leaves him behind.

Clinging to a floating piece of lifeboat in rough seas, he barely survives the night. A submarine surfaces nearby, and his joy turns to horror when he recognizes it as a Japanese U-boat.

Todd's troubles have just begun—but so has the race to save him.

As the US Navy launches a classified rescue mission, Todd is captive aboard the enemy submarine as it dodges depth charges and Allied ships. A deadly game of cat-and-mouse unfolds, and its outcome may affect the balance of power in a war that threatens to consume them all.

Get your copy today at JohnJGobbell.com

NEVER MISS A NEW RELEASE

Sign up to receive exclusive updates from author
John J. Gobbell.

**Join today at
SevernRiverPublishing.com/John-J-Gobbell**

ALSO BY JOHN J. GOBBELL

The Todd Ingram Series

The Last Lieutenant

A Code For Tomorrow

When Duty Whispers Low

The Neptune Strategy

Edge of Valor

Dead Man Launch

Other Books

A Call to Colors

The Brutus Lie

Never miss a new release. Sign up to receive exclusive updates from author John J. Gobbell.

SevernRiverPublishing.com/John-J-Gobbell

ACKNOWLEDGMENTS

One's very essence is a product of continual involvement with family, friends, and God. As in the past, this book benefits mightily from those relationships. Two friends weren't aware of my existence during World War II; I was far too young and they were busy putting it all on the line, fighting the enemy. I was privileged to know Alvin P. Cluster who served aboard PT boats in the Solomons and Gordon Curtis who flew Wildcats at the Battle of Midway. Sadly, both have since passed but were of enormous assistance in developing the original background for this story. Dick Bertea, a Marine fighter pilot of the Korean era, also helped with aviation scenes. Dr. Fred Milford once again filled in on historical and technical details. Two more Marines, my late brother Bill Gobbell, and Gordon Hanscom, filled me in on things that the Marine Corps does, while Dr. Russell J. Striff, a glutton for punishment over four books once again provided medical details. Retired Navy commander George A. Wallace, was very helpful in Naval affairs and Keiko Hallop lent fantastic advice in areas of music. I must also thank the Historical Societies of Hollywood, Long Beach, and San Pedro for their willingness to provide details about their respective cities in 1943.

Please don't hesitate to visit my website at www.JohnJGobbell.com to see photos of actual ships, locations, people, and equipment portrayed herein. Simply click on the book cover on the main page to find material for this particular work. There, you'll even find a photo of the venerated proximity fuze.

As before, my wife, Janine, carried me through this project with not just strong editorial comment, but with love, understanding and compassion.

John J. Gobbell
  Newport Beach, California
  John@JohnJGobbell.com

ABOUT THE AUTHOR

JOHN J. GOBBELL is a former Navy Lieutenant who saw duty as a destroyer weapons officer. His ship served in the South China Sea, granting him membership in the exclusive *Tonkin Gulf Yacht Club*. As an executive recruiter, his clients included military/commercial aerospace companies giving him insight into character development under a historical thriller format. An award-winning author, John has published eight novels. The books in his popular Todd Ingram series are based on the U.S Navy in the Pacific theater of World War II. John and his wife Janine live in Newport Beach, California.

john@johnjgobbell.com.

Printed in Poland
by Amazon Fulfillment
Poland Sp. z o.o., Wrocław
14 December 2021

285755ec-a58c-4b14-b48f-53d3097b03bbR02